The Good Vet

Joseph Ward

First edition.

ISBN 9798866866861

Bertington House Publishing 2024

Thank you to my editors, the wonderful Jayne, Pat and Karolyn.
Thank you to the real Mac and Anna for your inspiration and time.
Thank you to the world of animals for making life complete.
And of course, little Cooper.

'The more I learn about people, the more I like my dog.'

Mark Twain

Kevin

Kevin, who I've known for seven years, is about to die.

It's not his fault, or my own, but a sad part of life for little ones like him. A cruel, twisted toll brought down on him by an unknown power, delivering him into my hands for his final judgement. My kindness paying out for his betrayal.

We blame it on cancer this time, we can even give it a name.

Mast Cells, ruthless and un-hinged, multiplied and seeded throughout his small body as we watched on, bystanders to their malignancy, standing helpless on the shore as he drifted away from us. All the while he played in the garden, chased balls and sniffed out his friends, as well as enjoying television shows with his owner he just didn't seem to understand the storyline to.

It's heartbreaking, but it's life. It is, sadly, the defining moment of Kevin's life.

We've tried surgery, and chemotherapy, but unfortunately nothing has worked. The small spot that started as a pimple has now grown and spread down through his neck, invading into his chest and his little spleen. He doesn't know it of course — Kevin is a French Bull Dog — but as he tires easily, struggling to find the energy for the park anymore, time has grown short for him, and he has made his final trip to the vets to see me. A lost young soul, pulled back to land. Loved and not forgotten. Torn back from his fate.

I like Kevin. All vets like dogs with human names. But Kevin is a charming fellow, a soft furry slab of canine who never caused anyone a day's pain in his life, forever keen to see the treat jar or get a tickle from the receptionist behind the counter. To say he's one of my favourite patients wouldn't be far off the truth, and we've grown close over the last few months. I'll find myself thinking about him while I cycle home, or sit on the sofa after a day of trying to hide my dismay, seeing his tumour getting bigger or more painful as I measure it. While all the while Kevin is just intent on sniffing about my shoes, curious to know what other patients I've been seeing that day.

'I don't know how you do it.' says his owner as we sign the forms together for his euthanasia, making sure we've the right cremation option worked out for him.

'It's hard.' I say, checking the form a final time whilst Kevin licks my arm. 'But it's easier knowing we're helping him out, you know?'

'Maybe you're right.' She cups a hand under his chin and kisses his forehead. 'I'm so sorry Kevin, mummy loves you and always will okay.'

We spend the next few minutes chatting it over, with Kevin being fussed and getting treats while I reassure his owner it's all going to be okay. After a short period, she steps out and heads through the reception area to the car park. She's chosen not to be there at the time. It's a difficult memory she'd prefer not to have and so the nurse steps in as I get things ready. Some people can't cope with this, I get that.

'You alright Kev? It'll be okay little mate.'

Soon enough he realises I've brought doughnuts through from the back, and while I busy myself with the cannula in his leg, checking the port and flushing saline through, he bursts with excitement as the jam and chocolate explode out through the icing, and I gently inject the solution into his vein.

His dark blue eyes soften into a distant gaze, his head getting heavy.

Shortly after, Kevin has passed away.

Part One

Chapter One

The older I get, the more I enjoy the peace of this empty building.

A quiet reception. Consulting rooms cloaked in darkness. Diluted bleach stifling the air. It tells me its quiet tale of life and death. Of animals and people. Of our hopes and fears.

It tells me we're going to be okay for another day.

It's late October and sunlight has filled the horizon, spilling to the Northumberland coast and painting it bright for another day. From out there at sea it must look warm and cosy. The yellow rays falling onto the stone harbour and its lighthouse, the fishing boats like toys in the marina as they gently sway in the tide. But the icy frost was not one for dwelling in and I had hurried inside, through the darkness to the kitchen. A warm coffee pulling me in.

Slowly but surely the place comes to life. Doors open and lights shine on. Coats are hung up and scrubs are taken off pegs, stethoscopes found and hung around shoulders. Drip sets and the drugs they await have found their way out of cupboards and onto worktops, and all now nestle amongst fresh cups of tea and ringing phones. The hushed, solemn reception I walked into this morning has soon filled with noisy dogs, barging in through the doors to loudly announce themselves, scrabbling over the scales to the desk for check in; while cats sit in boxes, judging the mood and plotting quiet plans. Oblivious to the day they're about to have.

Drinking in one final ounce of tranquility before the morning sprints away from me, I look out through the small square window of the consult room door, out into the fur laden chaos, before opening it to call my first patient of the day.

It's not until later then, my seventh and last consultation of the morning, when Ralph, a four-year-old Staffordshire Bull Terrier trots in with a sore eye. His owner, Mr. Gregory, has been treating it at home over the weekend, reluctantly making the appointment after his partner badgered him into it this morning. He's a cool dog, a medium sized example in the varied world of canine breeds, and, despite the fact he won't open his left eye, is still grinning from ear to ear, happy to be the centre of our attention.

'In you get Ralph. He alright?'

Mr Gregory is sullen, I've met him before and expect nothing more, but Ralph plants two heavy front feet on my chest as I kneel to say hello. I love this dog, however his attempt at a French-kiss is waved away as I stand back up.

Most folks will figure Staffies for bad eggs — difficult dogs in a world of friendly Spaniels, bouncy Labradors and Teacup Chihuahuas. Sure, they get a bad reputation when things go wrong, mainly because of their bite power or when they've fallen into the wrong hands, but one look at Ralph will tell you he belongs in the majority. Soft lumps of muscle who would rather headbutt you for a treat than give even a hint of a grumble. But I guess they don't make the headlines, and the myth goes on for so many. Despite their attempts at furry romance.

'Just an infection that's all, don't know why I can't just pick up drops I had last time son.'

I shine a blue light in, fluorescing the deep ulcer I've just stained with dye. The ulcer that could cost him an eye if untreated. Mr. Gregory ignores it.

'Think I could have told you all that Mark.'

'It's Mac.'

'Mac. Daft name for a fella your size. Me Granda was called Mac. Wiry little bloke. Half a life on the boats. Smelled like fish guts and salt most of the time when he was on shore.' He grunted. 'Guess this'll all set me back a fortune at the front desk, will it?'

Sighing inside, there's always one who tries to make your day, I take him through the bill while he grudgingly acknowledges, grumbling and moaning out of the consult room without thanks as he goes over to the reception desk, complaining all over again — loud enough to raise the eyebrow of my previous client — about how he's paid thirty pounds for ten minutes and all he got was some drops.

'In my day this wouldn't hav...'

I shut the door.

So much for my peaceful practice waiting room. So much for the grateful days of James Herriot I think. Still, Ralph's eye should be fine I guess. One more quiet success that goes unnoticed in my career.

I'm beginning to sound like his owner at this rate.

I type up his notes and click off the screen, heading through to the back of the practice to see what's on my op list. Average enough it turns out, even despite my morning coffee being spoiled by the invading thoughts of sea-salt and fish ends.

Following surgery, I'm sitting in my usual spot a few hours later, tucked away in the consult room, checking emails before I head out for lunch, when a receptionist comes past the door, stopping with a turn of the head and quick double take as she realises where I am.

She sticks her head around the wooden frame and into the room.

'Sorry to bother you Mac I know you're having a break. Got the council on the phone. Animal Welfare are wondering whether they can bring a dog down for a check-up, seems it's in a bad way.'

Jill anxiously drums on the door as I look back, coffee in mid-air, neither up nor down. She's about fifty years old: I seem to recall singing happy birthday next to a cake with a lot of well-placed candles on it sometime last year, but she still has more energy for the workday than most of the younger staff in the practice, myself included. We sit and shoot the breeze often enough on reception together, her updating me on her latest grandchild or ambitious hiking plans for her next weekend in the Lakes, me happy not to be stood in front of a client and be sitting down for once.

Normally I would sink into my chair at the prospect of an unscheduled appointment, another client probably worried about nothing after an anxious night of Googling, but the council team are usually pretty good at only bringing important things to our attention, so I put the cup down beside the computer, its desktop littered with reminders and open browsers, and stand up from the stool.

'Yeah, go on then Jill should be fine, only because it's you though.' A small wink accompanies the fake sigh at the end. 'Just tell them to come down and I'll get things cleared up in here.'

I square away the paperwork and log off emails, cleaning the consult table with a quick spray of disinfectant. The other vets are still through the back, split between dental work and the ultrasound machine, so for now I'm front of house for any emergencies — my overdue lunch trip was on the back burner. This morning's hastily made sandwiches would have to wait a little longer.

In the short time it takes to refill the coffee cup in the kitchen, heading lazily back to reception via the biscuit box, the Animal Welfare van has pulled up in the car park and a familiar hi-vis duo are unloading a crate — the biggest they have by the looks of it — from the back. Usually it's Skye I deal with, but today Steve, the team boss, is here as well. Nothing unusual I suppose; he'll often stick his head in the door to see what we're up to in the clinic, but they always travel solo. Odd. I hold the door open.

Skye, small and petite, dressed in khaki combats and her yellow council jacket is already taking the lead as they slide the crate through the waiting area and into my room, the linoleum squeaking anxiously as the plastic drags over it. One look at her face as she moves past and I can tell this isn't going to be an easy appointment. She's usually a fairly happy-go-lucky girl, so I know something's up when the normal cheery demeanor has been replaced by an out of character, steely frown. Steve doesn't look too delighted at the prospect of being here either, so following the pair in I skirt around the side of the room before turning back to face them. Skye is already talking before I can pick a stethoscope up.

'Thanks for fitting us in Mac, he's not been a great one to deal with, hell of a fight getting him into the crate. Don't reckon he's dangerous or anything but something must have spooked this guy rotten the way he was carrying on up there.'

They finally get the big box in the door and step away, the scuffed doorframe creaking painfully as Steve leans back against it, staring down at the crate. He fidgets as his colleague continues.

'Found him up at the back end of the dene, dog walker saw him and gave us a call, couldn't get near him apparently. Luckily enough by then he'd snagged his collar on a tree so we could get him and get a lead on without too much of an effort. Hasn't been nasty or anything, just petrified to get in there. Terrified of Steve too, so I dunno, guess he's maybe scared of blokes as well.

I look up at Steve and see he hasn't registered an argument against his colleague's statement, instead looking down at the box, hands in his jacket pockets, flicking what sounds like loose change amongst his van keys. Skye carried on, anxious now.

'Looks like there's wounds up around his head, couldn't tell you how long he's been stuck up there though, few hours at least maybe longer, God knows what happened to him before all that.'

She's normally so calm and collected, but this nervous, rapid report makes me think this must be serious. Not the usual lost dog she brings in for scanning, or frail old cat stuck up a tree for that matter. She's my normal go to for welfare jobs — bubbly, confident and not short of a strong opinion or two, so much so I reckon she'll be running the entire department soon enough. If she doesn't piss Steve off first with her enthusiasm.

He on the other hand still seems fairly relaxed, his usual quiet and distracted self, spending Skye's speech nodding and idly turning over the contents of his pockets once more. 'Yeah he's a bit of a nervous one mate so you watch yourself.' turning to his younger colleague.

'Look I'm going to go make a few calls from out in the van, get ahead of a few things. Give us a shout if you need a hand, okay? Reckon Mac's got this one.' and with a nod of the head, he disappeared out through the practice waiting area, over to the van parked outside.

I sigh and turn back to Skye. I guess when you're the male vet everyone thinks you've 'got this'. Some dated preconception that follows you round with the older clients. Admittedly I have a reputation in the practice as the go to for difficult patients, probably because of my size and calm demeanor, distilled down through years of experience and the short army career before entering practice. Things mostly tend to give up and roll over when they see me coming, but sometimes it'll go the other way and they react badly to my large, lumbering presence.

As I lift the cover over the front of the crate, however, I can see this isn't going to be the case.

The box is about 4ft long, and whatever's in there takes up most of the space: all I can see is one end of a large shivering dark mass, tucking itself under a blanket. A thick white tail pokes out, its short fur stained with mud. One of the other vets has stopped outside the room and is looking in, looking at the contents, looking at me. Raised eyebrows suggest she's glad to be on the other side of the glass.

'He's enormous Skye, how on earth did you get him in?'

I kneel, reaching my right hand out to one of the sides and its grey plastic clips. Skye shuffles left.

'Okay mate, let's see what we've got hey?'

We undo the top together and slowly lift it up and over onto the other end of the consult room. Standing back, and closer to the door in case the contents suddenly launch outwards, we both stand and stare with an impressed silence at the bulk of the dog under the material. Skye seeing him in the context of a smaller room, and myself because I rarely get such a big dog in the clinic.

'Seems alright to me Skye, you're definitely sure about the no aggression part?'

Keeping her fixed stare, she slowly drops down to her haunches, steadying herself against the wall with her hand behind her. She's ignored the slight. She's in her zone.

'I wonder if he was scared, you know what they can be like, let me see if I can get this blanket off for a minute.'

She reaches forward and pinches the middle of the fabric, pulling it gently back and over the bulk of the dog. The head previously pressed into the corner of the crate creeps upwards to peer over the edge, and then back towards the consult room door. Realising no one is there, it rotates, side glancing at the pair of us — both now backed up against the wall within reaching distance of the door handle.

Two big, soulful eyes stare back at us.

A large white face, hazily etched with a brown eye patch sits under white ears; one torn and bleeding, a mix of blood and serum dripping down a cheek to a small puddle underneath. Fresh cuts and old scars mottle the left side, but underneath, a handsome, strong dog looks between us. Working us out. Sizing us up.

Slowly and carefully tucking its paws back, a big, hulked set of shoulders emerges as the huge dog perches up on his elbows, fixing us both with its ongoing, distrustful stare.

After what seems like an age, the dog, who by pure size I'm guessing must be a male, breaks into a panting head bob, relaxing before us and forgiving the new intrusion into his space. We breathe a sigh of relief, perhaps we weren't going to get mauled after all, but as soon as we move again he stops, pricking his ears back, fixing us with the same dead eyed stare all over again.

'I don't know about you Mac, but I'm shitting myself.' Skye leans in and whispers.

I grunt a quiet acknowledgement, all the while keeping my eyes on the patient. Something tells me though he's not a bad dog, only scared, and as I crouch down and open my palms in front of him, all the while his ear dripping fresh blood into the crate, he grins again and lets a huge tongue fall out, a glimmer of excitement showing as the treat packet makes its way out from my back pocket.

'No sudden movements okay, I reckon he's alright. Let's see.'

Chapter Two

'Okay, so don't get mad but I've brought something home.'

I peered around into the living room at Anna, my partner, confirming she had been listening.

'Hello to you too dear then I guess.' comes the sarcastic response, 'What, or who have you brought this time?'

We've been here before, but only with cats and smaller items. The small kitten we fostered for the weekend, the seasonal moribund hedgehog, and the little un-well fluff ball of a cat who turned into a permanent fixture alongside our two larger moggies, Hooper and Quint.

'Yeah, it's a bit different dear, you better come have a look. Not much of a house pet I'm afraid.'

With a well-worn sigh Anna stands up and follows me out to the car, and I pull the boot hatch upwards.

'Meet Tank.'

Tank, as I've conservatively called him, is grinning from ear to ear, an expression greatly amplified by the huge cone he's wearing. His wounds are clipped and cleaned; his ear stitched back into place earlier this afternoon. The larger of the chest wounds have come together well under anaesthetic and the remaining smaller ones I'll keep clean and let heal naturally, nothing a decent course of antibiotics won't sort out was my old school thinking. He's still wearing a ridiculously undersized pet shirt to keep things neat, but given the day he's had he seems to appreciate its tight fit and constant hug.

'Jesus.' is all Anna can say.

We stare together a while, and Tank stares back.

Realising that he's on safe ground, he tentatively puts a big heavy paw down onto the driveway and eases himself slowly out, leaving the comfort of the car behind him. I walk forward and attach a lead to the old collar I found in the practice storeroom, bringing him out, over towards Anna and the house.

'Don't worry, he's been pretty friendly to everyone so far.'

She knows how to be around dogs, so stands still and lets him pad over for a sniff, simultaneously scraping everyone and everything with the big lampshade around his head.

'Hey big guy, what's your story?'

After the initial greetings and rubs have been accepted, and I fill her in on his day so far, he seems to relax, turning to look around at the house. It's not enormous by any stretch, but nestled into trees and standing alone at the end of a quiet leafy cul-de-sac it seems to meet his approval, and he confidently moves over to the open front door, eager to claim our territory for himself it would seem. Starting with the clean tiles.

'Nice try oaf.'

I wince as I hold him back, his hefty weight edging its way over to the entrance and the hallway beyond, before finally managing to wrestle him around to the side of the house, past the bins, and point him instead in the direction of the concrete path which goes round to the rear.

'Front's not for the big doggies I'm afraid. Come on mate, this way.'

This greatly pleases Quint the cat, who after appearing around the front door looks mildly perturbed at the hulk of muscle who just crash landed into his domain. Seeing me take it around the side of the house though, en-route to the utility room, cheers him somewhat and he goes back to cleaning his paws and tail before heading under the fence to our right. By now an extra set of yellow eyes peer at me through a bush, and lit up by the adjacent streetlights I realise our junior cat Paulie has been watching the proceedings the whole time, ducking quickly out of view as I struggle past with 60kg of Mastiff, through into the side of the house, clattering the doorframe as we go.

I nudged his back end in and shut the door behind us.

'Right, there you go fella, I'll come check on you in a minute and get you a bed, sound alright?'

Tank briefly looks up at me, neck craned around the difficult angle of the cone, before crashing it all back down again, sniffing out his clean new surroundings. Whilst he busies himself in the corner, scraping over the laminate as he goes, I get a set of blankets from the cupboard, and, along with an old double duvet make it as nice as possible for him. Padding over, he seems to have appreciated the sentiment and settles in, still quiet after his anaesthetic, but awake enough to know a safe home when he sees it.

The utility room is bright and open, the big window at the far side usually letting in a fair amount of natural light, but as the autumn sun set a few hours ago, taking its warmth away with it, the dark glass contrasts against the rest of the room, giving the place an artificial glow as he begins to shut his eyes over in the corner, nestled into his new bed.

I get a bowl and fill it with water, making a mental note to get a much bigger one in the next few days, before standing over him, now fast asleep. He looks happy. Tired and weary, but warm and safe as well. God knows when the last time he felt secure like this I wonder.

After a while the stertored breathing settles to quiet snores, and I look up and around at the room. It's been a while since I'd been in for a good look about: the place wanted painting again if I was honest, and the hurried job when we first moved in was starting to show. The faded pictures on the wall could do with updating: collages of vet school memories looking quietly back at me, as well as the cheerful framed posters from holidays Anna and I had taken over the years. Further to the right, standing to attention next to the light switch, my favourite photos taken back in the Army hung side by side.

Tank started to snort heavily again as I looked in closer at the uniformed, fresh-faced recruit staring back at me, surrounded by fellow officer trainees, all set for different deployments; myself to the Royal Army Veterinary Corps, them to Engineers, Parachute Regiment, all sorts.

I had of course been the odd one out. Not only for my size, but for my vocation: a newly qualified vet trudging through fields and hills with all the other recruits. Set for combat duty, not animal work. But it was still great fun, friends for life I'd told myself. We'd all drifted apart after officer training however, and there were only a few of the fresh young faces staring back at me from the wall I could put a name to.

Distant times Mac, distant times. Who knew that guy would end up in Northumberland, speying cats and vaccinating dogs. Still. There had been no Anna in the Army, and sleeping in a king-sized bed beat a tent in Afghanistan any day of the week. On cue I heard her in the kitchen, an out of tune song coming through as she opened the oven.

Yeah, not many regrets, a good innings so far, and as Tank let out a huge rippling fart that briefly woke him up from a deepening slumber, I nudged the picture straight and checked the remainder were all still in line.

'You staring at those bloody pictures again Army boy?' Anna shouted through the gap in the door. 'This chicken casserole isn't going to eat itself dear.'

I smiled and shut the light off, leaving the door ajar for Tank in case he got lonely later, before heading back through into the kitchen to where Anna was draining vegetables and plating up for dinner.

'It was 'Captain' Army boy when you met me dearest and don't forget it. We having any wine, or we being healthy?'

'Healthy this week Mac. You can have wine at the weekend.'

I sat down, pulling up a stool to the kitchen island we used as a dinner table. No point in getting a proper one for the two of us had been the reasoning when we moved in, albeit two years ago now.

'Still think it was you distracting me which took my eye off the ball in Selection you know, pretty sure I had the second phase in the bag until you came on the scene. I'd have been a proper tough guy soldier if you and your flirty ways hadn't turned up.'

To emphasize the point, I held up an oven mitt, flexing a bicep.

'Should never have walked into that bar in the first place.'

I smiled, sitting down at the counter, pushing half the cutlery back over to her side of the worktop.

'Yes, we all know, first Veterinary Corps officer into the SAS, blah blah blah. Stopped in his tracks by the sexy doctor he met on weekend leave. Or was it tripping over into the helicopter door and concussing himself, I can't seem to remember.' Anna sat down and pushed a plate back my way with a small grin appearing on her face. 'Don't forget the second time you met me was in A&E, weren't looking too clever when I fed you into my CT scanner were you.'

I took the oven mitt off, shrugging as I turned and threw it over my shoulder and back in the direction of the hob.

'Anyway Rambo. Eat your sprouts. And don't forget you're taking the bins out after this.'

We smiled and clinked water glasses. She was probably right. She was about most things. I couldn't complain about the way things had turned out if I was being honest, and sprouts or no sprouts, I much preferred the quiet rural life to being back in the Army; who knows where I'd be if I hadn't crashed out and back into real life with a bump, quite literally. Along with the few framed pictures, the scars above my right eye where I'd hit the helicopter door in Hereford were my only real reminder of days past. I mean, who was I kidding: from vet school to Special Forces? Get real Mac.

Still, I thought, rubbing my temple with one hand, pushing a few vegetables around the dinner plate with a fork in the other, it was good to have a scapegoat. Maybe it had been good timing Anna came along and took my eye off the ball back in that bar. Maybe it wasn't meant to be.

Chapter Three

'Come on then mate, down the path.'

Tank rustled the leaves with his side as he headed towards the river.

It was a week or so later, and leaving Anna back in the house to catch up on sleep we had snuck out and headed down into the dene, out into the countryside beyond the village. It wasn't long before we had found ourselves on a quiet country path, snaking past the miners' cottages and down to the river that flowed eastwards, where it would slow briefly to curve around the final few villages between it and the North Sea.

It hadn't taken long to motivate him that morning. As it turns out it was me who found myself rushed, as a lead was brought through and I drained an uncomfortably hot coffee in front of an impatient dog. A heavy front foot scuffing at the laminate. He was, despite this, turning out to be a great companion. I had been worried he'd have been difficult given the circumstances we found him in, but to take one look at him, bounding out through the back gate, past a startled ginger cat who had been trying to quietly hunt in the undergrowth, it was clear to see he had a sturdier personality than I had initially given him credit for.

He didn't even seem to mind other dogs, brushing up alongside the small golden spaniel, owned by a tweed clad gentleman whose name I was yet to remember, the four of us meeting at the entrance to the woods once more. The pair of them sniffing out each other's interesting ends for the third time this week.

No, he was quite the dog. The perfect excuse to escape out of the house after a long day in the clinic, or indeed an early morning leg stretch before the real world woke up around us.

Something told me I was going to have to work on my small talk though, there was only so much dull weather chat I could get past the locals, a subject not even the Spaniel's owner could stomach for more than a minute, gently tugging the lead away from us as I looked skywards for a second time, prompting us all to go our separate ways.

We continued on, and as I was dreamily struggling to think of a reason why I hadn't thought to own a dog before, Tank craned his neck round to look at me, and duly squatted himself down on the path. I sighed.

'The cat wouldn't do this though would it mate?'

He seemed to grin, scuffing his feet in the undergrowth about four feet away as I unfolded a bag and collected his giant offerings, saying a quiet thank you we were not too far away from the next bin.

'You all done pal?' I enquired.

He was, and we moved on down to the water, myself ambling along, looking up at the trees and the ever-changing colours of the autumn leaves above, and Tank, head down, sniffing out the mulch making up the undergrowth next to the path. The odd bird would dart out as he approached, and a brief moment of excitement reared up as a squirrel shot past his face, taking us both by surprise, but it was generally calm, the only soundtrack the gentle, trickling clatter of water moving a few feet below us, over and around the small rocks which made up the riverbed.

As we found ourselves further out into the countryside I could see the walk was beginning to take its toll, and the effort required to plod along was gradually stacking up. Deeper breaths were drawn in as we walked along, and it was another reminder he was only a week out of surgery, his wounds scabbing over and healing; stretching and straining as I ignored the advice I gave to clients week in and week out about resting up their patients, taking him out anyway.

'What a terrible dad eh? C'mon pal, short walk up here then we'll head back around and home yeah.'

We moved slowly up an incline and found ourselves out of the woods which hugged the river below, and up against a bare wire fence. It looks familiar enough — I think I took a wrong turn on the bike and ended up here a year or so ago — but it's a new one for Tank.

I can feel him starting to tense up as we move along beside the new and unfamiliar surroundings, the wind picking up around us now that we're out of the protective depths of the dene, bristling his short fur as it blows through from the west.

As we walk on, I stumble a step, and realising a lace has come undone I kneel and throw a couple of loops together before switching over to check the other boot. Moving to get up, resting a hand on the path to steady myself, Tank stands with his weight over me: his giant head resting above my neck, his right paw edged up and onto the boot I've retied, thick claws scratching the leather as he positions himself. I can feel him breathing faster, his coat brushing against me as his chest moves in and out, and the sound of a small but increasingly urgent whine comes with every breath.

I move awkwardly to the side and stand up.

'What's up Tank, seen another scary squirrel?' I joke as I gently shoulder him sidewards on the way upwards.

But looking down I can see he has a fixed stare to the distance.

At the end of his eye line I see a farmhouse and its outbuildings, one I've cycled past over the past two years, never giving it a second thought on the way to work. Up ahead, a worker is slowly moving what look like hay bales or silage around in a JCB, stacking them up against one of the larger outbuildings, and a small constantly droning beep comes from the machine as it reverses, making its way out over the field to reach us as we stand beside the fence.

'It's a tractor T, don't stress it, loads of them round here mate. And it's all the way over there anyway, okay?' With the words I clumsily place a palm down on his massive chunk of a head, aiming to reassure him.

Immediately he snaps backwards and hits me with a wide-eyed stare, the same look he had a week ago when I met him for the first time with Skye, and the whine has been replaced by a low grumble, resonating out as his upper lip quivers, readying to show me his long canines. I step back, rattling the wire of the fence, managing to scare him further.

'It's okay big guy, it's me remember, your new pal, alright?'

It takes about five seconds before his forehead relaxes and the terrified eyes soften into some recognition of me. A shameful, tentative look comes over him and he soon pads over, pushing his head into my hip as if to apologise. Deep down I know dogs don't feel remorse, but I can still feel the trust flooding back into him with every one of the big dull nudges. We stand for a while, looking out over the field to the farm, the plough lines focusing our gaze onto the buildings ahead. The tractor is out of view and around the side of the bigger building, only the dull crank of its gears still signaling its presence.

Stupidly it dawns on me where we are. Thinking back to the conversation with Skye a week ago, *'He was found in the dene, tied up to a branch, must have been stuck there for hours…'*

'Shit, I'm sorry Tank, dragging you up here like this. What am I thinking? Probably not far off where you were found.' I look down to meet his worried gaze, the stitched and scabby ear still twitching. 'Still, it's good to get back out there though yeah? We friends?'

He seems back with it, the noise of the machinery waning on the wind, and we turn to find the path to the house, a mile and half or so back in the direction we came, this time not along the riverside but skirting the fields above. Tucked in behind, warily tracking my footsteps, we soon hit the small trail behind the house, and it isn't long before we see a familiar ginger cat on the fence, tired of the hunt game and waiting for us to return home.

Unlatching the gate, guiding Tank through, I see Anna looking out from the kitchen window. She waves as Paulie runs past and through the open door ahead.

'You okay boys, fancy fresh coffee? I've just made one.'

'Yeah, would be great, cheers.' I kicked off my boots and hung up his lead, checking to see if the water bowl was still fresh, which it wasn't.

'Weirdest thing, probably nothing. Properly spooked up at the back of the dene, up near that farm, you know, the one with all the outbuildings attached? Clingy, terrified, not at all himself.' I turn and fill the bowl from the tap in the utility. 'Not seen him like that since I met him back in consults, right out of character. I think it must have been up near where he was left, where the Welfare team found him — only thing I can think of. Seems fine now.'

I look down. Paulie has come in and bumped the rear end of Tank, head down and drinking the fresh water. Sensible cat, making friends with the biggest thing in the house. Well, second biggest anyway.

'Makes me think. Big fella like him, what on earth's he doing out there in that state last week. Scared out of his wits. Guess we'll never know unless someone comes forward for him, which is unlikely.' I look over at him. 'Still, safe and sound bud, and you never know, Anna might even let you stay if you behave yourself.'

Tank looks up through the door and over to Anna, water dripping from the sides of his jowly mouth and down onto the light coloured floor, destined never to be clean again.

'We'll see young man. You can stop floating those big meaty dog farts up through the house for a start.'

As she gives him a smile back I can tell she's already falling in love with him though. It's the same smile I've seen a thousand times over the years when she's happy, usually when we're playfully falling out and making up over something stupid and silly. It would be difficult not to love him, his large dopey head with its cartoon like markings. How anyone could have ever been cruel to him I don't think I'll ever know: still, all sorts of people out there I guess. All sorts.

I take the coffee from Anna, still smiling, and we sit down at the bench to start the weekend together. No plans and no stress. It didn't get much better.

Chapter Four

'So you're going to keep him? Thought you were a cat person Mac?"

Sammy the nurse looks over the surgery table as I reach for another clamp. The splenectomy was going well but had been bleeding like all hell before I'd opened the dog up, the tumour rupturing into the abdomen sometime overnight at home. An eight-year-old bearded collie, Hunter, rushed in this morning white as a sheet and with a distended abdomen. We had him in theatre within fifteen minutes after squeezing in a litre of fluids during surgical prep.

'Yeah, he seems pretty cool. And Anna thankfully gets on with him well enough. Probably likes me taking him out the house so she can get some peace and quiet I guess. You wanna hand me another pack of swabs, this thing's still gushing out at the top end when I let go.'

'No worries, you want the eight pack or just four?'

'Nah four's fine.' I finally clamp around the small artery which was causing the problem. The blood flow visibly halts as I swab around it, 'The suture as well, it's all ready to come out.'

I get a ligature around the final vessel and remove the organ, the bottom end of which is heavily disfigured by a large mass, dropping it into the kidney dish Sammy has held up ready.

'Take that cancer.'

Sammy smiles. We both know it's not that simple, but at least Hunter isn't going to bleed to death today in the practice. Best case would be a benign tumour, but at worst, I've given him a few more short months before the disease pops up somewhere else, somewhere we didn't know about. One for the pathology lab to tell me about in a week or so, no point in worrying today. At least he'll get home to his family.

'You're hilarious Mac. You've also still got blood all over your face you mucky pup.' She places the dish in the corner of the theatre, twisting her face as she does so, 'that's minging that.'

I smile and get on with stitching things up, the conversation turning back to my new found dog ownership skills and a dictated hospital plan for Hunter, and the next ten or so minutes tick by as we quickly forget all about the gruesome mass sat wobbling in the dish next to us. Best not to think about it is our unspoken consensus.

It's not half eleven then, sitting down in the office with another filter coffee — my third of the morning — and I drop a stack of notes onto the desk, ready to type up everything I've done through the morning so far and hopefully get stuck into the ever-increasing e-mail and phone call list.

It was a straightforward morning apart from the spleen, two bitch spays and a cat castrate for a local charity and it's only taken three hours, freeing me up for a good clear run at some admin before afternoon consults. The bane of any vet's life.

The sound of footsteps on linoleum distract me though as I look up through the internal window into the prep room, and see one of the part-time receptionists heading my way, a phone pressed to her ear. It's not Jill this time, something about a day in Keswick with a trip up Cat Bells was the topic of conversation when I last saw her, and so the easy job of tracking me down has fallen to one of her colleagues, Joan. Her eyes dart up and immediately my heart sinks a level, knowing my peaceful down time is about to be converted into something else.

'Hang on he's in the office I'll ask him.' Her voice floats through to me as she walks.

I drop down in my chair, pretending to busy myself with an email, but to no avail.

Without a knock, a head appears around the doorframe, accompanied by the strong aroma of cigarette smoke. Jill one, Joan nil in the receptionist play-offs I think.

'Mac I've got Skye on the phone, they've picked up another dog in a bad way, around the corner in one of the back streets, can she bring it in?'

Trying hard not to let out a sigh, Joan knows the answer before I've even looked up. Pushing back the paperwork to another late-night, I get up to follow her through the practice on her way to the front desk. A sympathetic look from the dental room watches me go.

I divert into the consult room next to reception, cleaning the table with a few wipes of disinfectant spray and dropping the wet paper towel into the bin. No sooner has the lid dropped back down Skye's voice comes into range, urgently calling out to reception staff as the front door slams behind her.

I'm quickly greeted by the sight of an armful of blankets, a small brown tail flopping out from under her right arm.

She rushes past and places it on the table, unfolding the bundle to reveal a lifeless body.

'Sorry, I got here as soon as I could.' Skye stutters, 'I think it would have been too late whatever we did though.'

She pauses, visibly upset, the adrenaline of her drive here starting to wear off. Looking up she half composes herself again.

'Member of the public found her in one of the bins behind the takeaway on Eleanor Street about half an hour ago, called straight up. Why she called us and not you I've no idea, maybe you could have done something quicker. I dunno, God, this is awful.'

She retreated to the chair in the corner and sat down heavily, lifting her hands, both painted red with the blood soaked through from the cotton blanket, not realising she'd already smeared it up and across her cheek.

'I think she was still alive when I got there so I bundled her up and started heading over. Sorry, what a mess. Van's no better either: blood everywhere, all over the front seat and console.'

A mess is an understatement. A small brown dog, short hair streaked red with blood from a large wound on the neck, as well as various puncture marks in and around the torso, lies before us. The nails of the front paws are torn to shreds, split to the bone, and the left forelimb itself is fractured mid-way. All amongst a mess of lacerated flesh and tendon.

A large, ragged flap of skin on the right side is torn open and crudely extends down into the abdomen, and I can see the muscles of her underside exposed and shredded to a pulp, chewed and discarded. The skin of the thorax is bubbly and crinkly to touch, and now, having stood up again, I notice Skye touching the odd texture, small blisters of air popping out through the puncture marks as she strokes. She looks up to see me staring back at her.

'Subcutaneous emphysema Skye, air trapped under the skin, the chest is open inside and the air is escaping as you touch it.'

She looks back down, holding her hand still now, allowing it to gently settle on the crinkly fur.

I wipe away most of the congealed blood around the throat, revealing the crude cut to the right side of the neck around the jugular. Compared to the rest of the frenzied rips and punctures around the legs and torso, the cut is accurate and well intentioned, like something I could do myself in surgery.

Sharp, clean wound edges are present, slicing their way through the strap like muscles of the neck on the right side, and prizing the skin apart we both see the soft fleshy tubular ends of the jugular vein, flaccid, barely supported by the heavy clot of blood which formed inside as the dog's life slowly slipped away and her heart stopped pumping. Lifting and looking deeper, I can see the deeper muscles of the neck shielding the larger structures within.

'Skye, I hate to say it, but this last bit looks deliberate, don't you think?'

I sigh looking down over the rest of the dog. Skye remains still, silently taking in the mess in front of her.

'She's either bled to death through the neck, or the air in the chest cavity has collapsed the lungs, killing her that way. I guess a postmortem might help us out, but from here it doesn't look like much of an accident. The people who found her say anything?'

She shakes her head and I go on. Pointing around the head with a gloved finger I draw Skye's attention back to the rest of the smaller, older wounds.

'Marks here around the eyes and ears look old, previous injuries starting to repair. Probably happened a while ago there from the look of it, but these have got to be new, today if anything. They've all bled recently. The chest wounds are going to be recent as well, you don't survive long in life with a pneumothorax.'

I look in her mouth. No injuries, just a row of clean teeth, she couldn't have been more than a few years old, if that.

'Hate to say it, but the neck is the last injury, designed to finish her off. Looks pretty major to me.'

Skye nods along, she's not an idiot, she would have known what I was going to say, but she still can't raise her gaze up to meet my own, to acknowledge what I'm saying, instead quietly staring down at the body between us.

'Probably a bigger dog did most of the damage. Then someone's panicked, tried to kill her out of mercy's sake. Dumped her thinking she wouldn't be found. Whatever's had a hold the first time must have been tossing her about like a rag doll. I guess she fought it off initially, but this time it broke her leg, crushed her chest. Probably lay gasping. Then they've realised and cut her throat. Not great. Not great at all'.

We stand silently for ten seconds or so. I hand Skye a paper towel and point to her face, letting her know about the blood smear, and she runs it under the tap before wiping it off and turning back. She isn't wearing make-up today.

'Jesus Christ, this is awful.' she mumbles, shell shocked by the situation in front of us. 'I've never seen anything like this before, have you?'

'Not really. I mean I've seen dog fights in the park, more than my fair share, but this looks relentless, planned, like she's been thrown in like a bit of bait. Something real nasty must have been doing this. I dread to think the size of it given the damage. And some awful person has stood and watched the whole thing. Makes my blood run cold thinking about it. '

I hold the bin open, and she throws in the blood-stained paper towel.

'You want to check and see if it's chipped?'

I reach down into my consult room cupboard and take out the microchip reader.

'I doubt it but you never know I guess.'

I turn it on, sweeping it over the body of the small dog. At around the point of the shoulders however it bleeps, giving me the fifteen-digit code, unique to each animal.

I note it down, passing it through for Joan to check the national database for the details. About two or three minutes later she comes back with a name and address local to the practice, as well as a phone number, all about five minutes away in the car, or van in Skye's case.

'Look, can you hold onto this little one while I get my head around all this. I'll go make a visit and see what's going on. Surely there's no one daft enough to kill their own micro-chipped dog and not expect anyone to realise?'

I sigh, folding the blanket back over.

'I dunno, there's some stupid people out there, and to be fair they may have forgotten she'd been chipped in the first place. Tell the police where you're going though, might not be the friendliest person in the world if they've done this.' gesturing back down to the table.

'Yeah, you're right, I'll need to speak to them anyway, may as well see if they can be there for a door knock on this one, just in case like you say. I'll let you know how I get on. You're in all day right?'

I nod, and she departs back out through the front door of the building, phone to her ear to the office, or the police. Lifting the corner of the blanket, glancing over the dog again I can scarcely believe the mess it's in, struggling to think of a dog in a worse state. I'd seen some wrecks of course in my time in the Veterinary Corps; dogs blasted by shrapnel or pot-shotted by cowardly enemies, but the viciousness and the precision of the cruelty was unique to anything I'd ever come across in this quiet corner of the UK.

Nasty folks out there I told myself, very nasty.

I shuddered as I lay the blanket back over her.

It was later in the day, after a routine set of consults, mostly boosters and the odd ear infection, that I received a phone call from Skye, presumably as she finished work for the evening.

'That was bloody awful Mac, wait till you hear this. Turns out the dog had been re-homed. The address was its former owner, an old lady who'd given her up because she was struggling to walk it anymore with her arthritis. The son puts an advert on Gumtree as "free to a good home", next day a man turned up and adopted her. All about a month ago. She was off to live with a family just down the coast.'

She paused, taking a breath.

'God it broke my heart to tell her what happened Mac. I've got the police going round tomorrow to take a statement; I felt terrible, the look on her face when she realised her beloved dog had ended up in the wrong hands, I didn't know what to say, she didn't know what to do with herself.'

The sound of paperwork and keys, her van starting in the background, reminded me Skye had pulled a late one after an already long day, run off her feet trying to tie up the loose ends with the dog. I look up into the waiting room. Mr. Gregory and Ralph sat at the end, one miserable, one delighted to be here.

'That and I've had the son on the phone raising hell about it as well. What an absolute mess, not the friendliest of conversations but he needed to rant I suppose. The police didn't sound too interested but hopefully they need to show it some respect; potential for escalation if it's someone out practicing, see what they can come up with tomorrow I guess. Needless to say Mac, this goes nowhere, not even the staff room.'

Shutting the door to the consult room I lean back on the worktop beside the computer.

'Sounds awful Skye, you okay? Can't have been easy to deal with your end. Rest of the staff are still in the dark and I can make sure it stays that way. Let me know how you get on though, or if there's anything I can do to help. If you reckon a postmortem will help let me know and I'll get it organised.'

'Not sure that's going to help, we already know it's something brutal. I don't think intricate details are going to get us anywhere if I'm honest. Let me speak to the Police tomorrow and get back to you.'

We signed off the conversation not long after and I hung up the phone, pausing as I replaced the handset. How anyone could do it to the dog, to any dog, I dreaded to think. Checking my scrubs pocket, I still had the scrap of paper with the microchip number, and I stuck it into the search button of the practice software, hitting return. Instantly it brings up the file of the dog.

'Bella'. I didn't recognise the surname as a regular.

We haven't seen it in about 6 months, since its vaccines, but sure enough the animal description matches the lifeless corpse lying out cold in the freezer room. One of my colleagues had seen it, but the year before I had speyed it as a happy six-month-old, hadn't even had a season yet.

I slump into my chair. What a waste, not even two years old. Headed off for a happy new life with a new family. Instead caged into God knows what with a miserable end to her life. The pen I'm holding has snapped before I even realised what I'm doing, and looking down my right hand is smeared with its ink. I launch the rest against the far wall and stand up. This wasn't the usual thing I could bury deep down, not this.

I collect myself and call Ralph in from the waiting room.

'Now there's a man that's had a bad day.'

Mr. Gregory has spied the broken pen and spilled ink. Ralph instead has the treat jar in his eyeline.

'This town will do that to you son if you let it.'

I nod and check Ralph's eye, still quiet and distracted by the dog, showing Mr. Gregory the ulcer has gone. I take the raised eyebrow as a thank-you, turning and dipping into the treats for Ralph before he jumps down to the floor more delicately than I would expect.

'Saw that young terrier in the car park earlier. Warden near as knocked me down in such a hurry when I was making me appointment. Half a mind to say until I saw state of it.'

'It's a bad business Mr. Gregory. Very bad.'

'Aye son. You don't want dogfighting round here.'

'I'm not sure it was that.'

'Oh aye? Not the first time it's been here. Stain the streets red if you let it.'

I felt a wet nose against my hand. More treats required for a smiling Ralph.

'Sure it's nothing. It'll be a misunderstanding.'

I absently tickle the thick brown head appearing between my legs.

'Hmm, just you watch Mac. You keep that tall head down you hear. There's a dark tide in this town.'

He turns and heads out the door, forgetting to pay his consult fee while he's at it. I cancel it off. He's given me more than enough to think about, never mind chasing him down the street with the card machine. What did he say? *'Not the first time it's been here.'*

No point in dwelling on it, but as I cycle home I still haven't shrugged off the afternoon's angry feelings. Anna picks up on it too having barely touched any dinner, but I feel mildly better as she turns in for the night, leaving me channel hopping on the sofa before bed with a promise I'll be up soon. I've left out the part about what I'd like to do if I caught the culprit of course, but she could see from the look in my eyes, as I poured a second whiskey, it was a question best left alone for now.

As I sat and drained the remainder of single malt, the nagging, gnawing feeling was tugging away at me.

First Tank with his sketchy history and old battle scars, and now this poor little dog. I'd seen all sorts so far in my career: neglect, fights, trauma cases or horrific disease states gone far too far, irresponsible owners I'd like to put in the freezer instead of their pet, but something about the vicious end to the her life tore off a piece of me I knew I would never get back, and something told me there could be more to come, something worse, something this was the beginning of.

'Stain the streets red if you let it.'

Or it was just the whisky and the long day.

I put the tumbler back on the kitchen worktop ready to find the dishwasher in the morning, and hit the lights before heading quietly up the stairs to bed. Before long I was hemmed in by a cat and a warm duvet. The day fading away into darkness as I drifted off and forgot about the details — hopefully deep enough not to be woken again by thoughts of them during the night.

Chapter Five

'The nice thing about it is it's completely organic. A good selling point to the clients.'

The drug rep was in trying to flog natural remedies. Something about deep sea minerals was the latest buzz for joint care, and the environment. The other vets looked equally as unenthralled as they looked over the free merchandise. Biscuits and bullshit. A running joke in the practice.

'So we can set you up with an account if you like, it comes with our tiered reward system for sales.'

The question was directed to me. They all did it. For some reason I always had the final say, despite having the narrowest treatment choice in the clinical staff. What works works I reckon. Old habits die hard.

'Yeah mate we can give it a go. What's it for again, otitis?'

I knew fine well what it was for, but the mistake deflated him anyway. Mac on top. Good bargaining chip.

'It's a joint supplement Max.'

It's Mac you twat. Well played.

'Ok we'll try the month and see what the clients think. Anything else good?'

The answer was no, so I took another cake and wandered back through to the consult room, taking the free pen and notepad with me. Could I gift that to Anna? No probably not, she'd noticed the company logo immediately on her backpack after the conference grab last year. I paid for that one despite all the other birthday gifts.

I logged in to the computer to check my afternoon, brushing crumbs away from the keyboard and into a pile. As I swept them into the bin, the front door of the practice opened and shut. Figuring it for the departing rep, I scrolled down the screen and onto my prescription list.

An urgent local accent sounded from the front desk. I stepped out.

It wasn't the rep.

A hunched figure rests both hands on the counter, and hearing my door open he looks round and meets me with a fixed, haunted stare, his red eyes soaking me up. A man with a lot on his mind.

'Are you Mac?'

He looks familiar, but I can't seem to place him. Perhaps I've had him in consults a while back. One of the many thousands of faces I must have seen over the past year.

'I'm Carl, you saw my mam's dog the other day.'

Still no further forwards, I see a lot of mam's dogs, I raise my eyebrows in a friendly manner, but this only brings him further in, now quietly whispering, 'The one found in the bins mate, you know, Bella.'

'Oh, okay, hi mate.'

He apologises for the confusion.

'Do you want to come through, there anything I can help with?'

Moving through into the consult room behind me, we turn to face each other over the table. I have a nervous clear up, slotting my ophthalmoscope back into its charger and tidying away a few leaflets, while all the while Carl fidgets and searches the floor, before looking up and launching into a speech — something it sounds like he has been practicing over and over before he arrived.

'Look what it is is, I feel shitty mate. I found the new home for her and look what's happened, had the whole bloody family at me since the police and the dog warden came round, but the guy was so genuine when I met up with him. I just wanted to know a bit more, see if I could make myself feel any better about it if that's even possible. I know you're not allowed to give too many details out like, confidentiality and all that…'

He tails off and goes back to looking at the floor.

'I don't think there's too much you could have done mate, you weren't to know what was going to happen.' A white lie I think, screaming at him on the inside for giving up the dog so irresponsibly.

'Not exactly common, I don't think anyone would have thought that was going to happen, especially round here, not exactly the big city, is it?'

This doesn't seem to have helped. He still seems agitated and bordering on distress. I can see the sweat beading on his forehead and neck as he looks up again.

'Shit mate, it's not that. I know I've fucked up and let everyone down. To be honest I've…'

'What is it?' I lean down on the table between us, open body language, urging him on.

'… to be honest mate I've come here to warn you.' He continues, raising both hands to his head. 'Fuck. I'm sorry mate. What a mess.'

He finds the plastic chair I keep in the corner of the consult room and sits down with his head in his hands. A short time goes by and he picks a small piece of dirt from his shoelace, flicking it into the corner of the room. Thanks Carl.

'Well, it was just after the police and the dog warden came down, Mam called me all upset like, giving me a right earful about what happened. Said I needed to speak to the cops, tell them everything, see if they could find the guy who took her. After all I met him and handed the dog over and all that eh.'

He shifts in the seat, the sweat settling into his collar, turning it a darker shade of navy blue.

'Thing is, I didn't, did I? Fucking smart arse here phoned up the number I had from the Gumtree ad. Same guy, answers all innocent like, so I tell him I know what's going on and what the fuck did he do to Mam's dog. I start telling him what I'm gonna do to him, and he better start running. I'm no mug like so I don't mind telling the guy.'

By this point Carl has looked back up from the point he was fixed to on the floor, the yellow stain which won't shift no matter how hard we scrub it. It annoys me every time I look at it. I switch back up to meet his eye line again. Shoulders set back now, bristling with all the same confidence he must have had on the phone.

'I goes on like this letting him have it, full on, at least a minute or so. Only when I run out of gas and stop, he asks me if I'm finished. Starts laughing at me down the line. Sick man. Fucking sick. Full on laughing at me. Tells me to calm down and watch out like. Tells me I better forget this number ever existed. Then hangs up. Number blocked so I can't even ring it back like.'

He's calmer now he's unburdened a bit, and the sweat has settled into a darkened high tide mark on his collar, but he still nervously bounces a left knee up and down, his palm resting on it. He looks up at the ceiling and exhales with a swear word attached to the deep escaping breath.

'That's not all mate. Mac isn't it? Mind if I call you Mac? That wasn't all Mac. So I'm sitting watching the match last night; having a beer and trying to forget about it, pretend the whole bloody thing never happened. Next thing I know there's a knock on the door, nothing mad like, so I get up thinking it's one of the neighbours or something. Nice gentle knock nothing serious. So anyways, I open the door. Same guy's there, full on man, just pure staring at me. Behind him is this two other lads, one's small and lean like, the other one's this huge fella, all tattoos and muscles, like one of them MMA freaks. All three of them staring at me, before I know it we're in the house and I'm getting proper laid into on the floor by the two of them.'

He lifts his shirt to show off some impressive black and blue bruising around both sides of his ribs and abdomen. A fleeting image of the dog flashes into mind, battered and torn as it lay on the table I'm resting my weight on.

'When they're finished like I'm dragged up onto the sofa, thank fuck the missus was out like was all I could think, and the guys in me face telling me to forget this ever happened. Forget all about who he was and the dog and everything man.'

Carl looks pale again having relived the ordeal, so I tear off some paper towel from the dispenser, handing it to him to soak up some of the sweat he's poured out: whatever hasn't already leached into his top.

'Sounds awful mate. Sure you can't go to the police? Think they won't help?'

'No way pal. I've fucked up enough letting the dog go get killed, I'm not gonna let them come round and do the same to me Mam, no way like. No mate, I came to warn you, make sure you stay out these guys way in case you were thinking about anything heroic. Mam always said you lot at the vets were nice, so I'm warning you, stay away from the whole mess. If the cops come asking, tell them what you know and leave it, these guys aren't messing about.'

He unzips his jacket pocket and brings out a smartphone, unlocks the screen and starts swiping. Getting up from the chair he holds the phone up to my face. Initially it looks blurry, but I realise it's only slow and unpixelating. I take it from him.

A lean rat like face takes up the screen, and stares gauntly downwards.

'That's him mate. I don't look like much but I'm a security freak, got a small desktop camera on the laptop, captures everything if I ask it to. Well I got this off it after he left. Got it in case anyone breaks into the house you know, but it got him crystal clear on his way out see. Want you to know what to look out for. They've got nothing on you pal, but in case, you know?'

I hand the phone back and spend the next few minutes chatting, calming him down, making sure he's okay before he heads back out. The offer of a glass of water is declined, something tells me Carl usually takes something stronger, but it's only kind words that bring his blood pressure back down this time around.

A few words later, and with a firm handshake, he heads out, not before leaving me one of his business cards.

I'm supposed to get lunch and take a break, but I spend five or so minutes staring quietly at my blank computer screen taking in what has happened. I'm also mulling over the faintest feeling of recognition of the face on the screen, trying to pin it down. Nothing comes to me, and I can't seem to confirm a feeling of familiarity with the image either way.

The silence is eventually broken by the door opening, Jill beaming in with a smile and a cup of coffee in her hand, sliding it over the desk towards me. I don't give away any details, I'd be as well as announcing it all with a megaphone to the staff if I told her, and in between diverting the chat to her hike in the lakes the day before and the afternoon appointments, I follow her back out with the tea tray, taking my coffee through to the back instead, checking I'm not needed to help.

Within a few minutes or so I've forgotten about Carl and his mam, slipping into the familiar humour of the practice, joining in with the debate and ribbing over one of the nurse's new partner and his misfortune to be coming on a staff night out at the weekend. I've near enough let the screen image slip from my mind as I drink coffee and banter with colleagues, so it's not until later the feeling starts creeping back in as I bike home. Where do I know that face from? An old client? Somewhere else?

The next evening after consults are finished, I get changed for the ride home.

We've shut all the lights out and I've sent the last nurse home after locking up. The car park is pretty well empty. A few office lights from across the street still glare away in neon, and I assume any of the remaining cars are the workers from over the road. It isn't unusual to get cornered by a client late on, so checking no one has snuck a pet around the corner, I grab my bike from inside the side exit, unlatch the door and wheel it out; pushing out into the street as I fumble and check everything's zipped up.

As I turn into the main road a set of headlights appears behind me in the distance. I'm a slow commuter so it's common for cars to appear behind me, and I edge closer to the parked cars, waiting for it to pass around and into the avenue ahead which leads the way out of town. Still at a fairly laboured pace, enough to keep my balance, I look back over my right shoulder to check I'm in the clear or see if it's is pulling off into a side street. I'm alarmed however to see it there, about a metre from my back tyre idling along behind me, full beams.

I slow, pulling in beside the nearest parked car to rest a foot down. As I do, the car, a dark BMW, closes the small gap, blocking the way back into the road. The engine noise dies back as it slows to a stop, inches away from my handlebars.

It's dark and I can't see the driver, the glare of my own light stopping the dull glow reaching me from within. I faintly hear the mechanical whine of the window as it comes down, and a gust of sweet smoke breezes out from the interior. A lean silhouette presents black against the streetlight from the other side, and I struggle to make out the features as it turns towards me.

A dark hoodie and scarf cover most of the face.

'You wanna leave the little bin doggy alone pal and back the fuck off like. We divvin' like grasses in this town, so divvin' make us come back and find ye.' The voice inside warns, muffled by the face covering.

The left hand comes up from the gearstick, presenting a gun gesture as the electric window closes upwards.

I'm struggling with balance, still edged into a narrow gap between parked cars, so when the passenger door kicks open it easily throws me down and onto the nearest car, my bike clattering on top of me as it falls as well. As I grapple with gravity I hear it reversing down the street, the full beams obscuring the number plate, before it screeches off into a side road about a hundred yards further down the avenue.

I look around to see if anyone else is watching, but not even a front door has opened or a security light has come on: I'm alone in the street, hemmed in by parked cars and the trees lining the avenue all the way down to the Port turn-off.

What the hell just happened? What madman threatens a guy on his bike, let alone the local vet over a dog?

I brush down my jacket, checking zips and seeing if anything has torn, simultaneously playing back the short one-sided conversation in my head. My padded glove was torn on the heel of my left palm, presumably as I'd stopped myself on the tarmac, but I was unscathed save my pride and a scratch on the side of the bike.

Did he use the word '*us*'? Something about '*make us come back for you*'?

I'd had worse. No doubt about it. You don't get a free ride in the army when you're seen as the big country boy that was for sure. But it was par for the course, the same bravado which follows any group of men trying to show off to each other. But call you out in the street for doing your job, for taking care of animals? Bizarre. Not had that one before. Not in this town anyway.

I mulled it over and decided to let it slide. No point in letting it brew up to the point of anxiety. Same way I dealt with the guys in the army, testing you for weaknesses, seeing what the big college fella would put up with. It usually always fizzled out by itself and faded away. The odd guy needed hurled through a hedgerow here and there when the ranking officers weren't looking, but that was life. The guy in the BMW didn't look like he would take much difficulty throwing.

Wait and see Mac.

Wait and see.

I found the pedals again and pushed off into the road, half looking ahead, half watching over my shoulder, wincing every time pressure went through my aching hand.

Definitely going to hurt tomorrow.

Chapter Six

Skye was always drawn to this spot.

Peaceful, quiet, trees and wildlife surrounding her, it made the perfect office away from the office. A little island of calm.

She blew off the steam from her thermos. The smell of the coffee still strong from within as it found its way out into the air of the countryside around her. It fogged the corner of the iPad that currently had her work emails open.

This time around it was another boring email from payroll, trying to sort out her pension contributions. A subject dragging on far beyond Skye's usual patience for admin. Reminding herself it was worth it in the long run, when she finally hung up the jacket and dog lead, she courteously replied to the drones in head office for what seemed like the tenth time and powered down the tablet, slipping it back into the cover on the passenger seat.

One of the perks of life on the road was taking a break whenever and wherever you liked, and Skye was always drawn back to this secluded lay-by off the A192. She would try to stop here at least once a week to escape the bustle of work and to remind herself of the better things in life: namely taking the dog for a walk and not seeing other human beings.

Although young, late twenties, she wasn't one for late nights and dirty stop-outs, usually preferring dog walks and country pubs with friends instead of the cocktails and dance floors which occupied most of her co-workers back in the office. It was probably the same reason she was still single as well, albeit not for the want of her friends trying: just the perfect dog walk loving man hadn't shown up yet, only uninteresting office boys and the weirdos with huskies and German shepherds who thought themselves wild and interesting, unbeknownst to them however they just smelled like wet dog and fleecy jacket.

Shuddering at the thought and checking the side mirror for any lurking dog walkers, she screwed the lid back on the mug and picked up her phone, which had pinged with a message notification while she had been daydreaming.

A flutter of excitement flowed up inside as Mac's name appeared and the screen came to life. She swiped it open and clicked into messages.

She definitely had a sweet spot for her favourite vet and could still remember the disappointment in finding out the sullen soulful Scotsman was partnered up and settled down with an annoyingly perfect woman. What had made it worse still was the time she met his partner Anna in the supermarket, realising how nice she was: Skye couldn't even fantasise about hating her, stealing Mac off for romantic walks and pub lunches. No, Mac, albeit tall and delicious in his gruff Scottish ways, was most definitely off the market, and she would have to keep on looking. Whilst still avoiding creeps with Dobermans who smelled like raw meat. She opened the message.

It was a typical Mac text, short and to the point:

'Hi Skye, Mac at the vets here, any news on the terrier dog you brought in?'

Despite emailing and messaging countless times about work, and the multiple cases they shared together, he always formally reminded you of his name and that he was from the vets. Some odd Herriot style professionalism which never let you in to his world. She knew he was ex-army: he briefly mentioned an honourable discharge after a training injury one time, but it was about the extent of her knowledge on him beyond the practice. The ongoing frustration of it all made Skye want to tease him open even more, to see what lay beyond the thick veneer of intrigue he always laid down by only speaking about work. She could still remember the acute red tinge of embarrassment when they all met in the supermarket, his delightful partner rambling informally, Mac shrinking back to the vegetable aisle to look at the onions. A stark contrast to the strong professional she knew from the vets.

'No news yet Mac, Steve took over handling the case as the senior dog warden so I'm out of the loop. Has he been in contact yet for your witness statement? He'll usually need that for the case to proceed to a prosecution. If he doesn't let me know and I'll chase it up for you. Skye x'

She always put a kiss on the end of texts to cheer him up, as well as embarrass him: even if it was only the two of them reading the messages it still made her smile to do it.

She closed the phone case and pocketed it into her high vis jacket, starting the van engine — break over and onto the next appointment of the morning. A recheck on a potential welfare case she had started a few weeks ago. Nothing serious but it still warranted a second look: the never-ending caseload of a warden it would seem.

Despite the long empty road either side of her she still indicated right, back into town and cheerier for the warm coffee and short escape from work, her favourite spot working its magic once again. Making a mental note to catch Steve about the case next time she saw him, she added it to her lengthy list of work things to do.

Still, there were worse things in life. Blind dates with whippet owners who still lived at home with their mothers for a start.

***

I picked up the phone from behind the computer screen where I usually tucked it during consults, and typed in the code to open it up. It had purred a small vibration during the last consult, a booster check up with Mrs. Debtford and her aptly named Jack Russell called Barrel. She had not noticed it springing to life, too busy telling me about her husband's hip operation and how Barrel's increasingly large abdominal circumference could be attributed solely to his lack of dog walking, not her daily sumptuous portions for him, but it still irked my professionalism when it silently went off behind me mid conversation.

Scrolling down, I found messages and opened it up. It was a reply from Skye to the text I had sent two consults ago, and reading down it didn't have the right answers to the question I had asked. It ended with the usual 'x' from Skye, and even though she was just one of those friendly people in life I wished she wouldn't. Despite Anna being relaxed and easy in our relationship, probably because she's safe in the knowledge I'm punching well above my weight, it always panicked me to think she might come across the message thread with all those unrequited kisses.

To play it down I always kept my openings or replies short and formal, and never talked about anything other than work.

No doubt they would have a great laugh about my insecurity if they got the chance. I already had the impression an outgoing and confident girl like Skye has no lack of suitors, chuckling every time she teases the stuffy vet down at the practice, safe in the knowledge yet another affluent date is lined up for the weekend ahead. No Mac, you're better off with your simple life, and thank your lucky stars while you're at it Anna isn't the high-maintenance woman you would struggle to keep a hold of.

I'd about died of fright when we bumped into Skye in the supermarket; only a quick diversion off to the fresh produce had saved any awkwardness. Pretty smooth on my part I had thought. Although I had nothing to hide, it wouldn't have been far beyond Anna to tease me constantly about the over friendly dog warden.

It was a worry Steve hadn't been in contact. What I thought would be an urgent matter for a relatively quiet animal welfare team, didn't seem to be the big headline news that Skye or I thought it ought to be, so I open my email browser and send off a short and polite update enquiry to the Welfare team, FAO Steve, and close it down before my next consult; this time making sure my phone is silent and well hidden.

It was Friday lunchtime in the practice, which usually meant a treat lunch, sometimes taken care of by the boss, but more often, whoever was free first after morning surgery would head out into town and go to a local sandwich shop. Today it was my turn, so as I clicked off the final consult, and as the nurses tidied up and prepped theatre for Monday, I zipped up my jacket against the wind and walked the short distance to the town centre, the order list and both hands dug deep down into my front pockets.

After about five minutes, I had crossed the road over into the square, dodging the market stalls selling everything from secondhand DVDs to knock-off candles, and headed into the nice deli with its hand painted sign and wooden tables out the front. Few had taken up the offer of al fresco dining today given the weather, so I joined the queue snaking inside, eyeing up the remaining rolls and wraps to see if I could satisfy the order from the staff. A bit of small talk later at the front of the line, I loaded up a carrier bag, turning to weave past the other customers who were still either sat down or queuing around the tables.

I padded myself down to check my pockets for my wallet, a nervous habit I have when leaving any shop: call it 'welcome to your thirties' anxiety if you will. Satisfied it was still there, I reach to the handle, only to have my hand cracked on the knuckles as the door pushes open and a gust of air swooshes in following it.

I'm a tough enough guy, but it hurts, and the f word falls out, shocking the pair of old women sitting to my left, still nursing cups of tea as they catch up on gossip, the remnants of morning scones scattered between them.

'Sorry ladies, apologies.' I utter, turning to focus my attention on the figure swaggering in, firing a look which sums up my lack of enthusiasm at his brisk entry. Refraining from the urge to give out a decent piece of my mind, all too aware I'm wearing a jacket with the vet practice logo on it, I eye up the little fellow in front of me.

'You should be more careful mate, no need.'

Deep and Scottish, a bit of granite in there.

I'm met by an unpleasant grin set below small dark eyes. Moving past me and still smirking, I catch the rancid odour of sweat combined with the sweet smell of cannabis. A day's grime festering out from under a stained tracksuit.

'What ye ganna de about it vet boy like?' drawls the man, turning and heading up the to the counter to place an order, ignoring the queue around him. I flex my neck sideways, letting it click, and decide to leave it alone. Not worth it I think. Turning back to the door for a second time, this time catching the more sympathetic eyes of the two old women on my way, I head out into the market square and back along the road to the practice. I'm not easily riled, but it's annoying having to maintain professionalism and not bite back, especially so soon after getting knocked off the bike a few days ago.

Later on after lunch I'm still annoyed, and the nurses have all noticed it.

'You alright Mac, not saying much?' Sammy asks as she picks up coffee mugs to make a round.

'Just the idiots in this town as per usual Sammy, can't seem to move for them sometimes. Looks like I've a few in this afternoon looking at the list. Wish me luck eh.'

Sammy smiles, 'Ha, you'll be fine, give them the usual Mac charm. Or is it only the old dears that one works on?'

She winks and cheerily moves round collecting the rest of the mugs, taking final orders as I head into consults and power up the screen to check for messages, dragging the cursor over to my first client of the afternoon, opening their file.

As I turn round to the waiting room however, I get a sudden flashback to Carl and his mother's dog, the red plastic chair in the corner reminding me: slumped with his head in his hands, the sweat collecting on his collar. I ponder on it for a few seconds before the feeling of déjà vu hits me, the phone picture flashing into my mind. Immediately, the nagging feeling I've had for the past few days lifts as I realise the man from the deli is the same ratty face from Carl's home security footage.

The more I piece it together, the more I recognise him from around the town centre: the betting shop when I have the occasional weekend flutter, smoking outside the bar opposite the main supermarket as I walk past for lunch, and something about the silhouette in the BMW who knocked me over. Had he meant to try and spook me in the deli? Was he trying to front me out on purpose now? It was bold to tempt fate by taunting me, but I guess I must seem like the easy-going gentle giant when I'm holding puppies on our social media, or wobbling along the street trying to keep balance on my bike in the wind.

The thoughts whirled around in my head during consults, which turned out to be straightforward and full of nice cases for a change. A litter of kittens from the previous week with a serious case of cat flu were all purring and playful, and the owner was gratefully dropping off a bottle of wine to add to the Christmas party collection as I dispensed their next worming. The rest of the afternoon petered itself out with boosters and phone calls, and before long I was getting changed, wheeling out my bike for the thirty minutes or so trip back home.

Heading out into the avenue, I switched on my beam, lighting the familiar darkness and the gaps the lampposts failed to cover. My eyes were gradually beginning to focus in, still square from looking at computer screens most of the day, and soon enough, up ahead in the beam, I see a double-parked car ahead, lights off, exhaust pipe smoking an off-white haze into the wintry night's air.

I check behind and overtake sharply, but no sooner have I passed it I'm illuminated by headlights and the sound of the car's engine revving up behind me. Moments later the roar is closing in behind and to the outside, jerking in front with just metres to spare. I do well enough not to spill over the handlebars, into what I can see is the same BMW from before, only I now notice a mismatched rear panel, grey and grimy against the darker bodywork.

The door didn't open this time. Instead, the window slides down once more to reveal the same lean silhouette, dimly illuminated by the radio console and the dash lights, the face inside betrayed by the lack of other lights around us.

My new unpleasant friend from the deli and Carl's grainy phone screen stares back: dark eyes sunken above high unattractive cheekbones.

'Seems like yer still digging about where yous ain't wanted, you and yer pet bitch from the council, the young 'un Skye.'

He barked, the same rough whiney accent as this afternoon. I catch a glimpse of uneven discoloured teeth as the lips hiss out the final syllables.

'Boss told me t'tell you fella it stops right now like, otherwise it ain't me and you on the street anymore, it's me and the lads round your fancy house in the dene wi that fit doctor tart ye gan home to every night. Trust me pal, dead pets will be the last of yer worries by the time a've been through ye with the fighting dogs.'

He stopped talking and I stared back through the window into those piggy eyes, feeling menacing, but probably looking ridiculous with a bike helmet clipped under my chin.

Raising up his left hand into the same pistol shape as before I resisted the temptation to grab it and pull him through the passenger side window: to stamp the life out of him there and then. I didn't know who else was watching us now, or worse, our home, so I stared dead eyed back at him as he hit the button to raise the window, before driving off, far slower than last time, and far easier for me to read the number plate as he drove away down the street.

About eighty yards down the avenue though he turned right without signaling, and I stepped down hard on the pedals to set off after him into the back streets. Lights off and tucking in close, I managed to keep up in the small narrow streets, far enough back as he turned off into another street, eventually slowing and stopping in one of the quieter avenues of terraced council houses. I hung back and edged an angled view from about fifty yards away, watching as he hit the key fob on the car and entered the house adjacent. Letting a few minutes go by to make sure he hadn't forgotten anything, I slowly cycled past, making a note of the number before heading back to the main road and out of town towards home, my mind racing.

Later, and after Anna had gone to bed to read and get an early night, I'm sitting with another whisky in front of the television — far too many already this month — and I'm idly flicking through channels, mulling over what to do. Dinner had been quiet, small talk about each other's days. Anna, I guess, thought I'd had another rough day and didn't want to probe it any further, and we watched the next episode of The Sopranos; something we'd been working through for months. Anna for the first time, but myself enjoying it all over again once more.

It did its best to distract me from the events of a few hours before, but watching those familiar characters, full of bravado and aggression, a world of macho and toughened charisma, none of it was the antidote I needed to settle down, and I found myself stewing with the dark malt, running things over and over again in my mind.

The urge to go over there and tear the little runt apart was strong. He was a tiny guy. I was a big angry Scotsman. I didn't think the match up was going to be a problem.

But what he'd said about the house, about Anna, about our life: I didn't want to risk it all by being hotheaded, a full-on maniac. And what if I went to the police? They'd have a word, scare him off. But the rest of them, the unknown entity I'd have to constantly worry about and look over my shoulder for; I didn't think it was worth the risk. Not for the sake of my own personal satisfaction or to prove a point. But then there was the other side. The animals. Tank. Bella. Hung on a tree in the dene. Torn apart and left for dead. And what about those yet to still meet their fate at the hands of whoever these people were? Go to the police about them? Would the police already know and be dealing with it?

I drained the whisky and decided to sleep on it. Skye had already said she'd be chasing Steve up so I figured it was worth just speaking to her tomorrow, to see what was happening — before I made any more mountains out of molehills.

I still didn't sleep well however. I had the nagging feeling things were about to get much worse before they got better.

Chapter Seven

The coffee machine clicked and hissed, steam twisting its way through the small pod before I clunked it out with the handle. It was 2 p.m. so whisky was out. Anna wouldn't be happy if a liquid lunch meant a below standard dinner later.

It was Wednesday afternoon, a half day from work, and I took the mug through to the sitting room, nestling into the sofa with my laptop. Yesterday's email to Steve the dog warden was still lacking a reply — frustrating enough — but I suppose he was a busy guy: the whole thing was a big deal and would take him some time. Still, it had left its unanswered questions in my mind, and with the new threats festering from last night, there were even more in there.

A rain shower outside had put an end to my plans for a garden tidy up, so after a quick leg stretch with Tank in the dene I had made the brew and cleared a space on the busy coffee table, putting my feet up beside a warm ginger cat. Much to the cat's annoyance however, I had also dragged Tank's bed into the living room, and he gratefully flopped down in front of the warm radiator. His big flappy snores grumbled rhythmically after about five minutes, soon accompanied by deep rhythmical purrs from Quint who had nestled back down beside me in a huff, mildly upset he wasn't allowed to sit on the laptop itself.

Anna wouldn't be back until after six p.m. so I had myself a few hours to kill before tidying up and making dinner.

Spurred on by recent events I had decided to research dog fighting. My two after work 'warnings', Tank, the Jack Russell Bella, as well as Carl and his visit from the shady local gangsters, had sealed the deal for me. All of it had got me thinking about the bigger picture. There was something out there these people were trying to protect. There had to be. Otherwise why bother with their threats?

I was familiar with fight wounds, dog behaviour and its hierarchy, and I wasn't an idiot when it came to gambling and the knowledge there was a murky criminal sub-world into which normal society didn't venture. But how did it work? If this was dog fighting surely there would be structure to it all. Not some local runt running about town tearing it up at will, threatening the local vets while he was at it.

There would be something out there. Some pattern repeating throughout the underworld, something which would be a tried and tested method. Sure I wasn't daft enough to expect a blueprint of a dog-fighting organisation on the internet, but I figured at least there would be enough out there to piece some form of an idea together.

So I sat, coffee mug in one hand, the other working the laptop, and trawled through whatever I could find. God help me if anyone ever looked at my browser history, some of the stuff out there was sickening, but after getting the hang of it: the lingo, the tactics, and most of all the mindset, it was easy enough to tap into what I was looking for.

After a few hours, the sharp autumn light coming in from the garden was beginning to fade. A second coffee was drained, its cold mug sat back on the table beside my rested feet. Tank's snores had settled into the occasional sigh, and Quint had long since departed to search for a warm radiator of his own.

There was a fair idea of how things worked now, gained through a combination of online documentaries, news articles, social media groups and threads. A lot of it was circumstantial, or pure conjecture, but a lot of repeated and cross-referenced information had formed itself into a decent picture of it all.

The whole thing was terrifying.

The basic premise was always the same. To have a dogfight you needed to have at least two dogs: one to be a winner and one to be a loser. It also follows that in any sport when you have victory and defeat, you can also place bets on who's beating who, and you can apply odds to make those bets more attractive. The higher the odds; the higher the returns on your investment.

Now, with any prizefight you usually have an undercard — a series of lesser fights building up to the main event. This makes the evening more of a spectacle and gets the punters in the mood for the big showdown at the end. Financially speaking, it also means more bets, and more money changing hands. If a punter wins early on, you have multiple more opportunities to win money back off him, and you can set your odds accordingly, depending on how desperate you are for re-investment.

Translate this to dog fighting. You need multiple dogs to make an event. You need strong, battle-hardened dogs you can rely on to win, and you also need weaker dogs you can rely on to lose. There's no point in having your undercard full of tough guys taking on tough guys. They take a long time to train: losing multiple good dogs in any one event isn't a sustainable business model. Consequently you also need a supply of weak dogs. These can be the dogs which haven't trained well and aren't worth the investment, or easier still, dogs you pick up off the street: strays or rehomes. Nobody misses them. Nobody expects the cruelest of worlds to take them in. Nobody thinks to ask questions.

So, you've got your participants, what next.

Next you need spectators. As an illegal enterprise you can't advertise a dogfight, so you rely on word of mouth amongst trusted clientele. You need to know there won't be any surprise visits from the police or the RSPCA, so it's best to find your punters from the less scrupulous side of the law. Organised crime goes hand in hand with your new venture: love of violence, love of money, as well as macho showing off. It's also a good place to do lucrative side business and make contacts in the underworld. Avoid inviting the careless or the drug dependent in society; they're much more likely to get arrested and turn you in as part of a plea deal.

And of course, avoid wives and girlfriends. Nothing ruins a dogfight more than emotions. This was a testosterone show after all.

So you've got your fighters. You've got your trusted criminal spectators. Next you need a location. It's a no brainer not to do this in the middle of the town centre or the suburbs: you need to consider your noise pollution, your neighbours and your clientele. Nothing screams an organised naughty boys club more than a load of high-end motors, parked up in an industrial estate or abandoned pub. So your ideal location requires acreage; a quiet country retreat to cater for noise. Also, multiple escape routes in case of any unwanted blue lights and attention. Generally speaking, your best bet will be farm buildings — either abandoned, or better, owned by a farmer you can control easily when required. They also have the added benefit of ample disposal avenues; losing participants need to go somewhere, and worst case, any unruly clientele can also be quietly dealt with. Just don't expect an EU subsidy anytime soon.

Next up you need the buzz.

No one's going to come to your event to see some dreary one-sided fight over in seconds, so you create legends. You create myths. Myths of monstrous dogs so evil and powerful they can't be beaten. So strong and tenacious they must be worth betting the big money on. You create matched up prize fights so tantalising that powerful people will be bending over backwards to be in your pocket and get themselves an invite. Big enough players who will travel the distance to see your all conquering killing machine do his business. Big enough players who might also do business with you, or think of you when they need a lucrative favour in the future. A dogfight with the local nobodies invited isn't going to have the big bets you can take a decent cut from: so, the bigger the spectacle, the bigger the prizes and rewards.

Add all these ingredients together and you can have a successful dog-fighting network. It takes time to get it up and running, but once initiated it becomes a melting pot of organised crime which pays healthy dividends. A sustained effort and you can become the ringmaster of a neat criminal clubhouse, the R&R for organised crime, the meeting of minds and provider of blood sports for the bloodthirsty.

It all of course takes more than one person. You need activity and you need help. You need silence at the right times, and you also need the occasional noise too. You need to pick your crew carefully; the stakes are high, but the rewards are higher once the gig is up and running. You need a team around you that takes orders and isn't afraid to get their hands dirty — so you need your dog trainers, your dog snatchers, and you need your tech help too. You also need dirt on everybody to keep them quiet and in-line, and of course you need muscle to keep things on track.

You have the team and those ingredients, and you might have yourselves a decent dog-fighting ring…

I shut the laptop closed and sat back into the sofa, arms raised and behind my head, staring up at the ceiling. My mind was racing at the possibilities of what might be going on.

A past life of adrenaline, risk and excitement was flaring up inside me, one I had worked hard to forget about. One that had brought more than enough trouble back home.

I figured out eventually there would be no harm in digging deeper. If there was no local dog fighting circuit, no harm would come of it, no one to offend if no one was involved. Just some local isolated idiots harming animals. Not exactly ideal in the community, but hardly the recipe for a major local crime syndicate. I did have to seriously think of the consequences however, not so much for myself but for my family: Anna, the pets, our life in the idyllic little house we'd bought and nurtured. Tread carefully with this one Mac. If it isn't some Walter Mitty fantasy and turns out to be the real thing, things could go south very quickly indeed.

I picked up an empty notebook I'd been saving for something noteworthy and took down a few pointers for myself on how to start. Being a complete novice at any form of investigation was of course the major stumbling block. Spending twelve years in clinical veterinary practice doesn't prepare you for breaking open the criminal underworld, and nothing screams greenhorn in the police department like a guy wearing a scrub-top and a stethoscope around his neck. Logic, however, would hopefully be my saving grace.

Forget working out locations. There are hundreds of potential sites for dog fighting, and even if this thing existed, I could spend years searching for something that wasn't exactly going to be sign-posted or obvious in the first place. Trudging about, raising suspicion, offending people while I was at it was the quickest way to make a fool of myself.

Then there was tapping into local organised crime. Forget it. Absolute non-starter. If anyone for one minute would accept that a squeaky-clean vet suddenly wanted to go dogfighting and laying bets, it would coincide with hell freezing over. A fairly good way to get struck off the Royal College register while I was at it. I can see the look on Anna's face when the conversation comes up at the dinner table.

No, the safest bet was to quietly find the crew responsible, or at least one of the vulnerable junior members, and go from there. My scummy new friend for instance if he would oblige me.

From what I could tell with online research, everything about this was usually as close knit as possible, so I wouldn't be expecting a heart to heart in the pub anytime soon. I guess it would depend on how organised any potential gang were. If this was dog-fighting, it was in something of a fledgling state.

The messiness of what I had seen so far had suggested so. Surely a slick run, tight knit syndicate wouldn't be making the sloppy errors which had splashed out into the community so far, would it? A well-run outfit wouldn't be doing their dirty laundry in public, ditching dogs in alleyways, and losing them out in the dene?

I eased out of the sofa and nudged Tank awake with my foot, edging him out into the kitchen. Dragging his enormous bed back into the side extension was met with a disgruntled stare, but it was nothing compared to the look Anna would give me if she realised the big hairy beast had been asleep in the living room for two hours. Everyone waited patiently as I flicked the vacuum over the carpet, before getting food containers from the cupboard and filling everyone's bowls for dinner service in the kitchen, as well as for Tank in his new side palace around the corner.

All animals fed and watered, I cleaned up the worktop and laid out dinner ingredients, setting to work getting things ready for when Anna would appear in an hour or so wondering what I had been doing with my afternoon. The research had put me in a darker mood, so I scrolled down through my music library and started up an acoustic play-list to match the downbeat rhythm of the chopping board as it rocked back and forth with every knife stroke.

Old, familiar feelings of rage and revenge were mixing themselves up against each other, feelings I pushed way down over time. Buried down under layers of good living and hard work, somehow they were clawing their way back through the sanctitude.

Still, at least Anna would be home soon, to distract me from myself as only she could. I threw the rest of dinner into the pan and set it all on a low simmer.

I looked across the room; Tank was staring at me from the side entrance, lead in mouth, grinning at me with a look of excited anticipation.

'C'mon then mate. Quick one before she gets home yeah.'

Chapter Eight

Skye checked the side mirrors of the van.

The dark BMW, its rear door a mismatched grey, still followed on, now only three cars back.

Sometimes edging out for an overtake, then tucking back in, it had been with her most of the morning, following her every move around town. Even when she stopped for a call it sat, far away, making no attempt to disguise itself: exhaust smoking in the late autumn morning.

The crouched, dark silhouette behind the wheel was always too blurry to recognise, the bumpy moving image in the mirror never still enough to catch a glimpse of the face under the hoodie.

What was it doing?

Steve's number was on speed-dial on the van's dashboard, ready to press the green call icon as she drove out of town. The saloon sat two behind her now in the long convoy of vehicles that waited behind a tractor. It edged out once more. Then back in. The grey door catching the sunlight as it bounced off the wet tarmac.

She slowed and indicated left, to her favourite layby.

It was a relief then when it drove past her on the A192, snaking into the distance with the long line of traffic as she pulled in. Had she been imagining it? Was it just a coincidence tied into her day?

She turned the engine off, the noise drifting off into the countryside around her. She reached into the glovebox for her iPad and set about checking her inbox, pouring out a coffee from her thermos. The warm comforting smell soothed her rattled nerves.

Another pension email demanding attention, and still no reply from Steve about the terrier when she checked her phone messages, she idly sipped at the cup, breaking half a biscuit from the stash in her rucksack and breathing in the frosty air from the open driver's side window. The lay-by was empty, as it usually was, and apart from the constant drone of traffic behind her, she was able to pick out a few bird songs from the hedgerow and the trees beyond the front wheel.

In and amongst the soft sounds from nature, and the bustle of leaves moving gently in the wind around the van, she gradually became aware of an engine slowing down through its gears, slowly coming to a halt on the road behind her. This sound unfortunately always signaled the end of her breaks. There was a strict no idling policy from the bosses back at the council, with all time on the road to be accounted for. She didn't like to take the chance of being reported by a local busy body and so she would move on when joined in her normally quiet and peaceful spot.

Getting ready to turn the keys in the engine she eyed up the side mirror, ready to stand down if it was a U-turn. To her dismay however, the car slowing down had the same mis-matched rear driver's side door she'd been seeing all morning, and signaling right, the BMW idled jolted forward as a space opened in the oncoming traffic.

It crept in slowly behind her, tucking rear and left so she couldn't see the driver's side door, only hearing it open and shut as she fumbled to turn the key and find the window control on the door, acutely aware how open and exposed she was by herself in the lay-by. Trapped and blocked by the car behind.

As the window edged up at a painfully slow mechanical pace, Skye caught sight of a dark figure moving quickly along the side of the van. The adrenaline suddenly shot ice cold through her as she remembered it was still unlocked, and reaching for the fob still in the ignition, the door burst open and she was pulled out onto the dirt of the lay-by. Birds shot from the hedgerow as she clattered to the ground, and the peaceful song was shattered with panicked squawks and flapping wings thrashing the leaves as they escaped the branches.

Looking up to catch a glimpse of her attacker, a small lean figure stooped over her, face covered by a ski mask and hood, breathing heavily with the exertion of pulling her down from the van. Still dazed, she was pulled up from her fetal position and thrown back against the vehicle's side, thudding her head off the plastic trim and metal doorframe.

Defensively raising her arms up to either side of her head she soon felt a heavy, crushing kick under her right elbow which crumpled her back down into the dirt. Shooting pains like lightening exploded out from her ribs as she gulped mouthfuls of now increasingly painful air. As the initial shock wore off, she opened her eyes to find a glinting blade inches from her nose. Serrated on one side, clean brushed steel the other.

Another surge of adrenaline flooded in as she writhed to get up, but a strong, wiry arm pinned her against the van.

'You wanna watch what questions you g'an asking missy,' the thick accented voice growled at her, 'a won't think nowt of slitting your pretty little throat and feeding ye to the dogs like.'

The blade was withdrawn, and a heavy slap caught Skye around the cheek, knocking her back down into the cold mud beside her front tyre.

'I haven't done anything! I don't know what you're on about! Please I've done nothing wrong!'

This brought rage back into the figure, and another kick to the ribs curled Skye back up into a small ball, eyes tight shut and arms around her head. She felt the small sharp metallic point of the knife pressing against her temple, and she squeezed herself tighter into a knot on the ground.

'Fucking bin dog man! Ye fucking leaving it alone ye slag! Next time ah'l bring the dogs, make a reet fucking mess of ye!'

The blade was lifted but Skye lay still, eyes screwed tightly shut, body braced surely for another kick into the ribs or abdomen.

As the seconds passed and the sound of blood rushing through her head calmed, she heard the car engine revving and whining as it reversed speedily back away from the van. Tyres spun and dirt flew. She opened her eyes only to see it drifting back onto the tarmac, back out in the direction of town.

Checking her sides and dabbing her temple for blood she looked upwards and breathed in. The adrenaline flood was replaced by shooting pains in the ribs, and after two failed attempts, she pulled herself up to the driver's seat of the van and dragged herself in, hastily locking it with shaking hands — dirty with the mud and grit of the layby — before finally hugging herself over the steering wheel.

As the pain eased into duller waves with every breath, she looked up through teary eyes and over the hedgerow into the fields beyond. Trying to comprehend what had happened, the screams from the attacker started to come back to her.

'The little bin dog. Leave it alone.'

What mess had she stumbled herself into? The only people who knew about the slaughtered dog were Steve, Mac and the member of the public who called it in. After that, the previous owners of the dog and a few of the vet practice staff if Mac hadn't been as careful as she'd asked. Who on earth would be trying to protect and stop an investigation? Surely the police officer Steve had spoken to wouldn't have been letting it slip this early in an enquiry?

No, it didn't make any sense. Everyone involved was on the side of the dog. Surely no one else could have got wind of it this early on?

The sinking realisation that Bella could be part of something much bigger started to weigh down.

She'd had idle threats from cases she'd investigated, but never this, never from one animal. No, she had to speak to Steve, she had to speak to Mac, to warn them. In case they were next.

Chapter Nine

Destination country, France. Check.

Method of travel, ferry. Check.

Taking your dog overseas so it can experience a new place to defecate. Check.

I stamped the final page of the health certificate, filing it behind the computer for the owner to pick up later. Twelve certified pages of text customs would glaze over at the border before waving them through. Twelve pages that cost over a hundred pounds to produce.

I wonder, only for a minute, if Hooper would like a trip to France. Take Quint as well. Comedy cat berets to embarrass Anna in the channel tunnel. No, probably not. They were happy with pooping in Northumberland.

The initial rush of morning consults was settling down, and I took five minutes to top up my mug from the pot in the kitchen, idly waiting for the next appointment to call in.

I hadn't heard from Skye as promised, and after the incident on the ride home I was keen to see if she had gotten anything further, so I picked up the phone and dialled her work mobile. It went straight through to voicemail.

'Hi Skye, it's Mac from the vets. Wondering if you'd had any developments on the terrier dog, anything back from your investigation or the police; let me know, it's been mildly interesting at this end.'

I hung up and took a sip of coffee. Not the greatest today, clearly the work experience kid was doing the rounds, but as I lowered the mug back down to the desk my phone rang, vibrating against the worktop, slowly making its way over to the sink.

'Skye. That was quick, barely finished leaving you a message. Busy at work are you?'

'Something like that Mac.' she sounded a bit quiet and distracted. 'Wanted to let you know I'm not looking at the terrier anymore, Steve took it over, made it a 'priority' case. I hadn't gotten far with it to be honest. Did I tell you already? I can't remember.'

'Yeah, I think you mentioned it. Shame, I was keen to follow it up.'

'You said it had gotten interesting? What do you mean?'

'Well, nothing.' I lied. 'Some guy giving me hassle, telling me to leave it. Same guy Carl, the owner's son had been scared of I think. Bit of a runt, I'm not particularly worried about it if I'm honest. He did say something interesting though, like it was all part of a bigger picture, that I should leave it alone. Not that I was digging into it anyway, I thought it was only you and Steve who knew about it so far. But he was keen to press it, like it was some big deal if I were to poke my nose into it.'

The line remained quiet.

'You still there?'

'Sorry Mac. Sorry.' Skye still sounded faint, tearful. Nothing like her usual strong and confident self, the girl I was used to bossing me about with her high viz jacket and clipboard.

'Everything okay?'

'Sorry Mac.' A sigh from the other end. 'I'm actually not at work today, I had to take the day off. I got attacked yesterday while I was out on the job, they got me while I was taking a break out in the van.

'Shit Skye, sounds awful, you hurt?'

'Nothing except my pride and a few bruises. I got away lightly, reckon it could have been a lot worse.'

'Well what did the police say, you did call them didn't you?'

'Well, no, that was it, the whole thing was a threat, said if I went to the police they'd be back. Said it was all to do with the terrier dog I brought to you and I should drop it, reckoned they'd be back if I kept at it. Next thing I knew it was over and he was gone.'

'He? You sure?'

I made sure the door to the consult room was shut and no one was hanging around outside listening, the work experience for a start.

'Look Skye if I'm honest I had the same. Near enough knocked me off my bike last night getting home. Same guy, it's happened twice. Telling me to leave it and forget about it all. Knew where I lived and everything, telling me they'd be back if I stuck my nose into anything else.'

'Shit, what are we going to do Mac?'

'Well, we're going to leave it alone don't you think? And I suggest you do the same, warn Steve too. Last thing we need is him getting his head kicked in as well while he's out on duty. Didn't the police follow all this up?'

'I think it's been shut down, lack of evidence, I don't know. Like I say it's Steve's case now. All I knew is some uniform came round initially to take some details, which I gave, as much as I could, then some detective flashing a badge was in Steve's office and that's the last I heard of it. Hasn't told me anything extra since he took the case. Same with Tank, your dog. Said he'd investigate it but never did, doesn't seem interested in any bigger picture, or if he is, he's keeping it all quiet for now. Perhaps it is part of something bigger, something no one's telling us about.'

'Well, I think it's got to be more than Tank and the terrier. The way we've both been threatened. Got to be something else don't you think? I'm not planning on getting myself into any more trouble mind, and I'd suggest you do the same if I were you.'

'Mac you're 6ft and the rest. What trouble are you going to get into? I'm the one who should be worried.'

'Exactly. I'm a big thick farm boy. Anna's not though, and neither are you. Sounds like you found out more than what they're capable of; I sure as hell don't want the same thing happening at my house as she gets home. No, I'm dropping it and I suggest we both stay well clear, and for God's sake go to the police if it happens again.'

'Look I know you're right. But that big picture, what if there's other animals they're killing or maiming. I can't sit by and let it happen. I couldn't live with myself.'

'Well, we'll have to hope Steve pulls his finger out won't we. He's head of department isn't he, if he's not getting things done who is?'

'I dunno. The way he's been so quiet about it.'

'Give him time Skye and stay out of it. Sounds like we've both got targets on our backs with whoever's doing this. Don't whatever you do give them reason to come back for you okay?'

'Okay Mac. But keep me posted.'

'I will, you too, and stay safe.'

'I will. And thanks for calling me.'

With that we ended the conversation. She sounded worried, but there wasn't much I could do about it right now. It was terrifying what had happened, and the thought of it happening to Anna filled me with dread.

I drained the coffee mug in front of me, bitter and cold, and tucked it behind my computer screen, readying for a final few consults before going into theatre.

Instead I stared at the screen. For all the advice I'd given to Skye, to leave it, to stay away from them, I wasn't sure myself I was done with it. The nagging feeling I wasn't going to let it be sat and persisted in my mind all afternoon. Perhaps Skye had the same feeling and was selling me the same story. Perhaps we'd both keep pulling at the threads of it, picking away until it either crashed down around us, or even on top of us.

The answer for me came later in the day, far quicker than I would have wished for.

I'd kept a free half hour for reporting lab results and calling a few owners, and after printing off a drugs label for my last patient, shouting round the corner to reception, I picked up a handset and walked through to the office to get a bit of peace and quiet. I was keen to make the most of it. Get my admin done and I could have a prompt finish at six, get home and see Anna before taking Tank out before it was only streetlights left.

My hand on the office door handle, I sighed as my name was called out from reception. I turned to face Joan, who had followed me through to the back.

'Sorry Mac, walk in, think you can fit in a dog bite? Don't think it's too serious but the guy wants it seen now.'

Kissing my free time goodbye, I turned and walked back in the direction of the consult room, slotting the phone back into its charger on the way past. Everyone knew fine well I couldn't say no to an emergency consult, so they only had to ask, but it was still annoying as time slipped away from me. The waft of tobacco from Joan's latest cigarette lingered in the corridor as I went through and edged past Sammy as she stood at the blood machine, carefully pipetting samples for the afternoon courier.

'No rest for the wicked eh Mac?'

'You're not kidding. You seen Jill back since she went to the lakes? Never ending streak of Joan here it seems.'

No reply but I stifled a laugh as Sammy acted out falling over, presumably a hill in the Lake District somewhere involving my favourite receptionist. I mimed fake disapproval back at her as I ducked into the consult room.

I logged back into the computer and dragged up the waiting room icon to read the animal's file. 'New client.' Brilliant, some dog which hadn't seen the vets for a decade, and an owner who will complain about money all the way through. I checked the table was clean, picked up a stethoscope and walked out into the waiting room.

'Markwell?'

I looked out over the waiting room to the far side, and my heart sank when I saw the owner, just what I needed. A runty frame and ratty features sat clothed in a matching grey tracksuit, faded black socks tucked into scuffed black trainers. A sly smile widened; the man from the deli, the BMW last night and probably Skye yesterday, was walking over to me with a timid looking Staffordshire Bull Terrier on a choke lead, its ear torn and streaked with dried blood. I let him pass, following him into the consult room.

'We meet again Mr Vet.'

'You're taking the piss, right?'

Despite standing tall over him, he looked relaxed as he sat in the corner chair and unleashed the staffy, which sat cowering beside him, its ear a mess.

'You g'an turn away an animal in need or summat? Big softy like you, animals in pain man, needs your help. Just cause we've a misunderstanding doesn't mean ma little girl needs sufferin' does it?'

He knew fine well I'd look at the animal, and he nudged it over to me with the sole of his trainer. 'G'an on girl, see the vet.'

The petite staffy came across and nestled in between my knees as I knelt beside it, cupping its head in one hand, holding up its damaged ear in the other. Swallowing my pride, I examined it. A small sharp cut to the left ear, neat and clean, which must have bled like hell after it happened.

'Not much like a dog attack, what did you say happened to it?'

I looked up at David Markwell, legs splayed and hunched over the edge of the chair with his eyes fixed on me. I looked down to where his hands met to see a small blade moving playfully between his fingers, one side serrated, the other sharp and clean.

'You did this to her?'

I stood up tall, towering over him as he rose from the chair, a creepy sadistic grin on his face.

'Told you, didn't I? We'd be coming for ye if ye didn't leave it alone. Wait till your own pretty little bitch gets that face slit cause of yer smart questions.'

He moved towards me and raised the knife, not to strike with but to make a point at me instead. I knew around the corner reception were sitting taking phone calls, and a few metres beyond the rear of the consult room the nurses were cleaning up in the prep room after surgery. On cue I heard Sammy's laughter at the end of the corridor. To make a commotion would be to invite a whole heap of drama I didn't need.

'You think a won't visit your country house with your pretty wife do ye? Can'nt be there all the time.'

To make the point he raised the blade and drew it slowly to one side. I looked down, the dog sat hunched on the floor not daring to look up, pressed against my leg, her bad ear clotted and dry. She was safe now.

Markwell snorted.

'Keep the bitch, plenty more where she came from.'

I couldn't take it anymore. His rancid breath and stinking clothes. The poor dog he had mutilated to make a point, and the thought of the terrier bleeding to death as it lay gasping from its chest wounds and slit throat. I didn't care if he knocked me off my bike fifty times, a hundred; touch one hair on Anna's head, or another innocent animal, I'd break him in half right there.

He stabbed a finger into my chest to make his point. I couldn't believe the guy, for an unformed runt he had balls of steel. God knows what backing he had to be this confident, or maybe he was stupid after all.

'Cat got yer tongue like man?'

I snapped.

I grabbed the hand he held the blade in, twisting it till he loosened his grip, slowly releasing it to me. With my other hand I took him by the throat and pushed him up against the wall, slow enough not to make a noise, strong enough he couldn't breathe or shout out for help. Below us the staffy looked up and twitched her tail, confused her master was under attack, probably happy about it as well. I leant in and spoke quietly into his ear.

'You're messing with the wrong fucking vet pal. I'd finish you here if it wasn't for the mess you'd make you wee runt. You stay well clear of me, my family, Skye the dog warden. I catch you doing otherwise I put you to sleep myself, you hear me?'

I moved the blade up to his chest, letting the tip press harder and harder against his stained grey tracksuit, and he winced as it threatened to pierce through the skin. A flashback to the terrier, collapsed lungs and its slow inevitable death, to push harder would do the same to Markwell. Payback in the cruelest of ways. It would be so easy.

But not here, not now and not ever. I snapped out of it, 'Not again Mac, come on.' I dropped the knife between us, letting it clatter away into the corner beside the door.

Instead, I squeezed harder on his neck as he gurgled and choked, keeping eye contact as I gripped him. Fair play to the guy, he was a tough little human, and when I finally let go he was still grinning, albeit red in the face, eyes streaming.

'We'll see how tough ye are mate.' He choked through tears and phlegm. 'We'll see. Keep the dog. Nay fucking use to me anyway, soft as shite man, not even good enough for bait.' He lunged at the staffy but she jumped out of the way behind me.

I stood tall and folded my arms, resisting all urges to fold him in half and squash the life out of him. If I'd been alone in the practice or elsewhere, God knows what I'd have done.

'Be seeing you around mate, divvin' get too comfortable ye hear.'

He picked the blade up, making a quick exit from the room. Not long after Joan put her head round the door.

'Is the dog staying in then, it need stitches?'

I collected myself, 'No, a misunderstanding, it's a stray he found, couldn't keep it.' I looked around to make sure the dog was still behind me.

'Call Steve the warden for me, will you? Skye's off today. See if we can get it picked up and some funds for treatment, tell him it's fine, needs antibiotics and some TLC. A good home and it'll be sorted.'

'Righto Mac.' She paused. 'Are you okay lovey, you look flustered.'

'Nothing a decent coffee won't fix. I'm fine. Guy just rubbed me up the wrong way. Nothing new for this town.'

I wasn't fine though. Threatening the guy was a mistake, albeit satisfying, but I'd probably brought a world of trouble down on myself, and potentially Anna. Why did I have to react? I knew why of course, I had the triggers as did anyone, I'd had them since school and fine-tuned them in the army; the inability to walk away from a bully or a fight no matter how stupid it was. Daft mentality for being 6ft 5 but there you go.

This guy had gone right ahead and pushed all the right buttons though, maybe on purpose, or by accident, maybe he was that kind of guy, a small man mentality with a point to prove. But I'd given him a reason to keep going, keep pushing.

Hopefully it was him by himself. Hopefully whatever group he was part of wasn't interested in goading the local vet, I mean why would you? You run a dog-fighting ring, bringing extra heat onto yourselves wasn't the wisest business model.

But the feeling this wasn't over, that it was just getting started, that threatening Markwell wasn't the end of the line and that he wouldn't let it drop, even if it was all just personal to him. The feeling gnawed me all afternoon and into the evening as I made my way back home.

Later, as we tidied up the kitchen together, Anna chatted away as she brewed a pot of coffee and took out the side plates for dessert, something sweet we'd sit and enjoy in front of the television; more calories than I deserved for the day, I don't think squeezing necks counted as exercise. I was quiet enough but said the right things at the right times, enough to keep Anna's rundown of her day more than a one-sided monologue, but not too much I interrupted the flow of the hospital politics rant. She opened the cutlery drawer and took out two forks, then moved over to the fridge and rustled about before emerging with a cheesecake. Not my favourite by any stretch, but better than watching the Sopranos empty handed while Anna tucked in.

'I'll just take the bin out, won't be long okay.'

'Yep no bother I'll bring yours through, see you in a bit.'

I flipped up the bin lid and removed the bag, before tying it and heading out into the hallway to find the front door keys.

Our bin was tucked away around the side of the garage, so I fumbled past the recycling to get to it before wheeling it over to the front corner of the driveway. It was freezing cold tonight and my breath smoked in the light from the front door. I bristled and shivered as the wind sent icy air down the back of my shirt.

I turned back around to the house, keen to get in, when suddenly the space in front of me lit up bright as a car's full beams shot through the cloud of condensing air, illuminating it all.

I held up a cupped hand back into the street, but all I could see was the two bright lights glaring back at me from across the tarmac. The engine behind them revved and strained, and the focus of the light shifted as the car crept forward and turned to its left, gradually swinging to face parallel to the house. The driver's side window was already down, the familiar silhouette of my unpleasant new friend Davey Markwell glaring back at me.

'Big mistake calling me out fella. Big mistake. Tall fellas like you got the habit of coming down hard like.'

I lent down and stared him out. The rodent like features had a sharper, nastier glare to them now.

'Know where you live divvin' I? Told you I'd see ye around.'

With the end of the sentence he flicked an arm and threw something from the car. Instinctively without thinking I caught it in both hands. As I took hold and looked down I was met with the sight of my own fingers, smeared red and sticky with blood, holding the unmistakable fur and cartilage of a dog's ear. I quickly looked back at Markwell.

'Plenty more where that came from ya cunt.'

I lunged for the car but he hit the accelerator, and I only succeeded in fumbling the rear door handle before he sped off up the closed street, losing my balance and hitting the road.

I rolled over and got up, brushing the leaves away before heading back into the house, straight to the kitchen sink to wash the blood from my hands.

Anna duly looked up at me from the sofa as I came back into the living room.

'You been fighting with the wheelie bin again dear? What was all that noise out the front?'

'Ah nothing, let it get away from me on the driveway, nothing major. Coffee ready?' I checked my hands once more.

'Yeah, it's over there. Sit down.' Anna smiled as she picked a leaf off my leg. 'Get the remote though first will you.'

We sat down and flicked into evening mode. Coffee, dessert, and television. Soon to be joined by one or all the cats while Tank snuffled around in the kitchen and side extension, tired from a day of being a huge dog. About ten minutes into the first episode though I realised I hadn't taken a single thing in. I'd been staring blankly at the screen in front of us.

'You going to eat that, or should I help you out?'

'Oh sorry, miles away, no I'm fine, it'll be delicious.'

I spent the next forty minutes or so drifting in and out. My adrenaline was still up from the confrontation on the driveway, and the realisation was slowly dawning. I was going to have to act before things came home to roost. What was the guy playing at? Not many people knew I had been in the army as well as being a vet, and it was only family and Anna who knew about getting so far in Selection. But still, he was playing with fire threatening me over a dog. Just what was he trying to protect? What would he stop at?

No, it was time to stop this guy.

The only question was how, and how hard.

Chapter Ten

Monday in the practice couldn't have gotten off to a worse start. I'd been tetchy all weekend deciding what to do about Markwell, still seething since our encounter on the driveway.

Anna had picked up on it by Saturday evening, wisely making alternative arrangements for the next day, but unwittingly leaving me to stew and quietly come up with a plan as I sat alone in the house, only the dog for company. In retrospect, if she'd hung around, distracting me from dark thoughts I wouldn't have gotten so far with it: but by the time she'd arrived home, tired and cheery from a pleasant day out with her parents, I was calmer and more focused. I knew what to do with him.

The only question was whether I had the bottle to go through with it.

As the evening went on however, we had relaxed on the sofa as she talked me through her normal Sunday, and I had climbed down from the heights I had reached alone in the house earlier. Getting into bed, along with a warm ginger cat, the ideas had become more and more far-fetched and distant as I drifted off to sleep. Thank God for perspective I thought.

Monday morning, however, had sent my psyche well and truly off the rails again: the peaceful feeling wrapped around me last night was shattered to pieces, and all by midday.

It was routine consults until about 10am, and after I was expecting a visit from Skye for a follow up on Tank; basically an official okay from the council that he was under the correct care. He'd been reluctant to get in the car, but by the time we'd arrived at the clinic he'd been happy enough to flop down into one of the large walk-in kennels through the back, watching the rest of the clinic go by. All between big snorts and stretches.

I'd finished signing a booster card and was readying to send the bill through to the front, when the main door of the practice opened and shut, followed by the sound of raised words at the reception desk. Figuring it for another emergency, I headed out into the waiting room to be met by a high-viz jacket holding another bundle of blankets.

This time it was Mark, Skye and Steve's colleague who made up the local trio of welfare officers, and I quickly ushered him through to the consult room.

'Hi Mac, long gone I'm afraid. Looks like it's been hit by a car, all beat up on one side and a broken front leg on the other. Something on the ear as well. Was coming in to see if one of the nurses would check it over but I guess if you're here you may as well have a look if that's alright?'

He put the bundle down on the table between us, something mildly familiar about the shape of it. I shook the idea off and looked up.

'Yeah, okay, haven't got too long though Mark. You know what the story is with it?'

'Found in the street by a group of kids, the parents called it in. Was getting there when the owner turned up, nasty foul mouth guy, said he'd just got it back, didn't seem so happy I was taking it away either. Don't be surprised if he turns up here mind. Was on his way to get the car keys, stormed off into a house off the back lane shouting and swearing.'

'Doesn't surprise me at all, guy probably thinks he's going to get a vet's bill. You get a name for him, you met him before?'

'Afraid not, sorry Mac, like I say he was coming down. It should be chipped anyway.'

I looked down, one brown paw sticking out of the bundle, and I turned to get some gloves from behind the computer. By the time I'd got them on and turned back, Mark had taken away the blankets.

A small Staffordshire Bull Terrier. With a cut on its left ear.

The same dog from Friday, which three days ago had cowered beneath me as Davey Markwell had sat across from us, issuing his vile threats to me.

'Fuck.' I exclaimed, 'Fucking fuck.' I banged the table with a heavy fist, shocking Mark while I was at it. His normally friendly expression was replaced instead by an open mouth, shell-shocked look.

'I had this dog in on Friday, I sent it across to Animal Welfare, Steve picked it up himself and took it to kennels, how the hell is it back here already?'

Mark was taken aback but came to a realisation.

'The only intake from Friday got picked up the next day, owner came forward, showed ID and everything, Steve signed it out himself and told me as much this morning when we were going through kennel rounds.' Mark looked apologetic, although it wasn't any of his fault, 'Look, sorry Mac, I didn't realise. Sounds like it got out and was hit by a car. Owner wasn't exactly too helpful with any of the information I'm afraid.'

'No, it's okay. Jesus what a mess.' I held my hands up. 'My fault, I overreacted. Just frustrating that's all. It was right here in this room fit and well apart from the ear.'

I decided to keep the part about Markwell's threats to myself, no point in muddying the waters at this point if I didn't have to. As yesterday's feelings of revenge and bile began to soar up again, the fewer links back to Davey the better. I sighed heavily, letting some of the tension ease its way out along with the big exhale of air.

'Look, you can get going if you want, I'll tidy this little one up and pop her into storage. If you need I'll get a report written up in the next few days for it; I've a fair idea who the owner might be so I'll look out for him, see what he wants to do with it. If he even cares.'

'Yeah okay. Don't get too stressed about it okay, it's not you, you're only following the protocol we gave you. Let me get a case number and an invoice sheet to you later in the week, see where we're at from there. Tell me as well if I need to speak to the owner okay.'

He wrote a note in his book before replacing it into a side pocket.

'Skye wasn't too far behind me I don't think, she's in checking the big dog you fostered, is she?'

'Yeah, a follow up for the rehome. Said we'd do it today. I guess I'll follow you out there if she's not going to be long.'

Mark exited, and I turned back to the table.

How the hell had Markwell got his hands on her again so quickly? Surely Steve wasn't daft enough to give the dog back over so easily. Maybe I should have told him about the threats, instead of beating around the bush like an idiot. I looked over the wounds; the ear had clearly been bleeding again, but now the chest was bruised and bloody, and with the front left leg broken at the elbow joint, prising it upwards I could see more wounds underneath. No way it was a road traffic accident. No way. Fucking Markwell. I'd crush him next time I saw him.

I sighed, my head in my arms on the table beside the dog. I'd as good as killed her sending her back into the system without warning Steve of who Davey was, and now I'd have to deal with him again when he turned up at the practice. If he had the nerve to show his face.

I wrapped her up and took her through to the back, ready to sort out aftercare. By the time I got to the front desk Skye was standing in the waiting room with a smile on her face, seemingly feeling much better after last week's ordeal.

'Hi Mac, you ready? Figured we could trot him outside so I can see how he's getting on with you if that's okay?'

I was still distracted, but soon enough snapped into the reality of the conversation, letting out a small smile.

'Uh yeah sure, wait a second, I'll go get him, probably needs a pee anyway by now, guy drinks water by the trough full, never-ending cycle with him. I'll meet you out in the car park, won't be long alright?'

I went through to kennels and found his lead, shaking off the last five minutes as I hooked it on to the thick collar. Sensing a toilet break as well as freedom, I near enough rode him through the practice on the way out to the front door, stopping to apologise to the old lady and her cat basket as Tank barged past to the double doors at the front of the building.

I managed to stop him in time before he went through the glass, and with one hand on the handle looked up into the car park, ready to let him out. Skye was stood in the middle of the tarmac beside her van, staring straight ahead, dead still — high-vis vest gently flapping in the breeze.

Beyond her was a dark BMW with a mismatched grey panel door. The driver's side window was down and Davey Markwell was mouthing off. I couldn't hear what he was saying, but it looked animated and angry. She was transfixed, body language terrified.

Tank could see it all as well. Ears back, eyes piercing through the glass he was emitting the same low growl as he had done back at the farm near the dene.

The car park itself was empty aside for Markwell and the council van, and as I tried to squeeze past Tank to get out, eager to help Skye, he sensed the moment and went for it, throwing me off balance and back into the practice as he lunged through the open door, racing toward the car. Markwell clearly saw it as well, getting the window up before Tank slammed both paws into the side of the door with such a force the whole thing rocked back and forth.

Skye was still frozen to the spot as I finally picked myself up, running out to the pair of them and picking the end of the lead up. I hauled him backwards away from the dented car door and back towards her. Checking she was okay, I turned back to Markwell, who realising I wasn't stupid enough to let him get mauled in the practice car park, had rolled down the window, staring out again at us from the relative safety of the front seat.

'See you found that pathetic little brown bitch again. Still think it was an accident, like the other dumb fuck from the council like?' He turned to Skye, 'Couldn't believe how easy it was to get her back off ye man, thanks for that darling. Owe ye one like.' He leered.

Tank was prowling on a relaxed lead, not taking his eyes off Markwell for a second as he paced back and forth in between us.

'I warned ye stay out of it. Look at the pair of ye, poking yer noses into me business again, what did I tell ye eh? Ye stay, the fuck, out of me way.'

I could feel Skye move in close behind me. Clearly terrified of this thug and his show.

To give him his due he was pretty unpleasant, I wouldn't want to meet him down a dark alley if I was a regular guy or didn't have 60kg of Mastiff ready to tear him apart. But staring at him now, in the cold light of day, I couldn't help but wish I'd choked the life out of him on Friday while I had the chance. I couldn't believe I'd spent last night talking myself out of dealing with him the way I wanted to, the army way, the Mac way.

No, staring at him now, sat in his cheap, battered car, dishing out threats against Skye and my family, I realised one thing. He was going down. The whole lot of them were going down. Screw Steve and his dead-end investigation, this guy and his shithole fight club were going to regret ever meeting me.

As he finally ran out of steam and realised we weren't biting, he started the car, stuttering it to life as Tank edged forwards, and slowly reversed it out of the car park before accelerating down the avenue, repeating his pathetic pistol gesture with his right hand as he left.

I turned to Skye, still shaking, putting a hand on her shoulder. Even Tank moved up close next to her.

'Well let's not put that in Tank's report shall we, eh?'

The joke was too soon. Even I was shaken up, more so by Tank's aggression than anything else, but it was a good few seconds before Skye snapped out of the trance she was in. Tears were in her eyes and dropping down to her yellow vest, and as I squeezed her shoulder harder and gave a few nice words, she turned in and bear hugged me whilst the sobs kicked in. I had no choice but to wrap an arm around her small frame.

'Hey, it's okay Skye, he's gone alright, we're not gonna see him again you hear? I'll make sure of it okay? You won't have to see him again.'

She squeezed me harder in between sobs. Struggling to get her words out.

'It was him, the guy who attacked me, I'm sure of it, same voice, same creepy body language, same smell even. God, I feel so small, so stupid.'

I pushed her away and held both her shoulders in my hands whilst I looked at her.

'Skye. Look at me, okay. That's the end of it. I promise. It's going to get dealt with. You've got to promise me you won't worry anymore.'

She wasn't convinced, but as the hug went on and gradually lost its intensity, she calmed, slowly loosening her grip. By the time the old lady with the cat basket exited the practice, and Tank had pricked his ears up at the prospect of a new unrequited cat friendship, Skye was back to normal, wiping the tears away with a sleeve and padding her pockets for the van keys.

'Sorry Mac, I guess I'm not as strong as I thought I was. You must think I'm an idiot,' and turning to Tank, 'and as for you, better be a one off. Dickhead or no dickhead we can't have you trashing cars up and expecting to get signed off, okay?'

Tank head butted her squarely in the hip, and in the direction of the van. She turned and looked at me.

'I meant what I said Skye. I'll get it sorted.'

David

You can still stop this. You can turn back.

The maze of terraced houses was dull, the brickwork barely visible in the faltering streetlight. This murky little community, this hive of avenues, it was morbidly quiet tonight; it barely noticed as I walked through. Only the shadows came with me. The bitter frost had sealed everything else inside.

You don't have to do this.

I found the street I was looking for. Bins overflowed from the back of each house, their alleyways a battleground for the residents against the council each week. I counted down the doors until I found where I was supposed to be. A backyard strewn with rubbish and dog-cages. A rusted latch that lifted easily into the mess. A wooden gate that squeaked shut as I closed it behind me.

You can find another way.

Light shines out from a mud-spattered window. The back of a greasy head is framed by the glow from a flat-screen television. It's still, to one side. A lonely, burnt-out cigarette dangles in one hand, the other rests over a beer can, its contents spilled out over the sofa. The owner was asleep.

Last chance Mac.

I try the kitchen door and it opens. I move inside and stand quietly, listening for movement, for company, for other signs of life in this reeking house. Nothing.

I was alone with David Markwell.

I move into the living room and close the blinds.

It was late Tuesday, Anna was away for the evening with her parents and staying over after a meal out, and I had free rein over my evening. What I hadn't explained to her was how I was choosing to spend it, how I was gambling my future on vitriol and revenge. I had considered bringing Tank, but only for a few seconds; his big lumbering presence would stand out like a sore thumb in the quiet back streets of town. No, this was a trip out for one. A quiet sojourn, with devastating consequences for at least one of us in this house.

I bend down closer to the gaunt face asleep in front of me, angelic in its peacefulness, rat like in all its other features.

He breathes back at me. Stale, humid beer. Laced with tobacco. Perhaps something else. Something toxic.

I stare at him in the silence of the back room. The aroma of cigarette smoke still lingers, and the foul odours of unwashed bachelorhood lift around the house. I could walk away. Hope his last visit was the end of it. But then I remembered Bella. I remember the threats against Anna. I remember his vile grin as I nearly choked the life out of him in the vets. No, guys like this didn't quit. Guys like this needed stamped out. Fuck it. Only one thing for it.

'Rise and shine beautiful.'

A look of confusion appears as the eyes open and shift side to side, and in the daze I see them register my midriff, the look of puzzlement spreading as a full white bodysuit fills his view.

The view isn't there for long: with a short backswing and flick from the wrist, I snap a metal bar I found in the yard straight into his jawline, seeing it all collapse sideways as the lights go out. A small trickle of blood comes from the right side of the mouth, but overall, it's not an impressive result.

Disappointed but pragmatic, I shift the little figure back upright from the sofa and get to work.

A short while later, and after checking around the remainder of the small house, making sure the front and back door are locked, I have Davey sat on a dining chair, the old wooden style with arms, like the type you'd sit your granddad at on Christmas day. Duct tape has made short work of any movement he had planned.

I'd decided against a sedative, anything traceable was a mistake, so for now I'm waiting until the blackout wears off. Having never hit anyone with a pipe before it was an open-ended question.

I look around. The room wasn't a glamorous one by any stretch. Flaking paint amongst damp walls was the decorative style, mould furring its way around the corners. I lifted a collection of tabloids on the table. Underneath was an old plate, swimming with rot. Vile.

Eventually though, I get fed up waiting, so filling a pint glass with cold water from the kitchen tap, I throw it square in Davey's face, gradually seeing the semblance of his consciousness reappear. Like the previous wake up but much, much groggier, the eyes open again and the mouth moves about, initially trying to form words and sentences, but eventually it focuses on the effort required to spit out the large blood clot from beside the tongue, and what I assume are a few molar teeth from my Wimbledon inspired jawbreaker.

Mumbling, chewing, and choking on the swelling he manages to focus in, testing his forearms, lightly tugging backwards and trying to flex his elbows against the duct tape, and I see the moment of panic click into place. A violent surge bursts out from the figure as he struggles against his restraints.

Luckily, I've also used my duct tape on the ankles, and to stop any trips backwards, I've nailed the dining chair into the wooden floorboards. One long nail into each leg: for a deadbeat he'd had quite the decent toolbox.

'Good luck Davey boy, you aren't going anywhere.'

I turn up the television volume, drowning out the dull moans and whimpers coming from the chair; just in case the next-door neighbours were still up and feeling inquisitive.

This was going quite well I thought.

'Now then mate, we're going to have a game of show and tell, and I'm not taking no for an answer. I can assume this is yours?'

I hold an iPhone to his face. The flicker in his eyes gives him away.

'Let's make this nice and easy, tell me the pin yeah?'

No surprises, and a few minutes later, he hasn't helped me with the passcode, but once he sits still enough the facial recognition clicks in, and the home screen lights up as it lets me in. Davey scowls from across the room.

I leave him where he is, still chewing his tongue and groaning, and sit on the opposite armchair to scroll through the apps. He's not stupid enough to have any incriminating texts, and the phone's messenger app is equally unhelpful. Impressively, he has more than a few lusty pictures with a good-looking brunette. The lack of name replaced with a crude nickname however suggests this is more of a casual acquaintance than Davey's bride to be, so I move on. Ticking off the apps as I go, I get to WhatsApp on the last page of scrolling and open the messages screen. A few names show up as contacts and group chats; the good-looking brunette makes an appearance again, 'you swine Davey boy,' but as I scroll down, fifth on the list is an interesting enough looking group.

Standing out by its name alone, I click on the morbidly titled 'BloodSport' and search through its reams of messages. Spliced intermittently with picture messages and file caches I can already tell it's what I'm looking for. I flick back up to the top for the group info icon: it shows me there are nine members of this group, a few names, but mostly phone numbers or abbreviations.

A pained groan drifts over from the chair.

Davey has finally spat out the blood clot. A trickle of fresh blood follows it out.

I check he isn't wriggling his way free from the duct tape and settle back. Pages and pages move past as I scroll down. There is way more information here than I can take in all at once. Most of it is only banter, inconsequential to what I want, but as more and more dates and locations flash up along the timeline, as well as all the disturbing pictures that will hopefully prove incriminating, it slowly dawns on me.

This was way beyond a few dogs.

The realisation of what was occurring, what my sleepless nights had been wrought with, were all confirmed as I read down through the group. This was worse than I could have imagined. I look at Davey, he can sense what I'm thinking.

A blood-stained grin shows an appearance, quickly replaced by a twisted grimace. A splintered mandible isn't worth smiling for it seems.

The next step was the trickier part. I could sit and read through at my leisure, with no one the wiser if I downloaded it, but I still wanted to know what was coming. No use in seeing what Davey and his pals had done in the past. If I wanted to shut this thing down once and for all I needed to know what they were planning in the future — enough to incriminate themselves into police custody and out of my life forever.

A flash of panic surged as I thought back to the threats against Anna, what they had done to Skye. I shook it off and focused. Stick to the script Mac. Don't back out now.

Ideally I would take the phone with me, let it scoop up messages and feed me information as it went. But it posed two problems. The police could track any missing phone as soon as they realised it was gone; a sure-fire way to find out who was responsible, and secondly, the group members would ditch the chat as soon as they realised it was an open link to them. No, I had another way.

I check Davey is an admin and add the number of a burner phone, one I picked up from the supermarket with cash. The cheapest smartphone I could find. Pay as you go.

'Sorry lads, new number, caught the missus trying to get into me old one, not ready for that yet like! D.'

Luckily an instant reply comes back in the group with laughing emojis, and after scrolling back up to check Davey's writing style, I give the banter back and forth until it's taken up a few screens worth of pages, aiming to distract the conversation away from the addition of the new number. After the chat quietens, and after exporting all the old files as a cache to the burner, I've deleted the real 'Davey' from the chat, leaving in my own quiet decoy. Not as stupid as I look sometimes.

Turning my attention back to the figure on the dining chair behind me, he's still groggy and confused, eyes darting around his own living room, wondering what the hell has happened here in the last ten minutes. Who his attacker was.

As I pull the hood down from the suit however he soon tunes into his reality. The gravity of it hitting harder than any iron bar ever could. The nails beneath him strain and flex the floorboards as wild trashing accompanies the panicked cries escaping the broken jaw. It's pitiful.

'I did tell you I was the wrong vet to be messing around with Davey, but you wouldn't listen, would you?'

I sat down in front of him, a smaller of his wooden chairs pulled round to face him.

'Turning up at my house, running me off my bike, threatening my partner and as good as killing that dog in front of me? I guess I don't blame you for not knowing, why would you?'

Not many did.

I leaned in, creaking the chair as I got closer. Both palms open, relaxing the mood.

'You like jokes Davey? Yeah? Well, here's one for you. You heard the one about the army vet who passed Selection?'

His eyes widened, the pupils flaring as he realised who I was, what I could do to him.

I reached into the bag, pulling out my party piece. It was what's called a three-way tap. A plastic cannula with three ends for attaching a syringe. A T-shaped lever on top allowed you to change the direction of fluid or air flow to one of three ways.

'It's a shit joke, but I like the punch line. Trouble is it's going to leave you a bit deflated.'

He was still confused. Panicked about what was next. But as I took out the 50ml syringe and large bore grey needle normally reserved for cattle work, I think the message started to sink in. He'd pissed off the wrong man, the wrong profession. The thrashing restarted and it took a gentle tap against the broken jaw to bring him back into line and settle him down. His eyes were burning into mine now.

'I know what you're thinking Davey. You'll get me back. One way or another. Clumsily run me over in your clapped-out BMW, jump me outside my house as I leave for work one day. Get a few of the lads to hit me in the street if I'm out walking with Anna.'

He focused and nodded, straining at the neck and sweating profusely, however it was difficult to come across as threatening when you were tied to a chair with your jaw hanging off.

'Problem is it relies on you leaving here, doesn't it? Here's how it's going to go then. I'm a fair guy, I like to give people a chance. So I thought why don't I give you the same chance you gave that dog eh? You know the one. Bella? Or perhaps you never even bothered to learn her name. She's the one you've been so intent on me forgetting. Thing is Davey, I didn't forget. I haven't stopped thinking about what you did to her.'

Davey was panicking now. He knew exactly what was coming.

'You read the bible Davey? I don't. Never had much time for it if I'm honest. But there's a few good bits. Eye for an eye. That's one for a start. Or in your case it should be lung for a lung. You catch my drift?'

Even deadbeats had heard of Leviticus.

He was crying and looking upwards, desperately searching for salvation in the ceiling above. The hope had gone out of him. It was a sad sight. If I hadn't had to sit and cradle his victims as they lay lifeless on my consult room table I would have felt sorry for him.

But I had.

'Okay pal. Time to start. Don't worry, a little scratch as it goes in. Trust me, okay?'

What I didn't tell him about, however, was the finale.

'And remember Davey. You wanted it darker.'

He screamed.

Part Two

Chapter Twelve

Police Headquarters, East Newcastle.

You could mistake it for an office the way it looked. A trendy college, some benign building home to corporate management. Neatly cleared out by 5.p.m. in time for the cleaners to move through. Sterile and lifeless, polished every day. Gleaming as it slept next to the eastbound Coast Road.

Not this building though. This silver cage rattled all night. This one had a heartbeat all of its own.

Alice Rose, Detective Inspector, sat in her corner office, looking out over the back road to the trees and country park beyond. It was cold and windy, a threat of rain just holding back as she'd made her way in from the carpark, and now, tucked inside on the fourth floor — a morning's worth of paperwork on the desk in front of her — it was looking like a straight-forward day.

She had cleared her in-tray yesterday afternoon, making way for a few hours of case preparation.

It was a meticulous, exacting routine she always followed when due in court, and so, with the door locked and a fresh coffee poured, she turned the first page on her notes, ready to go through everything once more.

The file was heavy, and well read by many.

Ronnie Macfarlane.

Local hardman, enforcer, drug-runner, aspiring kingpin. There were many descriptions Alice could think of for him, all of them negative.

He would stand trial at Newcastle Crown Court tomorrow on charges of distributing cocaine in the region, and it had been a long time coming. Months of surveillance, informants and GPS tracking had led to his arrest in the spring. An armed raid executed at dawn whilst he had slept. And now, with her evidence distilled and manicured, Alice was going to make it count. She had let him slip two years ago on assault charges, evidence dropped from intimidated witnesses, but now she had him where she wanted him. Back in the dock.

She lifted the first page.

***

About an hour into reading, draining the dregs and placing the mug back down, she looked at the door, weighing her chances of getting from the office to the kitchen for a refill, running the gauntlet of junior officers that would always run the risk of questions and interruption. As she stared though, considering whether the caffeine hit was worth it, the daydream was interrupted by a desk phone bursting into life with its shrill, repetitive ring. She sighed.

'DI Rose speaking, how can I help?'

'Sorry to bother you ma'am. I have you as duty officer for serious crimes.' It was the switchboard operator downstairs. 'We've a suspicious death up in Northumberland, uniforms have put the door in and by the looks of it they're sending it straight up to Inspector level, probable murder. Sounds awful. Lad all tied up and tortured they reckon.'

'Sounds grisly. You got any more details? Who's the uniform?'

Alice swapped the phone to her other ear.

'It's PC Kelly, out of Blyth, first responder to a welfare concern from the public. Door went in about an hour ago and they came straight back out by the sounds of it. Scene was a shocker.' A pause on the line, keys tapping as the log was opened. 'Have you got a pen? I'll give you the address.'

She took the details, noting them down in the margins of her paperwork as she shrugged an arm into her jacket.

'Tell them to wait outside. Only ones in are SOCO if I'm not there first, okay?'

She stood up, patting down the breast pocket for her ID and car keys. She knew the area well enough, it was only about a twenty-minute drive up the A19, and at this time of day, she'd be the first grown up on scene if she was quick enough.

If there was one thing she hated above everything, it was playing catch up.

***

Only after an annoying wait at a railway crossing on the outskirts of town, drumming the steering wheel whilst a never-ending freight train rolled past, she was pulling up outside the terraced house on Delaval Street, reversing in behind a large grey unmarked forensics van being unloaded by white-suited figures. Twenty-four minutes since the call. Second adult there it turns out.

Boxes and briefcases were being taken into the taped off property, and the small, peaked tent that lay folded on the pavement would soon be enclosing the front door. Martin Kelly, whom she recognised from routine briefings together, stood to attention at the front, whilst two of his colleagues kept back a small crowd of onlookers at the end of the street. Wearing dressing gowns and armed with smartphones, they were documenting every move the forensics team took.

'Nothing interesting everyone.' Alice lied as she moved around the boot of her car, 'Best get moving along before you get moved along.'

Knowing the crowd would stand and gawp for at least another hour, she took her basic kit from the car and proceeded over to the front door, pausing next to PC Kelly.

'You the initial attending Martin?'

'Yes ma'am. Got here about an hour and a half ago, called for back-up once I smelled it was a dead body in there, and we gained entry about seventy-five minutes ago. Fella called David Markwell if you've heard of him. Got a brief look around; established he was a goner and there was no one else, then came out and made the call. Looks well above my rank in there Ma'am, no disrespect to myself but you'll see what I mean when you get in.'

He shifted on the spot, checking his shoulder tag nervously before looking back at Alice, as if to make sure he hadn't received a promotion since he'd started speaking.

'SOCO have been here about twenty minutes setting up, but they're heading in officially if you're ready now. I think I heard them say something about calling the duty pathologist to come and have a look before they get him moved.'

'Sounds all very sensible Martin, thank-you.'

Alice fumbled with the zip on her white suit before bringing it up over her own jacket, talking as she slipped covers on over her leather work shoes.

'I checked the roster; it's Dr Ballingry on-call so we'll see if he can make an appearance. If you would be so kind as to look out for him and let me know when he arrives. In the meantime, try keep the locals back if you can, but gently okay, you know what it's like round here. If there's a commotion they'll all be out and we'll never get anything done this afternoon.'

'Okay ma'am. And good luck in there, I mean it. Never seen anything like it, and that's saying something.'

Alice checked the paper suit and shoe-covers once more and looked into the property. Even with the front door open, the stench of rotten flesh was still strong, causing her to gag underneath the mask. How on earth had the neighbours not noticed sooner? Surely it would've found its way through a crack in the wall by now? Terraced houses weren't exactly airtight she thought.

Stepping down the hallway on raised footplates laid out by the forensics team, she gingerly made her way through to the back of the house where the other suits had congregated. She stopped in her tracks.

'Jesus Christ.'

'I know ma'am.'

She held a hand up to her mouth.

'What on earth ...'

The scene was not pleasant to say the least. In the middle of the floor, backing into the rear window, a single wooden dining chair had been nailed into bare floorboards. Around its four legs, pools of blood had collected, some larger than others, but all had lost their glossy sheen with time, and the dark red puddles which had once flowed so readily had now wrinkled like washed up jellyfish.

Hung forward was a lean corpse, head jilted to the left, awkwardly balanced above a substantial neck wound, no doubt the source of the curdling blood below. Life had long since left it; even without being a pathologist DI Rose could tell by the blanching that this sorry soul had been sat for some time. Both ankles were bound to the chair legs with duct tape, and two thin, tattooed wrists were tightly taped to the armrests, propping up the figure as he held court over his own demise.

'May I?'

Moving around to his front, taking care not to disturb her colleagues, she hunched down, looking back up at the hollowed-out face, trying not to let her eyes fall to the gruesomely open neck wound below. She edged closer, the stench now lost on her as she focused, trying to start her process. Don't get lost in the scene Alice.

'This jaw looks weird, broken you think?'

She reached and touched the bruising, flinching back as she felt the bones crunch underneath.

'Any weapon in here, anything you've found so far?'

'Nothing yet boss. Had an initial recce and nothing jumping out as a weapon. We did notice blood patterning on the sofa there behind you though.' she turned to look, 'you see that spray there, moving horizontally at the top of the back cushion? Can't be certain, but I'd be sure the blow that did for the jaw was delivered there. We'll take samples of course. If it's his saliva and blood in the swab, good chance it came from a blow across the mouth. No big signs of a struggle, potentially might be talking a surprise attack.'

Alice stood up and carefully walked around the room. They were right of course, no sign of a commotion, so unless the attacker had a good tidy up once they were finished it has a good chance of this being a stealthy assault. It was eerily quiet in the room, a chemical smell hanging amongst the rot.

'Nails have moved.'

The officer called back to her, now hunched down with a light shone on the floor beneath the body. A dull glare came from the blood as he swept over it.

'What?'

'The nails have moved.'

Alice looked at him, pointing at the bottom of the chair legs with the beam.

'Moved in and out; mostly back and forth, but some side to side. Reckon he was awake enough at some point to struggle. Takes a fair jolt to rip a nail out, can only see the tops but they look like they'll be decent enough lengths. Once body's moved we'll get them out and analysed.'

He paused, reaching down for a swab stick, twisting the seal off with gloved fingers as he talked.

'Might get a few bits of the attacker's skin on there if we're lucky. Nails always take a few cells when you hold to whack them in. Could be a goldmine for you.'

Alice was always surprised how excited these people got on scene — swab this, dust that — it never failed to amaze her. She looked at the ceiling.

'You been upstairs yet?'

'Yeah, nothing much going on. If I was taking a guess I'd say it was undisturbed, but we'll do the checks, certainly no sign of a struggle or anyone rifling through drawers up there. You'll have to corroborate, but no obvious empty spaces where the TVs been pinched.'

She went upstairs, treading the uncarpeted boards and taking care not to brush the walls. Right enough, despite it being the typical unwashed bachelor pad, there was no sign of commotion or theft. Checking the downstairs front room confirmed her initial suspicions that most, if not all the events, had taken place in the property's back room.

She moved back through.

The white suits seemed to have multiplied, and were bustling around carefully, taking their samples and checking for fingerprints on doors and surfaces, all the while Alice stared pensively at the figure in front of her. Amongst the blood and the bruises, her eyes were drawn down to a small, perfect circle under the right armpit about three inches down. A small trickle of dried blood had dripped south, lucky not to have washed away in the tide from the neck wound above. Peering in closely it looked like a small hole. Like a track mark but larger.

'One of you lot got a pen light I can borrow?'

Gathering round they lit up the patch of skin, and careful not to get too close for the awful smell that was coming back in waves, they stared at the neatly congealed hole in the chest wall.

'Beats me. Too big for a needle. Too small for a knife or anything. An incidental? Wait for the doc I say, see what he thinks.'

The officer clicked the light off and stood up, the paper suit rustling as he stretched a stiff arm towards the ceiling.

'Reckons he'll be about an hour or so, hold up back at the mortuary. Not that we're going anywhere for a while, enough here to keep us going till the weekend if we're not careful.'

The officer went back to swabbing, leaving Alice to stare at the body in the dim light.

Dr Ballingry's delay was not the news she wanted to hear. Time was tight today, especially with tomorrow's court case, but she was also loath to give up the case to another DI for the sake of a few hours.

'Look guys, not ideal but realistically I'm going to have to head before the pathologist gets here. I'll get a word in with uniforms on the way out, get door to doors started and I'll send up a couple of DCs to liaise with you after the doc's been. You make sure he sees the chest mark, okay? I'll be catching up with him at the mortuary when he does the PM.'

Alice loosened the collar of the white suit and removed her gloves, placing them into an evidence bag for future reference.

'I'm in the office all day trial prepping, so if a DC can't answer your questions call the switchboard and they'll put you through, ok?'

'Not a problem ma'am, mind the lights on the way out.'

She retraced her steps to the front door, walking over the footplates and out into the street. The cordon was still holding tight as she got in the car. The uniforms looked hassled behind her.

Looking down, avoiding the stares of the onlookers at the end of the street, she started making a few notes in her notebook.

Her last murder was about a year ago and hadn't exactly stretched her professional ability.

A single male victim outside a pub in Heaton, stabbed three times with the fatal blow hitting the heart, the man had bled to death on the street in minutes shortly before being found by a group of students. Enter Alice.

Attacker and victim had been well acquainted, an argument brewing over a low value drug's debt before it escalated to violence, spilling out on to the street in the worst possible way.

It had only taken forty-eight hours worth of police work to pin down the motive and CCTV images, and a further twenty-four to track the attacker to a rural village out in Northumberland, courtesy of his credit card. One solid hour of questioning, before he'd had chance to sleep or think was all it had taken for Alice to break his implausible alibi and have him return ten minutes later with a signed confession courtesy of his solicitor. Textbook interview. Case closed.

Sentenced to twenty years at her Majesty's pleasure, the case had been satisfying, but hardly worthy of a well-plotted crime novel or TV show.

The house behind her though would surely provide a bit more of a challenge; its innocent façade hiding a torrent of terrors.

Probable torture, forensic awareness, and of course void of an initial presenting motive, the figure in the chair had piqued her interest. And in this quiet, coastal Northumberland town? Big news to say the least. It would boil down to some petty motive and macho justice, they always did, but something about the hollow figure — nailed down, punctured and drained. Something at the back of her mind said this was going to be a once in a career case.

The guy looked like a domesticated dead-beat, and the house hardly backed up any thoughts of high-level organised crime, but the scene. The little chest injury, his broken jaw and the open throat left to spill out onto the floor. The precision of the cut. Everything about it was teeing up into something special — she could feel all the ingredients there as she closed her notebook shut, tossing it onto the passenger seat.

She looked back at the street, framed in the rear-view mirror. The crowds had turned and headed back inside as interest waned and rain started to spatter. A forensic tent had provided enough to keep them out only for so long. Who knew what they had been expecting?

She turned the key in the ignition and signalled out, to join their exit from the street, while looking only once at the house and its sole victim. She shuddered, as a fleeting image of the open neck flashed back into her mind. It was a dull drive back down to the station in Newcastle, but with this and tomorrow's court case, something told her it was going to be a long night ahead.

Chapter Thirteen

Newcastle Quayside.

The Millenium Bridge tilted opposite, framing the Baltic behind it. To its right the Tyne Bridge and the rest of the country beyond.

All lost on Alice.

She walked down the steps of the courthouse, stopping dejectedly to check her phone for messages as it turned on, the screen flashing a bright logo before dying back to black. Yesterday's excitement at the murder scene was a long time ago now, and the evening's work afterwards was a peaceful blur in contrast to the mayhem which had just occurred.

The day so far couldn't have been any worse, a complete farce from start to finish — beginning with paperwork failing to turn up from the station, through to a verdict of mistrial due to the glaring technicality on the evidence supplied. Having been through the case with a fine toothcomb it had been heart wrenching to sit and watch from the gallery, as crown prosecution barristers flapped and panicked as the defence pointed out the errors, systematically dismantling her case piece by piece in front of her.

Gut wrenching.

Soul destroying.

How they had pinpointed it so accurately, and quickly, she'd never know, but it had clearly escaped her attention, and of the normally watertight KC prosecuting. They had avoided eye contact on the way out of the courtroom as the scolding words of the judge rang out loudly in their ears, too embarrassed to acknowledge their failings to one another as they pushed through doors. No doubt in the next few days they'd sit and hash out the details over a conference call, but for now she was making a sharp exit from the courthouse before any of the reporters inside had chance to catch up with her.

It had begun with the evidence for the prosecution. Dates of submission had been mis-recorded on the paperwork, meaning they were inadmissible and thus voiding them from the prosecution's evidence. No reliable timeline, no reliable evidence the Judge commented. Alice could scarcely believe what she was hearing as the defence team pointed out the mistakes, stacking them up one by one for an open-mouthed jury.

Shifting from the warm comfort of a well-presented case and into a heart stopping shambles, icy cold shivers had run down her spine when she pulled out her own documents, realising the two mismatched. How on earth? It would have been conceivable to try arguing the incompetence and resubmit, but by the time the second error was pointed out the judge was in no mood for discussions from the gallery.

The mobile phone evidence, GPS tracking and digital extractions, was the centre of her case. It had constituted the strongest proof by far of the defendant's movement, as well as repeated contact between members of the alleged drug distribution network. It showed communication, organisation, and correlated meeting times with transport which had been stopped and seized. Watertight evidence in Alice's favour, and indeed the whole case.

The phone number however was wrong, by a single digit, and had been immediately seized upon by the defence with a withering display of legal craftsmanship; first in congratulating the police work for tracking and tracing it so meticulously, proving its invaluable worth, then crippling the case by showing her error.

As the smile had widened on the defendant's face, realising he couldn't be linked to the phone, her head had sunk quietly into her hands. She had signed and submitted the evidence, and her shocked face quickly turned red when the court's attention turned to her in the gallery. A mistake rarely forgivable even for a novice police officer, it couldn't escape the Judge's attention to give her a strong piece of his mind as he dismissed the case; namely for wasting court time with this ineptitude, and fouling up what was an open goal against a defendant who had escaped the same Judge's justice time and time again over the years.

There was no choice but to turn him back out on to the streets. Back to rebuild his reign. Back to torment Alice.

She was quick to leave the building, looking left to the carpark as she exited the final set of double doors, the thought of walking back into the station filling her with dread.

Bad news travelled fast in a regional force, and the same colleagues who had wished her well that morning would no doubt be quietly judging upon her return. It was tempting to turn right and walk into town, some coffee shop or café to lose herself for the day. Spend a few hours lost in a newspaper or magazine, wait till the buzz had died down.

No, better to face this head on. Better to show them she wasn't scared. She pocketed the phone and stepped down to the pavement.

The Millenium Bridge was moving in front of her now, easing back down into position over the Tyne, the boat it had let through now floating towards the North Sea. The physics of jumping on board from the walkway flashed through her mind. One way to avoid the gossip for sure. One way to end up on the slab at the mortuary as well however.

As it moved further eastwards and out of view, hugging the Gateshead shore, the sound of footsteps got louder and heavier behind her. Ronnie Macfarlane had followed her outside.

A big man, bulking out an expensive but off the rack two-piece suit, the same grin from inside the courtroom was still spread widely over his face, and he held an uncomfortable eye contact until she looked down to her shoes.

'Think you should be arrested for wasting police time DI Rose.' A hefty, pointed pronunciation of the 'D' and 'I'.

A chuckle escaped. He had obviously amused himself.

'Silly error with the mobile number like, surprised you let it slip past to be honest, figured you a highflyer. Was sure like when I got out of bed this morning I was gonna be spending next few years in the big house. Seems a shame now, forking out a day's rate on my solicitor seens as he tore yous to shreds in twenty minutes. Nay chance I can put in for a rebate on my legal fees like?'

Ronnie smirked as he lifted a cigarette up to his lips and lit the tip, making no effort to blow the smoke in a different direction away from her. She kept quiet, learning a long time ago better to not engage with his type, determined not to look back and increase his satisfaction with the day's events.

He called out once again.

'Only hope you do a better job with Davey. Good lad like.' Ronnie shouted down the steps. A thin smile revealing straight white teeth.

It didn't take long though for the penny to drop, the smile turning downwards with it. The half cigarette fell to the pavement and soon found its way under a scuffed leather sole. Clearly the court budget hadn't stretched to footwear this week.

'What do you know about that then? We only found Davey yesterday.'

He squirmed the ash into the concrete before it scattered to the road. Trying to form words before Alice beat him to it.

'We'll be in touch Ronnie. Don't go booking your celebrations too soon you hear?'

Not so smart now are we.

Chapter Fourteen

'Saw you sneaking out the canteen DI Rose, how's a nice girl like you supposed to do a day's police work with just salad? You'll never catch the bad guys on just lettuce power.'

The voice flowed from an open door.

Solitude was rare in this place Alice thought.

It had been a hurried, vacant lunch. Dodging the gossip and the fake concern, she had weaved her way through the canteen on her way back to the office, avoiding eye contact and her colleagues' flimsy attempts at conversation starters. Only her reflection in the glass reminded her of yesterday as she stared outwards, over the carpark, over the trees and into the country park. The serenity calming her.

The door had knocked four minutes later, the voice following it.

She sighed and flicked an elastic band at the woman in the window, watching it ping back into the shelves before she turned round. The hopeful gaze of Alex Jamieson was smiling back at her, eyebrows raised and an open mouth grin — his default greeting — and he slipped in, pressing the door shut with both hands behind him.

'You okay?'

More fake concern.

'Fine thank you Alex. What can I do for you?'

Keep it brisk, get him out.

Her strategy failed instantly as he slid into the chair opposite. Scooting it round to face her he relaxed and leaned back. Picking up her favourite biro, he dangled it over her notepad. She shuffled upright.

'Sucked about the case Alice, what the hell happened? You've been chasing that boy Macfarlane ever since he slipped the assault charge on his ex, thought you had him wrapped up this time, no?'

The biro landed, leaving a blue trail as he bumped it into the margin.

Alex had always known she was a clean freak.

They had been part of the same intake at Police College, top of the class from the first few weeks, and their gentle rivalry had been simmering away over the years as they saw their promotions come in together. It was always hard to pick between them as they competed for cases: Alice with her casework, Alex with his politics and networking. Occasionally the heat would boil over, but for now the atmosphere in the kitchen was at a truce as they sat opposite.

'I'd be reading the riot act to my team if they'd messed a big one up like that for me. Who was it this time, that idiot Andy Jordan?'

He eased back in the chair, gazing past Alice's left shoulder and out of the window beyond, jealous his own office only overlooked the bins. The biro was back against his temple, and not too far away from inking the sharp haircut he regularly paid through the nose for in the city centre. She was pained to admit it suited him well, but she'd never tell him, keep it for the army of swooning WPCs and secretaries paying out constant compliments as he charmed his way around the station.

'The day he makes sergeant I'll eat my golf hat in one sitting, the guy's a liability.'

A wry grin tweaked on Alex's mouth, quickly pursing into a friendly concerned look as he suppressed the locker room urge to crow.

Read: if you can't control your team Alice, the career's going nowhere.

'Unfortunately, Alex, I don't seem to have anyone else to blame.' She looked back up from the desk. 'Thought I had it watertight, had it sewn up with the mobile phone data: perfect tracking of his movements for shipments, dealers, even the bit on the side he thought he was keeping quiet. Wrong bloody number by one digit, couldn't pin a thing on him. Everything else was circumstantial, surveillance not convincing enough to nail him to it without mobile GPS.' She let out a small sigh. 'How he slipped this one I'll never know, friends in useful places would seem most likely. And the circus with the case files turning up late didn't help. Icing on the overall incompetence cake — as far as the judge was concerned he didn't have any choice but to throw it all out. I don't blame him. Bloody annoying.'

Alice drummed the desk with the fingers on her right hand,

'Still, might turn out useful. Now he thinks he's bulletproof he might get lazy I suppose. Slipped while he was gloating though, mentioned yesterday's Markwell murder. Thought it was strange. You ever come across those two in the same sentence before?'

'Can't say I have Alice. You know what that town's like, everyone knows everyone up there, never mind the dodgy ones, probably in each other's pocket more than we know. If Markwell's anything like the other dregs spilling out on a daily basis it's some deal gone wrong. Two low level traders fighting it out for a patch of council estate we wouldn't even send a blue light to. I can keep my ear to the ground, see if any of my sources throw you anything good up. Don't be holding out for miracles though.'

DI Alex Jamieson and his 'sources'. Alice smiled to herself. If she had a pound for every time Alex mentioned his sources at a team meeting she'd be weekly shopping at Waitrose instead of Sainsbury's for sure. She hadn't worked out yet if they all existed or if it was one of his plays to impress the guys, but they rarely threw anything good up for anyone else but himself.

'I'll bear it in mind thanks Alex, you hear anything you let me know,' trying to hide the doubt in her voice, 'leave Ronnie alone though. I want the guy running carefree in the community, and the faster the better so I can trip him up. Watch him crash land right into my lap.'

'Sure he'd love to spend time in your lap.' Alex leered humorously. 'As would we all.'

'Whatever. Pervert. You weren't convincing at Police College and you still aren't now.'

'Ok hotshot. Whatever you say. Seriously though, you throw up any leads on Markwell, rumour has it was a juicy one? Bumped into that 'first on scene' rookie PC Kelly, said it was a right knees up in there. Fella all tied up with some bizarre injuries he hadn't seen before.'

He looked expectantly, but she wasn't budging. She knew fine well what 'bumped into' meant. Kelly had been shooting his mouth off in the locker room and a receptive audience had been lapping it up. If Alex could take any of the credit for her investigation he wouldn't hesitate to name drop or edge his way into her work if he could, something she had fallen for in the past, losing brownie points to the locker room network, time and time again. Making a mental note to deal with Kelly before the day was out, she reached over and whipped the biro out as it got dangerously close to her note pad again, placing it safely back into her pen-pot.

'Nothing yet. Got the initial feelers out and waiting for the lab tests to trickle in. I'll get down to see Dr Ballingry when he gets the post-mortem started, hopefully get a bit more from there, might even get a motive soon hopefully. Like you say just some old local rivalry flaring up. He wasn't exactly the social elite. Probably some macho torture crap copied from a mini-series we've never heard of. See how your sources work out and let me know.'

'You're still hanging off Ballingry's every sacred word?' Alex scoffed. 'Guy's a relic, soon to be replaced. The days of the pathologist to the rescue are long gone Alice. Don't think I've had anything useful from that department in years. Anyway, it's all on Wikipedia and TV now, reckon I'll pick up more at the initial scene than those guys do in a week of poking livers and pickling eyeballs. Nobody's convicting on post-mortem data anymore, any idiot with a smartphone and decent internet knows how to fool a pathologist to make it look like something else.'

He looked up, a gentle shrug and raised eyebrow.

'We all know they only do that stuff for the death certificate and the families: the real deal is in the police work, not some body sitting cold on the slab.'

'Somebody still got a chip on their shoulder I see.' Alice smiled. 'Ever since Donald tore you apart in the courtroom last year you've been quite the sceptic, haven't you? Teach you not to move bodies at the crime scene before the pathologist gets there, naughty policeman. He still asks about you every time I see him you know, I'll tell him you were asking after him, shall I?'

She grinned as she saw DI Jamieson's inferiority complex squirming in the chair opposite. Ever since College she had known how to deflate him at just the right time, and now was no exception. Watching Dr Donald Ballingry, the regional forensic pathologist tear him a new one in court had been fine viewing, leading to weeks of fake rebukes in a gruff Scottish accent, something which had secretly riled the DI more than he let on. The fact he rescued the case — despite all the initial scene mistakes — had irked Alex further still, making him even more determined to debunk the good doctor's work whenever he could.

'Yeah yeah Alice.' playing it down, 'let me know though anyway, sounds like an interesting one. I'll keep my ear to the ground. Never know, you might want to thank me by taking me out to dinner sometime.'

'Chance would be a fine thing, we both know how your romances usually pan out, think I'll keep myself warm by other means if it's all the same to you.'

She tidied up the already tidy desk in front of her.

'Anyway, haven't you got work to do, or are you waiting for one of your 'sources' to magic you up some evidence? Go on, bugger off will you.'

'Your loss as always.' Alex stood up and opened the door to leave. 'Keep me posted: love a psycho murder'.

He shut the door and she pushed back, reclining in the chair. She liked Alex but the feeling she couldn't ever trust the guy was always there. It had been since their first weeks together.

The whole department knew they would be the two candidates for DCI when the boss retired in a few years, and failing an external appointment, the two of them would be fighting it out to impress the hierarchy. Alice with casework, Alex with his contacts and chess moves. Even despite the recent courtroom setback, she knew she would be the front-runner. The right face at the right time in a department screaming gender inequality.

Not for one minute was she going to relax though. Any help from him would be self-amplified, and so without obstructing herself too much, cracking cases without his interference would always be the way forward.

She picked up the phone to the Royal Victoria Infirmary, the region's main hospital, and was put through to the Pathology Department after the usual round of phone tennis with the switchboard. Confirming things were soon to be underway, she headed out into the maze of desks, quickly snaking past her juniors to find the stairwell down to the carpark.

Hopefully, Alice thought, as she cleared a space on the passenger seat for her case files, Dr Ballingry would have the good news the case needed right now.

Chapter Fifteen

The Mortuary.

Where the dead wait to tell their story.

Where life's ends are laid bare.

Not a regular occurrence for Alice these days, she opened the door to the building, attached to the city's main hospital, and proceeded over to the front desk to sign in. It was an unfamiliar receptionist who smiled to greet her, and after short introductions and small talk were exchanged, she picked up a receiver and dialled an internal line. A few minutes later the door to the right of the main entrance swung open, and it was the solid, squat figure of Dr Ballingry coming through, raising a hand to meet Alice as she stood up. A second hand enveloped the handshake, always the case with Donald, and a warm Scottish accent filled the room in greeting.

'How you doing Alice my darling eh, long time no see in these parts?'

'Can't complain Don, all the better for not seeing your ugly old mug out and about.'

A broad grin spreads over the forensic pathologist's face, and further amicable unpleasantries were exchanged as they moved through the building and into the changing rooms. Always the raconteur outside the lab, he brought Alice up to date on the latest changes in the department, but as they opened the door into the wet lab the tone changed, and Dr Ballingry, the professional, took centre stage.

Stood in front of a heavily reinforced steel table, fitted with a sink and drain at the far end, a shrouded shape lay beneath a white cloth, waiting patiently for the lab technician to get the last pieces of equipment together for their examination.

'I've done the boring stuff already Alice, including all the grim internal things I know you used to love so much back in the day,' a small smile creeps from Dr. Ballingry's mouth, 'but I've got you in to show you the business end.'

The material was peeled back to reveal a much cleaner version of the body Alice met a few days previously in Delaval Street. A large sutured incision ran up the midline of the abdomen and into the chest. Made this morning prior to the detective's arrival, organs had been checked to look for any corresponding internal injuries and pre-existing disease, before being stitched closed by the same technician who stood by, now firmly resolute.

'Nothing much interesting in the abdomen of course. Not the healthiest of livers I suppose, but not a factor in this case. No, the more interesting aspects are in the chest and head. If it wasn't for the tragedy of it, I'd be applauding the ingenuity. Fascinating all in all, not something I've dealt with in the forensic context before, and that's saying something.'

Dr Ballingry pointed with gloved fingers to two pinpoint injuries either side of the chest at the level of the elbow, dark concentrated circles of clotted blood, surrounded by cloud like bruising. All three of them moved closer in.

'I think you noticed these at the scene, didn't you? Or at least one of them.'

'Yeah, thought they were odd, what are we looking at exactly?'

'Needle insertions. Big fat needle insertions. My best guess would be a large bore cannula, normally only see these following a chest drain placement in a major trauma patient. A lot less bruising, and certainly no evidence of fixing in place, so I guess they weren't in for long, but enough to do the trick internally. I'll not repeat the pleasure of opening the chest back up, but I can tell you it was the textbook definition of a tension pneumothorax in there. Grade A collapsed lung bilaterally — both lungs left and right if you didn't know Alice — crushed to the point of minimal inflation, the sheer pressure of the air sucking in through these holes into a closed space. The heart was an impressive site as well, what would have been a clear silky pericardial sac was like a bubble wrapped ham by the time it had snap crackled and popped from the internal pressure.'

Donald stood back, emphasizing the point with outstretched arms closing inwards.

'The chest is an amazing place Alice, but forgiving it is not. You let all that air escape around the lungs, the internal pressure of your breathing makes it worse and worse until there's no space left for any organs. Imagine this poor chap's last few moments felt like a circus elephant was having a picnic on his breastbone. That was the party piece, but this …'

He pointed up, to the severed jugular vein on the left side of the neck.

'… This was the finishing move. You don't need thirty-seven years in forensic pathology to write this part of the PM report. Probably bled out and lost consciousness, what was left of it, within thirty seconds or so. The sadist in me thinks it was done after cardiac arrest set in from the pneumothorax — there's enough myocardial injury there to suggest so — but perhaps the optimist wins and it was a mercy kill when he'd suffered enough. All in all a bad way to go lassie. You're also looking at massive blunt initial trauma to the left jaw, CT scan showed it shattered under all that bruising. Not a mortal injury by any means, but enough to have ruined his weekend plans for sure.'

Alice scratched her forehead, the details all making for a grim summary as well as a confusing murder method. Donald was quick to pick up on it, resting a palm down on the cold steel.

'Look missy, don't go getting het up on the details, things like this always boil down to a mistake here or there. Ninety-nine percent of them mess it up somewhere along the line. No one's that perfect, we've seen it a hundred times or more. Find the slip up, you find your man, ask the DCI from back in the day.'

'Yes, I know you're right, but still. What a way to go. Never seen anything like it.'

She stepped back, unzipping the white overcoat as the technician wheeled a trolley around to the side of Markwell.

'Look, I'll get back to the station, chase up those mistakes. You let me know as soon as the report's in, will you?'

'Right ye are young 'un. I'll see you around.'

'Not if I see you first, you stay out of trouble okay.'

Alice turned to the door, not before one last long look at the mess of Davey Markwell's body. A cold shiver ran down her back as she walked out and into the mortuary changing room. Donald might be playing it cool, but by the time she sat down on the wooden bench, she was as white as a sheet.

Chapter Sixteen

'Thank you ladies and gentlemen for joining on such short notice. I appreciate this is an unusual one for us.'

Alice stood at the head of a long conference table, its room situated on the easterly side of the fourth floor at Police Headquarters. It was similar to what might be found in any corporate office up and down the country, grey fabric paneled walls tailoring a slick layout, but the PowerPoint behind her was definitely a niche subject: the murder of David Markwell. Assembled in front of her were her detective team, as well as the initial attending officers: PCs Martin Kelly, John Bolton and Graeme Talbot.

'We've got preliminary post-mortem and forensics from the scene, and I am currently awaiting final reports and toxicology from the victim, all within the next seven days hopefully. As you can see…' Alice clicked forward through her hastily assembled presentation, '…the victim was subject to violent and accurate assault wounds, presumably whilst in situ in the downstairs back room of the property. At this time we don't believe the body was moved post-mortem, or indeed post assault given the forensics on scene, so subject to further information we are currently only looking at one primary site. Our working hypothesis currently would either be an assailant known to the victim who entered through the front of the premises with permission, or, an unauthorised entry through the rear of the building. Given the volume of alcohol containers and drug paraphernalia in the room, it would be a reasonable assumption the victim was not entirely lucid at the beginning, or indeed during all of the assault, adding weight to the possibility of a surprise, targeted entry through the rear of the property.

I daresay when the toxicology report comes back we'll find Mr Markwell was not on the region's teetotal list for the evening.'

Others in the room nodded. A few of them had met and dealt with Davey Markwell before, so it would come as no surprise if he was under the influence of alcohol or something heavier at the point of the attack. Alice took a moment for a sip of water and placed the bottle back down on the table, continuing with her summary.

'Forensic searches through the rest of the property show no sign of unrest or frenzied searching, and correlating this with an ex-partner, there doesn't appear to be any obvious attempts or successes at burglary in regards to removal of belongings. Indeed, Mr. Markwell's smartphone was still on site, as well as other personal items including cash, credit cards, and some valuable electronics which would normally present an easy opportunity. This, I believe, adds weight to the motive of a punishment beating, or even the retrieval of important information from Davey himself: whatever that may be however, is not obvious. The lack of any initial macroscopic forensics from the scene shows us some scientific savvy, as well as the awareness to not remove items. We have of course submitted the smartphone to be unlocked and evaluated for information, so expect some digital forensics to be heading our way in the next few days once the lab has opened everything up for us.'

She clicked through the initial crime scene photos showing the back room from different angles, before stopping on a close up of the victim in the chair.

'The actual method of assault seems to be initially quite clumsy — a heavy head blow — however our colleague Dr Ballingry has pointed out a subsequent and fairly intricate injury which, at this point, may yield the most useful lines of enquiry given its nature.' Alice pointed out the chest wound.

'The final flourish it seems is this well aimed laceration to the jugular vein in the neck, although this may have been shortly post-mortem. I await a final report from Dr Ballingry for this, he was still undecided on the precise cause of death. I'll give that update when he makes his mind up. But that about sums up our initial walk through on the case.'

She sat down in front of her notes and looked back at the table, visibly relaxing after the formality required to deliver her information so succinctly.

They were by no means an inexperienced or green set of police officers, but the method and brutality of the attack had silenced the team, all sat quietly processing the information received. This was an unusual crime for the region — a step away from their normal day-to-day workload.

'So, what's the thinking boss? Bit big for that neck of the woods isn't it. I've come across him once or twice but never had him down for being a big player, I mean, he wasn't exactly a shut-in when it came to the local crime scene, but seems a big jump to be getting in deep enough for something like this to come back on him?'

Gavin Riley, one of the Detective Sergeants, raised a biro to his lip and tapped it there three times.

'No Gav you're not wrong. Far from it. I mean I've had his name mentioned a few times in relation to low level dealing, but nothing big enough to pin on him or to tie him in to anything bigger like organised crime. Out for himself most of the time.'

'So what's a guy like Davey Markwell into these days to get himself tied to a chair and have his throat slit, plus or minus whatever the lung thing you were on about.'

'The pneumothorax.' Alice clarified.

'Yeah, the pneumo-whatever it was. Bit of a funny way to kill a man if it's what's done for him. We looking for some deranged doctor or something you think?'

Alice gently shook her head and looked up at Gavin.

'It seems implausible, I mean, he was hardly mixing in the affluent social circles which would attract a high functioning individual, but that's what we've got to find out. What's he been into? Who's he pissed off, and why was it big enough for him to get dealt with in such a precise and brutal way?

'The ex say anything useful?' Samantha Bell, one of her other Sergeants at the end of the table.

'I think it was you speaking to her, was it Graeme? She was hanging around in the crowd outside the house on the first day no?' Alice looked at the uniforms at the end of the conference table.

Graeme Talbot, veteran PC and one of the initial attending officers, looked up, surprised to be spoken to.

'Ah yes ma'am. Yes, that was me. Pretty upset she was too. Had to take her to one side to get her calmed down. Seems like they recently called it a day. Her doing, I might add, but there was still an attachment there. I got a couple of probing questions in, see if anything might have slipped out if her distress was due to regret instead of true love, but I got the feeling she didn't have a clue what was going on. She knew he was a wrong 'un alright but was still pretty taken aback by it all. Kept muttering something about the dogs, or something — I couldn't catch it. She broke down in the end and went home with a friend. About as far as I got with her.'

'Thank you, PC Talbot,' Alice noted down the word 'dogs' in the margin of her notepad. Probably nothing, but you never know.

'I caught up with her the day after ma'am.' Andy Jordan, upright and smoothing his tie down.

'Oh, yes?'

'Can't say she was that emotional, well at least by the time I spoke to her anyway. If anything, she was more disinterested than anything. Took her round the house to check and see if anything was missing. She was itching to get home the whole time. Asked her about any trouble he might have been in, anyone he had any debts or grievances with. Nothing, not a scrap. Out the door as quick as she could.'

'Shame. You think she knew more?'

'Possibly. Just keen to get away. Scared maybe. Turned up to give us the impression she had helped perhaps. Maybe there's more there, maybe not. Be interesting to see what the tech lab come back with, see if there's any messages on Markwell's phone to say why they broke up. I can't say she mentioned anything about dogs though: just the token statement. No sign of an animal in the house, didn't seem the type either, could be wrong.'

'Okay. Fair enough. We'll come back to her if we need to. Like you say, if the unlocked phone brings us anything we can always stick her in an interview room and see if she trips up. Sounds sensible to me.'

Alice closed the laptop, and the power point shut down behind her to leave a glowing blue screen with 'no signal', written in small type in its centre.

'Anything else?'

Shaking heads and murmurs of 'no' came from around the table, and she proceeded to set tasks for the DCs as well as follow up enquiries for her two sergeants. It was currently slim pickings until the phone was unlocked, and nothing was sparking anyone's interest in any direction.

Meeting ended, she dismissed the team to disperse out into the office and back to work. All except Andy Jordan whom she held back. Her protégé.

'Andy. Dig into this dog thing for me, will you? Might be nothing. Might be a starter. A hunch I'm getting. See if there are any leads there. Excuse the pun.'

'Yes ma'am. Will do.'

'And something else.' Alice folded her arms and looked over Andy's shoulder for door hangers. 'DI Jamieson started sniffing around this one. You know what he's like with his sources and the over friendliness eventually turning into point scoring. I know you're something of a hit in the locker room, keep your ear to the ground for me, okay? Let me know if he comes asking questions. Nothing serious, I'm just on edge after the Macfarlane case went south so quickly. Probably nothing, but this must be flawless, okay?'

'Yes boss. Team Rose all the way.'

'Yes alright 'Twilight boy'. Get out of here. Go on.'

Andy smiled as he turned and shut the door behind him, and Alice looked down at her minimal notes from the meeting: it was not the quick start she had hoped for, but then it wasn't your regular cut-and-shut murder.

There were a few threads of course. The chest injury, the brutality inflicted, the chilling accuracy which could rule out ninety-five percent of Markwell's clumsy backstreet acquaintances. No, all there she thought. All lingering in the shadows. All quietly waiting for her to scratch into and pick away at. You wait and see Alice, these things always come together eventually.

'Find the slip up, find your man.' repeating Donald's words.

If only sooner rather than later though. She shut the notepad.

Chapter Seventeen

I came to from the daze.

I'd got home an hour ago and sat down with a coffee. A half day, a promise of free time. Instead, I'd lapsed into the trance, a dull unease washing over me as I thought about Markwell and stared at a blank television screen. A black reflection with me in the middle.

I absently picked up the mug. It was stone cold, not even worth a trip to the microwave. I put it back down.

For a Wednesday, my morning had been uneventful: consults racing by, faster and faster as my blood pressure refused to settle. Thankfully, no damage had been done. No one had noticed by the time I packed up to leave.

Normally on a day like today I'd be out in the garden, fixing up the continual project of our house, tidying leaves or tackling the lawn, but the crushing heavy clouds above had driven me inside to the kettle and the living room. The wind viciously whipping at me as I made my way in from the car.

Usually I'd relish the house to myself, a quiet couple of hours without any interruptions, however the past few days had been a world away from man jobs or mundane housework, replaced instead by a haze of panic and anguish over the events a few nights ago. Not for Davey, but selfishly, more for myself.

After finishing up with him I'd made a swift exit back the way I had entered, taking ten minutes or so to clean up and trying to leave as little or no evidence as I could.

The worry though, the constant worry, was I'd left something behind, or had been seen on my way out through the back streets. At the time I wouldn't have looked out of place. Another quiet figure moving through the back streets in a dead-end part of town. But as time went past and a body was discovered, questions would be asked, doors would be knocked on, and memories would come flooding back to nosey neighbours who spent their idle time spying out of windows.

Although the street had been ghostly quiet by the time I'd left, in my mind curtains were now twitching and furrowed eyes peered out at me through the darkness, documenting my every move. Old clients, looking and wondering, what their vet was doing creeping around in the alleyways. And CCTV. What if there were CCTV, and I was caught bang to rights skulking about on camera somewhere.

It was unlikely, hardly an area of town worth monitoring, but my lack of sleep over the past few nights had been racked by intrusive thoughts and all the worst possibilities. Every time a door opened in the practice I thought I'd be looking up to see a police officer, and every engine driving past was a van ready to take me away.

Surprisingly, the guilt had been easier to deal with. Sure, it wasn't pleasant to have ended a life, but I'd done it a thousand times before, albeit with animals and a good deal more cleanly, and the process and emotion were all too familiar and easy to shut away. In life, as in work, you move from one place to another, leaving behind a sobbing, emotional family who've lost their beloved pet to cancer in one room, and into the next, where a small child holds her new puppy, full of love and questions: difficult not to develop a shut-out clause for your mentality in our line of business.

I can't say I'd ever met a more deserving specimen than Markwell though. If anything, I wish I'd made it more painful for him.

No, as psychopathic as it sounded, I didn't regret finishing him off so ceremoniously, not a bit. The guy was trash to me. I'd have difficulty explaining the sentiment to a police officer however, or indeed Anna, so hopefully things would stay quiet and I'd get away with it.

The less explaining the better.

This afternoon though — still battling with all the turmoil — I'd pushed down most of the anxiety, setting my time aside for research and planning.

Anna wouldn't be home until six-thirty or seven p.m., so I had myself a good few hours to sit and scroll through the WhatsApp group chat download from a few days before. I had left it alone until now, too busy worrying about everything else, but the time had come. I needed to get ahead of this thing, this non-stop monster that was living in my head.

Every time I had switched on the burner phone and released it from airplane mode, BloodSport pinged to life, reams of messages and media files coming through without abandon since I infiltrated the new contact into their group.

It had been a few days since the trip to see Davey, and slowly but surely the group was coming alive with chatter about his lack of input since. It was two days ago, Monday, when the pace really picked up however — as did my adrenaline — as I read through the pages of messages about what had been discovered. The group was in panic mode as the details filtered in of what I had done, how I had done it, and what state Davey had been left to fester in, by himself, all alone in the house.

A neighbour had called it in, the police discovering him a short while later still bound and lifeless. The group was buzzing all the way through with questions and theories, as well as a notable lack of empathy for Davey, but the question of who'd done it was still unanswered by the time I had scrolled through to the end.

Since last night, no further messages were on, and the chat was quiet. Silenced it would seem.

As I refilled a coffee cup, Quint rotated himself round on the sofa next to me, and I gradually pieced together a semblance of the group dynamic from the text.

Of the nine members, all men I'm guessing from the awfulness of them, six actively participated, perhaps the other three were technophobes or wallflowers when it came to voicing their thoughts. Of the five or six regular chat participants though, when you boiled down the banter and subtracted the chaff, two main players emerged as leading the group.

Davey was not one of them.

Looking back through his previous input it was mostly submissive and dutiful, which fitted in with the impression his lifestyle gave in general; he didn't seem to contribute any organisational power to the ongoing workings. Only taking their orders or trying to crack bad jokes.

'S' leads most of the organising and takes a decent grip on the group. He doesn't flag much questioning and the joking stops when he sends a message, even dishing out the occasional sharp rebuke to a member when required. I get the impression he might have above average knowledge of the medical world, offering his crude advice to the other less dominant members of the group.

Next is 'J', who seems equally as in charge, but slips into the banter more than his counterpart. With a naivety and charm about him it's difficult to pin down where he's coming from, a hint of the legal system, I'm not sure. Something about the way he answers questions or gives orders. Very clinical. Very methodical. A man used to being in charge for sure.

The overriding, frustrating theme of the research however, was a lack of real names and set locations. I get the feeling 'J' or 'S' has banned the specifics on the chat, as the void of useful information is clear to see. I do however find myself mentioned more than a few times around the time of the dog found in the bins, along with Skye, and Carl the owner's son. It had created quite the debate it seems, mostly anger at the stupidity of Davey for attempting such a novice disposal, as well as fury at him for leaving them open to the suspicion of the law.

It hadn't taken them long to work out where the body had gone, and the gift of the angry phone call from the previous owner had sparked the clampdown and scare tactics I first heard about, and fell victim to the night after. Gloating and jokes filled a few pages about how the vet had pissed his pants and fallen off his bike, the consensus being I had it coming for being a know it all and charging too much.

Only when 'S' put an end to the chat did it stop, reminding Davey not to get too carried away with himself or try it again. Enough was enough for the vet, and to leave Skye well alone.

'Seems like Davey was going rogue after all eh Quint?'

I reach over and grab a handful of cat to tickle.

Unfortunately, this wakes him up, which in turn livens up the rest of the animal household, forcing me into dishing out food for all of them. Meanwhile Tank whines at the door to be let out behind me.

I see him out into the garden for a pee and I slowly drain the cup of coffee I've been nursing over the last half an hour, heading back to the sofa to put a few finishing touches to the notes I've made in the notebook, discreetly replacing it back onto a high shelf when I'm done. There were a few things to get working on, a few ideas to calm the rushes of adrenaline hitting me in waves.

Looking out into the garden, Tank sails past after a leaf, stamping it down between two paws in the corner. Paulie is watching with me from behind the glass.

'He's an idiot mate.'

Paulie agrees, snaking between my legs as he heads out of the room and into the kitchen for round two of dinner. Whatever Hooper has left behind anyway.

The burner phone is powered down and goes back into a hollowed out veterinary dictionary beside the notebook and I shut the light off.

By the time I get back to the kitchen, Tank is pawing heavily at the side door to get back in, wet and muddy from the rain, the leaf stuck to the top of his head.

'Come on in then. You want dinner yet big fella?' I ask as he pads past me and over to the cat food, dirty paw prints following behind him as I flail the floor with an old towel.

Anna and I decided a few weeks ago he could stay for the long term; news which had been gladly received by him, so he thanks me again by buckling my knees with a wet head butt, causing me to tip half a container of dry food in his direction.

'Cheers Tank you big clown.'

He grins and sticks his large, cartoon-like head back down into his bowl, busying himself eating while I lean past him to open the fridge, taking out dinner ingredients. I flick the Bluetooth speaker sat on top of the microwave and select an easy-going playlist from my music library.

As I sort out a chopping board and open a few packets, the soothing tones of old indie music strum out into the kitchen, and I realise, looking over at Tank, it's the first time in days I haven't thought about Davey Markwell. Thought about leaving him behind in the empty house surrounded by blood. His neck drained below him.

Maybe it was going to be okay after all.

'Eh Tank? Sod him.'

I guess it paid to be a little dead inside.

Thanks veterinary career.

Chapter Eighteen

The phone rang on Alice's desk.

Her morning had been dull; moving paperwork from one tray to the next, tying up one lead after another without any progress. Markwell was stagnant. Not moving.

She reached over and picked up the receiver, Dr Ballingry's gravelly tones warmly greeting her on the other end of the line.

'Now lassie have I caught you at a bad time? Weren't rushing out the door to collar some thief were you, I know what rush you Polis are about these days.'

The use of the old Scottish term always cheered Alice up, taking her back to her formative days; watching police dramas from north of the border, thoughts of pints and whisky chasers, thoughts of simpler times.

'Not at all Donald, the opposite in fact. You've caught me at the perfect time, all yours as it happens.'

She could almost see the glaze in the Doctor's eyes as he pondered on the sentiment for a split second. She hurried him.

'It's the final report for Mr. Markwell I'm hoping? Wouldn't you normally send it over via internal mail, or is it something juicy you couldn't keep to yourself?'

'It's just the main headlines for you Alice before I send all the paperwork over.'

The formal tone had resumed.

'Just in case you wanted a head start on the type of suspect you might be looking for that's all.' There was a short pause on the line whilst the receiver was passed from one ear to the other, no doubt as Donald picked up his case notes, 'No, it seems to boil down to our chest injury, all the other stuff is impressive, but too crude and broad in the execution. I think any old sort could achieve it given the desire to, but the chest I think is the key to this one. Not necessarily as cause of death, still a mix up between the pneumothorax and the neck incision — a 'what came first' situation if you will — but the specifics of the thorax make it more significant.'

Alice reached over for her pen and paper, urging him to go ahead.

'There's something acutely medical about the injury and it's been bugging me since I saw it. No layperson would know how to create such a pathology without reading the odd textbook or two. Whoever placed that needle, and I'm assuming it was medical grade by the sharpness and neatness of the skin entry, we're not talking a bicycle pump here Alice, knew exactly where to place it and what to do with it. You don't accidently get a pneumothorax through such a wee hole without being very intentional. You're looking for someone with access to chest drains, syringes, cannulas and taps; a whole host of specialist inventory. And knowledge. I can't imagine the average man on the street would have the imagination, or the inclination, without some serious training.'

Donald paused, taking a short break. Alice heard papers shuffling on the other end of the line, as well as the clink of a cup hitting a saucer.

'No, someone has either researched in quite some detail, or done it before. Bloody odd way to kill a man if you ask me. Half reminded me of the time back in the eighties when we PM'd an unfortunate fellow with both his eyes removed. Clean out. Never seen such a thing. Wasn't cause of death of course but blow me down if it wasn't the most unusual PM I'd ever done. I'm older and grizzlier now, but it was still bad enough to stick in the mind for some time. Turns out Alice, sorry, stop me if this is irrelevant…'

'No no Donald, go ahead.'

'Well, turns out Alice, some jilted General Surgeon from Ninewells in Dundee had gone to town on his wife's lover. Sedated him, the whole nine yards. Bloody well took both eyes out of him before he woke him up and killed him. Stupid bugger kept the eyes though didn't he. Arrogant surgeon if you ask me. What was his name? For the life of me I can't remember. Made more than a few front pages I can tell you. A bit before your time young lady I expect.'

'And so what about this chest thing? I'm looking for some deranged surgeon with a vendetta against the low lives of the town?' She cut in, eager to move along now.

'Well not the finesse of an eye surgeon, but clever enough to know what he or she was doing, and careful enough not to kill him outright. Ingenious if you ask me, but yes, still odd. Much easier ways to bring a life to an end, and why cut the throat? Strikes me there was some symbolism to it. Usually is with the unusual ones. Your Dundee Surgeon couldn't bear the thought of those eyes that had looked at his wife, cut them out to teach him a lesson.'

He coughed a harsh cough, no doubt brought on by many enclosed years of breathing formalin-soaked air, before gathering himself with a sip of water and carrying on.

'Find the lesson and whatever it stands for, you'll be on to something. There'll be some wee nugget in the past this relates to.'

Alice turned the page over, shaking the pen as it faltered with the last few words.

'Find the lesson. Past.'

'Anyway lassie, a definite first for me, and hopefully a last. We'll see if I can't make it to retirement without another one like it. Good luck I say, hopefully might narrow down the suspect pool for you. I'd find out if he's pissed off some doctor or ICU nurse if I were you, few other people capable of it I imagine.'

They wrapped up with a few informalities and promises to hopefully not see each other too soon, and Alice replaced the receiver down, pushing back from the desk. One step forward, but two steps back on her motive.

Tossing the pad of paper back to its original position beside her in-tray, she stood up, walking over to the whiteboard on the far wall, obscured with pictures of the scene and associates of Davey. Picking up the blue marker pen, following the instructions of Dr Ballingry, she duly noted his suspicions in the suspect section: 'Medical. Symbolism. Punishment?'

And that was it, pretty much all she could think to write. How would a deadbeat like Davey Markwell have invited such an exquisite end to himself? It didn't make sense.

A short while later the clock had moved forward but progress hadn't. She had swapped the office for the conference room. The solitude for gathered company.

'Any other bright ideas?'

The same sentiments were being uttered around the table as the team received the pathology briefing.

How on earth had Davey managed to get himself done in in such a way was beyond anyone, but it opened new leads to chase. The few known associates they did have would be re-questioned — albeit oddly — to see if the deceased had any connections to anyone medical. Their agreed hope was such an unusual connection would flag up quickly; he was unlikely to be moving in social circles with doctors and nurses and so they were optimistic they might just catch a break with this one. Alice wasn't so sure.

'How are the forensics getting on, please tell me we're getting some positive news, anything from DNA analysis?'

Andy Jordan shuffled uncomfortably as the focus of the room turned towards him. Forensics had been his responsibility to liaise for, and so far there was a gaping chasm of useful information for him to report, one of the reasons he'd kept quiet so far in the meeting.

'Sorry Ma'am, nothing terribly good from it. Only type we've recovered so far is from the deceased. Currently we're waiting back on hair samples from the upstairs bedroom to correlate with the ex-partner, but it seems unlikely the attacker went up there, let alone got into bed. All entry points were sterile, the back door they're telling me showed signs of a recent bleach clean, streaks on the UPVC and chemical residue, so I guess either Mr. Markwell was a clean freak -—which seems unlikely from the rest of the property — or the attacker was forensically literate, cleaning as they left. You potentially might have a lead on a white fibre residue consistent with an overall, the type you see for decorating, but probably points towards a future lack of forensics if they were that clued up. They would be generic and difficult to trace. Ties in with our medical hypothesis though Ma'am.'

DC Jordan glanced up from his notes to the rest of the table, and then further to his right to look at DI Rose.

'Only useful thing not DNA, is the phone. The lab called me before to say they'd finally got it unlocked, so I'm hoping something useful will be on the extraction summary. Should have access to the files in the next few days once they've downloaded and decrypted everything on there.'

'Well at least something positive.'

Alice scrolled the last few notes in her notebook and looked up.

'Anything else good to cheer me up?'

It was a resounding negative, and she remained seated as they filed out behind her, dispersing into the office to find their desks, or more realistically over to the coffee machine. The open door framed them as they walked away.

What she wouldn't give for a break right now, some gold dust in the digital extraction, something solid she could build a foundation on. As soon as the thought came to her, however, the misery of her last case swarmed around it. Ronnie Macfarlane's gloating face accompanied it.

She shuddered thinking back to the confrontation outside the courthouse days before; she had half a mind to pull him in and shake him down over his verbal slip, mentioning Davey by name, but had thought better of it.

Better to let him sweat a little longer.

Chapter Nineteen

The label advertised it as vitamin rich. How rich Alice wondered? Rich enough to soak up last night's white wine fumes, the faint wisps that had her head space tainted and dull this morning?

Her own fault: stupid to accept an invitation for drinks on a weeknight but there you go.

The date had seemed promising. Yet, there it had been, two drinks in and the usual, inevitable cloud of boredom crept in. Cue more wine ordered. Cue more boasting. Career in finance, active lifestyle. All the same. There was a reason single men in their late thirties made poor first impressions.

The lid went back on the mineral water; screwed tight to avoid a spill. She gazed at the door. She wondered what Ronnie Macfarlane would be like on a date. Probably quite exciting in some ways. A shudder made its way up her back.

She was sat with Andy Jordan again, nervously thumbing his tie across the table after being called into the conference room alone. Much easier to have a one to one than wait for the next formal case conference she had thought, and she had caught him off guard at the coffee machine as he flicked his second sugar packet.

'Anything on Markwell's smartphone yet DC Jordan? Any nuggets to send us in the right direction by any chance?'

Sitting upright, his crumpled Next suit jacket was unbuttoned and open to reveal a plain white shirt with a monotone anthracite necktie. Not one for big fashion statements, Andy shuffled his frame around uncomfortably in the chair opposite his DI.

'Full report isn't in yet ma'am. Hence me waiting to brief you until it was all back in, but I am just in from the tech lab. Spent the morning dredging through all his messages. Nothing too interesting, usual string of adult material and flirty messages, no obvious kinks or quirks jumping out to suggest he was into anything or anyone which might have got him done over. Can't find any recents to suggest he was expecting anyone for the evening either. Activity goes dead a few days back, before the uniforms found him, which fits with the initial post-mortem and body decomposition. No one taking an interest in his lack of activity in the days leading up to his discovery either, no appointments scheduled or regular meetings he was missed at. Few pings on WhatsApp: his mum called him and left a voicemail, couple of text messages from the local takeaway. But nothing big to suggest he was the regular man about town people were missing.'

'And nothing on the medical angle we had? The unusual wound patterns? No links there?'

'Not that I can tell ma'am. Seems like a regular run of the mill low life so far. All except a couple of disturbing pictures in his albums. Messed up animal carcass pictures, what looks like a mutilated dog, a few bigger dogs with bite wounds. Twisted stuff. I've asked the lab to look at the origins if they can; whether he took them himself, or whether they were internet images or automatic downloads from messaging apps; should hopefully get it back in the next few days. Unfortunately ma'am, DI Jamieson was in the lab busy fast tracking his own cases and I couldn't get a foot in the door for our stuff, apologies.

'No need to apologise Andy, I'm well aware of what DI Jamieson is like down there, probably sweet talking the new secretary everyone knows he's been seeing on the side. I'll give them a ring and see if I can push things in our direction, you never know I might even give the silver-tongued DI a run for his money one of these days. Anything else before I release you back into the playground?'

'No ma'am not really. The lab tech was going on about some new software he had that recaptures old and deleted message threads. Lost me to be honest, but he reckoned he could uncover recent deleted chats or caches if they hadn't already been swamped in encryption. I dunno, we'll see, I'll let you know as soon as I get the full report back in. Do you want me to save it for the next meeting, or come directly to you?'

'Ideally direct Andy. I don't mind telling you things are currently thin on the ground leads wise and I can do with all the heads up I get. I might ring and get cc'd into the report so don't take offence if I'm one step ahead of you.'

'None taken ma'am, none at all.'

***

The clock in Alice's office read 1pm, the hour hand grinding its way up and past midday. Trouble was, it was a day later, and she was still getting nowhere. Twenty-four hours of malaise and lethargy hiding amongst her piles of disorganised notes.

Another unsatisfying salad had made its way down, accompanied by another flavoured water alongside her now towering stack of paperwork. She leaned over and powered up her desktop computer for the afternoon. Over lunch her mobile had pinged a notification from the lab, but being a casefile, it would only download on the secure network in the office. She logged onto the server, and scrolling past office circulars and usual HR reminders, she found the email and opened it. Andy was the main recipient with herself copied in as the overseeing case officer in charge, but shifting her gaze down the list, next to her name was DI Jamieson's, on a 'request to view' query.

'What the hell?'

Alice picked up the phone and dialled the lab's extension.

'Hi, it's DI Rose here, checking my case emails, and there's a marker in for DI Jamieson. Any reason or just an unfortunate error? Please tell me you're not sending these out to all of the department, are you?'

A nervous silence on the line accompanied a sound of paper shuffling, and the receiver was picked up to remove the call from speakerphone.

'Sorry ma'am, the DI called yesterday, I took the call and he wanted a copy of the results for another case he was working up, something about a shared interest he was wanting to keep an eye on, an associate of the deceased. Sorry, I should have checked. Protocol says put it as a request for the officer in charge, but seens as you're in the same office I figured it was going to be a formality. Is it a problem? I can take it off if you'd prefer?'

'In future if you can take him off that would be great. Nothing personal, just a sensitive case at the moment, the less eyes on this one the better. Do me a favour as well, if any other officers come asking about the case or any of my others, can you let me know? Thanks.'

Without waiting for the reply she replaced the receiver and stared at the screen. She was sure it was the secretary Alex had been seeing in his spare time, as well as during office hours. Odd though she thought. He was forever playing office politics, but trying to snoop on her cases as well? She had him for a gossip but this was getting underhand. It wasn't like him to stab you in the back; he was usually too busy making himself look good to bother being sly about it.

Still, she thought, no point going to the DCI with it yet, for all she knew he was keeping tabs on her as well after the Macfarlane debacle, or was that paranoia setting in? Doubts creeping in as she worked her way along the career ladder? Probably nothing, probably Alex's way of power playing her next time they were in the office kitchen together, showing her up in front of colleagues to come across as the big man. She took a mental note to remind him the secretary had a boyfriend on the force's regional rugby team next time she saw him, and it wasn't just him who could play politics when required.

Mulling it a while longer, she scrolled down through the email. Lots of repetition from DC Jordan's initial report to her a day back, but at the bottom there was the addendum with new findings. Mainly deleted conversations and the image origins Andy had spoken about as an area of interest.

The attached image files were a selection from the smartphone, no doubt the whole album files were sitting on a secure USB in the lab for later use if required. As promised they made for unpleasant viewing: dismembered dogs, what looked like fight wounds, and one in particular — what looked like a terrier, its throat slit and ragged with bites. They mostly varied in origin, but worryingly, a minority were marked as original images, meaning Davey had taken the photos himself. More than a few were sourced from a deleted and recovered WhatsApp group. The aptly named 'BloodSport'.

Mr Markwell had shared to, as well as downloaded from it, and they all showed similar pictures of injured dogs in varying states of distress.

'Jesus Christ.' Alice muttered as she filtered through the images, flicking faster and faster as it became clear they were all much the same, 'What the hell is wrong with some people.'

The door knocked in front of her, and Andy Jordan's head and right shoulder appeared around the doorframe, eager it would seem for the rest of him to follow. 'Okay to come in ma'am?'

She nodded. He took the seat in front of her.

'Don't suppose you checked your emails yet ma'am, I saw you were copied into the latest lab report on the Markwell case, I finished up lunch early and started going through it, figured I'd come check in with you now we both had it.'

'Yes Andy, started looking at some of the images now. Some disturbing pictures there, you weren't wrong. Nothing flagged up in the house about this did it, nothing came back on the searches so far no?'

'No nothing yet ma'am, it might all be nothing, but I was thinking it might be worth exploring as a potential line of enquiry, some violent stuff in there; it doesn't take too much of a leap in imagination to get to Mr Markwell's endpoint. More so if you read through that 'BloodSport' group.'

The puzzled look on her face told him she obviously hadn't gotten that far into the report and attached files yet.

'Sorry ma'am, I jumped straight in given I'd already looked through the image files. BloodSport. If you ask me it's some kind of dog-fighting group, and not just for voyeurs, looks like some ongoing active organisation there. I can see why it's been deleted. No names yet, but we should ask the lab if they can retrieve the phone numbers for us.'

'Not as daft as you look Andy, good logic. Show's you're following the right things.'

Alice smiled as she let her guard down, before remembering her rank and switching back to her usual mode.

'One question though, when was it deleted?

'When?'

'Yes Sherlock, when?

'I don't follow ma'am.'

'Well, when was the last time you deleted a conversation off your phone? Hardly ever is what I'm guessing. What would be the point? It's your phone, and you're the one looking at it. Especially if you're apparently single like the victim Mr Markwell. Nothing to hide, so who's he supposed to be deleting things from?'

Andy nodded, starting to twig what Alice was thinking.

'We need to know when the conversation was deleted. For example, if he's deleted it a while back, what's the significance; has he left the group for bad reasons and this is his payback, or was there something on there incriminating enough to get him killed? Or here's a theory, whoever did for him went through his phone and deleted anything that could provide evidence of their motives. Get back to the lab, find out when it was deleted, and find the owners of those phone numbers. If it's the only thing missing from the phone chances are it's the best link to cracking this case.'

'Yes ma'am, on it right away. I'll make it my only priority this afternoon.'

'Good lad. Nothing else you hear?'

'Yes ma'am. Oh, and one other thing. I noticed DI Jamieson was a copy request for the results, am I to report to him as well, or just yourself. Wasn't aware he was working this as well.'

'No Andy, just me. I'll keep DI Jamieson in the loop where required.

That'll be all for now.'

He raised himself up out of the chair and left the room. She took another sip of the flavoured water, mountain berries to be precise, and a short buzz of adrenaline fluttered up inside as the dregs of last night's alcohol were filtered and forgotten. The reassuring, familiar feeling of evidence slowly fitting into place filled her with new confidence, and turning back to the desktop, she opened the 'BloodSport' transcripts, to read it all back from its grisly start.

Chapter Twenty

'At the garage now guys.'

Blood Sport had come through.

In amongst the putrid chat, the dark images and awful video content, was the location of a previous meeting. It was the obvious next step for me.

It had taken some scrolling: nestled in its rotten company a month ago was a screenshot of a map, pinpointing a fight, surrounded by invites and excitement. Their depravity was overwhelming. It was time to get ahead of them.

Anna was out for drinks with colleagues, the kind that promised to go late into the night, and I had an empty pass for the evening. I had left the mobile at home, cycling into town via one of the many un-lit wagonways which existed in the area, figuring it best not to leave a trace of my movements in case something about this dark little adventure went wrong.

I approached the area and identified the garage, where it sat on a large industrial estate.

The place itself was a run-down looking affair, I had street viewed the area the day before, to get my bearings, and so it all looked familiar enough as I slowly cycled past the shadowy buildings. If it was still in use it didn't show: a crusty front sign sat precariously above a creaky looking metal roller door advertising bodywork repairs and custom re-sprays on most types of vehicles. The padlock on the front however was still shiny and well maintained, and with a gentle tug I established it wasn't going to be so easy to gain access.

Stashing my bike in the nearest, darkest alleyway I could find, I moved around to the rear of the building: a chain-link fence was all that surrounded a small yard, one containing an empty skip and a few wooden pallets. Fairly tidy and not much sign of any day-to-day usage occurring, I took a guess it would be vacant and not under the watch of any alarm system. Making my way along, methodically checking as I went, it didn't take long to find the loose bottom segment big enough to slide under and into the small concrete space.

There was a wooden door on the building, set neatly into the blockwork of the garage structure. No handle on either side suggested this was either a fire escape or one-way door; only a poorly maintained security light was set above, flickering a sparse dull light into the yard it was failing to protect.

Checking and finding it tightly shut I was sure I'd had a wasted trip, another dead end in this chase. However, looking up to the left and right I noticed two horizontal single pane windows. I tried the first of the two, and to my surprise, it creaked open after a gentle nudge: the latch inside had been left sitting away from its hinge, making it easy enough to swing it up ninety degrees and set it open. Good fortune favours the naïve it turns out.

Looking around to make sure there were no onlookers joining me, I eased my way up and into the rear of the building, finding a sturdy shelf and worktop on the other side I could drop a leg down on. This was too easy.

I had brought along a small torch, and trying not to flash it back towards the window, I flicked the switch and took my bearings. The space was much bigger than it looked from the front, the other side of the rusty roller door opening out into a wide and dusty expanse. Clearly it had long been stripped of any valuable machinery. The only indicators of its previous use were a few bits of sheet metal, as well as mismatched lengths of plastic piping stacked against the far wall, next to a commercial wheelie bin with its lid still propped open.

The colour scheme of the walls and the gritty concrete floor however gave a sense of lingering déjà vu.

I got the sense I had been in this building whilst looking at the WhatsApp group pictures. In the centre of the garage the faintly familiar space was clear and recently swept, devoid of any of the detritus cluttering the rest of the workspace, and it was easy enough to make out the four right-angled corners of a large square. I even recognised the broom discarded to the side.

A sharp, demarcated line suggested a larger structure had been placed on top of the makeshift arena — something which had been removed. Two metal rings, drilled and bolted into the concrete sat in each corner. I kicked down at the bearings, making a thick clinking sound as they rattled and echoed against their fixings in the shop floor.

In the centre of it all, however, was the most telling finding.

Pale stains spilled out and drained from a larger centre point. Difficult to tell the colour in the harsh artificial light of the torch, I knelt and sniffed at the ground, coming away with the faintest of metallic smells. I'd smelled it a thousand times before in my career: dried blood.

From the width of it, something, or someone had bled out heavily here in this building; whisked away for disposal, the evidence washed and scrubbed down afterwards. Looking into the corners, the only other tell-tale was a small dark red spot, crusting and peeling on the metalwork of one of the metal rings. It lifted easily, and on the fingertip of a latex glove it broke down to a red smear when dabbed in saliva. Not exactly CSI, but I was confident this was blood spatter.

The thought of dogs dying here, being torn apart whilst I had existed only miles away, filled me with an empty dread.

My eyes gradually adjusted to the dim interior, and I switched off the torch. The pale light from outside was enough to stop me from tripping and knocking things over as I moved around, and piecing things together it was becoming clear the group were well into the business of dog fighting.

Potentially not the biggest or most well organised yet, but they obviously weren't messing around either. From this, and the group chat, I had the feeling this wasn't going to be a one off.

Sure, they weren't in an established location, setting up fights on a regular schedule, but the clues were there to suggest they were on the up, and I guessed it wouldn't be long before they found a clientele and location they were happy with. Worse still, the baiting and trapping of local dogs to fuel their empire would pick up pace alongside their ability.

The empty dread was turning back to rage as I stared down at the stains beneath my feet. This thing had to stop.

Clearly the dog dumped and brought into the clinic had been a mistake, a screw up they wouldn't aim to repeat if they were going to make a success with this — so the urgency of my situation was now fuelled by the need to stop them before things got any worse.

Dealing with Davey had burned bridges with the police. Satisfying but not the cleverest of moves, there were multiple other ways to have dealt with things more smoothly. Not killing him for a start. But here I was, in the blood-spattered shell of a fighting ring, working out my next move.

Standing here in the dark wasn't the best one.

After a few more minutes fruitlessly searching the building, lifting pallets and sweeping aside the stacked cardboard, I realised the bloodstains were the only clue. I moved back over to the worktop in front of the window, easing it open once more.

As I swung my leg up and over the sill, a pile of letters caught my eye, weighted under another new looking padlock on the countertop.

Clear of the grime that dusted the rest of the worktop, I picked them up and shuffled through the stack, the torch between my teeth pointing down on to them as it illuminated the wording.

Mainly bills and circulars, they weren't too enlightening:

'To the Occupier',

'To the Occupier',

'To the Business Owner'

And second from last:

'Mr D Markwell and Mr S Trench'

Bingo. I turned it over. It was official and had a return address for a local machine parts company on the underside. I pocketed it before quietly making the return journey through the window, and out under the gap in the fence. Checking around to see I was alone, I moved to the alleyway and found my bike.

Cycling home, the cogs turned: 'Mr S Trench', who are you, how do you know Davey Markwell? And what are you doing receiving letters in a property where dog fighting occurred?

Later, and after Anna had gotten home and fallen into bed, glowing from cocktails and tired from pleasant company, I retrieved the letter from my jacket pocket and sat down to open it. I didn't need to be careful — I'd throw it in the log burner once I was done reading. I tore it open and tossed the ripped envelope towards the tumbler of single malt which was going down too well.

I drained the last few millimetres of a generous serving and opened out the letter which had been addressed to Markwell, and my new interest, Mr S Trench.

It was an invoice from a regional engineering firm, for parts ordered a while ago, and one which clearly hadn't been paid for past their initial deposit. The outstanding balance was marked in red at the bottom of the second page, following a stern warning about referral to debt collectors and blacklisting from the use of the company and other affiliates in the region. I guess the company didn't know the letters had been falling onto an empty concrete floor, so the last paragraph read 'third and final demand'.

Dated from two months ago, no doubt the authors had learned of its fate when the collection team had finally appeared to find the same rusty shutters and lack of activity, the same I had encountered earlier on this evening. Perhaps they'd even slid under the same wire fence and peered in through the same ill-fitting single pane window at the abandoned internal layout.

Most useful though was the full address, and the 'for attention of' at the head of the text.

'For attention of Mr David Markwell and Mr Simon Trench, QuickWorks Bodyshop.'

'We have tried contacting you on the following phone numbers and email addresses…'

I opened the leather notebook I had been jotting down details in since discovering the initial BloodSport group, and flicked through to my list of the known members from the contact details.

It was embarrassingly short: D Markwell.

At least the phone numbers from the letter matched to one from the group's contact list, a promising start.

I scrolled down my list to what I hoped would be the money-shot and looked at the number for 'S' in my notebook: one of the main organisers and ringleaders of the group. I was left disappointed as I traced over the eleven-digit mobile number, with only the first three matching up.

No name for the big player just yet, which figured. I couldn't see a budding criminal entrepreneur pressing metal and buffing bonnets, so when the number matched up to the group chat member 'ST', it all made more sense.

Quiet, infrequent in the chat, and submissive to 'S' and 'J', it figured Simon Trench was a lower player in this new ring of dogfighting debutantes. In business with the soft-brained Markwell, or out of business it would seem, 'ST' was clearly on the lower rungs of the ladder with this social group. Still though, a step in the right direction, another name to the list with another potential lead to follow up. This time I wouldn't be as forceful as I was with Davey. Nothing like creating a dead end to create a dead end I thought. No, a softer and less confrontational approach was in order once I tracked down this Trench character.

I shut the notebook, replacing it over on the shelf in the living room. After a second read of the letter to make sure nothing had been missed, I unlatched the log burner and tossed the crumpled paper along with the envelope onto the embers, stoking them up long enough to catch the paper and watch it set alight.

I figured I might as well sleep on the name, save starting over with a new set of research tonight and a fresh whisky. I didn't need my head swimming any more than it already was. No, today had been productive enough without adding any more fuel for my upcoming lack of sleep beside a contented Anna.

I flicked the lights off downstairs and quietly crept up the stairs and into a comfy bed. A job for another day I thought.

This thing was picking up pace now.

Chapter Twenty-One

'Ma'am?'

The door left ajar to DI Rose's office sounded with a knock, shortly followed by the figure of Andy Jordan.

'Yes, yes, come in.' she motioned. 'Sorry I was headed out and forgot something, don't think it's an open-door policy around here now.'

'Sorry to barge in ma'am, thought I'd catch you before the end of the day that's all.'

Alice motioned him in but didn't offer a seat, instead leaning back on her desk facing him, making clear enough this wasn't going to be a long visit. She had made plans for the evening, plans which didn't involve sitting around in the office listening to young detective constables drone on, so she folded her arms and tilted her head with an inquisitive, demanding slant.

'Sorry ma'am, be as quick as I can.'

He held up an A4 binder in between them.

'You told me to follow up on the timeline for the WhatsApp group yeah? Well, your hunch was right to follow it it seems. Lab downloaded all the actions on the phone for the past few days, tracing the deletion to around the time, or if not after, Markwell was deceased. He's either deleted it himself, or his attacker has done it for him.'

'Interesting. Any more?'

'Oh, not the interesting part ma'am. Not only was it deleted, but the whole thing was sent to another number: files, photos, audio, the whole lot. Now, the clever part is, the exact same phone number is entered into the group chat by Davey shortly before deletion. Some flimsy excuse about changing the phone number from him. Now, given he was most likely being tortured and murdered at the time, it seems daft he would simultaneously be swapping his phone number in the group whilst downloading the previous content, doesn't it? No, I'm guessing, and hopefully not too much of a stretch, whoever's killed him has stolen the data for themselves and planted a number in the group to receive any ongoing text and data.'

'The new phone, it wasn't found at the scene?'

'Nothing so far. Figured it disappeared along with the attacker. They haven't banked on us retrieving data from Markwell's phone either. Surely though ma'am, people in the group are going to question why a new phone pinged into the group at the time of his death though aren't they? Clearly they wouldn't know it was all downloaded — but a new convenient number pops up the same time their friend is dispatched? Can't imagine the group chat kept going much longer.'

'No, doesn't take a genius to work it out. You'd be a complete novice not to see it coming. Although it is a shame we can't see the on-going group discussion, don't suppose the wonder kids at the lab can do it for us can they?'

'No, I asked. Fully encrypted. Not even they can do it. Needs to be a direct add from the group itself. They could reactivate Markwell's number but it still wouldn't automatically find itself in the group again having been withdrawn the first time around. So we're frozen out — the only people seeing the group are the members, and obviously whoever's infiltrated into it so clumsily.'

Alice was still stood resting against the desk, arms pensively folded.

'I guess what we do know, is whatever information they downloaded to their own phone, is the same as what we see here. Whatever they're sifting through now, we can do the same. If we draw the same conclusions, we can guess their next move before they do it.'

Andy nodded. Although he was a DC he had been thinking the exact same thing. The attackers next move was probably sitting there in the downloaded information, staring right at them. Find it and you find them — DI Rose was worryingly good at reading his mind sometimes he thought.

'If you're short of overtime and haven't got a life this weekend I'll sign you off for it. Find me a decent lead by Monday morning and I'll make sure your appraisal next month mentions it.'

Andy nodded, hand on the door, turning as Alice spoke again.

'I'll put those numbers in for GPS tracing and identification before I go, see if we can't have enough for a fresh go with it after the weekend.'

'You're on ma'am. I'll see you for team debrief Monday morning nice and early. Get the gold star ready.'

He attempted a wink, but it came out as more of an awkward spasm. Luckily Alice had been looking down at her desk at the time so hadn't seen it by the time she looked up.

'Don't stay up too late DC Jordan. Monday morning, bright and early it is, you're first on the PowerPoint.'

'Yes ma'am'.

She let him close the door behind himself and picked up the phone to the lab. It was easy enough to order GPS tracking, standard practice for most cases involving any form of tech device these days, but this time she wanted to be sure of one thing.

'Hi, DI Rose up on four. You got the data files unlocked for DC Jordan?' She went on, listing the numbers she was interested in for tracking, 'And can I check the recipient list for this one,' going through the long list of details, 'Good, that's great, so to be clear, these are locked in for my eyes only, yes? Wonderful. You be sure to keep it this way as well, I hear a word of this list being anything but encrypted, or leaked into the department I'll be sure to knock on your door, okay? There's a lad.'

She rang off. It didn't suit her to make threats, but the way her evidence had slipped away with Ronnie Macfarlane, the next move had to be watertight.

She turned.

The board next to her loomed tall, taking up half of the wall. In the centre, the face of Davey Markwell looked out — thin, corrupted by lifestyle, shaped by his own poor choices. Who had wanted him dead? Who had hunted him down so ruthlessly, punctured and battered him, bled him dry in his own home? Who wanted him that badly; wanted his friends so desperately they'd risk being so naïve?

Alice was at a loss. Davey's face could only stare back at her, unable to speak out.

The next move in this game was coming and she could feel it. The only problem was, could they catch up in time to stop it?

Chapter Twenty-Two

I was getting ahead of them now. I was sure of it.

Simon Trench was simple enough to find on Facebook. An open profile and shared friendship with Davey was an easy thirty seconds work on a fake social media profile, his gleaming face staring back at me surrounded by a patriotic filter.

He was cut from the same cloth as Davey.

Moronic shares and public statements littered his page, alongside check ins with the boys down the pub and shout outs to the kids he seemingly saw every other weekend. The car body shop featured heavily until about five months previously, quickly replaced by an equipment sell off and big promises to prove everyone wrong and come back stronger than ever. The comments and likes were low on the ground, something told me he had had this coming and it shouldn't have been a big surprise for him.

Some people were like that I guess. Flush their life down the toilet and find anyone but themselves to blame for the situation they found themselves in.

Pictures were in abundance however, giving a nice clear-cut image of the man I'd be looking for. It didn't take long to work out his regular watering hole either. Check-ins, pictures on the terrace, his new romance with one of the older looking barmaids on the payroll: it all stacked together to make me think it wouldn't be difficult to track him down in real life.

So, it was a few nights later, and I decided to plan a 'drop in' when Anna was finishing her last night of on-call. I'd sometimes head for a beer after work on Fridays anyway, grab a couple of colleagues and sink a few if the week had been a tough one — so it wasn't unusual to suggest a trip for a few drinks, albeit this time into one of the less salubrious bars on the high street.

The promise of buying the first round had eventually sealed the deal, and it wasn't long before we were sat around a corner table. A solid view of the bar ahead of us.

Soon enough, and without too much of a wait, he showed up, taking a seat at the slot machine next to the bar with a pint in hand, feeding in spare change and dabbing at the flashing plastic buttons in front of him. He wasn't chatting much to the staff, something told me that particular relationship might have temporarily gone sour from his body language, emphasised more and more by the constant looks around and over to the optics behind her.

Maybe I was being a bit harsh.

Perhaps it was sitting in a rough patch, soon to be on the mend after a few glasses of Dutch courage. Perhaps he wasn't the big failure I had him pegged for in life. She didn't look convinced as she stared back at him between customers.

As the drinks went on and a second pint drained downwards, his attention went from the bar and slot machine, and more to his phone, scrolling through apps, before what looked like the pale earthy tones of a WhatsApp group chat dominated. Too far away, I excused myself and walked behind and over to the gents on the far side of the bar. WhatsApp, and the familiar group name sat at the top of his message list as I glanced over his shoulder.

I headed into a cubicle, and not one to miss an opportunity, took out the burner phone, heading to the only group chat on the phone. BloodSport.

Sure enough, 'ST' was active and chatting along with a few other members.

The subject was the arrival of new 'livestock': read that as either bait dogs or potential fighting pedigree for their stable. Normally Davey's responsibility, it had passed down to Simon to do intake and upkeep since Mr Markwell's untimely demise, and he was being urged to get over to the animals, to do an inspection and feed them all. After a lot of to and fro he eventually gave in, spoiling his attempt to make up with the barmaid, agreeing to be there within the hour.

Shit. I hastily turned off the phone and headed back out to the bar. A quick glance to my left confirmed Simon was still at the fruit machine, but as the dregs of the pint were drained, he stood up, his jacket quickly following from the stool.

I turned back to the table and held up my phone in my hand, the other apologetically open.

'Sorry guys I'm gonna have to make, Anna's headed back from work, sounded important. I'll stick a twenty behind the bar though, next round's on me alright? Catch you all Monday morning bright and breezy.'

Mutters of disapproval were soon replaced by the realisation a free round was on the way, and after a few goodbyes and promises not to stay out too late, I too had my jacket on, turning towards the exit.

I gave it ten seconds and headed out the side, standing in the doorway pretending to check my pockets. I looked about and discovered Simon heading to the small car park behind the pub. I had parked up off a side alley, so I got into the driver's seat, waiting for him to pull out in front of me.

About thirty seconds later a black Vauxhall Vectra, Trench at the wheel, edged out into the street and turned right towards the main road. Waiting for him to accelerate, I turned the ignition and pulled out, nosing into the junction far enough to see him drive away. He turned left in the distance as I let a car go past.

I followed from a few cars behind, through the main part of town and its empty market square, and we were both soon headed inland away from the coast, onto one of the bigger B roads and the dual carriageway linking the town southbound to Newcastle.

Shortly before the main turn off, a small country lane opened up and headed into darker unlit woodland, a large hedgerow shielding the glare of Simon's headlights as they swung at a right angle and into the distance along the new route. I slowed right down and held back, giving the car a few seconds to accelerate away and reach a bend in the lane, before I pulled in from behind the tall fence line. It was easy enough to follow on, the flashes of light against green leaves and tree trunks showed me Simon was still ahead, and still not changing direction. After a minute or so his speed had slowed, and without indicating he turned right onto an even smaller access road — headlights bumping up and down, as the front wheels dodged and dipped through the potholes on a rutted track.

I eased to a halt, shy of the entrance, and turned the engine off, the interior lights dimming as I turned the key anti-clockwise. No other cars were approaching so, tucked into the hedgerow, I got out and walked to a gap, watching as Simon made his way up to the darkened farm buildings, coming to a stop outside one of the smaller outhouses.

The farm sat in a small, flattened gully below the rest of the surrounding fields, protected from the wind as the landscape gently hugged around it. It gave me a decent enough overview from above, and I could just about see Simon lift a latch on a metal shed and disappear, pulling the door closed from the inside.

A square strip of light flickered into view around its frame, and over the fields came the accompanying sound of dogs barking: some deeper booming growls as well as lighter, piercing yaps. A big metallic clang and shouting came back, no doubt as a metal bar was whacked against their cages. The barking stopped immediately, the fields falling back to the hustle of crops gently swaying, with only the occasional chirp of a bird settling for the night after the sudden intrusion on to their farm.

Nothing happened for twenty minutes or so, and as I stood quietly, hands dug deeply down against the cold, I listened to the sounds of the night air around me. It was peaceful, as calm as the dusky yellow light spilling up from the city some ten miles or so to the south.

Ahead of me over the field the door soon unlatched and swung open, and as the artificial light flicked off a shadowy figure emerged and set it shut; still the hunched silhouette of Simon. I couldn't see anything like a padlock being fitted, no keys replaced in pockets, no alarms being activated, so it was safe to assume it was open access.

I had considered creeping up and confronting him, but the downsides significantly outweighed the benefits. The only gains would be the personal satisfaction of dealing with Mr Trench, as well as potentially freeing a few dogs. Much better however to gain more information and steer this thing back in the right direction. Towards the law.

He also had kids I thought. They didn't deserve a life without him, no matter how dark his hobbies were or how infrequently they might see him. Simon hadn't been on my radar for long enough to cause me any offence — all that could change however when I looked inside the shed.

He moved back over to the Vectra, my cue to move on.

As the door closed behind him I quickly came back from the hedge and started up my own car, making sure only the side lights were on as I moved further along a shallow curve in the lane. I was banking on him going back the way he came, but for good measure I tucked the car in and got into the back seat, ready to duck down if he carried on up the road and past me.

I soon saw the car's lights bouncing down the rutted track, briefly slowing to a halt at the junction before moving away in the opposite direction.

I got out and listened to the engine noise, constant and reducing as it moved away. Standing watch for the next ten minutes, in case he returned, I looked around at my surroundings. The evening birdsong had settled down again as the sun faded further back under the skyline, leaving only the brushing noise of crops as they swayed against each other in the field next to me. My eyes had settled and adjusted to the dark light, and with no sign of Simon returning I locked the car and walked back down the lane to the farm track's entrance.

It didn't take me long to reach the buildings, and I stopped and listened for noise or signs of life from the abandoned farmhouse. The black uncurtained windows however, covered in dust and framed by decaying wooden windowsills, confirmed I was the only one in the vicinity.

I moved to the smaller shed.

Snuffling and rustling sounds came from inside, but they soon halted as I lifted the latch upwards and pushed inside. The door creaked as it slowly swung open, and a tide of wet fur smells and old dog food came out with the air from within, accompanying the familiar fousty farm smell: hay with engine grease. I closed the door behind me, taking out the torch from my pocket, I flicked the stark LED light into the darkness.

Five pairs of yellow eyes looked back at me from various pens and cages.

One large dog stared back at me under a furrowed, agitated brow, whereas the rest were all open, bewildered, and set into timid faces; their ears backwards and heads hung low. At the end of the row however was one of life's idiots: a wagging tail and grinning from ear to ear, furiously padding at the ground in front of him.

I could tell this daft dog hadn't grasped his surroundings yet; clearly delighted to have a friend visiting his new digs. Food all over his face, and water tipped over in front of him, the hapless hound was probably a friendly family pet recently pinched off a local street or field, no doubt the subject of frantic social media pleas for his return.

The rest of the mutley crew, despite their scared and unsettled demeanours, were still in good shape. I looked around: the remainder of the shed was basic. A small kitchen unit and sink to one side, a mop and bucket to the other, as well as old, folded grain and feed bags from the previous farm work tucked behind the door. I looked up in the rafters of the shed, the ghostly fading glow of the strip light about ten foot above looking back at me. As I checked the corners, the eyes all still followed me around the room; mostly in fear, but a small shred of hope still shone through in their expressions.

There was no way I could get them out by myself. I didn't have the transport and I didn't have the hands required to separate them all if I removed them from the building. Taking them one by one, or even the smaller ones would no doubt raise more questions than I had answers for; for a start Anna would be perplexed coming home from on-call to find another scruffy little stray in the side extension, let alone five or six. I couldn't drop them at work either. I'd have to explain away to the other staff members how I had found them, a subject which would only open a whole new Pandora's box of problems for me.

It was with a heavy heart then I clicked off the torch, carefully creaking the door back open and out into the yard.

Latching the door as well as I could remember — surely Simon wouldn't be so mindful to know it's exact position — I started back off down the farm track and away from the outbuildings, the desperate sounds of scuffling and yelping starting up behind me as I walked.

It wasn't long, after a short drive along the dark back roads of the county, that I was pulling into the driveway at home. Lights were still off and I knew I had made it back before Anna, giving me the chance for a hasty tidy up in time for her late arrival. She breezed in about an hour after me, and as we opened a bottle of wine — toasting the end of the week — I put thoughts of the farm to the back of my mind.

After breakfast the next day, at the local café in the village where the crowds were light and the coffee was strong, I headed to the shops with a list for the weekend as Anna walked back ahead of me to get a head start on some chores. We'd tossed up whether to head and do a Parkrun, but late nights and stuffy heads from our nightcaps had sent us in the direction of comfort food instead. It was promising to be a typical lazy weekend — ideal after the week we had both had, and no plans meant no stress for the two of us; dog walks with Tank, nice meals, and more white wine if I could find it in the grocer on the corner of the main street.

One job I hadn't told Anna about was the short errand before shopping, and I slipped out the burner phone from my inside pocket and turned it on. God forbid if she ever looked in my jacket. We didn't have a suspicious relationship by any means. We'd been around long enough to know jealousy wasn't worth the hassle, but a second phone would leave me with some awkward explaining to do.

I dialled in the number for the council's emergency line. I'd figured it quicker going straight to the source, less likely to be fobbed off and less likely to get tracked down later by a council employee as opposed to a police officer. I asked for the animal welfare team, hoping they had a call handler and wouldn't end up speaking to the team direct, and so it was relief when an unfamiliar voice picked up the call in the office.

Masking my accent — never a strong point of mine — I gave a fake name and number.

'And how can I help you today? This line is reserved for emergencies Sir.'

'Ah yes, I know, I'm sorry, you see what it is is, I was out walking my dog up round the dual carriageway and I happened across this farm. Normally walk past it every other week or so but the damn dog couldn't help but drag me there. When I got close you see all I could hear was this barking from one of the outbuildings, right distressed they all sounded, must have five or six of them in there from the sound of it. I wouldn't normally call and bother you lot on a weekend, but the bugger of it is the whole place looks abandoned, couldn't see a living soul there, no sign of life. I love my dogs you see, well, all animals really, I'd hate to think the wee blighters had been left in there all night, no food or nothing.'

Carrying on, as gruff and local as I could manage, I left the location and a description of the farm.

'I hope I haven't got anyone in any trouble love, but you can see why I called hopefully.'

'Yes, no, thanks for calling. I'll pass it on to the duty warden this morning, see if I can't get it chased up as soon as possible for you. Poor little things, I expect they're okay and it's all a misunderstanding. A wee fuss over nothing. Do you want me to call and give you an update on Monday, when I get the chance?'

'No, you're okay, long as I know it's in hand that's all I need. Good luck to you love, have a lovely weekend you hear.'

I rang off and shut down the phone. I think it should do the trick. If you know what strings to pull with certain people you can get your way in life when you need to. There are also few jobsworths on the Animal Welfare team, and so I figured I had a pretty good chance of getting the dogs out, and into care, so long as Simon or the rest of the team hadn't had them moved on by this afternoon.

With any luck they would back it up with a Police visit and shut it all down before I had to take any more risks.

I ducked into the grocery and grabbed the essentials, along with the lonely bottle of Pinot Gris which sat last on the shelf. Kudos from Anna would ensue, it was a favourite, albeit a dangerous piece of knowledge to know it was now stocked so close to the house.

Kicking myself as usual for forgetting a bag I stuffed everything into bulging pockets, and along with a scratch card I headed out, back down the road for the short walk back to the house, dawdling in the idle hope Anna would have started the vacuuming before I got home.

The feeling of calm was starting to return to life. Hopefully this was my ticket out of this thing.

Hopefully, it meant I could walk away.

Chapter Twenty-Three

Skye's list for Saturday morning was slowly growing. On call weekends for the welfare team could be simple and straightforward, but equally you could find yourself crawling into bed at midnight with a head full of stress and a string of unanswered questions. It was shaping up for the latter as head office called and she picked up the notepad from the dashboard again, taking down details of what could easily be a prank call, but could also be a group of dogs in distress. Experience said not to ignore it, and she jotted down the words as the secretary read them out.

It was not so much an address, but a general description of the area: apparently the call in from the member of the public had been a bit vague and delivered in quite a bizarre accent, but Skye had a fair idea of where she was heading and put the call to the top of her list. The barking neighbour's dog and the stray cat with a limp would have to wait until later.

It was a short enough trip out of town. Tucked away along a small side road which departed the main route from the dual carriageway, it was an abandoned small holding nestled in amongst hedgerows and rolling fields, fairly non-descript. She was sure she'd driven past the place before and had a rough idea of the layout, so it wasn't long before the van was bumping along a rutted farm track, pulling up outside what appeared to be an old homestead with its own accompanying rusted and dilapidated outbuildings. Why this place hadn't been snapped up for a barn conversion was beyond her; a perfect quiet location nestling into a hillside, with its forested border and easy access to Newcastle to the south. Who knew Skye thought, who knew.

Jumping out of the van, the height of the step defeating a graceful exit, she clicked the key fob and headed quietly over to the outbuildings, listening intently for the reported yelps which were heard earlier.

Sure enough, the smallest of three sheds emitted a constant rustling, as well as quiet, muffled barks. She looked around, a rusty latch with no padlock was all that stopped access, and it squeaked open as Skye pulled the door outwards and peered inside into the gloomy interior, illuminated by the thin shafts of sunlight piercing through dusty air and onto the rough floor below.

As her eyes grew accustomed to the light inside, the dog noises were soon accompanied by the moving silhouettes of small four-legged figures in cages, mostly stood still and staring back at Skye, heads lowered and tails between their legs. All apart from the end kennel, where unbridled joy stared back at her, bouncing on the spot as she approached.

'Hello then lovelies, what are you all doing in here by yourselves eh?'

She looked around. Feedbags and blankets were set aside against the far wall, and hanging up from hooks were basic collars and chain leads. Not exactly luxury boarding kennels.

'I'll go make a call and be back okay.'

Aware of how alone she was and still shaken up by her last encounter by herself in the countryside, she walked out into the crisp cold air which blew around the farmyard.

The breeze itself was fresh enough, but soon the stench of rotten flesh had whipped up around her, and, following it round the side of the small building, she soon discovered a black bin bag, its end rippling in the wind. Nudging it open with the end of her boot, a small, stiff paw stuck out, rigid and extended, and she peeled open the bag to reveal a lifeless canine corpse, wounds around the chest and legs, the life drained from its eyes. Young, still in good body condition, it wasn't hard to make the link back to dog fighting again as she stood over it, staring down despairingly.

She took out her phone and opened the contacts. Steve would be at home or out on the golf course — one of the two — but something about his recent lack of interest and empathy told her not to ring him. Instead, she scrolled down to her contact from the police a few weeks ago: the first officer who had come out and taken a statement regarding the small terrier.

It went straight to voicemail, but a minute or so later, as she sat in the van making notes, her phone rang and the same officer was on the other end of the line.

'Hi is that Skye?'

'Speaking.'

'I got your voicemail; you've got another dog?'

'Yeah, sorry to bother you, it's all torn up like the others, only this time it's been dumped next to a load of live dogs, bit of a coincidence I'd say, thought I'd see if it would tie in with the others. The boss Steve has been following it up but I couldn't seem to get hold of him.' she lied. 'Figured I'd speak to the other side of the investigation straight away if I could, you're still in charge, aren't you?'

'In a manner of speaking. Our boss took charge of the last one after my initial enquiries, it was tying into some bigger case he was working on, don't ask me what, all I know was to defer to him if anything else came up. You want to give me some details?'

She filled the officer in, from the initial phone call to head office through to the putrid discovery in the bin-bag. She had the window down to the van, and the sound of barking and whining was getting louder as she spoke, the dogs obviously growing in confidence after their contact.

'And that about sums it up. What are you thinking?'

'It certainly sounds suspicious alright, and you're not wrong about a possible connection. I'll have to ring it in to the DI, but I can get moving with the dog team about recovering the live animals, should be able to house them in kennels until we know what to do with them. You'd be surprised what constitutes evidence these days Skye. You ok to sit tight and

I'll get a van along? Shouldn't be too long, I doubt dog units will be too stretched at this time on a Saturday without a match on.'

They finished up the conversation and Skye poured a fresh brew from the thermos, pushing back in the driver's seat. She had enough paperwork to be getting on with, so thirty minutes or so wouldn't hurt the schedule, but it was frustrating not to go back into the shed for fear of disrupting evidence, whilst the dogs all sat barking just metres away. Against all instincts, she wound up the window and turned on the radio to drown out the anxious barks and yelps.

Not long till the police turned up, not long.

Chapter Twenty-Four

The office was dark to walk into, the North East weather clearly not reading the memo, and Alice clicked the light. A stark, clinical glare filled the room. Any lingering thoughts of her pleasant weekend quickly disappeared as she sat down.

Visiting with family, Sunday lunch in Tynemouth, she had resisted the temptation to message Andy for a progress report, saving it instead for their case conference at 9am. Her own input, the phone tracking, was ready to read.

She found the files attached to internal emails. One for each number submitted, ten in total. The requested information was broken down into separate headers: registered owner and device origin, their ingoing and outgoing calls and messages, and finally, GPS locations set on a map, each with their own timelines attached.

Unsurprisingly, yet still equally frustrating, none of the phones had a registered owner except for Markwell, and the new and unfamiliar name of 'Simon Trench'.

The remainder were all from the same origin: same sequential IMEI numbers, all burner phones bought in batch. Itself a reliable enough indicator of organised criminality if ever there were one. It went to figure then that Markwell, and whoever this Trench was, were either daft enough to use their own phones or, low enough down on the list not to warrant shiny, new for-purpose burners.

The last number on the list, the 'infiltrator', was also an unregistered pre-paid device.

In contrast to the others however it did not make calls or receive them, did not send messages, and when looking at its GPS data, was turned on only for short periods and never in the same place twice, scattered throughout the region in remote locations. Clever phone, clever owner. It didn't even ping up on any public Wi-Fi, suggesting it was exclusively turned off and not emitting any signal.

Compared to the remainder of the phones with their own hotspots and patterns of use, it would appear like a ghost, periodically checking in before ducking its head back down below the visible waterline of data production and digital forensics. Its last activity was two days ago in a small village to the north of Newcastle, over the border into Northumberland.

Alice gazed quickly through the rest of the interim reports, mentally subdividing the jobs they would generate for the various team members at this morning's meeting, before heading through to the conference room a few minutes before nine o'clock.

The rest of the team were already sat around the table by the time she arrived, except for Andy who was stood beside his laptop at the head of them, next to the projector. His body language, energetic and caffeinated, suggested this would be an enlightening presentation, and so she made her way to the opposite end, raising a hand to indicate he could start.

'Good morning ma'am. Everyone. Thanks all for coming, hope everyone had a good weekend.'

He turned and faced the screen, clicker in hand, and scrolled through screenshots from the phone of Davey Markwell, explaining why the focus of the investigation was currently centred around the organisation referred to as 'BloodSport'.

'The main factor,' he went on to explain, 'is the appearance of this infiltrator number, which I've called Phone X for obvious reasons. DI Rose will take us through any intel on the numbers in the group in a short while, but here's my work from the weekend — it centres around the identification of locations and members, and to see if there are any clues as to Mr Markwell's attacker, or indeed any future direction of the gang.'

Andy continued to click through group chat screenshots until arriving on a Google map view.

'This here is a rare example of a slip up from them. Everything's tight lipped, pretty locked down in terms of any viable intelligence gathering, but reference to this location as a meet up point pings up a while back. Nothing much else comes up; if this is more of a social thread, then the main organisational details are occurring elsewhere, perhaps with fewer more select members, with other more encrypted devices. Just my initial thinking.'

Around the room pens quietly jotted down details into notebooks.

'Any idea who the main guys are then Andy?'

'Nothing concrete but this 'S' and 'J' lead it, like I say makes me think they have their own communications between themselves. 'RM' gets a few references in being the muscle, an enforcer of some kind, but the rest seem a bit submissive. Markwell himself isn't playing a huge role, gives out something of a backroom vibe. Gets into trouble a while back for dumping some poor dog which gets picked up by the local council, gets him some grief but nothing directly threatening from the members it would seem.'

'Owner of the dog?' DI Rose interjected.

'Probably some old dear … I can follow it up though? A disgruntled owner? Seems extreme for a murder motive though don't you think?'

'Stranger things have happened DC Jordan, trust me. Follow it up.'

'Yes boss.'

'Any other decent leads from it so far?'

'Not particularly ma'am. Like I say potentially more of a social, less select group. It does seem they were definitely into the organisation of dog fighting though. And, for whatever reason our attacker has specifically sought out and tracked down this aspect, given this was the sole focus of the infiltration. Chances are he or she could act on the same information from the group that we have; presumably except for phone tracking of course.'

'Okay, well before I get into it I want the Google map location checked out today, as well who owns or operates from it. DS Riley that's you, okay? I also want the dumped dog followed up as well. I want the names, addresses and alibis by the end of the day, okay?'

'Yes ma'am.'

'Okay. Turning from promising work by DC Jordan, unfortunately the phone tracking hasn't given us too much intelligence so far, only a few small nuggets to go on. The members seem fairly tech savvy from what I can tell — pre-paid unregistered burner phones bought in batch. Our only registered names are Davey Markwell, and one 'Simon Trench', or this 'ST' in the chat. He's not got a record but I want him picked up today and brought in for questioning as an associate of Markwell, see what he knows about the victim: motives, enemies, people he may have owed money to. I want a full shakedown. If he's stupid enough to not use an unregistered phone, hopefully he'll be simple enough to crack under questioning for us.'

Alice looked up at the table, all eyes were still on her.

'Anyone else got anything for us?'

The answer was no, so jobs dispensed, the team filed out of the conference room one by one, Gavin Riley leading the way. She felt a resurgence of energy given the leads opening in front of her. Not exactly a clear-cut motive, but at least it felt like the case was heading in the right direction after a stuttering start.

Simon Trench, she hoped, would begin to unravel this deadly puzzle.

Chapter Twenty-Five

Simon Trench, scratching at a week-old beard, stared down at his shoes in interview room three. Dry skin flaked down onto his collar as he worked the stubble on each side, and he clumsily brushed it onto the floor below. By contrast, his solicitor, tailored and fresh, was sat next to him, thumbing through a yellow legal pad, ready to make notes and prepare rebuttal questions should the need arise.

Simon had been advised he wasn't under arrest, but it would be 'appreciated' if he could help the police with their enquiries, and they sat and quietly waited for someone to enter the room. A single, empty paper coffee cup sat in front of him, and looking anxiously down at his watch, he wished he'd gone to the bathroom before agreeing to sit down. He'd been watching re-runs on television when he'd had the knock on the door, and as the seconds clicked past, he was beginning to think he shouldn't have answered.

'Good afternoon, Mr Trench.'

He looked up to see a smartly dressed woman, mid-thirties, followed in by a younger but soft around the edges colleague in a charcoal grey suit.

'If you don't mind we'll get started, things to do and all that. My name is Detective Inspector Alice Rose, and this is my colleague Detective Constable Andy Jordan. You're not under arrest so are free to leave at any time, but as was explained by the uniformed officers any help you can provide will be of great help. I'm sure your solicitor Mr Jackson explained this to you as well. Any questions?'

'Well yeah, what's all this about then?'

'We'll come to that. First, can I confirm you are indeed Simon Trench of 114 Whitbury Avenue?'

'Yeah yeah, I explained all that. Where your boys picked me up from, bit of a coincidence if it weren't me ain't it?'

Simon sneered and looked sideways at his solicitor. The humour was not reciprocated. Trevor Jackson had sat in enough interviews to know it didn't play well to be a smart arse, and especially not with Alice Rose, a woman he had seen tear grown men to shreds many a time before.

'Nice and short answers Simon today, keep it simple.'

He huffed and folded his arms, replying robotically.

'Yes, I am Simon Trench. Any other questions officer?'

'Yes, you're here after your name came up in relation to a one David Markwell, I believe you know him?'

'Know of him that's all like, can'nt say I had much to do with him, see him about town, in the pub, shit like that. Haven't seen him in a while, he doing alright, what's he up to these days. Getting into trouble is he, getting me into trouble like?'

'He's dead Mr Trench. Murdered. You're not aware?'

'Is he really? Well, reet shame isn't it. Family must be gutted like.'

Alice flicked an edge of the thin card file in front of her.

'Yes, I suspect they most probably are. In your knowledge of him 'around town', would you say you knew of any enemies he might have had, anyone he had disagreed with or fallen out with, business dealings gone south for instance?'

'Like I say Inspector, divvin' have much doing with the guy like, wouldn't know what crowd he's in or out with, can'nt help you really.'

'No idea at all?' Andy Jordan lifted his notes, drawing Simon's gaze to the left of the table where he sat.

'No 'Constable', can'nt say I do.'

Alice opened the file in front of her and picked up the first two sheets of A4 from the top. Trevor quietly sighed. He knew what was coming, establish a lie in the first few minutes then throw the suspect off course, putty in your hands for the remainder of the interview.

'Would you care to explain QuickWorks Bodyshop to us Mr Trench?' Alice rotated and pushed across a printout from Companies house, naming both Simon Trench and David Markwell.

Simon looked down, and the look on his face sank with it.

'Funny how you only 'know of' Mr Markwell and yet here you are on paper together, filing tax returns and claiming dividends from a body shop business right here in town. Seems odd you claim you didn't know he was dead. I'd imagine in fact it might be a good way of avoiding some of these debts the pair of you also seem to have?'

Simon shifted in his chair and picked up the empty coffee cup, the hollow charade buying him a few more seconds.

'Look alright, I kna the guy, doesn't mean a like him, follow him round town every day of the week does it. Pure business like.'

Alice lent forward, lowering her tone of voice.

'So why are you pretending to have nothing to do with a murder victim, is there something else to hide? Something you don't want us sniffing around in? Where were you in the days before we discovered his body?'

'Let's not get ahead of ourselves officers.' Trevor interjected. 'Can I remind us all this interview is not under caution, and my client is not under any obligation to come up with answers to your questions at the present moment.'

Alice sat back and opened her palms to Simon across the table.

'Surely you have some concerns though Mr Trench, your associate murdered whilst both of you share debts. What else were the two of you sharing and not telling us about? Wouldn't it be better to let us help, let us find out who killed your friend?'

'Told you he weren't my friend alright man. I'm done here,' turning to his side, 'nowts keeping me from heading is there?' Trevor raised his eyebrows and shook his head.

'It doesn't look good to not be helping us with our enquiries Simon.' Alice closed her file. 'Better to be on our side and not the side of suspicion wouldn't you say? Who knows what we might uncover by the time this is all through.'

Out of the corner of her eye she spied Andy thumbing the corners of his own case file, flicking through and lifting the page on the WhatsApp transcripts. She gently laid a hand on the stack of papers, closing it with a gentle pat.

'It's ok DC Jordan I think that's probably enough for one day, I'm sure if we think of anything else Mr Trench will be more than happy to help now we've cleared up his initial confusion.'

'Ma'am?'

But Alice didn't have to answer, and the solicitor didn't need any more cues to get his client out of the room; he stood up and almost dragged Simon by the collar over to the interview room door. Trevor Jackson knew interviews like this were best kept as short as possible, informal or not.

'One last one Mr Trench if I may, I have here yourself and Davey are quite the animal lovers, dogs in particular, you talk about them in the workshop much?'

Simon froze...

'Only I sent a couple of officers down there earlier today. Deserted of course, but you know that. Place cleared out long ago. Couldn't help but notice some interesting floor arrangements in there. Dog leads and the like. Seems odd for a body shop. Keep pets, do we?'

Simon began to form a sentence, about to mouth a reply, before being pushed out by his solicitor, whispering adamantly in his ear as they both exited the interview room.

They closed their files as the door shut, and Alice took a sip of water, smiling as she put it back down.

'I don't understand Ma'am, we have him in the group chat mouthing off, clearly friends with Markwell, could have nailed him right there and then.'

'Nailed him for what exactly? Being in a dodgy group chat? Being better friends than we thought with a murder victim? No, let him loose, let him run back to his friends panicking. If he's as stupid as I think, next time we pick him up we can take his phone in evidence and retrieve a whole lot more data once he's done flapping after today.'

She lifted the corner of her file to make a note in one of the margins. Something she would forget to do later if she didn't.

'Don't get me wrong, I agree it would have been satisfying to watch him squirm, but we'd have lost half the case once they started shutting all the burner phones down. Better to leave it all out there, ticking away, leaving their electronic breadcrumbs for us to follow right to the source. And don't forget if we spook the group chat, we also spook your Phone X while we're at it.'

'Yes ma'am suppose you're right. Why mention the dogs though?'

'We want him panicking in the right direction Andy. Come on, have I taught you nothing in the last few years?'

'Sorry ma'am.'

'Right, well if that's everything go and be thick somewhere else okay. Can you go and follow up the dead dog like I asked you, see if it starts to get us anywhere.' She smiled, hopefully he knew she was joking about the thick part. Nothing disappointed her more than a soft snowflake in her team.

'And once you're done let's meet back here tomorrow when I've followed up the other things, okay?'

He nodded, the door clicking shut as he left, leaving her only the interview machine and case files for company. She reached across and pulled out the USB stick, pausing as a distant feeling washed over her.

Warm plastic heat, beautifully acrid, fanned out by the whirr of a tape recorder winding on another of the room's tired, ground out confessions. She sat back and pocketed the drive.

Analogue memories, playing in a digital age.

She shook it off and stood up.

Time for a coffee.

Chapter Twenty-Six

'Sorry detective, I'm confused, didn't you already receive it?'

The look on Andy's face had clearly suggested otherwise.

He stopped on the staircase, hand on the metal rail thinking back to the conversation that morning. The outer coating felt sticky against his palm as he looked up to the next flight, the knot in his stomach not getting any lighter as he made his way up to DI Rose's office, his sweat only adding to the layers on the already claggy black rubber. Perhaps its tacky texture was all down to timid DCs, nervously climbing through the building on the way to deal bad news to their superiors.

Last night's dinner with his girlfriend seemed like a different decade now, the steak and prosecco sitting heavy as he pushed through the door into the fourth floor main. He still hadn't got his facts straight as he weaved through the desks to the corner.

Out of office from 8am, his third stop on the road had been a corner shop, the street along from the Davey Markwell's house, tying up initial enquiries from the day of his discovery.

It was a long shot, but there was still a question mark if CCTV covered the route of the murderer, and the initial officer had made the sloppy mistake of not collecting the footage himself, relying instead on the shop owner to submit it in their own time. A mistake Andy had fallen for in his own uniform days.

The business was your regular sell-it-all shop. Heart of the community to those in the neighbouring avenues, it stocked everything from milk and bread through to SIM cards and lottery tickets.

Behind the counter had been a friendly enough sort, and he had asked questions about the first police visit as well as a few follow-ups on what he knew about the victim. When the subject turned to the CCTV coverage however, the cashier, who also turned out to be the shop owner, had taken on a puzzled look and scratched his ear.

'Yeah, it was a couple of days afterwards, one of your lot in uniform came back in for it, took the whole lot from the evening before through to the morning after, explained he was taking it down the station for analysis. Would have the storage drive back to me as soon as they'd finished and got what they need.'

Andy's mood was beginning to sink.

'I don't suppose you got the officers name did you, or the paperwork in return for collecting by any chance?'

'No nothing like that sorry pal, should I have? Sorry, all seemed kosher and above board with it being a uniform and all.'

'No no, you're fine. Probably a rookie who forgot the protocol. I'll clear it all up when I get back and let you know about the receipt for the drive. It'll be sitting in the evidence room waiting to be catalogued I imagine. Happens all the time believe me.'

Only it doesn't, and the sinking feeling was confirmed later that morning when he got back and headed down to evidence storage. The officer on duty logged in to the desk computer, running a finger down the screen as he searched through the evidence listings for the Markwell case.

'Let me see boss…' mouthing out evidence numbers silently as his eyes and fingertip made their way down, and then back up to the top as the page refreshed onto the second list.

It didn't take long.

'Nope, nothing, diddly squat pal. Nothing here marked as a storage drive or CD-ROM for the address. Sorry mate the owner was fobbing you off. If we had it, it would be here: even if it had been fast-tracked off the computer lab for analysis it'd still be logged as coming in first. Happens all the time people lying to the police, you should know that by now Constable.'

A sly grin accompanied the enunciation on DC Jordan's rank, but not rising to it he smiled and drummed the desk.

'Yeah, you're probably right. No harm in asking though was there. Catch you later Sergeant. Pleasure as always.'

He exited the office and arched back against the wall outside. Knowing what was next -— telling DI Rose — was not the soothing tonic his stomach needed right now, but better done sooner than later, he began trudging upstairs to see the boss. 'Not your fault Andy, nothing she can do except shout at you that's all, don't sweat it'. Yeah right.

Standing outside her office he composed himself before knocking, entering after the call from within.

'Sorry to disturb ma'am. Bit of an update on the Markwell case, and not the good kind unfortunately. I'll cut straight to the point if it's alright.'

'Well, you may as well do it sitting down I suppose,' Alice gestured to the chair she kept angled in front of her desk, 'come on then, what is this joyous news you've come to tell me DC Jordan?'

Andy shifted his weight.

'I think we're not the only ones in blue looking at the case ma'am. I mean, it would seem so after this morning.'

'Come again?'

'Well, I was out this morning, checking off loose ends from the initial intelligence gathering. Not much, couple of follow up questions, which it turns out didn't tell me much more. Thing is, when I went to chase up the CCTV footage from the shop, the one the street over from the house, turns out one of our lot has been in and scooped it up before us.'

'Who?'

'Well, that's the problem ma'am. I don't know. Didn't leave a name, didn't leave a receipt for evidence either. I've been down to storage as well and there's no trace of it, I looked like a right bell-end down there asking the question.'

'So, what, it's gone, someone's just gone ahead and lost it?'

'Well, worse don't you think? Sounds like someone downright went and pinched it. Cashier was pretty well convinced it was a copper as well. Full uniform so didn't think twice about it. Handed it all straight over there and then, no questions asked. Could be one of us, could be some clever clogs. Seems a risky tactic to go dressing up as a copper in the middle of an active crime scene though.'

'You're absolutely sure of this?'

'Afraid so ma'am.'

'Jesus. I didn't need this; meddling and subversion from some smart arse in the station. Surely they would know we'd be back to look for the footage at some point, no? Find the initial uniform doing the rounds on the day, see if it wasn't them and wring their neck if it was. Failing that, find out who's been bending their ear or has a favour owing from them. Honestly, this bloody station!'

She thought about throwing a pen at the window, but stopped and composed herself, remembering she was with a junior. She looked back up with a thin smile.

'Never mind eh. It'll turn up I suppose. Or at least I hope it will. Now, the other thing I asked you to do yesterday, track down the info about the dog Markwell had dealt with, you find anything there?'

'Ah well, not so much ma'am. Spent most of yesterday following up on the group chat files, wanted to be prepared for next time we had Trench in the hot seat.'

She tilted her gaze up.

'Don't forget taking your girlfriend out for dinner as well.'

'And taking… wait sorry ma'am?'

'Andy if you're going to skip out at 4.30pm on a Monday be sure not to tell the secretaries. They gossip more than the custody sergeant.'

He looked down, embarrassed.

'When I say follow something up, I mean follow something up okay?

Never mind trying to outsmart Trench next time around, I'll take care of that twit don't worry about it. Now get. I want the story on the dog, and I want it yesterday you hear?'

'Yes ma'am. Apologies, won't happen again.'

She pretended to log in to her computer and return to work. As soon as he had left though she placed her pen down on the nearest pad and screwed up the top layer of another.

First the Macfarlane debacle, and now this CCTV going missing. And in clear broad daylight from a uniform as well. Whoever said the boys in blue stuck together clearly hadn't worked in a police station, suffering the professional ignominy of a decent backstabbing.

She unfurled the paper, resting her head on a flat palm while she thought about it. A murder case of all things. It was going to surface later at some point, timed to perfection no doubt at her next promotion, but that thought didn't help her right now. Whoever had pinched the CCTV was either knowingly, or unwittingly, sitting on vital evidence; to spite her and the investigation. Damn them. Damn this petty little station.

It riled her the rest of the afternoon as she pored over the case notes for Markwell. The guy was a deadbeat, a nobody. Probably got his kicks killing animals and one had finally come back on him. Who was covering for him? Or being so petty as to screw up the investigation for their office politics?

She shut the case files and picked up her jacket. She was getting nowhere today, and the bad news had only managed to set her mind off down avenues which were not at all helpful. A good night's sleep after an evening of mindless reality TV would hopefully do the trick — Wednesday would hopefully prove a much more straightforward day.

Chapter Twenty-Seven

I couldn't shake the intrusive thoughts.

Not knowing what had happened on the farm: the dogs, Simon, even a few days later it was all getting too much. I couldn't get it out of my head. The wagging tail at the end, the spilled water bowl seeping into the torn feed sacks. Had the council answered the call?

All questions I needed answered.

Firstly, I couldn't phone Skye and ask about them: if they hadn't been picked up it would look downright suspicious, and if they had been, they clearly hadn't been taken to the vets, so how would I know? The group's chat had been quiet too. Nothing but mundane chatter and routine up-keep.

It was a catch-22 situation, so stupidly, I figured the easiest solution was heading back to have a look for myself. It was a Wednesday, my usual half-day from the practice, and so without any errands I had a clear run at the afternoon.

Animals fed and Tank taken for a short walk, I pushed my bike onto the driveway. It was a couple of miles so shouldn't take too long, and ditching the fluorescent yellow cycling jacket for a darker hoodie, I headed off.

When I arrived some twenty minutes later the farm looked as deserted as before, and tucking the bike in behind a gap in the hedgerow, I found myself walking up the same potholed farm track to the outbuildings I had been in a few nights ago. It was uncomfortable being here during daylight, so I moved over to the door, quietly listening.

The shuffling and grunting was absent, leaving only the gentle creak of corrugated iron sheets against the steel frame as the wind shifted the skeleton of the building to and fro. The latch I had so carefully replaced was hanging loose, its job taken care of by a zip tie. Attached to it was an official tag from Northumbria Police, with the words 'Do Not Enter' emblazoned in bold capital letters, set against a blue and white striped background behind the force insignia.

This was good news. Very good news.

It also explained why I hadn't heard anything regarding the dogs. Whereas our practice took care of the Northumberland County Council cases, another practice in the region oversaw the police dogs, and was their go-to point of contact for the force when dealing with their own cruelty cases.

It hopefully also meant the dog thefts would be investigated with more vigour; a paper trail from the farm buildings, the animal feed, or at best, Simon himself could have been caught in the act whilst at the shed. It also meant I could relax and stop trying to fight this thing. Taking revenge on Davey had been disturbingly satisfying and hadn't troubled my conscience far beyond the initial anxiety in the days after — brutalising animals and threatening my family had counter-balanced the harsh method of his disposal — but taking that energy on to a whole group? I'm not sure it was within my psychological remit. Or indeed a wise move altogether when they knew so much about my life.

No, this was a step in the right direction. Police involvement was the break I needed. Time to step away.

I eased up onto a railway sleeper and peered through the cracks in the sheet iron walls. I couldn't see much of the interior, dark and dusky with the dim outlines of the animal cages, but there was no sign of life from within.

A warm satisfied glow filled me, knowing the dogs were safe, and I stepped back, turning round into the yard.

'Alright Mac?'

An icy shot of adrenaline swept through me, freezing me to the spot. A big, bulky figure was stood about three metres away, covering the gap between the farm-track and myself; the tight gym t-shirt not leaving much doubt about the physique underneath. The clever grin on the man's face, widening by the second, told me he wasn't in any doubt about this physical mismatch either.

I'm a big guy from good stock. Broad in the shoulders and bulk around me too. But I don't lift weights and I don't train in the ring. Give me an axe and I'll swing it all day long for firewood, herd of cattle back on the farm wouldn't trouble me either; you show them who's boss and you're laughing. The residual stamina from my army days was still there and would be for life. But fighting? Never been a question I answer too often. Folks tend to leave big Scottish people alone, an unwritten rule of life.

But this guy seemed like he didn't want to follow the majority.

'Been sent down to show you a thing or two like. We figured it was you who ratted us out, figured you'd show your face sooner or later given the chance.'

The swinging door behind him told me he'd been waiting, expecting someone to show up. I couldn't work out how he had my name though, had Markwell been talking in the days before I'd finished him off?

The grin widened further still, and the arms opened out to cover the space between the farm track and my escape. Looks like we're getting into it.

Now, I'm no idiot. The guy will clearly knock seven shades out of me given the chance. If this thing develops into a full fight, odds are, despite any bulk and grit left in my genetics we're still looking at KO for Mac inside the first round. No point in denying it. The veins on his forearms and the massive neck tells me there's a good chance he's been lapping up the old steroids as well. You don't get this size on push-ups and protein shakes.

It's clearly going to have to be quick on my part. A quick mental flashback to an old physics equation tells me hit him hard, make it small, and make it in the right place. Something about surface area, force exerted and power: it was screaming out at me back from high school. No point landing a thud on the side of his head: it would bounce off no matter how grisly and Scottish I made it. No, pick a small point, hit it hard and hope for the best. Bob's your uncle, hopefully not your pallbearer.

The guy rushes me and starts winding up a haymaker punch: big arc with minimal elbow bend, swinging it round from his right side, up and over the point of his shoulder. There's no finesse here, he's clearly thinking this is a one-shot fight.

And he's right of course. Just he hasn't picked the right side.

I duck down, letting the arm sail through the air above my head — the power pulling him with it and sending him off balance. As momentum takes him to my right a knee joint presents itself side on, and I stand and stamp through it with a hefty cow-kick, spinning him further to the ground before buckling down further with the pain of the twisted and torn cartilage. It's not just milking you learn in the dairy parlour.

Resisting the urge to grapple him: guys like this probably have all sorts of wrestling moves tucked away in their arsenal, I follow the physics orders and find the next weak point on this slab of muscle. I'm wearing trainers, flimsy. Nice to cycle in, but terrible to try inflicting any real damage on a big gym freak like this, so if it's a hit and hope shot, I'm aiming for the windpipe.

I swing a leg round and connect, sending him backwards to the ground, grasping at the front of his neck and writhing his legs in a hopeless attempt to open his airways. I've clearly hit the jackpot. Stridored breathing gurgles and hisses around the folded trachea as it rasps against the tiniest of airflows, wheezing as a helpless set of hands claw at it from the outside.

I stand back and watch the sight.

A primeval rush of satisfaction hits me as I watch him struggling, and after thirty seconds or so, the life begins to fade. There wouldn't be much help I could give even if I wanted to: tracheostomy aside, this hunk of steroid flavoured beef was on a one-way ticket to meet his maker. Sad news for his gym direct debit, but good for me it turns out. If he'd got a good hold of me I'd be the one lying down there, twitching and lifeless.

I shake myself down as the adrenaline subsides and quickly check around the farm for an accomplice, but the yard is empty save for a few startled pigeons.

I look at the body in front of me. Who the hell was this guy, and how the hell did he know I was going to be here? He had to be from Bloodsport, but he had also known my name. Was the game up, was I a worse sleuth than I thought following Simon Trench to the yard? Surely they weren't so tech savvy they could trace phone numbers. Besides, I'd been careful all the way through up until now. It had to be the other night when I was last here, had to be.

Still, at least there was one way to find out.

I turned him over and felt around the back pockets on his tracksuit bottoms. Car keys and a wallet in one, a phone and billfold with about £200 tucked into it in the other.

I opened the wallet and took out the driver's license. 'Ronnie Macfarlane', a local address. Thirty-two years old, no points. I rolled him back over: the face matched the license.

'Sorry Ronnie, looks like it wasn't your day pal.'

I moved my attention to the phone. The screen was locked, but a quick flick and swipe up let me into facial id, and after turning it down to face the deceased, it came alive with a screen full of apps as I held it over him.

I found WhatsApp, and sure enough, Bloodsport was there on the list, Ronnie Macfarlane carrying the initials RM for his chat name. Which figured. He'd come across as the hard man in my previous notes. Another name to tick off my list, which was getting shorter by the day at my current rate: Markwell, Trench, and Macfarlane.

'Pace yourself Mac.'

I came back out and swiped through his messages, looking for any more clues. He wouldn't have acted alone to come here, surely there would be another group or separate message giving him instructions what to do?

BloodSport had been third on the list, second to a 'Carly', and topped off by messages from 'J'. Bingo. Looks like this was a side project from the boss himself. Looks like there was a hierarchy to this thing.

I clicked onto the message thread, but my heart froze as it turned into a video call. Shit. How the hell had I managed to do that? Tech skills of a five-year-old and the fat fingers of a Scottish farm boy it would seem.

I panicked, trying to find the cancel button, but as the burst of adrenaline slowed, I realised it was an incoming call from the boss himself — sitting remotely, impatiently waiting for a progress update.

I let it ring out for a few seconds, then decided to hit the accept button: holding the camera away from myself and up to the sky.

'Ronnie?' Fumbling and scratching noises came from the handset as 'J' positioned it at the other end.

'Ronnie what the fuck are you doing pal, all I'm seeing is sky mate. You got an update for me yet, any sign of that Scottish prick?'

The line went quiet and reverted to breath sounds, as well as the sound of a coffee mug being drained and hitting a desk. I bit the bullet, making the next move.

I reversed the camera from its selfie mode and started filming the ground. In the smaller inset picture I could see I was still focusing on the grass, but the larger video screen was a shirt and tie, the head cut off at the top.

'Ronnie what the fuck are you doing pal? Live up to the meat head stereotype why don't you.'

I peered closely from an angle. He was in an office, a lanyard and fuzzy name badge hanging loosely around his neck. It looked official, an emblem with words in bold black and white, printed in capitals. The camera edged in and out of focus but gradually settled as he sat still again.

'POLICE'.

Shit.

That explained a bit. 'J' was a copper. And plain clothes by the look of it, Detective rank minimum. Bent as a toilet u-bend, but still a copper. No wonder they were one step ahead of any investigations into the dog fighting. Shit.

'Ronnie I'm losing my patience here mate, please tell me this is a pocket answer you Muppet.'

I figured it was now or never, time to up the game, so I turned back round to Ronnie and swung the video picture over his body, as twisted and lifeless as it was, zooming into his expressionless face to let it sit there.

Ten seconds or so passed. 'J' had shut off his camera as soon as he realised, but the video call was still open, silently broadcasting the deathly image of Ronnie laid out in the yard.

'Fair play to you mate. Fair play.'

The tone of voice was calm and steady.

'Didn't see that one coming, didn't see that coming at all; man like Ronnie, figured he'd twist you round like an old paperclip, have you tied in all kinds of knots. Tougher than you look you big sack of shit. Fair play...'

Rustling from the other end of the line, the dark screen giving nothing away.

'Game's up though isn't it. You've nothing on us, and we've got everything on you. There's so much you think you got away with isn't there? Well tick-tock, tick-tock, the clock doesn't stop for you Mr Vet. You'll never know when but trust me we're coming for you, and sooner than you might think.'

The call ended.

The screen went back to the list of messages.

My mouth was dry, and I was stone cold. They knew everything, how? I must have made a mistake with Davey which had been shelved by this Detective for later use. Fuck. I'd walked right into it. Clearly they knew I was going to turn up here, hence Ronnie sent for dispatch purposes. But now what? Wait for a knock on the door, let the bent copper and his criminal friends send me down while they carried on?

Shit. Shit. Shit.

I focused on the phone, looking for anything more I could use to turn this mess around, anything at all, but at the same time I became aware of a rumbling engine noise from the other side of the farm track, approaching along the lane from the west.

I closed the phone down and wiped it off, doing the same for the wallet and hoping to hell I hadn't left any DNA on either the case or leather. Nothing I could do about it now though. Throwing it back down to Ronnie, I moved and quickly ducked behind the hedgerow of the track to trace its path along the edge of the field, my heart racing even more than when the phone call ended.

The engine noise lowered in frequency as the vehicle slowed down, and I caught sight of it turning into the track. A white van. Shit. My head was screaming at me now. I moved as fast as I could down the hedgerow until it came level, dropping down at the last second.

As it dipped a rear wheel into a pothole, I caught sight of the same markings I had seen on the shed's tag and on the blur of 'J's police badge: Northumbria Police. A follow up visit, forensics on the shed? 'J' surely couldn't have sent anything that quick, was he phoning Ronnie to send him away from the farm while his legitimate colleagues were on site? How involved was this guy?

As soon as it had passed me it would have about eighty yards before it reached the farmyard, as well as Ronnie Macfarlane's body lying out cold in the middle. Without doubt it would bring ten times as many more police vehicles turning up, all within a short space of time, so I made the decision and stood up, bursting into a sprint down the hedgerow to where the bike was stashed. If the occupants of the police car were at all inclined to look back they'd see me for sure — but the consequences of staying put weren't worth thinking about. No way was I explaining myself out of this one. 'J's threats were yet to materialise, but the last thing I needed was to find myself sitting in a hedge at a murder scene. University degrees and clean criminal records didn't get you a slap on the wrist for manslaughter. I had to get as much distance between myself and the farm as possible.

I reached the bike and turned it round. The van was slowing to a stop and the passenger side was opening, its occupant looking forward. Which was fair enough, there was a dead body in front of them.

Throwing it through the hedge, clattering it over the verge, I pedalled hard in the opposite direction, up the lane to a point I knew an old bridle way opened. I wasn't looking back now; it was full effort to get off the road and out of sight. Only when I got to the path did I realise what a shit state I was in: dripping with sweat and heart pounding.

Surrounded by the overgrown trees which hugged and strangled the path, I hung my head over the handlebars, gasping for each panicked breath. It was all I could do not to think about what had just happened, or for that matter, what terrifying things might happen next.

Part Three

Chapter Twenty-Eight

Alice drove under the sign for Berryhill Farm, wincing as the front wheels bounced erratically out of a pothole; one of the many which pockmarked the deserted track. Time to upgrade the transport choice she thought. One of the fancy lease options colleagues were always hinting at. Couldn't as well push for promotion in this old rust heap.

The chassis groaned on cue as it found another unforgiving rut, slowly aching its way along to the outbuildings.

Pulling in behind the SOCO van she got out and slipped on a pair of shoe covers, the end tearing slightly around her low heel. It would be fine she told herself. She walked over to the taped and tented area in the centre of the farmyard. A uniformed officer saw her and held a hand up in recognition.

'Evening ma'am. Sorry to keep you from getting home on time but you were first on the list of duty detectives for the night. Mind, saying that I almost got DI Jamieson after calling the victim's name into the station; seems he had an interest and was itching to come along, boss said stick to the protocol though, you know what he's like — hence here you are.'

'Oh yeah? Who's the victim? Bit out in the sticks here, aren't we?'

'Well, wasn't difficult ma'am. Wallet with a photo ID lying beside him. Attacker seems to have made little effort in clearing up after himself either, tossed everything back down and scarpered: phone, money, the lot. Can't see big signs of a struggle neither, all collapsed here on the ground, not massively obvious the method either ma'am…'

'Constable, the victim's name you were saying?'

'Oh yes sorry ma'am, carried away with myself as usual. Ronnie Macfarlane. Believe you might have had dealings in the past.'

Bad news travels fast in a regional headquarters it seems, but ignoring the dig she pushed on.

'Ronnie Macfarlane? Wasn't expecting that. You're sure?'

'Certain ma'am. Face matches the ID, and not many units like him around town either. I've come across him one or two times myself, wasn't exactly the shrinking violet in these parts our Ronnie.'

A radio sparked to life between them. The officer raised a hand in apology, the other lifting the handset to his mic, returning the call. Ignore the switchboard at your peril.

Thanking him as he talked, Alice walked past him to the tent.

A single, crisp white cube, dropped in the drab grey and brown oil painting that was the farmyard.

Sure enough, as she lifted the flap, Macfarlane lay out, presided over by a forensics officer, meticulously sampling and periodically taking close up pictures. The pained final expression on his face suggested it hadn't been the most pleasant of last moments for him either, and a fleeting surge of satisfaction pulsed through her as she took in the scene. She would, of course, rather have nailed him the conventional way, in a court of law, but seeing him lifeless, contorted, and unable to continue his cruel existence gave her the smallest moment of guilty pleasure.

She soon snapped out of it. He was a victim, she was a police officer.

'Anything interesting so far?'

Alice knelt beside Macfarlane as she spoke, resisting the temptation to reach out and touch him in his agonal state.

'Not so much ma'am. Nothing obvious like a stab or gunshot wound that I can tell, the ground's fairly organic and uneven so I'm not seeing any blood patterning or obvious spills. Yet to lift him though. Been wrong before.'

The officer pointed around the immediate surroundings, over to a disturbed patch of earth a few feet away.

'There's not much of a commotion so far as I can tell, dirt's dusted up over there, think I can about see a boot print matching his; looks like he might have twisted on the right side as he fell. Seems to have collapsed on the spot. Must have been a fair whack to get him down.'

He clicked a swab shut, placing it into a sealed bag with its own barcode.

'Gonna have a job moving him too; he's got to be 18 or 19 stone of pure muscle surely.'

'He was a big one alright was Ronnie.' Alice moved carefully around to the head end. 'May I?' Indicating to his scalp with a gloved finger.

'Be my guest, I've got the initial positional shots.'

She gently lifted the shaved head, rotating it as well she could against the stiffened neck muscles. Right enough, there was no blood or sign of injury, and she placed the thick skull and its contents back down on the earth.

'Bit bizarre. You'd think at least one or more headshots would be needed to drop him. You see anything else on the initial?'

'Well for a big fella I'd expect the larynx to sit more prominently. Looks dropped and recessed. Can't tell as much because of the neck tattoo, but I dunno, there's petechiation, sorry, bruising, around the Adam's apple.'

'I know what petechiation is young man.'

She smiled and shone a pen-torch down and on to the front of Ronnie's throat. Right enough it was darker and bruised against the rest of the skin, albeit shielded by a large skull tattoo and its shading, a death mask for the trauma underneath. The officer was right. It looked smaller and collapsed, like it had been pushed in with some force.

'You think it's relevant?'

'Could be. His hands were up around his throat when we got here and set up, I moved them after photographs and initial sweep of the scene. Like he was clawing his neck or pulling at something. No sign of a ligature or blunt marking. Bit odd. Pathologist will tell us though. Never know, maybe the silly git choked on his lunch and collapsed.'

'I highly doubt it don't you?'

'I'm joking, obviously.' He pointed lower down the body.

'Knee's twisted too. Reckon might have floored him first, giving us our twisted boot prints over there. Might help with the theory of how you could drop a big bloke like Ronnie.'

'Maybe. Maybe.'

Alice moved round and took the scene in one last time, before lifting the tent flap back open and walking out into the empty farmyard. She couldn't help wondering why Ronnie Macfarlane had been here in the first place. Why this farm? What the hell was he doing up here in the middle of nowhere getting himself killed? Who on earth could take down a big hard nut like Ronnie? Couldn't be many locals out there could get the better of him.

Stepping out to check the rest of the yard, she was stopped by a call from within the tent. SOCO clearly had other plans for her.

'Sorry ma'am. Do you want the smartphone to take away, or should I bag it all up with the rest of his personal stuff?'

'Bag it up. I've not had too much luck with evidence recently, I'll let you lot handle it. Who's your senior on this, is it Diane?'

'Yeah it's the boss in charge.'

'OK well tell her I'll catch up with her as soon as it's feasible, you got anything else for me? You know when the pathologist is getting here?'

'I don't think he'll be here until after six. Something about a specimen hold up at the lab he had to oversee, said to keep the scene locked down until he got here. You know what Ballingry's like, can't lift a fingernail without his say so if he's in charge. I'll already be in the shit for moving the hands so reckon I'm sitting tight till the doc's had a look.'

'Right you are. I'll see Diane back at the station for debrief when she's collected all the initials, unless she's around?'

'Back to the lab for a bigger bag. Didn't realise he was such a big bugger until we got here. Stick around if you want. Probably need a hand moving him once the docs been and had a look.'

'No you're okay. Days of me shifting stiffs are long gone. There's got to be some perks with the rank. No, I'll get back and start the case file. Lord knows where we begin with this one though.'

She dropped the flap back down and drank in the scene. Nothing but empty buildings and debris scattered amongst each other, the sky overhead matching the rusted texture of the place. Checking the car was still intact from the drive in, she eased back in.

Surely it couldn't be a coincidence, could it? Davey Markwell, and now Ronnie Macfarlane? Ronnie Macfarlane, the man who had dropped himself in it the day after Markwell had been discovered, murdered himself in bizarre and unusual circumstances. There had to be a link. Had to be.

She indicated left, for Newcastle.

Sod's law, she had wanted at least one interesting case, there were now two to deal with, and another late night was stretching out in front of her.

Chapter Twenty-Nine

For a Wednesday afternoon it was going slowly for Skye, too slowly in fact, and most of her morning had been taken up preparing for court.

She had been called as witness for the prosecution on a welfare case against a local dog breeder. It was an insult to most of the breeding community to call him a breeder, but he bred dogs, called himself a breeder, and so he dragged their good names down with him.

The main case was his treatment, or lack of, with his kenneled dogs. She had been part of a raid organised by the RSPCA and the police some months ago, but it was only now that the case was being brought to trial. Three separate counts of cruelty were under question; however, her involvement was limited to the third of the three animals: an unfortunate French Bulldog who had been bred to the point of exhaustion. Never having seen the end of a vet's stethoscope, or indeed a clean kennel, she was keen to make this testimony count.

As she flicked back through the pictures and the vet's report, her eyes were drawn down to Mac's signature on his evidence statement. He had examined the animal in his usual calm and collected manner, carefully turning her around on the consult room table to record various measurements and observations, taking care not to scare her in her already timid state. He had obviously been moved by her condition, holding her like a lamb in the crook of his arm while he chatted back to her and typed notes one handed, every now and then stopping to tickle her ear and feed her a treat. If she hadn't already had a huge sweet spot for Mac, the sight of him holding the emaciated little girl in a big Scottish forearm would have easily swung her in his direction. Still, best not to go there she thought.

It did, however, take her mind to the Jack Russell, jolting her back to the attack in the lay-by as well as the encounter in the car park at the vets. Near enough three weeks had passed, the ribs still twinging when she raised her arms high enough. But it was the dent to her confidence which was still the biggest injury: she hadn't been back to the scene, nowhere near it in fact, and Mac was the only person she had briefly confided in. Normally she would have mentioned it to Steve, her father figure in the office, but there was something about him recently, something telling her not to bother.

Deep down she knew she should have gone to the police, but as time moved forward and the injuries healed it was becoming less of a big deal, and her anxieties gradually dulled back with the banality of day-to-day life. She hadn't seen or heard from her attacker in the weeks gone by, and there was no sign of the BMW following her either, despite constantly checking her wing mirror every time she was out in the works van. Was Mac right? Had it been dealt with?

No, as time went by and everything settled, she felt more and more like leaving it all alone, hoping the whole thing would never come back.

Bella still niggled her though. More so the lack of progress on her case, or for that fact, the lack of anyone telling her what was going on with it. Same with the cache of dogs up at the farm from Saturday. Since Steve incorporated it into his workload she hadn't heard a thing about them. He was good at it his job, no doubt about it, but she would still like to have been involved in some way, mainly because she had been the primary contact on both cases. To lose touch felt like abandoning them, stupid she told herself, but the thought swirled anxiously around her head as she sat in front of the Bulldog's case notes.

As she flicked over the first page again, going over it for the third time, she looked up to see the main external door swing open, followed shortly by Steve's burly figure coming into the office, snaking his way around the desks and over to his private office in the far corner.

Should she, thought Skye? He was probably busy with something else. He certainly looked it: a furrowed brow framing a stern look forward, but as her gran always used to say to her, or indeed anyone who was listening, *'Shy bairns get nowt hinny'*.

She smiled inside, pushing back her chair to stand and follow her own weaving path over to the corner, reaching it as Steve turned to take his jacket off and hang it up, hand on the door, ready to shut himself in.

'Could I get a word Steve? Won't take long.'

'Yeah sure, come in. What is it? The court case coming up?' He sat down and leaned back in his tattered faux leather office chair. He looked tired, his mind somewhere else.

'No, but it did make me think about it.' She stepped forward and thought better of it; the flimsy plastic chair in front of Steve's desk didn't look particularly sturdy, or indeed clean.

'Right, so what is it.' Steve snipped sharply, a temper creeping in. 'You're not going to ask me about the workplace pension scheme again are you, I've only just got my head around my own, never mind how it works for the rest of you lot. Why they thought I should be liaso..'

'No no. Not that again. Don't worry.' Skye held both hands up. 'No, it was to see how things were getting on with the Jack Russell. You know, the one from a few weeks ago I took to the vets, the one with its throat slit.'

'Oh that. Yeah, sorry Skye, I had been meaning to tell you. A dead end. No pun intended. Talked it over with the investigating detective, friend of mine from the golf club would you believe. They couldn't get anything from the woman's son, wouldn't give up a dime so they dropped it, insufficient evidence if he wasn't willing. Talked to him a few times apparently but nothing came of it in the end.'

'This the same detective who breezed through the office and tossed a card at me?'

Skye padded her pockets for her wallet but realised it was back at her desk, the business card tucked inside.

'Probably. They're busy people Skye. Much as we'd like it they aren't going to blow the budget on investigating a dog murder, no matter how gruesome.'

'But what if it escalates?' Skye was thinking back to her attack a few weeks ago. Dangerous people. Should she have gone to the police instead of waiting for Steve to fill her in on what was happening? Something about the detective's lack of interest though hadn't exactly filled her with much confidence.

'It's a local idiot Skye. Hopefully we'll never see the likes again. Best to try and forget about it.' His smile only lasted a few seconds.

'And what about Saturday? The dogs up at Berryhill farm? Didn't you think it was a bit out of the ordinary? The anonymous tip off for stolen dogs?'

'Skye, I told you to leave that one well alone. I'll deal with it, okay? Why don't you get focused for the court case and leave me to deal with Berryhill. Whole thing's probably some mixed up old farmer.'

'Mixed up old farmer my eye. Did you even check the microchips? What about the dead one round the back? More than just some daft old farmer. If I were allowed an opinion, one anyone would bother listening to, I'd say the terrier was part of the same problem.' She leant forward on the chair, both hands gripping the plastic. 'I mean come on, when have we ever seen mutilated dogs on our patch before? You honestly think this is all a couple of coincidences? If you're too busy with everyone's pensions or the office work I'll be happy to take it back off you if you want me to.'

Skye was getting more than irate now, and the tension in the office had reached an uncomfortable level, as had her tone of voice. Looking out of the large office window she could see one of the secretaries looking up and over in their direction. Steve leant forward and placed both hands on the table.

'I resent the accusation Skye; you know me well enough to know I won't cut corners on a case. But if the police say they can't follow it up, they can't follow it up. Okay? We're not some wild set of vigilantes in high-viz. We can't just go round throwing out theories on dog fighting and be expecting them to stick.'

'So you do think it's something bigger. You do think this is dog fighting?'

'It was a turn of phrase Skye. And I'd advise you to keep your nose out of it. It's in hand and I'd prefer it stayed that way.' Steve sighed and looked out of the window, catching the secretary's eye and causing her to look down.

'I like you, I like your work, but sometimes you're a massive pain in the arse with all the questions Skye. Leave this one to me, okay? I'll let you know if I need you.'

He motioned her out of the room, reminding her to shut the door on her way out. She could feel her cheeks burning after the confrontation: Steve was normally so approachable and friendly, so affable and easy to work with. What was going on, what was making him act in such a bizarre way, had he been attacked too? Warned off like she had a few weeks ago? Is that why he was being so protective over the dogs from the farm, to protect Skye, or himself?

She had half a mind to go back in and come clean about the assault, in the small hope he would open up to her. But as she paused, weighing it up, she thought better of it, quickly turning back to the main office. The same secretary was clearly trying to catch her eye, so she walked over.

'Eeee you alright pet?' she gazed up, eager to get the gossip, 'Don't you worry about Steve, he's been in a bad mood all afternoon. Took a phone call and stormed out, that was him coming back in. You probably just caught him at the wrong moment love, I shouldn't worry about it.'

She held up a box of chocolates, intent to get a response it would seem.

'You don't think it's anything to do with that body, do you? One they found up on the Berryhill farm, same as all of them dogs?'

She tutted away to herself.

'My Mark's on the force, text me to say there was some poor bloke found up there battered and dead. He shouldn't you know, but when they're stood about waiting for the science bods to turn up they get bored, you know how it is. Come to think of it I wasn't supposed to tell you. You didn't hear it from me, okay? Here, have a caramel triangle pet. You look like you could do with one, day you're having.'

Skye obliged, unwrapping the chocolate as she headed back over to her desk and sat down. A dead body? Up at Berryhill farm? What on earth was going on, was that why Steve was suddenly so stressed, worried he was next?

She sat and stared down in a daze at her case file for the court case, reading the same sentence over and over, taking none of it in. Idly, she threw the caramel wrapper into the bin. It bounced out. Perhaps she should go to the police, perhaps not. It had been weeks, but the fear of the threats still lingered there, deep down in her psyche. She looked to the secretary for reassurance, but only a smile and a wink were returned. No, this was best left in her head for now.

Chapter Thirty

Macfarlane's case file. Thick and dog-eared, it had seen many a day out in the office over the years, tilted down off the shelf and getting heavier every time; each officer, landing it on their desk with a heavy thud, aiming to close it for good. Banish it to storage while its subject rotted in a cell. Take the glory of sending him down.

Alice, it seemed, would have the final say. His murder the guttural epilogue to a life misspent. The chapter most colleagues had wanted to edit.

She had requested all the previous case notes on prior investigations, namely his domestic assaults and later the drug charges she had failed to prosecute, and all now sat in their entirety, neatly in the folder before her. The court case was still fresh and raw, nine days having passed, and it still irked her to think of his childish gloating on the courtroom steps as he hinted at his other connections. But putting it to the back of her mind she focused on the task — finding his attacker.

Ronnie Macfarlane was a local through and through. Born and raised in the county he had never left, completing his education on the streets as opposed to the classroom. He was a renowned hard man and hot head, and never far away from trouble. Standing at over six foot and built like the proverbial, he had been in more fights and trouble than was good for him in his early days; giving him a fearsome reputation.

Over time the arrest rate had gradually slowed down, usually meaning more and more involvement in organised crime for a dishonest man like

Ronnie, taking a back seat from bar room brawls and local street enforcement in favour of overseeing from above. He kept fit though. Sources had him as a regular at the local MMA club — even venturing into regional competitions — so it was a surprise to everyone he had been so easily killed up at the farm.

Something told her she was looking for a special individual in this case. Not your average brawler. Preliminary forensics had indicated blunt force trauma to the knee and throat; well-placed blows designed to immobilise and render unconscious, or in this case dead. Couldn't be many attackers around like that, had he pissed someone off at a tournament fight? Some other criminal gang?

She turned another page, his many associates listed on top of each other.

She still hadn't forgotten his words at the courthouse either.

'I hope you do a better job with Davey…' and the sheepish look which followed.

Clearly he had links to Markwell.

Question was though, did they share the same attacker? If they did, what was the link between the two of them? How was it strong enough to end up with them both killed within two weeks of one another? Perhaps Ronnie was himself looking into Davey's murder, uncovering something bad enough to get himself terminated so ceremoniously. And what of the location, what on earth was he doing out in the middle of nowhere in broad daylight?

She began sorting into potential links, siding those which were irrelevant.

Everything from that first arrest through to her recent failed drugs case was included, and it was interesting to see case notes from older colleagues through the years. Every dealing with the force was recorded, from traffic offences through to dropped assault charges, cannabis warnings and a closed investigation three years ago over witness intimidation. Half the office had dealt with him at one time or another — even the DCI back in the day — but nothing serious ever stuck on the guy. Alex had gone closest with the witness intimidation case, but it had only fizzled out due to 'lack of evidence' for the CPS. Guy was like Teflon. No wonder he'd wriggled out of her drugs case. Probably also why he was taking such an interest now. His failures three years ago didn't look so bad after a collapsed drugs trial.

Weird how he was still checking in though, copying himself into emails from the lab whenever Macfarlane was mentioned.

What was it he said?

'Rumour has it was a juicy one.'

His usual smarmy look to follow it up.

Guess he still had a point to prove after his own failure. She got it: a defendant outdoes you and sometimes you can't let it go. You spend the next few years looking for the loose ends you missed the first time around, anything to take the case back to the CPS for another go at it.

After two coffees, sure enough, she had her potential leads marked out, carefully noted in her workbook. Known potential associates, local interests; there was more enough for the team to be getting stuck into for the next few days — even before any ties to Markwell.

***

It was later that afternoon when Diane Petty, senior forensics officer to the station, knocked on the door of her office and promptly entered, sitting down opposite Alice. Initial pleasantries were exchanged, but it wasn't long before talk moved onto Ronnie.

The investigation into the Macfarlane murder was at the earliest of stages, so any preliminary forensics would be brief: the organic swabs, post-mortem examinations would all take time. A cursory run down of the scene only, the objective for them was to focus and fast track any evidence where it was deemed most important: accelerate the investigation, or at least steer it away from the dead ends most cases threw up along the path to conviction.

Small talk over, Diane set out her paperwork in front of Alice.

'Well, as indicated by the initial scene analysis it doesn't look like there was any prolonged struggle, no evidence of blood patterning, no discarded weapons, no obvious self-defence injuries noted either. The victim is still awaiting his post-mortem exam at the RVI, but the initial exam would suggest blunt force trauma times two: front of neck and lateral right knee. The pathologist will have to confirm it, but I think a crushing injury to the larynx is your working murder method at present, nothing else obvious to sway it in another direction that we could see. I expect Dr Ballingry will have an opinion to give shortly.'

'Yes, I expect he will if I know him as well as I think I do.' Alice smiled to herself.

'Anything digital back yet?'

'No ma'am. Put in for submission this morning so we can expect an extraction in the next few days, unless we want it fast-tracked?'

'Potentially. This could be a second victim from a single attacker, so it might be useful to link the two if we can. Any way they can look for particular things, or is it all or nothing? I'm interested in a WhatsApp group which might link to another victim.'

'I can certainly ask them to prioritise. It shouldn't be too difficult to stick it to the front of the queue, they can't argue if it's murder. Priority one on the list if we want it to be.'

'I think it would be wise. Anything else of interest at the scene?' Alice shifted in her seat ready to move.

'Not especially ma'am. We swabbed in the kennels to see if the scenes were linked. I wasn't on the initial, but figured it could be involved, so we went in and dusted it down. Mostly dog hair, nothing too interesting yet.'

Alice looked up, confused.

'Kennels? What kennels?'

'The dog kennels ma'am. From the recovered stolen dogs a few days before, reported on the Saturday — we had a cursory exam, it was a low-grade priority then, DI Jamieson didn't seem interested in the forensic aspect, only tying up his loose ends. I think we were there all of thirty minutes before he dismissed us. Said he'd "give us a call" if he had any further requirement. Didn't think much of it until this murder turning up at the same scene. Ironically, it was the team heading back to clear it out who discovered Macfarlane.'

Diane looked apologetically at Alice.

'Sorry ma'am, I thought you would have already known, no intention to muddy the waters.'

'No no, not at all. Never realised there was another scene that's all. My mistake.'

Alice pondered, briefly thinking back to the previous case meetings and the evidence on Davey Markwell's smartphone, namely the mutilated dog pictures, as well as the group chat.

'I don't suppose there was any evidence of dog fighting going on up there was there Diane?'

'Nothing jumped out immediately. Looked like storage for them: cages, feed, blankets etc. Animal welfare team from the council had been called in, think they were being rounded up and taken down to our kennels for a check with whatever vets the dog unit use. I didn't think anything of it. The initial attending officer had called it in for forensics, then when DI Jamieson turned up it just died out. Packed it up mostly and left the scene not long after.'

Odd, how Alex had turned up: must have been a slow Saturday Alice thought to herself, didn't have him pegged as taking an interest in animals. Only the golf course and his own career.

'Okay, well that's enough I guess. I'll see if I can attend the post-mortem, and you be sure to let me know when the digital files come back. If I can link these two cases, I'll get more manpower and a bigger overtime budget, instead of Andy Jordan sitting in over the weekend by himself, scratching his arse and getting crisp crumbs on the case notes.'

Diane laughed. She had previous with Andy Jordan, amicable enough, but the image of him scattering his pack lunch over case files wasn't a world away from her encounters with him.

They exchanged goodbyes and Alice let the officer out, shutting the door behind her as she went. Instead of sitting down, she went over to the window and looked out over the houses to the country park.

Was this the same attacker? Could it all be related to dog fighting? And if so, what had caused the sudden vendetta? Surely a small dog couldn't spark such venom, could it? No, there had to be another angle Alice thought, had to be.

Chapter Thirty-One

Andy was in a good mood. His brother had come through on tickets for the match last night, and although frozen to marrow by a sharp wind flooding through the Gallowgate, it had been a solid win. A solid night out. Even if it was just the League Cup.

He knocked on DI Rose's door, entering after the call from within.

'Afternoon ma'am,' he sat down presumptively, 'I've got the digital forensics back for Macfarlane's phone. Didn't take much, no deletions, all there once they unlocked it.'

'And?'

'Good and bad news. We can tie him to the dog-fighting group easily enough. He's our 'RM' in the BloodSport group chat, previously active, his albums full of some awful pictures of dogs — not too far away from the stuff we found on Markwell's phone.'

'And the bad news?'

'Well, it's clearly a burner with nothing much else on there. He's been deleted from the chat, and probably not long after he was murdered from what I can tell. Externally though there's none of the spy work we saw with Davey from Phone X, so it looks like they're getting wise, deleting as they go.'

'Shame, still at least we have the promise of Simon Trench's device I guess. Any big updates after Markwell? We haven't had any insight into the group for at least ten days, any chat from them about Davey's murder?'

'Unfortunately not ma'am. If anything the chat's been quiet recently, there was an uproar after Davey but it soon settled down, not entirely sure they missed him too much. Not much of anything from anyone. A few bits of social here and there but no plans or organising. Like we reckoned maybe it's not the main thread, or the big players discuss their business elsewhere on other devices. Last event on the phone is a video call from 'J', and that's about it, all goes quiet not long after. No messages or anything though to suggest what it was about.'

'Or they're not stupid, and knew we'd find it eventually and stopped incriminating themselves, knew we'd be reading it for clues. Makes me wonder why the GPS is still active though, maybe they don't reckon on us being that smart, or you think they're keeping it all going for Phone X? Anything which might be a set of breadcrumbs on there for whoever this infiltrator is?'

'Not so much ma'am. But I guess we don't know what's been going on since Macfarlane caught it.'

'This is true. They had Davey as a one off and were happy to let it slide. They must be bricking themselves now Macfarlane is gone. From what I can gather he was the muscle in all this, must have taken something almighty to bring him down so easily. Any other messages on there, any instructions or anything to send him to the farm that day?'

'No it's a clean phone. Like I say, probably his burner phone and the personal is sitting at home somewhere. If they're as tech literate as we suspect, he left it behind to keep his digital footprint static. Only extra on there is random chat with some girl called Carly, not entirely sure it's relevant ma'am. If we can get a warrant and search his property it might have what we need on there. Think it's possible?'

'Anything's possible Andy when you're owed a few favours. Leave it with me, in the meantime I want to turn the screw on that smart-arse Simon Trench. I think it's time to play our trump card with him; tell him what we know and see what excuses he can come up with, there's enough on the group chat to more than shake him up don't you think?'

Andy nodded, trying not to show he too was excited by the opportunity to have another crack at Trench.

'See if we can't catch him by surprise somewhere, I don't want that cute solicitor Trevor Jackson keeping him out of trouble either, for all we know he's the one reporting it all back to the rest of the group. No, the sooner we get him sat at a table with a stock legal advisor the better. Not exactly fair police work but we need the run on him before the lawyer shuts it down. If he drops a name on our suspect, it'll unravel this whole group quicker than you can say doggy day-care.'

'You want to get a warrant on his home address as well, in case he's hiding something else?'

'No no, I think he'll crack fine without it. Go pick him up and I'll see about getting one on Macfarlane's sorted out instead, that's where the treasure will be. If Trench drops a stinker we'll hold him and search his house while he's in the cells.'

Andy stood up and left, while Alice picked up the phone and began organising the warrant paperwork, one she would carry out herself as soon as it was sent over, so long as the judge was in a better mood than her previous encounter with him. Something about Simon Trench told her she'd enjoy playing with him this time. She had him right where she wanted him — she was sure of it.

***

It turned out to be an hour later when she was given the chance. It hadn't taken DC Jordan long to track him down to a local garage, panel beating an old Mondeo out in the back yard. By all accounts he hadn't been over the moon to see Andy stroll round the corner, warrant card in hand. But here he was, settled in interview room three; this time having declined the offer of a machine coffee.

'Simon. Good of you to join us. Sorry we couldn't contact your solicitor, but seeing as this is an informal chat you'll be okay with the duty won't you? There's a lad.'

Alice turned the interview machine on.

'Just mostly going over old ground on this one, we do appreciate you coming in.'

Simon Trench was a lot more uptight this time around, and on guard to Alice's faux friendly attitude. He was dressed in an oil-stained hoodie, the grime under his fingernails suggesting he hadn't had time to consider much of an excuse before being ushered to the station in a patrol car. Better to go quietly than kick up a fuss in front of his new employer he had thought, and he had picked up his day sack and keys and got in the car.

'Divvin' think there's anything new I'm gan add like. Still can'nt say I know any more about Davey than last time, damn shame for the guy like but divvin' see how I can help to be honest.'

'Oh, I don't know about that, a few more things have come up. Are we going to dance around like last time, or will you admit you're friends with Ronnie Macfarlane as well as David Markwell?'

Simon leaned back in his chair and held his hands up in front of the detectives.

'Whoa, look man alreet. First Davey now Ronnie, I barely kna the guys, okay? Yeah see them in the pub like, bit of business with Davey back in the day ya kna, but I divvin' know why I'm in the shop getting asked questions about them.'

'You're aware Ronnie was found murdered at Berryhill farm a few days ago are you, enough of a mate to know that?'

'Look I'm nay idiot, course I heard about it like, half the town's talking about it. Hard to keep them quiet when it's a mad nutter like Ronnie like. Just cause I kna the guys though, doesn't mean I kna what happened does it?'

He looked down and exhaled. The solicitor looked confused, out of her depth, but kept a gaze on her notebook, writing a few more lines.

'You were all more than just mates though weren't you, Simon?' Andy opened his case file in front of him. Alice had agreed to let him have this part of the interview. If the junior officer can outsmart you heaven knows what cards the DI is holding.

'Seems like you've been holding back on us…'

Simon looked up and sneered at Andy.

'Look mate, pardon me French, but fuck off yeah? Getting sick of the smarmy looks sitting above that cheap suit.'

Andy recoiled but came back quickly enough, pulling out a stack of A4 sheets and placing them on the table, rotating them slowly to face Simon before pushing them across the table.

'The name 'BloodSport' mean anything to you Simon?'

Simon froze like a pint of ice cubes had been spilled down his back, before placing an elbow on the table and leaning across, managing to regain his composure. The beads of sweat forming still gave him away however.

'Can'nt say I do pal. What's that when it's at home like?'

Andy pushed on, pointing at the numbers on the sheet.

'None of these phone numbers or names mean anything to you, not this one, 'ST'?'

Andy pointed at Simon's own number on the page, scrolling across to his own texts in the group chat transcript. 'Quite the exciting read this group chat isn't it DI Rose.'

'Nope, nowt mate. Think ye've got the wrong lad as usual like.'

He looked at Alice with a raised eyebrow, a sneer escaping from the side of his mouth as he changed the subject.

'Fucking hilarious when you fucked up at Ronnie's trial man, I were laughing all day when I heard about it. Fucking pigs man.'

Simon stood up, looking calmly at his fingernails as he moved to the door. Still playing it all remarkably cool Alice thought, worryingly so.

'Look if all ye've got are bits of paper wi random phone numbers and code names I think I'll be off like. Divvin' think I'm under arrest here, so I'll be leaving if that's okay like.' He turned to his lawyer, 'Alreet with you ringer?'

As he turned and put his hand on the door handle, a phone rang out. Padding down his leg, he reached into the side pocket on his right. Pulling out a mobile he looked at the screen, *'CALLER WITHHELD'*.

He looked up at Alice, holding her own ringing phone, pointing the screen at him.

'Still think it's not you in the group chat Simon?'

This time there was no playing it safe for Simon Trench. The colour drained from his face, the oil stains highlighting it even more.

'Now sit down before I arrest you for obstructing police business.'

He looked at the door, clearly weighing up his chances of getting out unscathed. She could sense what he was thinking.

'If you think you'll make it back through the custody suite without being stopped Simon you've another thing coming. Now sit.'

He obliged, sinking back down in his chair and placing both hands on the table, palms up.

'Look alright man ye've got to believe me, I'm nowt to do with what's happened to Davey and Ronnie alright, I'm as much in the dark as you are, nay one tells me anything like, it's a social group, nowt happens from it. C'mon guys, look at me man, ye think I could take down a big fucker like Ronnie? Guy was a beast man for god's sake.'

'So why have we got locations on there you're linked to, locations with blood spatter and dog chains? Locations linked directly to your name? We've got you named here as going to check on a dog kennel. Same kennel gets phoned in by a 'concerned citizen', same kennel where your friend Macfarlane turns up murdered four days later. C'mon Simon, pull the other one, you're up to your neck in this mess, and now someone's tearing through you one by one, picking you off, watching your group and taking you at will. Trust me, the more you help us the more we can help you before you go down the same dark hole as Davey and Ronnie.'

'Aye and what's in it for me exactly, I rat them out an help you, I'm next on the list, either theirs or his, it dissn't matter man.'

'And who is this mystery figure exactly?'

'I divvin' know honestly, I'm not exactly high on the pecking order in this thing of ours am I like, all I know is some lad is pissed off at us, and ain't exactly been shy in coming forward like. Honestly, ye've got to believe me man. Nay one's talking to little Simon like. They divvin' tell me anything: only know things when I need to know, that's how they like to keep it man.'

He picked at the dirt under his thumbnail, wiping it on the table.

'All I got told was to act normal and they would get it all sorted like, I reckons they know who it is but they ain't letting on.'

'And so who exactly is 'they'? Your bosses, your mates? Come on Simon, you expect us to leave it? You think they won't throw you under a bus as soon as look at you? No one knows you're here; if you let us know we'll look favourably on it when it comes to the Crown Prosecution Service — a good word from us and I doubt you'll see any charges. Like you say, what have we got against you, all we want is the murderer.'

'Trust me chicken they'll find out soon enough I was here, I know how it works in a place like this, nay one can keep things like this quiet for long, you divvin' kna who you're dealing with.'

'It's not 'chicken', it's Detective Inspector Rose, and I can assure you this investigation is fully watertight Simon.'

Alice wasn't so sure however, the missing CCTV, a nagging feeling someone was watching her every step in the investigation, the confidence brewing across the table from her again.

'Watertight like your case against Macfarlane that fell through? I weren't joking; we all had a good laugh about it like, and not only because it were funny, but the look on your face in court when it happened man. They were good enough to let me in on it like. Trust me 'Inspector', there's things in play here, things I'm gan to stay on the right side of, and from where I'm sitting it ain't talking to ye like.'

The elation of hitting Simon with BloodSport had all but gone.

Was someone sabotaging her from the inside or was this just a clever bluff to throw her off the scent? She wasn't sure anymore, especially with the smug interviewee sat across from her, arms folded over his chest, puffed out and ready for round two. Would Simon be capable of this intelligent play? She began to question herself; she'd been so sure he'd crack under pressure, yet here he was again matching her at her own game. A back street panel beater, grimy and grinning over the tabletop at her.

'I'll take it on board Mr Trench. But I'd choose carefully who you intend to side with in the future, people have a habit of making mistakes in my experience, and trust me, I'm there to catch them when they do.'

The interview had clearly come to a stalemate, even the bewildered solicitor who had no idea what she'd walked into was packing up her writing pad and tucking a pen into her breast pocket.

'If you want to come clean Simon and talk to us before this gets too big for you, you let us know. Sounds like you're in bed with the wrong people, if this attacker doesn't get you, your friends will.'

'Look officers, nay offence like, but knowing what I do, I'd rather take me chances out there on the streets than in here with ye lot any day. At least I've got a fighting chance out there, not like in here like some daft cunt waiting for it. Nah, not a chance I'm talking like, ye can stick your deals where the sun divvin' shine. Come get me when ye've got something decent, cause it seems yer all talk. Am I wrong like? Fucking pair of ye man, look at ye's.'

He wasn't wrong. Everyone knew it. He soon walked out, trailed by his solicitor, no doubt never to meet again. Alice shut the door and turned to Andy.

'We can kiss the group chat goodbye, and no point in tracking those burner phones either, they'll be destroyed before the day's out if he runs back to them. Damn it. I really thought he'd turn.'

'What did he mean by all that 'powers we didn't know about' stuff ma'am? Think he's grasping at straws to cover his own back or is there some truth to it? All the sitting in here like a lame duck stuff, who's he scared of if it isn't our attacker?'

'I'm not sure Andy, bit of a curveball, and a specific one for that matter. This doesn't go beyond these four walls for now. I need to have think about how we proceed; this and the CCTV nonsense has got me wondering about a few things.'

'Okay boss. Under the hat. Mum's the word.'

'Your mum and your Granny DC Jordan. Not a peep.'

Chapter Thirty-Two

A cold machine coffee was down to its dregs, and idling between emails, Alice had a cloud in her brain. One that caffeine wasn't shifting. Nothing was.

She had been filling out performance reviews. Slowly.

She was also trying, and failing, not to think about Simon Trench and the trainwreck of an interview yesterday. Self-satisfied idiot. She could forget Chief Inspector if that dimwit could derail her so easily. What was wrong with her this month?

The door knocked and Andy Jordan's head appeared.

'Please tell me you're making progress Andy, I'm going round in circles with this mystery man's motive.'

'Some ma'am, mostly background, but possibly something. I've been digging into that dog like you asked, the one found dead, the one Davey gets mentioned for in the group chat and seems to be heavily linked to. Turns out some useful stuff after all.'

Alice closed her laptop.

'I'm listening.'

'Ok so I punched it into the call log for those few days when it's on the chat, and sure enough, it was picked up by an Animal Welfare team at the council and taken to the local vets, where it was pronounced dead. Some vet there reckoned it was intentional, throat cut and punctured lungs or something, so the council worker phoned the police and reported it as suspicious. Part of a bigger concern potentially for the public, potential maniac on the loose practising on animals, 'escalation' was the word used in the initial contact report. So anyway, uniform goes out and takes a statement from the Welfare officer, and files it for CID to follow up.'

'And was it followed up?'

'Well, this is the awkward part, it's taken up by one of the DCs on Jamieson's team for the initial work up. Case opened, interview with the previous owner, informal interview with the Animal Welfare officer, file written up. Case closed.'

'And the outcome?'

'Well, that's it. I spoke to the DC, and DI Jamieson set it on the back burner, didn't think there was enough to take to the CPS until there was more evidence or chance of a prosecution. Apparently when they talked to the previous owners the description matched well enough to Markwell, so being murdered and all they happily called it a dead end, an isolated incident.'

'And they didn't pick it up as a potential motive and think to send it our way, who was this DC?'

'Well I asked ma'am. Turns out the last owner is some old biddy, and the son, Carl he's called, was scared half to death of Markwell. Suspicion was he'd had the frighteners put on him, wasn't capable of it, wasn't keen on talking about it either. Thought it was a bit of a quick conclusion myself. Got the feeling the DC was of the same mind as well, but Jamieson, sorry, DI Jamieson had left it there to come back to. Don't think he was too interested in a dead dog was the thinking.'

'Did you speak to the Animal Welfare officer?'

'Well, it got passed up the chain there as well, to some head of department, Steve someone or other. Tried tracking him down but he never seems to be at his desk or capable of returning a phone call for that matter. I'll keep at him, but I think he's given up on it as well. Like he doesn't want the work of uncovering a dog fighting ring on his patch.'

'Well look, why don't I see if I can find him, harder to avoid two of us I suspect. Nothing else from the initial report to the police, the one from the junior welfare officer?'

'Not especially ma'am. The dog was pretty beat up, had its throat slit apparently.'

'Like Markwell.'

'Ma'am?'

'Markwell had his throat cut, the final injury, or at least what Dr Ballingry thought at the post-mortem. Anything else, any chest injuries noted?'

'Not specifically included on the report, just the mention of a punctured lung by the vet in the contact report. I gather they need to authorise a post-mortem from management, it's not cheap apparently. They send them off to one of the big universities and not much change from a grand for a doggy PM apparently. Bit of a stretch for the average council budget, especially when there's no one to chase a conviction against.'

'It does makes me think the attack on Davey was linked, I mean after all, who cuts throats if not to make a statement? Eye for an eye potentially? And the lung thing.'

She shuddered at the thought of it again, thinking back to the words of Donald Ballingry: '*snap crackled and popped from the internal pressure*'.

'I think it's worth talking to the family again, the son, Carl. Make sure he's not some closet hero in his spare time. If it stinks, we'll get a warrant, okay? If he's sitting on a burner phone it's case closed for Markwell.'

'Will do ma'am. Will you speak to DI Jamieson, or should I?'

'I'll tackle Alex. He knows he can't fob me off that easily.'

Andy headed out and shut the door. The news was encouraging and discouraging in equal measures. It strengthened the motive linking Markwell and the dog, but it sounded like more dead ends were being thrown up left right and centre. The lack of proper follow up set them back, as would the evidence trail which was steadily going cold, if she could even work out where the dog was. But at least there were new avenues for them to explore, not just a ghost appearing in a group of untraceable burner phones.

'Alex, it's Alice, have you got a minute?'

'Yeah, on the phone though; I'm out on a case, can't rush up and fall into your loving arms if that's what you're after?'

Alice winced at the thought.

'On the phone is fine Alex.'

She waited while he talked away from the phone, giving direction to another officer before coming on the line.

'Okay I'm all yours, how can I help?'

'I think one of your team picked up a lead from council Animal Welfare a while ago, dog found dead and taken into the vets by one of the junior officers, referred to us as a potential escalation concern given the nature of the injuries.'

'Oh yeah, dead end, I didn't have anything to do with it apart from looking at the paperwork: not enough for the CPS so we called it quits, file's still there, barely open, just nowhere to go with it sadly. Shame.'

'And you didn't think to mention to me it traced back to Davey Markwell, seems he was the one took it away from the owner for a promise of a better life, then put the wind right up them when they came asking about it after the fact.'

'Look Davey was no angel, what's it got to do with his murder though? As far as the DC could tell he just adopted the dog off them. The whole family was a whole bunch of wet lettuces. Last he spoke to them they wanted no more action taken on it. I hardly think they mounted a vigilante group for the sake of a mutt Alice.'

'I've got evidence here suggesting it was Davey killed and dumped it. I also know both Davey and the dog had their throats slit, got to be more than a coincidence don't you think?'

'Come off it Alice, guy was a loser, probably had a hundred enemies. I doubt anyone was going to get too worked up over a small dog.'

'Did you get any word back from the senior Animal Welfare officer, this Steve? Any other suspicious activity they're picking up on in the region? One of our potential angles is Davey was mixed up in organised dog fighting, you heard anything along those lines?'

'I can't say I have Alice,' Alex shouted away from the phone, something about witness statements, coming back with a whisper. 'Pardon the stereotype, I thought it was all cockney gangsters and travelers did that stuff. Look if it helps, I'll chase it up again if it makes you feel any better, but don't hold your breath. I think this Steve might knock around at the golf club, if I can't get him officially I'll see if I can catch him there: if one of my DCs has dropped the ball on it you've got my word I'll be first in line to kick his arse, sound okay?'

She sighed; if it was Alex's old boys' network, it was better than nothing.

'Okay but keep me in the loop, this is important, I don't want it being one of those things I have to come chasing you for weeks down the line, you hear anything you let me know, okay?'

'I will be straight on the phone, day or night Alice.'

'Creep. I'll talk to you later.'

Alice hung up. She hated being reliant on colleagues, but she would have to wait on this one. If the case was linked to organised dog fighting, she didn't want to go antagonising the region's animal welfare team and getting the cold shoulder, or worse, the murder being handed to the supervision of Alex as part of an on-going case he'd inflated to boost his own work ego. No, she'd wait it out a few days and see what he could come back with.

Later, as she was leaving for home, Andy called.

'Just checking in ma'am. I tracked down the family, the little dog? They weren't overly keen to talk to me, but I got a bit out of the son Carl, the one who was mentioned. He was sure enough it was Davey took the dog off their hands in the first place, but after that he was all a bit shy with the details.'

The sound of a car unlocking and opening came down the line, and a pause while Andy eased into the seat, a small groan as a seatbelt was pulled round and clicked into place.

'Think the whole thing hurt his pride if I'm honest, which is fair enough; getting your mum's dog killed isn't exactly one for the family compendium. Asked him if Davey had been in contact after the incident, he reckoned he hadn't, but I could tell he wanted the whole thing going away. Got an alibi to check for the murder but it sounds watertight: working away on a specialist construction job down south for a week; the same week Davey was getting his throat cut.'

Alice murmured. Not a positive reassurance for her junior.

'I think DI Jamieson was right ma'am, he sounds like a dead end. The family have been tight lipped about the whole thing, so unless the animal welfare team is suddenly out dealing retribution, it's all making this revenge motive a little weaker.'

'Ok thanks Andy. Get home and have a night off; good work today I'll see you tomorrow.'

'Thanks ma'am. Bright and early.'

He rang off. Alice liked DC Jordan. Not the sharpest in the office but he could put a shift in when it counted and his instincts were good enough, lacking in logic every now and then, but it would come.

Back to square one on her attacker however. Alex was smarmy and smooth, but he wasn't one to run a poor investigation. If his DC had done the digging, chances are it had been done right. She sighed. There was nothing like the excitement of a case unfolding before your eyes, and there was also nothing like the hollow despair when the same leads slammed shut again. She knew another long night of head scratching lay ahead, so buttoning up her overcoat and flicking the light switch, she put a hand on the door, ready to leave for the drive home. She patted her breast pocket. Empty.

'Bloody phone.'

She stepped back to the desk and leaned over to pick it up, looking back up at the white board on the wall as she turned, now cast in shadow with a lonely single column of light hitting it from the streetlights. It had picked out three words. The three words she had written after her phone call with Dr Ballingry.

Medical.

Symbolism.

Punishment.

It dawned on her. The words from Donald echoing around in her head, the thick Scottish accent spelling it out as she stood alone in the darkness, *'find out if he's pissed off some doctor or ICU nurse if I were you, not many other people would be capable of that I imagine.'*

The fleeting, graphic image of Davey on the mortuary slab, head turned, eyes open staring at her above an open chest accompanied the voice.

'Dogs you idiot. Dogs. Who helps dogs.'

She fumbled around in the dark for the marker pen, eager not to lose her train of thought. Making her way over she flicked the plastic top off, sending it tumbling down on to the carpet and under the desk where it would lay until tomorrow.

Thick, bold capitals spelled out her fourth word on the list:

Only three letters.

'Vet.'

Chapter Thirty-Three

Friday morning, after a night of racing thoughts and disrupted sleep, Alice walked through the front entrance of the council's main regional office on her way to the third floor.

It was a drab, red bricked millennial building, aching with over-spend.

She'd left Andy back at the office for this one, setting him loose on the background checks for her new hunch from the evening before. She had also spied the substantial snack pile he'd brought and had wanted to make sure ground zero stayed firmly at his desk, not scattered on her passenger seat.

She had phoned ahead to make sure Steve was going to be in, confirming as much again as she enquired at the reception desk, before being directed upstairs to the shared office. It didn't take long before he appeared, lanyard around his neck, sitting itself over a neat shirt and tie.

'Hi Steve, my name's Detective Inspector Alice Rose, I was wondering if I could ask you a few questions about a case you've been overseeing?'

'Can do, not sure how much help I'll be, I'm generally here to oversee the office work and admin, don't see too much time out on the street these days.'

'Oh sorry, I was told you were the man to speak to about this one, a small dog found mutilated a few weeks back. I was informed you had taken over the investigation from a junior officer that's all; it might be relevant to a case I'm working on; wondering if I could take a few more details to correlate?'

'Oh right, that one. I remember nothing much came of it if I'm honest, followed up its microchip to an old lady, said she'd rehomed it on Gumtree. Well, her son had anyway, she was mad at him for obvious reasons when we'd explained what happened to it. I never did track the son down though, quite the elusive character.'

'And any ideas if it was linked to something else, any clues? Quite a grim discovery even around these parts, can't be a common occurrence can it, that kind of thing?'

'Can't say anything else has come up, sorry I can't be of any more help.'

He moved to get away but Alice persisted, drawing him back in.

'Anything else suspicious lately while you've been out and about?'

'Like I say officer, I'm usually stuck behind a desk in here most of the day, don't see much sunlight until it's time to hit the road at five. I went through all this with the Detective Constable when it first came up, what was his name? Ah I can't remember, young fella, in a rush, keen to tie up all the loose ends and be out of here, can't say I was blown away by his work ethic mind.'

'Did you mention it to anyone else in the office? You discuss the injuries with anyone else apart from the Detective? Or anyone else come asking about it for that matter?'

'No, it was all over and done with after the first statement, I didn't have anything else to chase up, and given it was on your lot's radar I figured it best not get too involved in case I messed up an on-going investigation, you know how it is.'

'And you haven't come across Mr Markwell before?'

'Can't say I have darling.'

Alice pushed on,

'The name Simon Trench mean anything to you Steve, he come up in conversation anywhere around town?'

'Look Inspector, I can't add anything extra to what the young DC hasn't already taken away. If you've nothing else I better be getting on with the office work, okay?'

The conversation fizzled out soon after, despite her persistence, with Steve making his excuses and striding back to his office, leaving her with the only option to turn and head back down to her car, muttering as she went.

'That's a council salary I could do without paying for.'

It was looking like a pointless visit after all.

Making her way down the stairs, pausing only to let a porter past with a particularly heavy looking box of files, she pushed open the double doors and walked over to her car. The grey, darkening skies overhead reflecting her mood.

About halfway though she turned, the sound of footsteps running up behind her.

A young woman, baggily clad in a reflective vest and khaki combats, stopped about three metres away, out of breath. Attractive in an un-cared for way Alice thought. Her perfume drifted over.

'Sorry officer, sorry to rush up on you, I couldn't help overhearing your conversation with the boss, Steve?'

'Oh yes, and you are?'

'Sorry,' she looked flustered, still breathing hard. 'My name's Skye, I'm one of the Animal Welfare team. I was initially involved with the dog you were talking about that's all. I'm not normally like this, but I couldn't help but think Steve wasn't being too helpful with you.'

Skye went on to explain about speaking to the son, and the horrific injuries to the dog.

'And then Steve, well, just took over. Shut me out. Said he'd be dealing with it from there on in. Hasn't mentioned it since. Normally you can't shut the guy up: likes to know what you're up to, what you've been doing, who you've been talking to for your cases. Controlling, but in a nice way, like you can go to him for advice if you need it, no problem. But this, shut the whole thing down. I asked him about it again a few days ago, being worried about dog fighting and all, and he just snapped at me to stay out of it. Said it was 'in hand'.'

She nervously toyed with a lock of blonde hair, tucking it behind an ear and smoothing it down.

'I'd seen him talking to the other police officer, the one who flashed a badge at the reception desk who he looked all chummy with, it was like old buddies the way they were carrying on. But apart from that nothing. Same thing with the dogs up at Berryhill farm. I was first to respond to the call, but next thing I know he's taken care of it and I'm back on stray cat duty.'

'Berryhill farm? What do you know about it?'

'Member of the public called in a concern about dogs being mistreated. I turned up to find them all in the farm shed, I'm not there an hour before Steve turns up and sends me on another errand. He was hopping mad I'd called the police. I was thinking it was to do with more dog fighting, told me to stop interfering and get on my way, stop 'making mountains out of molehills' he called it. Honestly, he's been acting all sorts of weird recently.'

Skye looked down at her feet and fumbled with her lanyard.

'To be honest, it's not the only thing. I should have reported it at the time, but not long after the first dog I got attacked while I was out having a break in the van. Nothing too serious, shook me up enough though. Guy told me to leave the thing well alone, the 'bin dog' he called it, or I'd be getting another visit. Told me he'd be bringing the dogs.'

Alice, not known for her tactility, reached out a hand of reassurance, resting it on Skye's shoulder.

'Listen, nothing's too small to come to the police, certainly not that. I can get someone to speak to you if you want? Even if it just helps you get closure okay? Can you remember any details?'

'No, it was all so quick I can't remember too much. I just don't know how they knew who I was, I only picked the thing up and took it to the vets before it died, asked the old owner a few questions before Steve took it over. God, if I could just leave the whole mess alone.'

The lock of hair had made its way loose again and was brushing against her cheek, below eyes beginning to redden.

'Sorry, I shouldn't have bothered you; I don't want it taken further I just want someone to understand I think something bigger is going on. No one seems to be listening to me — the way Steve's been going on I wouldn't be surprised if he's been threatened as well, he's been nothing but irritable the past few days, nothing at all like his normal self.'

Skye's tough exterior had slipped, and the red eyes had finally given way to tears.

'You must think I'm an idiot.'

'Not at all. Not at all.' Alice withdrew her hand and reached into her inside pocket for a card. 'We can do whatever you feel comfortable with for the attack okay. It's entirely up to you. You only need to call and I can make it happen. You need to promise me though you won't think it's a bother, it's what we're here for.'

She held out the card.

'And if you think of any more details you need to let me know. It might be a bigger help than you think.'

Skye took it and turned it over in her hand, smiling.

'We want you to feel safe. And Steve as well, okay? No matter how moody he is.'

'Thank-you.' she smiled, 'You've been much more helpful than the other policeman. Wouldn't even stop to hear a word once he was done speaking to Steve, I don't think he was taking it too seriously.'

'Well look I'll have a word with the DC. I know it was the one of the younger officers, I'll remind them not to be so rushed. You know what these up and comers are like, think they can do everything in a hurry. You have my word we're not all so hasty.'

Skye reached into the pocket on her cargo pants and pulled out another business card.

'He didn't come across as green, bit older when I think back.' Squinting down at the card. 'He tossed me this though on his way past. DI Alex Jamieson. Bit of a creep if I'm honest. I assume he's one of yours.'

'Uh yes, yes of course. I know Alex. Sorry, I thought it was a younger officer who had been following this one up.'

She turned the card over in her hand before handing it back to Skye. Alex had written his personal mobile on the back, underlined.

'One more thing Skye, you must meet all sorts of people in your line of work, you work much alongside vets? Had a name come up this morning, local guy, works not far from here, I think he looked at the first dog you had turn up, Mac his name is. You had much to do with him?"

'Mac? Yeah, sure, all the time. Looks at most of my cases for me when I ask him to, why?'

Skye's heart quickened a pace. A fleeting memory of their embrace in the car park after Markwell's threats. Feeling safe and warm. Feeling like Davey meant nothing when Mac was around.

'It's nothing really, his name has come up with something I'm looking at. Couldn't work the guy out for myself, mysterious lot those vets it turns out. You know him outside of work at all?'

'Only that he keeps himself to himself, nice life out in the country with his partner. Always helpful though, nice guy if you need help with anything, sure he'd have a chat with you if you caught up with him. Is it about the terrier? Was there anything new?'

'Potentially. Just a tenuous link I thought he could have helped with. Anyway, like I say, yet to catch up with him. Best not to mention it if you see him. You keep that card safe, and let me know if you change your mind on taking things further? Nothing's a bother, okay?'

She made excuses to leave, turning back to carry on across the car park and over to her car. As she got in she tossed the work folder on the front seat and stared ahead, the key hovering in front of the ignition. She paused, thinking back to the business card Skye had shown her. Strange, she thought, she could have sworn it was a DC doing the investigation. What had Alex been going on about before? He clearly had her pegged for an idiot if he thought she wasn't going to follow up her leads on a murder case.

'Honestly this job, may as well work in a bloody primary school sometimes.'

Realising she was talking to nobody but the car stereo, she turned the key, the engine coming to life after a brief stutter, and she decided to let it settle while she checked her phone's inbox. At least one bit of good news had come her way, the warrant on Macfarlane's property had finally been authorised by the local magistrate. She dialled the number for Andy Jordan and he picked up after three rings, clearly eating his pack lunch.

'Andy put your crisps down, the warrant came through for Ronnie. The magistrate must have changed his mind about me. Out front in ten, I'm driving.'

She swung round to the entrance of the council car park and out into the main road, no sign of Skye anymore, presumably she'd gone back inside or headed off on her own break.

She mulled over their conversation as she drove south. It was a big deal to threaten her over the dog, but if it was Markwell, it backed up the theory he'd been out making waves, pointing the finger and making threats. Trouble was, had he threatened the wrong person, or was his own group finally fed up with him: hiding their revenge amongst a rogue vigilante story?

The cogs kept whirring as she pulled into the station, slowing for the barrier to rise and let her in, and soon enough she was met by the sight of Andy Jordan on the kerbside, brushing light coloured crumbs from his suit. He ducked down and opened the door as she approached.

'You have the warrant ma'am?'

'Certainly do, pain in the arse the delay getting it from the judge, I think he's still looking down on me since the trial collapse. Anyway, get in, better late than never I suppose. You better not be trailing sandwich crumbs in here young man.'

Alice urged him on to the front seat. It was a clean car, albeit dated. Andy looked concerned.

'You ever think about upgrading the wheels ma'am?' struggling round to find the seatbelt behind him. 'Some pretty good deals out there you know, something fitting the image of a potential DCI.'

'There's nothing wrong with 'the wheels' DC Jordan. Perhaps I've better things to spend my money on than leaseholds for expensive German cars. You might be able to upgrade those suits if you took more care of your monthlies by the way.'

'Point taken ma'am.'

Andy looked ahead and flattened down his tie. His girlfriend had bought him the suit.

'So, what is it we're looking for anyway?'

'Well, I want to look around for starters. See if we can't find a personal mobile to back up the idea he was sent there by a higher power, or powers. The burner phones are probably a dead end now, even deader once Simon Trench got home and blew the whistle on them.'

She grunted, struggling with a difficult gear as they edged off from a traffic light.

'I wouldn't complain if we happened across anything from the drugs trial either, something to counteract my disaster in court would be handy. Speaking of which, if there was someone feeding him inside information about cases I want to know about it, I don't mind telling you that smug git Trench rubbed me up the wrong way with his smarmy boasting. He'll live to regret it. Or not if we don't catch this attacker.'

'Yeah, that was a funny one, especially with the CCTV going missing on Markwell.'

'Exactly Andy. Sooner I iron it out the better as far as I'm concerned.'

'You're not wrong.'

'So anyway, did you get the background on the vet, that Mac guy I wanted this morning?'

He nodded, taking out a notebook and leafing over to the pages near the rear. She could see lines of handwriting, interspersed with question marks and arrows, his usual mind map of thought processes: sometimes useful, sometimes not.

'Yeah. Took a bit of digging I must say, few phone calls and waited a bit for people to get back to me. Turns out he's not your usual fluffy James Herriot, I mean don't get me wrong, nothing horrendous lurking, but I don't think I'd mess around too much with him. No record on file but there is a warning from Police Scotland on record north of the border.'

'Oh?'

'I'll come back to that ma'am. Anyway, he's had a normal upbringing, family of farmers up in North Fife, he gets a scholarship to a private school which sees him all the way through to university, place at the vet college in Edinburgh. Fast forward five years and he's joined the army after graduation, Officer school then into the Veterinary Corps, does his time with the military dogs down south then takes a tour to Afghanistan along the way. Doesn't seem shy either ma'am, supporting the dog units at forward bases for six months. He wasn't sat brushing parade horses back at Sandringham ma'am — proper down and dirty in the desert.'

'Jeez. Didn't realise the army even had that.' Alice stared ahead at the dual carriageway.

'Not all ma'am. Tracked down his superior in the Veterinary Corps. Turns out, three months after they returned to base in the UK he had his application in for SAS Selection.'

'Eh? Isn't that soldiers only? How's a vet doing that?'

'Turns out no, anyone can apply if you're in the Army, and this guy did. Made it all the way through the first phase, the nasty beasting part down in Hereford you see on the tele.'

'So, what's he doing here in Northumberland? Bit of a change in direction, no?'

'Well, that's it. Finished the first phase on one attempt, before getting himself hospitalised in Hereford, details weren't all there on paper, but the gist of it was a head injury and then unfit for active duty; he got medically discharged and returned to his unit. Served his time out then took the civilian option. Looks like he moved up here for a job and stayed put. Hasn't found any trouble either from what I could tell.'

'And the police caution, from north of the border?'

'Probably nothing ma'am. Sounds like they weren't too interested. It's down as a self-defence but he still ended up with a decent talking to. Nearly went to court until the Procurator Fiscal up there saw sense.'

Alice indicated left, onto the dual carriageway.

'Well, turns out he was on a night out in Edinburgh, walking home with a group of mates back to halls in first year. Crossing the Meadows they're set on by a group of blokes out for a fight, picking on the easy student targets, only this guy Mac doesn't see it that way. Knocks three of them clean out and breaks the other one's arm on the way down. Didn't run though, called the police and waited for the ambulance: apparently they turned up and he good as shrugged his shoulders, said they had it coming.'

'Took out four attackers?'

'Well, he's 6ft5 ma'am. All solid farm boy as well, used to pushing cattle about all day. Seems genuine though, popped them all once and called 999, like I say, almost got taken to court until they saw sense and realised he was just defending the group he was with. Took them months to drop the charges though, can't have been a fun wait for him.'

'No, still. Nice guy or not, we're talking a capable individual even back then, never mind stick him in the army and put him into SAS Selection. What you thinking, we got enough to bring him in for a chat?'

'I dunno ma'am, up to you, I still can't see it though. Guy spends his day playing with cats and dogs before heading back to his nice house in the countryside. What's he want to get involved with all this for? And besides, how would he know who to go after?'

'Isn't there a mention of him in the group chat? Davey wants to have a go at him?'

Alice's mind flashed back to the words in her office. Punishment, Symbolism.

'Quickly warned off though remember. I think they had the sense to leave him alone.'

'Not if Davey went rogue though and tried something off the books.'

She thought about Skye's words, her attack in the layby.

'Potentially.'

'Right, well before we go disturbing the local vet population and looking ridiculous, I want you to go do more digging, write this down okay: I want bank statements, any unusual purchases, specifically phones or anything that might come close to a forensic clean up kit for Markwell. It's tenuous but I'll need more background. And find the commanding officer again, see if we can't get any more information on him okay, anything pointing back to more violence. If he' a suspect, we need to know why: you don't escalate from your normal day to day life to cold-blooded murderer. You give me a reason and I'll give you a warrant. So far this is all conjecture. I need concrete, not quicksand.'

'Yes ma'am.'

It was a further twenty-minute drive from the station to Ronnie Macfarlane's property, a terraced house in the avenues of the town, and it didn't take long before they were pulling off the A19 and onto a slip road leading in. They hadn't spoken much more about the vet, but their thoughts weren't too far away as they approached the town he worked in, and more importantly, Davey had died in.

Hedgerows turned to pavements, trees to lampposts, and soon they were stopped at a railway crossing waiting for the tail end of a freight train to make its way past. They followed Alice around the North East.

'Can't say I'm too fond of this place ma'am, never saw the attraction myself.'

'I don't know Andy it's not all bad, I think we only tend to see the rotten side of it.'

She looked up at the deserted workman's club next to the tracks.

'Not a bad place back in the day by all accounts. Just the industry left and the low lives like Macfarlane and Markwell took over, peddling criminality over hard work.'

'I dunno ma'am, you'll not catch me here on a Saturday night; give me the quayside with a tipsy metro ride home any day of the week.'

'Long time since I tried that DC Jordan. Right, is it this street or the next?'

'Next one. Dead end after the mini roundabout that way.'

Alice signalled left and took the car into the narrower row of terraces, edging past a badly double-parked car with its hazard lights on. Two men were unloading boxes and weren't in a hurry about it. She carried on another fifty yards before turning right onto Macfarlane's Street, checking the house number she'd written on the back of her hand.

Ahead though she recognised a familiar car, Andy did as well.

'Is that who I think it is ma'am?'

'I think you might be right, what the hell is he doing here? The warrant's been live an hour, no way he's hijacked it from us.'

Alice pulled up alongside Alex Jamieson's 5 series BMW. It was empty save for a pair of sunglasses resting on the dashboard. Flash git.

'Let's get out, see what's going on. Let me go in first though.'

They parked and got out, walking to the open doored house and stepping over the threshold into a starkly lit hallway. There was no sign of Alex or anyone else on the ground floor as they quietly moved around, but drawers were pulled open, with envelopes and personal belongings strewn down on to the floor. Floorboards soon creaked above them, no doubt as DI Jamieson moved around from room to room, and the sound of more cupboards and drawers dragging open screeched their way down the stairs.

They looked at each other with puzzled looks, what was he doing up there?

After a minute or so the footsteps walked over in the direction of the upstairs hallway and made their way down towards them, standing motionless in the rear living room of the property. Alice moved out into the hall as he reached the bottom of the stairs.

'Jesus Christ Alice, you nearly gave me a flipping heart attack. What on earth are you doing here, is that Jordan behind you as well?'

He looked startled, a pale shade of himself as the colour drained away from him.

'I might ask you the same question Alex; we're here executing an hour old search warrant, how on earth do you find yourself in an unlocked property by yourself, searching through a murder victim's belongings?'

Alex had composed himself and was holding a phone up.

'In the area, source of mine said Macfarlane had been burgled, so I headed round to check the place over and secure it. Door was wide open when I got here, place in a right mess, checking no one was still upstairs when you arrived.'

Alice glared unsympathetically at him. She had half a mind to check his pockets herself, but he'd only wriggle out of complying.

'Bit of a coincidence don't you think, place gets turned over as soon as we get a warrant?'

'Life's full of coincidences Alice.' Alex looked down at the mess on the floor. 'Good thing I was in the area, god knows what else would've been out the door if I hadn't turned up.'

'You care to name this source of yours for us Alex? Or do I have to get the DCI to ask you?'

'You know he's not going to do it Alice, come on now.'

She knew fine well he was right, old boys club and all that.

'Well look if you're here to secure the place I may as well head off. Let me know if you find anything, can't say I spied anything good on my way round.'

She watched with a sinking feeling as he headed out of the door, clicking his key fob as he turned right and walked to his car. She knew damn well it wasn't a coincidence he was in the area. Either he'd been given the heads up on the warrant, or worse, was snooping around on her cases as usual. Didn't the man have anything better to do with his time than harass and disrupt her?

They searched the house but to no avail. No mobiles or incriminating evidence. No laptops or hard drives. Nothing but a wasted afternoon for an Inspector and her Constable. Dejected and frustrated they got back in the car.

'Well, that was a complete bust ma'am if you don't mind me saying.'

'No you're not wrong. Bit of a wasted trip.' Alice drummed the top of the steering wheel with both hands and stared ahead, letting a thought grow in her mind. The sun was beginning to set around the roofs of the terraced houses, casting a sharp row of shadows on the harled wall opposite them.

'Where did you say the corner shop was Andy, the one near Davey's house? Wouldn't mind a drink before we head back. I'm buying.'

They drove the short distance to the shop after Andy gave directions, as well as a drinks order. It turns out Markwell and Macfarlane weren't too far removed from one another in their residences, as well as their social lives. Alice grabbed her purse and headed in, looking left at the counter as she passed inside. A face looked up, framed by lottery tickets and an open shelf of cigarettes.

'Afternoon. Are you the owner?' She flashed her warrant card at the man behind the counter, who sighed as he saw another official ID.

'Look, if this is about the Markwell lad I already talked to at least three of your lot, I'm running out of things I can tell you officer. You'll have to excuse me I've got things to get done through the back.'

He moved around the side of the counter, clearly a feeble excuse to get away from Alice, but she grabbed two drinks and a packet of gum and held them up.

'Look, just these and I'll be on my way, one thing though…'

She put the drinks down on the counter and retrieved her phone from her bag, opening her camera album and flicking through the photos before holding it up to the owner.

'The officer who took the CCTV away a few weeks ago. Is this him?'

The shopkeeper took out some glasses from his top pocket and put them on, squinting at the image on the screen.

'Yeah, that's him why? Any chance he's gonna bring my USB stick back as well? They don't grow on trees you know.'

She flashed her debit card for a payment, pocketing the gum before picking up the drinks.

'Oh, I'll make sure he gets back in touch. Don't worry about it.'

She got back in the car and held a drink in front of Andy. He took it, checking the side mirror as they edged out on to the street.

'Not a bad shop that one ma'am. Nice enough guy.'

'Very nice guy, helpful as well. Very helpful indeed.'

The journey back passed in silence. Andy checking his phone as the countryside rolled past them on the A19, Alice staring ahead, driving on autopilot again as her mind now raced on to other things.

What the hell was he up to, what was the game this time?

Chapter Thirty-Four

Wednesday afternoon, I had gotten back to the house, and despite the cool weather and wind in the air I had been dripping with sweat from the ride home, relentless and panicked all the way back as I made my way through bridleways and back paths to the house.

Killing another member of the gang hadn't been the plan for obvious reasons.

This time I told myself it was self-defence, fight or flight. If I hadn't of taken him down I would have been a smear on the farmyard if he'd had even half a chance with me.

Davey had been personal, a threat against my family and revenge for the dog, a worthless nobody who didn't deserve life. But that had been it, violence over I told myself. The rest of it was to be stealthy and smooth, and all with a quiet resolution. Not another death. The feeling things had escalated well beyond my control was slowly sinking in.

It didn't improve as I held my head under the shower either, washing myself clean of all the dirt, sweat, and guilt. The video call from 'J' had sealed my hollowed out feeling.

They knew who I was and what I had done, and apparently, they could prove it all.

The gang were clearly on the defensive. It had been a mistake returning to the farm; they'd guessed right enough someone would come back, and there I was, walking straight into it. I thought I hadn't left any traces with Davey, hadn't told anyone or left any digital footprints I could think of. I'd been sterile all the way through. I'd been so careful in entering and leaving the property, so how did they know it was me? And 'J,' whoever he was, a police ID around his neck. There was no way this was good news.

Still, at least I had the group chat, my burner phone was untraceable.

I had gotten out the shower and sat down with Tank, it had been too early for a whisky, so I'd put the kettle on instead, going back to my notes. Grinding down a couple of paracetamols, I brushed the white powder into the coffee while it brewed on the countertop.

I wasn't any further forward in naming names, only Davey Markwell, Simon Trench and now this Ronnie Macfarlane character. I didn't recognise him, hadn't seen him around town, never dealt with the guy before. I had already decided to stay away from him online — better not to leave a trace or a connection for someone to pick up later — so I went back into my original notebook.

The chat had been mundane and run of the mill, even since I had dispatched Davey, and the clues had been achingly hard to come by except for finding his workshop. Hopefully now, with Ronnie gone, things would spark up again. They'd drop a crumb I could pick up and follow, finally put this thing to bed quietly and without any more confrontation.

I read the notes over and over, but still nothing was jumping out, so I'd closed everything down and signalled to Tank we'd go for a walk out the back. My head spinning despite the painkillers and strong caffeine hit.

That evening after a quiet dinner with Anna, she had headed into the office to finish off some paperwork, and I made the honest excuse of taking Tank back out again for another leg stretch before bed. I'd grabbed his lead and we headed though the unlatched back gate, out into the dene, picking up the well-worn path heading east through the trees and down to the coast.

A few hundred yards away from the house I'd turned back, making sure she hadn't changed her mind to follow us out, and seeing I was alone, took the burner from my pocket and turned it on.

The group chat had sprung alive with reams of messages. For a Wednesday evening they clearly all had had nothing better to do, and I was their number one topic of discussion. They were panicking about the chat too, sure it would be uncovered by the Police and traced once Ronnie's device was seized: 'J' had assured them however he had a quiet mole in forensics, and they were safe for now.

'Got that department wrapped round my finger lads, any ins and outs and I'd know about it trust me.'

Ronnie, I noted, had already been removed from the members. The group was livid.

'Fucking vet. Who does he think he is. First Davey, now Ronnie...'

'We got to do something J, nvr mind shopping him for Davey, this prick is going down...'

'J' was more in control than the rest, as was 'S', steering them away from their hysterics. One of the members had even suggested getting me in the vet's car park.

'No, we sit tight. We'll think of a plan. Don't forget we've got Saturday to come as well. First event so we can't be getting distracted okay. The vet can wait. Davey got sloppy, and Ronnie got unlucky. The rest of us he has nothing on so let's all be patient alright? If he starts making public noises, he knows we've got him pinned for Davey. That'll be enough to keep him quiet till we think of what to do.'

The rest of the group had quietened down and their excitement had subsided. But I couldn't help but thinking. Saturday? What was happening on Saturday: their 'first event'? As I'd walked home I had started to hatch a plan, a way to get myself out of this mess once and for all. All I had to do was figure out what it was and how to use it to my advantage.

Thursday had passed with no word in the group chat, discovered on another fruitless walk with Tank, but as Friday evening plunged into darkness once again I had headed out into the dene, phone tucked away in my pocket once more. Powering it up, the WhatsApp icon showed me unread messages — bingo.

'Right lads I've got the site confirmed for tomorrow night.'

It was 'S', clearly in charge of running Saturday's show, dealing out tasks to the group.

'I want no fuck ups alright? Big night for us so it's got to go as smoothly as possible, okay? Some important people coming along, we can't afford to look like a bunch of amateurs in front of this lot otherwise they'll be taking their money elsewhere in the future.'

A list of jobs had been given out, along with the timings of the evening.

'You've forgotten to tell them where it is mate ya daft cunt.' J had interrupted.

'Oh yeah. Sorry. I only just got it confirmed, had a couple of favours owing, hence the lateness of it. It's Strandwell farm. I'll get the postcode and send it along soon. But remember that we don't go telling any old dickhead. This is our first VIP event. No local trash allowed alright? 7pm start. Any problems, you tell me with plenty time to spare you hear?'

The group had all agreed. I'd powered down the phone and headed back to the house, Tank gently plodding along behind me.

Strandwell farm.

It had sounded familiar. Perhaps I'd been past it on a walk. I wasn't sure. Nothing a quick look on Google wouldn't sort out, and I'd spent the rest of Friday evening mulling over a plan in my head. It wasn't until Anna had gone to bed and a second malt whisky had made its way down the hatch that I finally had something viable to go with.

So now, here I was, twenty-four hours later, and it was early Saturday evening; Anna out the house and with a good few hours to spare. I'd a decent idea of how to play things out, and so, as six thirty ticked past I walked out of the back door, through the gate and into the dene.

I whistled for Tank, hoping to feed him and make sure he was secure before I left, but there was no sign of him. As I descended into the woods, the late afternoon sun tucked under the skyline with only its dull glow coming through the trees above. He was probably in the house somewhere along with the cats, tucked up near a radiator, ingratiating himself to his new feline friends. I reckoned he'd be fine until I got back.

I'd worked out last night where the farm was; close enough I didn't need to bother with the car, but far enough away to take about twenty minutes on foot.

Dressed in dark clothes, the aim tonight was to be out of sight and to collect information. I figured if I could catch them all in the act — finally working out who the elusive 'S' and 'J' were — I had a chance of getting this thing straightened out once and for all. At least that was the plan anyway. Gather enough evidence on video and let it do the talking. Finally get out of this thing without any more trouble. No more confrontations. No more death.

As it was, it took around twenty-five minutes to reach the farm. I'd forgotten about the detour around the stone bridge as it crossed the dene to the east, and trudging up makeshift paths to the field's edge on the other side had been slow muddy progress. It was bitterly cold, and every breath steamed up in front of me as I moved through the trees and along hedgerows by torchlight. As I got closer to the farm, a few hundred yards or so out, I shut off the beam and got by on the dull moonlight starting to break through the cloud cover above, cursing every ten feet or so as I stumbled over yet another rut in the field.

The air was ghostly still, any wind which might have blown through earlier in the day was long gone as I crept into the yard, each footstep sounding ten times louder than back in the dene. It was close to 7pm, but the outbuildings and farmhouse were still dark and unlit, with no sign of movement in or around them as I made my way forward.

Strange I thought — even a clandestine club like BloodSport would be making noise, especially if they had their VIPs in town. Where on earth were they? Had I misread the messages, got the wrong location, the wrong time?

As I looked backwards to the track, searching for any headlights or movement to indicate an arrival, the low sound of whimpering escaped the larger of the outbuildings.

Unmistakeably canine, it soon quietened down, before starting around twenty seconds later, this time louder and more persistent, and accompanied by the faint rattling of metal against metal, a sound I'd heard many times before: a cage door being worked over.

I moved closer and soon found myself against the back wall of the wooden building. It was total darkness, not even a single light came from within, but the sound of the dog struggling inside kept going, getting more desperate as it went on.

'Ah shit.' I thought to myself. Not the reason I was here. I was supposed to be spying on an up-and-coming dog fighting ring, not out rescuing more of the local dog population. Still, there was a tinge of relief realising I didn't have to come up against them again tonight. What had happened to the meet exactly? I cursed myself for not bringing the phone; it would have been easy to check if it had been cancelled or not, but here I was, stuck out in the darkness with one of the forgotten contestants, freezing my arse off.

Still, I figured. No point in leaving empty handed.

I checked again for any late arrivals, and then moved around to the only side of the building with an entrance: a small door set into a larger pair of corrugated iron openings; the kind big enough you could drive a combine through. It was open, and gently lowering the handle I moved in and closed it behind me.

The sound of the whimpering was echoing around inside the shed. The place felt huge within, the air was stale and metallic, not what I was expecting for a farmyard — more like an old abattoir from the smell of it — and it gave the place an unpleasant feeling as I stood inside the dark void.

'Hello?'

The whimpering stopped with a sharp yelp as the door swung shut behind me.

'Let me get a light on pal. Get you out of here ok?'

I padded my jacket down, trying to remember which pocket I'd put the torch back into, and eventually found it. I pointed it straight ahead, in the direction of the noise, and was rewarded with a view over a large concrete pit, beyond which a single metal cage sat on the opposite side. Inside, a large, thirty-to-forty-kilogram male Bull Terrier stood staring back at me, one eye scarred shut, its mouth stained red with blood. At its feet lay a small golden haired terrier dog — torn and blooded, glistening from a recent kill.

No doubt by the dog which stood over it.

The cage door was open.

'What in the fuck?' I let out in the darkness, the dog eyeing me up across the pit.

No sooner had the words left my mouth however when the inside of the shed burst into artificial light, and the whole picture was laid bare to me: the easy trap I had walked into.

Either side of the pit I counted five figures, all stocky and male, all wearing balaclavas, all staring back at me with arms folded. One of the five stepped forward.

'Welcome Mac. You're right on time.'

'Shite.' I whispered to myself.

I glanced around. No easy exit to the front or to the back but there was still a good enough distance between me and the group, so turning on my heel I pushed back towards the small door.

What I hadn't seen was the guy behind. Dressed all in black and in a matching balaclava, he had a baseball bat raised and already swinging towards my head. I turned away from the hit, but too late. The splintering impact sent me flying backwards, and by the time I hit the concrete, the lights were well and truly out.

Chapter Thirty-Five

The first thing I can focus on as I come round is a sharp noise, piercing through the middle of my head from ear to ear. It splits through the blackness, whirling round, and I slowly push myself up from the floor. In and amongst the darkness I gradually find myself, as the shrill ringing slowly subsides to an eery echo, accompanied by the gritty, grainy feel of the concrete under my palms.

My hands are tied at the wrist with tape, and the only option I have is to roll over onto my back and fill my lungs with air, tainted by the blood in my throat and upper airways. A bright strip-light above starts to come into focus, and all too sudden a soundtrack of voices and rattling chains flicks on. Someone has pressed the play button on a horrible industrial nightmare.

I carefully push back on my elbows as far as I can, hitting a concrete wall. Aware of more voices around me, I look upwards and see looming figures, four or five of them emerging from the light, coming into focus along with my hazy peripheral vision. It dawns on me I'm lying prostrate in the concrete pit. The same one I had looked out over earlier on.

'Wakey wakey beautiful.' calls one of the stockier figures, a mocking voice.

'Good of you to eventually join us Mac.'

A sharper edge accompanies the violent effort of tossing a pail of water down in my direction.

Most of it hits me, soaking my upper half and jolting me back to my senses as I look around at them. I can't recognise or place any of them. Even beneath the face coverings I get the impression no one is smiling.

The shorter, stocky figure breaks the deadlock, sitting down on the edge of the pit.

'To be honest mate, it's nice to have you here. We were all starting to get a bit bored with the usual events; it's nice to liven things up a bit, different species for a change, you know.'

I can see the wool of the balaclava spread in what I assume to be a grin, accompanied by a cruel crinkling of crow's feet around the eyes.

'You see mate, we realised what you were up to not long after Davey, bumbling your way through a shop's CCTV. So after you confirmed your stupidity by killing Ronnie it didn't take long to reel you into coming here. You lot think you're so smart don't you you vets, couldn't possibly be out thought by the likes of us eh?'

He jabs a thumb backwards into his chest.

'But see where you went wrong was your arrogance, quietly getting away with him like that, creeping around the backstreets at night, adding numbers into the chat. Thought you had us all on a string with your sneaky wiretap into our group didn't you? I'd applaud you if it weren't for the fucking cheek of it mate. I mean how fucking thick do you think us lot are not to notice you bell-end. Fucking thing was bloody popping up active two days after Davey was in the fucking ground.'

Shit. I hadn't thought. Two ticks my downfall. Damn technology.

He stood up and turned between the group before turning back, to address me again.

'None of us much missed Davey to be honest, rat featured cunt that he was, probably did us a favour in the end; forever running about town mouthing off, a bloody liability waiting to happen — but he had his uses every now and then. But you couldn't let it go, could you? If you'd left it there we'd have let you off, I mean one of us would have done it to him eventually. But you just had to poke the rest of the bear, didn't you? Tugging at all the little threads till one came loose again and you could go running to your girlfriend at Animal Welfare? Fucking idiot. Well look at you now. See where that got you. Hook line and fucking sinker pal.'

He stood back up and moved round the corner of the pit until he was behind me, crouching down again.

'Wait until you see who we've got for you next.'

I was now fully awake, sharply aware as the sound of wood dragged behind me, bumping over debris on the edge of the concrete pit. Its sides were about six foot deep and sunken into the floor of the industrial barn. It was still dark outside, but looking up, through narrow broken gaps in the corrugated iron roof I could see shafts of moonlight hitting the flecks of dust way up high in the roof space. Peaceful embers dancing in the rays, oblivious to the horror down below them.

My attention came quickly back down however when a pallet appeared into view from the side, making its way in front of me. A hooded figure swung it round over the edge, lowering it down onto the pit floor; resting it back against the far wall — forming a ramp reaching halfway up the brick wall of the pit, its two ropes loosely draped over the side.

'Starting to get your attention aren't we big fella,' came the call again behind me. I could tell he was pacing back and forth from the shifting position of his voice.

'Bet you're wondering what all this fuss is about, why you've got the gang all here, all this special effort? Why we reeled you in with all the fake VIP shit?'

He posed the question but didn't wait for the answer. Footsteps walked a short distance behind me and stopped, followed by a metallic rattling as sheet metal scraped against concrete and old hinges groaned open. The small clink of a dog lead fastening into a thick ring came down over the rim of the pit and filled me with dread, shortly followed by the scrabbling of nails and feet on the dusty dry concrete. The husk of a phlegmy grunt came round as a neck strained against its leash, growing louder behind me, echoing off the wall of the pit. The sound shifting as whatever it was came into my eye-line.

I'm a calm guy — panic rarely sets with a personality like mine, but the sight of the squat muscled bull breed dog again, ears tipped and teeth filed, the good eye bulging as every inch of its powerful hind limbs strained to move forward against the chain that held it back — every bit of it filled my chest and guts with toxic adrenaline as the sight of it loomed larger and larger in front of me.

It wasn't the biggest dog I'd seen in my life, Tank would be twice its size easily, but with a lean shredded muscle mass and scarred skin wrapped tight over its frame, it was certainly the meanest looking canine I'd come across. This wasn't your friendly family pet who trotted into the clinic every year for boosters, looking for the treat jar. This was a proper animal, a beastly throwback to its untamed ancestors; kept in the dark and brought out on special occasions to kill, before returning to its caged lair. This thing's purpose in life was eat, sleep, and maim — and make smaller killing machines every once and a while if it was allowed.

The blood vessels in its remaining eye strained harder as it was lowered down onto the ramp, and a second hooded figure jumped down after it to fit a thicker, stronger chain to its collar, looping it back through a floor level iron ring on the wall, giving the holder on the other end the ability to pull it back across the floor at a right angle from above.

The beast ignored him as he jumped up the makeshift ramp and onto the ledge of the pit, and it kept its glare solely on me about ten feet away, still prostrate on the floor in front of it — still unable to move from dead legs, hands bound tight behind my back with duct tape. As I struggled it only relaxed more, safe in the knowledge I wasn't going anywhere anytime soon.

'Thought we'd introduce you to the resident champ seen as you're so interested in what we do. Finally put a name to the face for you eh you fucking smart arse.'

The figure walked between the group theatrically, emphasising his point.

'Don't look so clever now do you vet? You still think you've got the better of us now, you over educated twat?'

With the last sentence I could hear the venom as it was spat out from under the balaclava, and the humour and mirth which had been mumbling around the pit from the other onlookers faded away to a stony silence, one matched only by the freezing cold air in the barn.

'This, my son, is Caesar. Reigning champ of the North-East. Twenty-seven fights in and twenty-seven wins, and I don't have to explain to you they were knockouts do I. This isn't a tickling competition.'

Caesar paced up and down, and had I been feeling anthropomorphic I'd have sworn he was lapping up the attention as his credentials were being listed.

'You see every scar he's got? Each one made him a little bit meaner, a little bit harder. Fuck those poodles you piss about with every day, those fucking kittens and cockapoos. This is a real dog son. A real dog who's about to teach you a lesson I think you'll understand; a lesson in your own anatomy, a lesson in humility, payback for Ronnie. Caesar is gonna make you wish it was him who'd knocked you out. Trust me son, he's gonna make you wish a lot of things.'

With the last sentence he reached down and patted my shoulder, and gave a low whisper,

'Why don't we make it a nice slow lesson eh. Our speciality.'

With a flick of the shoulder and wrist the chain was whipped against the side of the pit and Caesar flicked back into focus. The pacing gait halted, and with every tug of the chain tighter against his collar he pushed back sharply, tighter and tighter against its metallic grip, edging across the inches between us.

With a lightening ferocity, the previous grumbles and groans snapped into sharp barks, giving me an all too perfect view of filed sharp canines and molars, all held up by gum lines etched ragged with the scars from previous battles. The front paws clawed against concrete in an attempt to burst forward, and all too quickly the chain was slackened by its keeper, allowing short leaps forward, inch by inch — their motion halted by the iron hoop drilled into the far wall behind him.

Looking past Caesar, I could see the tiny trickles of cement dust fall around its base as it resisted the thrashing of canine muscle mass wrenching and twisting at it. I hoped to God the thing didn't rip out the wall; I wasn't ready for this yet.

I pulled my legs as far up to my chest as possible, but this was soon met with a blow from a long metal bar swung directly from above, the resulting impact deadening the leg all over again, leaving it flat on the ground in front of an advancing and snapping canine.

In no time at all he was inches from my feet, and what had previously been un-aimed warning bites into thin air, were now getting dangerously close. Unable to move I looked in horror as the chain was loosened again, and with a look of excited realisation, Caesar leapt forward and grabbed a sharp mouthful of material, shredding at my trouser leg.

I managed to gain control, pulling back, to be met only with further loosening of the chain. He felt the slack, and realising his opportunity, walked backwards like a seasoned pro before taking a run up straight back at me.

To give the chain holder credit, and in what was a well-practiced move, he allowed the teeth to snap centimetres from my face, turned and pressed firmly up against the pit wall. I let out a cry of fear, justified I thought, but it was met by howls of laughter and joy from the crowd above, and Caesar was dragged backwards into the centre of the pit.

Heart racing as I realised I'd been temporarily spared, I looked back at the dog, obviously in on the joke as he stood panting and grinning, staring back at me through one eye. He knew the best was yet to come. He'd done this before — hopefully not with a human I thought. The hooded figure above could obviously read what I was thinking.

'He's not the champ for no reason mate, true showman this one — likes to put on a show. Especially against his weaker opponents. No point in ending things early, is there Caesar?'

Acknowledging his name and grinning wider, Caesar stretched out his front legs and took a commanding stance in the pit.

'He made short work of that imp Davey dumped in the bins you know, clever little thing mind, gave up early and played dead. No fun for old Caesar though, he likes some sport — likes to hear them scream and suffer. Likes to make sure they know who's boss.'

The group was clearly relaxing and getting into it now, something which didn't bode well for me. I looked around at the pit, the sides high above me. Even if my legs were working, which they weren't, it was going to be a struggle to get out in one go, never mind with my hands bound to the wall behind me. Despair was starting to sink in deeper and deeper. It looked like there was going to be no way out for me this time. I had well and truly fucked up by coming here tonight. What was Anna going to think when I disappeared off the face of the earth, coming home to a dark house and no partner, just emptiness? Why had I gotten myself into this mess? Why?

Up above, the attention was focusing back down into the pit.

'Right boys we've had the previews, what's say we get some bets on? Now we know the outcome, vet boy here's a goner no matter what, but I got any takers on the fucker lasting twenty minutes with old Caesar here? Ten? Cheeky five-minute job? Dunno about you lot I reckon he's in a playful mood. I'm betting twenty-five minutes, who's with me, eh?'

I'm not normally a betting man, but I didn't fancy my chances against him much either; I'd have been taking the shorter odds for sure if I was up there. No way I was going to get out of this looking pretty, even after a minute of Caesar and those filed teeth — I had to think of a way out, and fast.

Looking around the pit, it was bare save a few worrying looking stains on the ground, but each of the three walls had an iron loop, one of which was tethering a settled and panting Caesar.

If there was one on each of them, surely there would be a fourth on the wall holding me up. Too busy focusing on the terror in front of me I hadn't moved around, and it wasn't long before my hands felt the loop of metal and traced it back to its anchor in the concrete.

Fixed solid there was no chance of movement; it was a fair assumption Caesar's opponents had writhed against the same solid base, but feeling underneath the metal was rough and sharp, scarred from its previous battles with chains. Slowly I ground the tape over the surface, gradually feeling it fraying and tearing apart as it weakened its grip around me.

The conversation above peaked in its animation before gradually the hubbub subsided, and the focus returned down towards me.

'Seems we have a few bets big guy. Seems we can't agree how tough you are, so this'll be good I reckon. I'm feeling lucky on twenty-five, got a few thinking Caesar is in a quick mood though so watch this space... Right boys, start the clock!'

The chain whipped and he lunged forwards. I could feel I was about a third of the way through the tape layers, and it felt like it was getting looser the more I was able to move and wriggle now everyone's eyes were on Caesar.

'Not too fast you idiot we want our money's worth, you want him round his throat within the first minute you fuck?'

The screams and goads got louder from above, and the stamping on the side of the pit created a loud echo in the barn that was only drowned out by the rippling clang of the chain against the wall, and the snap as it strained against the iron loop. Caesar knew the game was on and pulled himself forward inch-by-inch, grabbing and biting mouthfuls of air as he prepared to sink into my leg.

The banging above got louder as each of the crowd jeered and clenched their fists, wide eyed with anticipation of the inevitable blood shed they were about to witness…

… all but one.

As I desperately ground the tape against the sharp metal spurs of the iron, working it down to its last few fibres, I looked up to see one of the gang, not looking into the pit, but instead to his left and out into the darkness.

The stomping of feet was turning into a frenzy of jeering and shouting, but the dull, methodical thudding and creaking of wood crept from behind them, up past the confused spectator, and down into the pit where it became clearer and easier to separate from the cries of the other gang members.

One by one they moved their attention to the far wall of the barn, and after twenty seconds or so only the holder of the chain was concentrating — mesmerised by Caesar's thrashing against the iron as he claimed the inches of concrete between us with every flex of his hindlimbs. The thudding beyond them became more frenzied, and suddenly the almighty sound of splitting wood crashed in through the darkness and a rush of bitterly cold air flew between us into the barn.

Now, every one of the group was turned to face the commotion, and before I knew it the chain was slack, Caesar lunging full speed towards me from the centre of the pit, unleashed from his shackles and accelerating fast towards me.

As he moved, everything else disappeared; the group, the noises, the cold air and panic flooding down around me from up above; my full attention was wired into deflecting the oncoming freight train of sharp teeth and heavy muscle mass closing the gap between us. With a final leap he jumped, jaws wide open as the tape binding my hands finally gave way, and I felt the rush of air move past me as canine teeth snapped shut millimetres from my face.

We both flew back into the wall, connecting hard as we looked at one another hit the brickwork. My final image, before blackness descended and I slumped back down into the pit, was Caesar, confused and panicked as his neck whipped round at a horrid angle, twenty-seven fights leaving him nowhere but broken on the floor, just another victim in all this.

As I fought hard against the black swirls and bright stars which were filling my vision, they were soon soundtracked by shrieks and cries of agony from above. But before I could piece the confusion together, the world closed in, leaving me out cold, this time without any promise I would wake up again.

***

What seemed like a lifetime later, the same industrial nightmare cranked up around me, and the dull lights started to register from my periphery once more. I couldn't see and I couldn't move, but the cries of pain which were my previous lullaby had been replaced instead by guttural choking and struggling, the sound of flesh tearing and animal grunting, and all too soon my heart was racing as I realised Caesar must be alive. Was I listening to my own death, was I so numb I couldn't tell anymore?

More cries echoed around in my head as vision started to blurrily return; slowly widening into view from a fuzzy centre point ahead of me. The shapes became clearer in front of me; my own legs sprawled out, framed through the fingers of my left hand as it lay draped over my face, gradually moving apart as I screamed at the muscles from inside to move and get up. I could only twitch them however, flat out on the concrete and not going anywhere anytime soon.

Instead, I concentrated on the field of view slowly coming back into focus. It wasn't good. The shape of a large dog padded around and stepped between a mass of bodies as it grunted its way around the pit, snuffling at the hazy figures laid out horizontally before me.

Waves of confusion began. Even in my groggy collapsed state I knew I should be alone down here; I was supposed to be the VIP in town tonight. What was going on?

The animal turned and came closer, halting about a foot away, a massive head filling my vision. I could feel its breath on my skin, tainted with the metallic tang of its blood laced saliva, the smell of it taking me back to the clinic briefly before dropping me right into the reality of what was happening. This wasn't Caesar. I had watched him break and fall before me. He was dead.

As the fog continued to lift I could soon see two large eyes staring back at me, half framed in a brindle patch beneath a scarred ear, both above a handsome grin. The head nudged me. A giant tongue licked my forehead.

This was Tank.

Blood smeared and panting heavily, but it was Tank.

The memories of the thudding and crashing, wood splitting and the gang turning terrified as Caesar ran at me all rapidly returned. Slowly it starts to piece together. As I push back and get up — the adrenaline and confidence of having 60kg of Mastiff in front of me — I look beyond him. Three bodies lie around us. Two clearly dead, and one other, barely breathing to my right. Thinking back to the house, missing as I had glanced back, I realise he must have followed my scent over the fields to the farm, and the splitting sound was him crashing through the wall.

Blood is still trickling down in long rivulets over the side of the pit; I can only imagine the fight which took place whilst I was out cold. With the sight of torn necks and shredded flesh, never mind the amount of blood still dripping from Tank's mouth, my mind is distracted as I hear a shuffle of feet above us.

'Think you're tough do you, eh?'

The voice shouts down into the pit from above. The same as before.

'Think you're clever with the big dog do you, eh? Dumb fuck, still down there though aren't you, still ain't looking too clever Mac mate, despite the mess your hound's made.'

I look up. Two figures stand tall on the other side of the pit, still wearing dark balaclavas and holding metal bars, both with wide stances, safe in the knowledge they were up high and away from the carnage. Why hadn't they helped their friends?

'Seems we underestimated your friend here, isn't he the timid beast we tied up in the woods a few weeks back, 'nowt but a big family mutt? Guess he needed the right motivation in life; looks like he could have been quite the moneymaker from where I'm standing. Might have even given old Caesar a run for his money by the looks of it, what you think J?'

'J' shuffled side to side, sullen and not in the mood for small talk; clearly not as recovered as his friend.

'Think you've upset my sensitive friend here Mac. We can live without the chum bait you've left us down there, liabilities most of them, but Caesar was a special guy, a lot of time went into him, a lot of effort. Effort we're gonna need paid back one way or the other.'

The figure boldly stepped forward and sat down on the edge of the pit, legs dangling close to the bloodstains. Tank stiffened and bristled, ready to meet him head on. Something about the guy was familiar, even the accent, muffled through material of the balaclava, it had a familiar tone.

'Why don't you come down here and we'll talk it out? Think I fancy our chances better than before.'

I was getting the strength back in my legs, as well as my confidence. 'Can even take a bet on it if you like, what you reckon Tank, five minutes, ten, twenty?'

I grinned, but realising the left side of my face was in agony, rapidly swelling up as the bruising developed under my eye and along my jaw, I went back to looking more serious, matching the stares of the two figures above me.

'No, we're good thanks, think we've about got the advantage with you down there. Dogs aren't so good at getting out of there we find, so either you come up and we deal with you first, or you put him on the chain and we sort him out, your choice vet.'

He was right. I didn't rate my chances against two of them by myself, and Tank was a liability down here until I got him out: I couldn't leave him, and I'd struggle to lift him with the state I was still in. I looked over at him and he reciprocated the feeling, tilting his big head, looking back at me.

I'd about started to think of a plan when Tank straightened his head and ran at me, and with three feet between us, jumped and planted his big back feet into my rapidly adjusting arms, carrying the movement with a second leap, up and over the side of the pit, clearing it with a few inches to spare. He turned, pawing at the side of the pit above the ramp, and I didn't need asking twice, jumping and scrabbling myself up and over the edge as he stood by, growling at the two figures on the other side.

It was probably the threat of what he had already done which kept 'S' and 'J' back, and we stood fifteen or so feet apart from each other across the pit, Tank and I breathing heavily, my face swollen and getting worse as the minutes went on. They both stood still, poised to move if Tank made a move on them, keeping a tight grip on the makeshift weapons they'd been holding since the commotion had started.

'Looks like a stalemate situation don't you think?'

I tried not to groan in between the words. My ribs were stabbing me with every lung full of air that went in.

'I think I'll decline your previous offer if it's all the same. Unless you fancy your chances with Tank here?'

They were motionless, not engaging, and slowly we started to move around the pit towards the hole Tank had so violently created before. As I bent down to ease through, they glared back at me from beneath their balaclavas, knowing full well they couldn't do anything with the balance of power shifted. We moved out into the dark, the open air a stark contrast to the deathly claustrophobia of the fighting pit behind us.

I stood up tall in the farmyard, quietly groaning as the new injuries stretched out over my bones, something unpleasant clicking in my neck as I looked skywards. It was all quiet apart from the panting of Tank, and as I ducked and looked back, making sure we weren't about to be followed, soon enough he pulled my sleeve away.

I took the hint — I didn't fancy round two given the state I was in, and we began the slow limping run back across the field, Tank guarding our escape all the way as the lights of the village grew nearer in the distance.

Part Four

Chapter Thirty-Six

Sunday, yesterday, had been a blur.

Anna hadn't seen me arriving home on Saturday evening, which was lucky. Given the state I was in I don't think I would have had time to think of a back story, never mind collect myself and calm down. As it was she had been at her sister's dropping off a birthday present, deciding they'd head out for dinner after I hadn't responded to a call or her messages. Small mercies it would seem.

I'd near enough crawled into the dark house, having run back from the farm, a bounding dog ahead of me most of the way, turning his head every few yards to check I was still there and not falling behind. I'd only realised how tired I was as I put the key in the door, Tank barging past me and downstairs to his water bowl, the taste of blood and exhaustion in his mouth. Or perhaps it was satisfaction; he didn't seem too upset by what had happened, whereas I on the other hand was in breakdown mode, warning lights all over the dashboard.

I'd sat on the floor, a trembling pint of water in my right hand, leaning back against one of the kitchen units and staring at the wall for what turned out to be a good ten minutes before Tank came back through from the side of the house and sniffed me over.

'It's okay boy, we'll be fine.' I had lied, patting his head.

Hooper the larger of the three cats had appeared, and oblivious to the state I was in, was taking the opportunity to ask for a second dinner, annoyed Tank was getting more attention, angrily pawing at the food cupboard over to our left.

I remember briefly checking Tank over for any wounds, making sure he was unscathed before heading upstairs to the bathroom, pulling off my bloodied clothes ready for a shower.

I stood, head under the hot water jet for what seemed like hours, snapping out of my trance as the headlights of Anna's car appeared on the driveway through the frosted window, flicking off as the engine died. I turned the water tap and got out. Standing in front of the fogged-up mirror I wiped enough away to see the reflection looking back at me.

The left side of my face was a rash of cuts and bruising, presumably where I'd hit the concrete floor before being dragged across it, and feeling the back of my head there was a nice swelling from where I'd first been knocked out. Most of it was hidden by hair, but I'm sure if she looked close enough Anna would see the scab I was now painfully picking at with my fingers. My ribs and back were a messy cloud of dark blue bruising; they must have really laid into me after they'd knocked me out, but luckily, as I checked lower down, I couldn't find any dog bites or deeper cuts.

The bathroom door knocked. Anna.

'You in there Mac? Bit early for bed, isn't it? What are you up to in the shower, you in a bad mood because I had dinner without you, is that it?'

I opened the bathroom door and let the view do the talking.

'Bloody hell. What on earth's happened to you?'

'It's nothing. Fell off my bike heading back across the dene. Must have hit a rock or something and gone sideways, can't remember it if I'm honest. Woke up in one of those small gullies beside the trail with the bike on top of me. Was my own fault, getting dark and hadn't put the light on.'

The lie was getting accepted, Anna's concern overriding any questions she might have had. She edged past me and looked at the other side.

'Lucky Tank was with me, running alongside. Woke up with him trying to drag me out by a leg. Clever dog.'

'Jesus Mac, it's all up your back, how fast were you going? Looks like you've had a fight with a grizzly bear from this angle, you land in a hawthorn bush or something?'

I winced as she pressed hard on one of the grazes. Typical doctor.

'Thanks. No, only good old tree roots and rocks. Honestly, I'll be fine, just need to take a few paracetamols and get a good night's sleep. More worried about what the clients will think on Monday morning in consults if I'm honest. Must look like a right thug.'

'Yeah, it's not your best look. Come on, get in the bedroom, I'll help you get changed.'

She fussed me through and grabbed a loose t-shirt. Medic mode had been fully engaged.

'Honestly Mac you need to grow up, stop flying around like you're twenty years old. You're not some army boy on a mission anymore, I need you all in one piece remember.'

The rest of the evening had followed a similar vein. Concern mixed with admonishment for being so stupid. If only she had known the real reason I thought. I nodded along. She'd let me have a large whisky, not the best idea she'd told me in case I was concussed and fell into a coma — I hoped she was joking — and we'd had an early night. Surprisingly, I'd gone out like a light. Probably the mix of alcohol with exhaustion. But it was Sunday my anxiety kicked in again.

I was given a pass to do nothing on account of being injured, so as she busied herself around the house with jobs, heading out later to do the shopping, I sat on the sofa and mulled over the previous night's events, idly flicking through the sports channels and watching comedy re-runs.

I couldn't get over how stupid I had been, to think I could have remained anonymous in the group chat for a start — my trick with the burner phone was looking pretty daft the more and more I thought about it now.

They'd clearly got something on me from Markwell's murder, they had to have done, 'J' as good as said it when he'd called Ronnie's phone and I'd picked up. But what was it he had, CCTV, DNA? Surely forensics would create a paper trail not even a bent copper could get rid of. No, it had to be something untraceable, a one off he could keep hidden to use on me at the right time. Maybe it was something I could get still back. Had they mentioned it last night? The whole thing was a blur now.

I spent most of the day either racking my brains as to how I'd messed up in the first place, or worrying what was coming next from the two I'd left behind.

Something told me it was 'S' and 'J'. It had to be. The way they'd done all the talking. The way they'd stood back and watched Tank and I struggle with the rest of the gang in the pit. It had to be them, overseeing and directing, watching and waiting as the rest of the crew did the dirty work. God help me if there were more of them out there — two I could deal with, anymore and I didn't want to think about it.

So, what now?

There was no way this would be the end of it.

They knew who I was. They knew where I lived and where I worked. They knew what I had done, what Tank had done. They also had solid evidence on me for Markwell's murder. They would be coming for me no doubt about it.

I would. I had for that matter.

They also knew they remained anonymous. Save for the fact I knew one of them was a policeman that was about it. I didn't have the ability to track phones or see through balaclavas, I didn't have the time or wherewithal to look up acquaintances of Markwell or Macfarlane. I could track Simon Trench down again I suppose, but something told me he was long gone. No sign of him last night and no word from him in the chat. If the actual police had had the same thoughts as I'd had, they'd probably pulled him in.

The police. God. What if they had interviewed Simon Trench and he'd named me? Tracked down through his business links to Markwell? 'J' could have been coaching them all the way through. Perhaps he was even in charge of the whole Davey investigation — then I was really screwed. Jesus. The anxiety was killing me now. It was the same if not worse than the days after killing Davey. I had to get out of the house.

'Anna?' A murmur of a response came back from the kitchen next door. 'I'm going to take Tank for a walk, ok? See if I can't stretch out some of these bruises.'

I picked up a set of keys, and checking she wasn't looking, the burner phone from inside the dictionary on the living room shelf.

'Yeah ok. Don't be too long though I've got a dinner planned. And don't get on your bloody bike okay.'

I whistled for Tank and he came padding up the stairs with his lead in his mouth. He looked as calm and untroubled as ever, despite committing a triple murder the day before. I could take a lesson from him; he clearly didn't think it was a big deal, or if he did, he'd taken it in his stride. I guess he didn't have the burden of foresight though, the worry of what was still to happen, or how things might come to an end.

'Must be nice inside there eh pal.' I patted his fat head and opened the door, all the time pushing down the thoughts that I'd have to eventually deal with Tank and his aggression problems: not exactly a reliable family pet it was turning out. At least he was on my side I guess, perhaps I could worry about that one later.

Terrible vet advice Mac, just terrible.

He turned and eyed me up as I squatted under the wooden beam of the fence, breaking into a grinning smile, his big tongue falling out from his mouth as he panted and turned back around to the path ahead.

About a mile from the house my anxiety soon got the better of me, and I pulled out the burner phone from my pocket and turned it on. Understandably the group chat was empty of any updates. I guessed they were all either dead or knew better.

I stopped in the middle of the path, surrounded by bright skies and winter tranquility, letting Tank sniff his way around the grass over on the other side of the tall trees running along the track. My fingers hovered over the screen momentarily, and, willing myself on, I wrote out a short message in the group. My first and only:

'What's next?'

I pressed the arrow to send it. Seconds later the two ticks appeared alongside it. I looked up. Tank had found himself a nice patch of green, squatting tentatively over some wet grass, ready to leave some business for me to pick up.

I looked down at the screen. 'J' was typing straight away. My heart skipped a beat as the message flashed up:

'Wait and see. It's going to be good.'

The adrenaline surge amplified. It could mean anything. Tank was plodding back over, lighter for his efforts, and duly head butted me in the thigh, finding a painful new bruise with his temple.

I shut the phone down as quickly as I could. I wasn't going to dialogue with them; it wouldn't solve anything at this stage.

For a moment I wish I'd ended it last night at the farm, instead of running away, turned back and finished it once and for all; but there was no use dwelling on what I had and hadn't done when I'd had the chance. Unless I had some genius brainwave anytime soon I was going to have to sit and wait — be ready for whatever came my way.

It was terrifying.

***

Monday morning came around after yet another sleepless night. I looked like shit in the bathroom mirror as I brushed my teeth and checked over the bruises from Saturday. Not only was the left side of my face a mess from the kicking I'd had, but I also had bags under my eyes from a long night of tossing and turning. The brainwave had not come, and I was off to work, ready to explain the scrapes and bruises to a whole new audience. Try to get through another day ridden with churning anxiety and worry.

Luckily there wasn't a taxing caseload in the clinic, and I'd got through to lunchtime without too many questions, repeating the same story about falling off my bike to whoever asked, and hiding away in the office whenever there wasn't an animal to see.

By one o'clock I'd poured a coffee and taken a seat in the consult room, ready to reply to emails and write up the repeat prescriptions, when a knock on the door behind me caused me to look up to the small square window.

Steve the dog warden looked back at me, smiling. I gestured him in.

'Christ what happened to you Mac? Get on the wrong side of the nurses or something?'

I repeated the spiel about the bike and coming off in the dene, for about the twentieth time; I had it down to about ten seconds start to finish. Steve didn't look overly empathetic by the time I was through with it. Seemingly finding it funny, a grin crept into the corner of his mouth and he put a pile of paperwork on to the table between us.

'Well, anyway, Lance Armstrong, I need a few signatures on a witness statement, the Jack Russell you looked at for Skye.'

'Can't say I remember writing anything.' He turned the thin stack of paper around to face me on the table. 'Now you mention it I've been chasing Skye for what seems like weeks trying to follow the whole thing up. Poor things still in the freezer you know. No one even claimed her in the end.'

'Ah sorry Mac, my fault. Took over the investigation not long after it started, Skye was taking on too much so I thought I'd ease her workload, poor thing was reaching burnout.'

'Seemed okay to me last time I saw her. Did you get anywhere at least?'

'Can't say we did in the end. Took it to the police but it turned into a dead end; couldn't get a statement out of anyone who was involved, especially the son of hers, Carl he was called. Got the advice back to shut it all down, sign it off as a lost cause. Anyway, this is me tidying up the loose ends. Prepared something for you to sign if it's okay, get the case filed away so I can get on with other things.'

Steve took the lid off a biro and pushed the paperwork further my way.

'If you don't mind…'

'I dunno if I'm happy about this mate, think I'd like a bit more time to go through it if I can, you want to leave it with me and I'll read it later on, check I'm happy with everything before I sign it?'

Steve didn't exactly look thrilled by the prospect of having to wait any longer. A look of frustration was clear from the scowling face and arms folded across his chest.

'I don't know what you're going to change, like I told you, thing's a lost cause, but if you will be difficult... you're getting as bad as Skye.'

'Well I'm not being difficult, just want things to be right before I attach my name to them okay?'

'Be quick about it then, I'm trying to have this thing closed before the end of the week if I can remember.' Steve pulled another piece of paper out from his jacket, a single A4 folded three times. 'I also need you to sign an ownership form for that big beast you adopted from us, the mastiff a month ago. What have you named him, Tank was it?'

I took the form and signed it. He was officially ours. My first dog.

'I take it his case was a dead end as well?' The tone of my voice, with the sarcasm sneaking through wasn't lost on Steve, who looked up at me through raised eyebrows as he checked the form.

'Something like that.' He turned to the door, holding the handle, before turning back.

'You want to be careful with dogs like him, have a habit of getting unmanageable, I wouldn't want to see him getting you into any trouble.'

'I think I can handle a dog Steve, it's not my first day on the job.'

'Not what I've heard. You watch out for that bike okay.' And he left the consult room, the front door of the practice sounding not long after.

'Prick.' I muttered out loud, no one to hear it anyway except the ophthalmoscope. 'Last thing I sodding need, cheek off the bloody dog warden.'

I looked up. A nurse was staring at me through the window, wittering away to myself in an empty room. She tilted her head and raised an eyebrow, clearly taking enjoyment out of my temporary madness, before moving on down the corridor to the prep room.

'Great, that's me mental as well.'

I started thumbing through the witness statement. It turned out to be fairly accurate and I couldn't argue with its contents or change too much. Damn Steve, he was overstepping his mark with this one; just a shame he had this paperwork all spot on. I took out a biro and started jotting notes in the margins, anything to change it around for my own satisfaction.

I was on the third page however as I stopped and stared ahead, a flashback to the conversation with Steve from moments before: how had he known what I'd called Tank? Skye must have let it slip in the office; didn't think it would have been much of a talking point but there you go. I got back to the statement, and after five minutes or so I had it looking the way I wanted it, tucking it back in behind the computer screen in the area I used as a desk tidy. Ironically, at the same time, a small business card fell out between the wires and I picked it up. It was from Carl, who had rehomed the dog to Davey Markwell all those weeks ago.

I turned it around in my hand for a moment, wondering should I or shouldn't I, before deciding it was fine to call. Besides, case was closed anyhow, it couldn't do any harm.

'Carl?'

'Yeah, who's this?' The voice on the other end of the line was sharp and abrupt.

'It's Mac. From the vets. We spoke a few weeks back, do you remember?'

'Oh yeah Mac,' the tone softened, 'yeah sorry mate. Didn't know who the strange number was there for a minute. How you doing mate? No trouble found you I hope?'

'No, no,' I lied. 'It's all quiet here. Just running through my witness statement for the council, they're tying up the loose ends, something they always do, saw your name and thought I'd give you a ring to see if you'd heard anything about it. Have you?'

'No mate. It's all been quiet here too. Haven't heard a peep since the initial council lass, Steph was her name? And the PC who came round with her? They reckoned I was getting a follow up but never heard anything in the end. Probably for the best, the less said about it the better. Me mam's still at my throat for it, definitely off the Christmas card list this year. What bout you? Any news like?'

'No, much the same as you.' I picked up the first page of the statement and leafed through it again. 'You sure no one got in contact, no one from the police again?'

'Nah mate, not really, had some lad sniffing round the other day, chubby fella in a cheap suit, Detective Jordan someone or other, but by that point I was all up for forgetting it, good as got the feeling the first-time round. Nah it was only that Steph lass that took it seriously first time.'

'Skye.'

'Sorry yeah, Skye. Knew it was something like that. Shame, wouldn't have minded talking to her again if you know what I mean.'

I ignored the comment and pushed on.

'No one called Steve, her senior?'

'Nah honestly mate that was it.' He was sounding distracted now. 'Been a good few weeks 'an all like I said. Anyway, I better get on, shit to do, on a big contract at the moment mate. It's good to hear from you Mac, you're a top lad eh. Keep up the good work yeah.'

He rang off without waiting for a reply.

Odd. I could have sworn Steve told me he'd been chasing Carl up for a statement. What was it he had said, '*couldn't get a statement, especially out of the son.'?* Why did I get the feeling someone had dropped the ball on this one? Still, the more I thought about it, maybe it was better they weren't digging into it too much. You never know what they might find if they turned up the link to Markwell. God this was getting confusing.

Chapter Thirty-Seven

Monday Morning.

Police Headquarters, East Newcastle.

Still feeling like square one.

Only a trip to her parents for Sunday lunch, out to the west in a small village outside of Corbridge had stopped her sneaking in yesterday; her father insisting they go for a good long walk around the hills after dinner. Still, looking around the office, it had done her some good.

In amongst the stock questions about why she hadn't settled down yet, or what was slowing the promotion to DCI, Alice had had plenty of time to digest last week's progress, thinking hard on the questions Friday had thrown up as they'd strolled through the fields above the house.

She'd set a case conference for 10am. She would lead, Andy Jordan would back it up with his work on the dog fighting ring and the digital forensics. The other detectives hadn't so far contributed any positives, but it was good to bounce ideas off their analytical minds, even if they were lagging far behind. The feeling Alice and Andy had been going round in circles hadn't escaped her, chipping away all weekend, and she was looking forward to a different perspective on everything.

'*Sometimes you just need to come up here and think about it pet.*' Her dad had duly remarked the day before, his uncanny ability to read her thoughts as they had climbed over stiles together.

The two murders were officially linked and under the same investigation, so as the clock moved round to the top of the hour, she gathered up both files and moved out into the corridor, over to the conference room. On the way she looked over to Alex's office: the door shut and the room behind it in darkness. Maybe he was out on a case. Maybe he was trying to avoid her after Friday's encounter in the empty house, who knew, but she was relishing the opportunity to find out — with or without the DCI's help.

'Good morning ladies and gentlemen. Thank you again for joining us.'

Alice moved round and headed up the table, the power point bright behind her. It was Andy's turn to look relaxed, thumbing his notes and staring dead ahead towards the screen, a blank expression painted over his face. The rest of them shuffled uncomfortably as she closed the blinds and turned to address them, dimming the lights as she spoke.

'Davey Markwell. Ronnie Macfarlane. As you may or may not be aware we are incorporating both murders under the same investigation. Given the evidence which you are about to see I have codenamed the operation 'BloodSport'. It will make sense by the time we have finished, so don't get panicky, but yes, it is all to do with the group chat.'

Alice looked down at her laptop and moved forward through the pages.

'Since we last met a week ago there have been developments. Unless you've had your head in the sand you'll know Ronnie Macfarlane was found dead on Wednesday.'

Everyone nodded. No one on the team was sheltered enough they hadn't heard.

'So why are we investigating the pair of them together, lovers tiff?'

Andy smiled at DS Riley's input; he had a poor poker face and a love of bad jokes. Alice looked up and ignored him, carrying on.

'Digital forensics from Ronnie's burner phone confirm him as RM in the BloodSport group, linking him directly to Markwell.'

Samantha Bell lifted the corner of her transcripts to make a note.

'Ronnie was also found dead at the same site as a cache of dogs, picked up four days before by the dog team after an anonymous tip off to the council the same day. The same site our previous interest Simon Trench is directed to in the chat for some donkey work. Now, it doesn't take a genius to work out what he was doing there at the same time as being the muscle for a dog fighting organization, tidying up most likely, or looking for clues on the person who shopped them. Problem is, for whatever reason, someone's had the same idea and he's come off worse for it.'

'Any forensics on the kennels we can use ma'am?' Gavin Riley again, tapping a biro against his head, probably the same one as last week. It looked empty from where she was standing.

'Pending sadly. Dogs went to the back of the queue it would seem at the forensics lab, somewhere behind burglary and airbag saliva. DI Jamieson oversaw the signatures and they were delayed it would seem, I've had it fast-tracked this morning.'

Alice looked up at Andy Jordan, who raised an eyebrow in return.

Gavin continued,

'So, I get Macfarlane. Muscle in the group chat and done over at the dog site or whatever it was. But how are we linking whatever happened to Markwell to the dog fighting?'

'Andy, you want to help us out on this one?'

'Uh yes ma'am. Hang on.' He stood up and leafed through his notes, heading round to the head of the table alongside Alice.

'In summary it's two things.'

He scrolled forward through the PowerPoint, to the screenshots of the group chat.

'The appearance of Phone X if you recall. It appears in the chat around the time we believe Markwell was murdered, presumably added by the attacker, and whilst in situ with Markwell's own smartphone device. We've tracked it since and it's sporadic to say the least. Every couple of days it pings up, but never in the same place and never for more than a few minutes. Surveillance only. Thing never receives or makes any calls, uses very little data, a digital ghost in its own purgatory. Whoever placed it there knew to watch the group and knew the significance. The working hypothesis is they've twigged the cache of dogs and reported it, not sure why yet, but it's got to link to Macfarlane. We just haven't proved it as a non-coincidence yet.'

Samantha raised a hand but spoke before the invite was offered.

'You said there was two things Andy.'

Instead Alice looked up to answer.

'The injuries to Markwell.'

'Ma'am?'

'The injuries to Markwell, save for the broken jaw, are near identical to the injuries inflicted on the dog Davey mutilated and dumped two weeks before his own murder. You recall the terrier in the group chat?'

Nods again.

'Chest injury causing the lungs to collapse, followed by throat laceration, both victims bleeding to death. The dog didn't have a PM but the first dog warden near said as much'

'Nasty.'

'Quite. Dr Ballingry said it was so intricate to the point it couldn't have been coincidence. Working motive for Markwell therefore was that he was done by the owner of the dog. It falls down however when you find out the owner was an old dear with the strength of a kitten. Immediate family alibis all check out as watertight as well. So, someone has found out about it and taken it up as a vigilante cause, but who? And why turn on the rest of the group as well?'

'So someone's out there hunting down a dog fighting group one by one?'

'Seems like it.'

'I'd say let them finish their work.' Gavin muttered, loud enough for the table to hear. 'Who the hell wants to see dogs fight anyway, I mean what the hell's wrong with people?'

'Thank you, DS Riley. Not the most useful of inputs but thank you.' Alice looked around the table. 'Anyone else got any thoughts on what we've covered so far?'

'Just thinking ma'am.' Samantha Bell again, 'you picked up Simon Trench didn't you? Won't he name names? He must know who's after them, doesn't he?'

'Problem there,' Andy spoke up again, 'Is whoever is in charge, and he as good as said there was; whoever is in charge has the frighteners on him so tight he's saying nothing. He knows we haven't technically got him for anything, an associative relationship up to this point, but whoever leads the group, this 'S' and 'J', has them terrified of making mistakes or talking. He was sweating bullets when the topic came up. I can't see him naming anyone anytime soon unfortunately.'

'Stick surveillance on him?'

'We thought about it, but given the fact he's had two interviews, if he's got any sense he'll be lying low for a while. Not sure it's the best way to spend the budget.'

'You ever think it's an inside job? The two leaders cleaning house? Markwell had clearly messed up and was getting sloppy, easy to make it look like a revenge killing in exchange for an easy exit from the organisation. Not sure about Macfarlane, perhaps he'd outlived his usefulness as well, figured they'd kill two birds with the same stone. We're never far off a conviction, maybe an easy way to sweep him under the rug before he tried a plea deal?'

'Bit of a clumsy way to do it no? Leaving bodies around the place? And why bother with the burner phone if they didn't think we'd find the deleted chat anyway. Doesn't make sense, does it?'

'Not if you're about to pin it on someone, someone you know will take the blame?'

'Trust you to add a new motive Gav.' Alice jotted it down in the margin of her notes, to echo her own thoughts from a few days ago.

'As ever ma'am, you're welcome.' He smiled, tapping the pen again. She could see the ink marks now on his middle finger. It did work.

'So what was the cause of death on Macfarlane in the end? Dr Ballingry have any pointers, niche injuries, any sign our psychopath was up to his old tricks again?'

'I don't think we're looking at a classic psychopath here, do you?'

'The guy tied down and slit the throat of Markwell: hardly the actions of an upstanding citizen wouldn't you say?'

'Psychopaths are categorised by lacking empathy, an inability to love or understand their actions. Remember, this is still a crime of passion. Whoever we are looking for just placed Davey below the dog in his affections.'

She flicked back to the picture of the dog, displaying it up on the screen behind them, seeing if any light bulbs came on in her colleagues' minds. Vet shaped ones in particular.

'There is a definitive enough display of emotion. Clearly some daylight between conscience and actions when it came to the method however, but whoever we are looking for still has a beating heart. Just it beats in favour of the little guy, or little dog in this instance. Wouldn't you say?'

'Perhaps.' Gavin still looked unconvinced. 'Any links to the method on Ronnie though?'

'Ronnie seems much more like a fight to the death. No real planning seems involved. Given the size of the guy I don't think whoever did for him was waiting for an opportunity to show off any finesse. This was two blows. Each brutal, and each well aimed. Snapped knee ligaments got him down to the ground, the blow to the neck enough to crush the larynx in on itself, stopping his airflow at the same time. No, whoever it was took the opportunity and took it quickly, I don't think there was much planning involved.'

'So what, he didn't mean to do it?'

'Oh, he meant to hit him alright. Only it all seems rushed. Potentially self-defence. Ronnie wasn't exactly some coy debutante in the local community you remember. No, if my hunch is right I'd say this wasn't on our suspect's agenda. I wouldn't even be surprised if Ronnie initiated it. Remember he's a big guy, a history of violence and a regular at an MMA club in town. Probably fancied his chances and met his match.'

'So we're looking for some giant, MMA defeating animal lover who has the technical nous to infiltrate and track down an organised crime group, as well as avoid and defeat our SOCO team? Come on. Bit far-fetched, isn't it? Surely that kind of suspect would have shown up on CCTV, creeping around before and after doing Markwell in, wouldn't he?'

Alice looked at Andy, sitting up and ready to speak, hoping a raised eyebrow would keep him quiet about their new person of interest. Instead however he had taken the bait over the surveillance footage.

'You'd think so.'

'Andy...'

'Sorry ma'am.'

The team looked round in unison, and then to the head of the table, at an exasperated Inspector.

'Well fine, I suppose you may as well tell them now, good a time as any.'

'Right you are.' Andy shuffled back up in his seat, shaking off the admonishment before it had a chance to sink in.

'Well, it looks like we've either a joker in the pack or some competition for the conviction. Either way, a uniform has had away with the initial scene CCTV in the days after — one of the corner shops around near Markwell's property. Can't find a record of it anywhere despite my best efforts. It never entered an evidence record and was never signed for, but still got lifted.'

'What, so our suspect has friends on the force?'

'Or, we're looking at a suspect on our side of the fence.' DS Bell pondered.

Alice was quick to interrupt, 'Either way people, it stays in this room. I hear a whisper of it in the corridors, each and every one of you will be in my office you hear?'

The murmurs went around the table. This added a different dimension to the investigation now that evidence tampering was involved.

'So, you know where we're at. I want bright ideas, with plenty of background, and I want them back in the room by Wednesday morning, okay? I realise we've still got very little on the attacker, but given the links to this group, I say we get them, and we get the whole thing, him included. Anyone got any other questions, no?'

Alice looked over at DS Riley, still tapping the pen on the notepad in front of him.

'I want you to dig deeper into Simon Trench for me. Every time we've pulled him he's had the same excuse to clam up, so next time I want something he can't walk away from, okay? If all else fails he's our way into the group; so we've got to be scarier prospects than his bosses. Find something solid, you understand Gavin?'

DS Riley acknowledged the task as the team filed out. All except for Andy Jordan and DS Samantha Bell, who were both asked to stay back.

'Extra duties ma'am?' Samantha was a previous protégé of Alice's, let out on a longer leash after passing her sergeant's exams two years ago, but she would still come back into the fold for sensitive tasks when required. Andy on the other hand was still her pet constable.

'I'm going to let you in on a few secrets Samantha. Nothing that goes beyond the three of us you hear?'

'Yes ma'am, as always. What's the job?'

'Andy and I took the interview with Simon Trench; this is definitely part of something bigger, no doubt about it. The guy was scared witless of the consequences of being a grass, so although we keep at him I doubt it's going to give us anything new even if Gavin comes through with the goods.'

'So what's the angle?'

'Well, it's no secret my case against Ronnie Macfarlane went south a few weeks ago. Seemed like carelessness from me at the time, but now this case has had its interference, a case he's directly involved with, I'm beginning to think he's got a friend on the force, much closer to home than I would like…'

'You got someone in mind for it?'

'More than just in mind.' She turned to Andy and held her hand in apology.

'Sorry Andy, what I didn't tell you on Friday was the shopkeeper confirmed it to me with a positive ID on a photo: our evidence hoarder. I've spent all weekend thinking about it and it's been making more and more sense.'

'Ma'am?'

Alice took her phone out and scrolled through to her photo albums, selecting the same one she had shown the shop owner, zooming in on one face. She held it up to Andy and Samantha.

'Bloody Hell you're kidding, aren't you? What's he doing sniffing around on this?'

'I haven't worked it out yet, but this goes nowhere d'you hear? You two know about it, and I've also discussed it with one of the DCIs on the Durham force. I'm waiting to hear back about a warrant issue from the Superintendent down there. In the meantime, I want some questions quietly answered.'

'Ma'am?'

'Samantha. First, I want his phone number and this one from the group chat looked at for their GPS data. I want to know if they ping together, and more than once. And the same for these two numbers.' Alice handed her a second piece of paper. 'Speak to Dianne Petty in the forensics lab, she's expecting this, and knows not to ask any questions, is that clear?'

'Yes ma'am, right away. So who's the second?'

'I'll answer that when you bring me back the data. For now I only want to see if they match my hunch okay?'

'Yes boss.' Alice turned her attention to her constable as Samantha took leave.

'So, before this next bit, you got anything on this vet for me, anything we can use for a warrant?'

Andy creaked in the chair he had sat back down on, squaring an elbow and pushing himself up straight.

'Well the guy seems clean this end. No unusual bank or phone activity, nothing on our Phone X locates to where he lives either, I mean it pops up near his home address once, but then it appears all over the place, can't say it could be anything other than a coincidence. Don't think a magistrate will give you a warrant based on that.'

Andy flicked a page in the notebook.

'Still, might be worth a chat, see how he reacts if you ask about it I guess.'

'Okay, we'll get something in the diary, better for two of us to be there for that one. Anything from his past, anything flagging as a potential red flag?'

'Well yeah, potentially ma'am. Tracked down the superior officer again, the one he had back in Afghanistan, turns out he wasn't the gentle giant he comes across as now. Fizzled out in the end when they saw sense, didn't make a disciplinary, but he almost got a Court Martial for decking one of his dog handlers. Found out apparently he'd been beating a dog instead of training it properly: this guy Mac was busy knocking seven shades of shit out of him when the rest of the team finally managed to pull him off the guy. The lad got binned to the UK and the vet gets a proper talking to.'

'Interesting. So, he doesn't mind violence when it comes to helping animals. Might be worth putting the squeeze on him, see what the reaction is when we mention the dog. How he felt about it etc. Still, be a bit of a jump. I guess he had the capability though; from what Dr Ballingry said we're looking for a very technically proficient killer, vets probably have all sorts of tricks we don't know about. Could be Andy, could be. But then why not come to the police? Why would he take it into his own hands?'

'Dunno ma'am. Not everyone enjoys working with us, do they? Could be there's a bad taste in his mouth from back in Edinburgh, when he gets held up for helping his mates. Worth a chat I'd say.'

'Yes, I think you're right. Just a shame he hasn't done anything obvious. Still, worth the trip. Anything else?'

'No ma'am, taken up most of my time to be fair.'

'Ok well look, next thing's a bit sensitive and I need you to be underhand. Put the vet back on the shelf for now, I want this leak sorted out first. I know the group's the key to all this. Pull the right string and the whole thing's going to come tumbling down on everyone, our vet included if they're on to him as well.'

'Righto ma'am. So what's the job?'

'I'll back you up 100% of the way, ok? I'll want this done even before the warrant comes out, incase I'm out of my depth and our mutual friend has friends down in Durham as well, we on the same page?'

'Not a problem ma'am, never liked the guy anyway if I'm honest.'

She wrote down a location, with two lockers to search. Entry wouldn't be difficult, he wasn't going to Fort Knox, and something told her it would be worth his effort.

'You report to me as soon as you're in and out, okay? No mucking about.'

'Yes ma'am.'

Alice closed the PowerPoint as Andy left, staring across the table into the quiet room. If she was right about what Samantha and Andy would find, it was going to be massive. Never mind a dog crazed murderer; this one was going to make a hell of a mess if it was true.

Chapter Thirty-Eight

Tuesday evening had come round quickly.

After a long, drawn-out shift I pulled up outside the house, hoping I could find some solace on a quiet night in with Anna, to get me away from the anxiety of the last two days, panicking over what was next. No form of resolution to my problems had been found in a busy day of work, and I was looking forward to shutting off, drinking whisky and getting an early night.

The head in the sand method was my default today. Salvation in healthy living was not.

Turning the headlights off I got out of the car, stepping on to the driveway.

Anna's Audi sat quietly next to the low wall. The heat from the engine had long since left it and it mirrored the darkness from the rest of the property. As my old estate car whirred and ticked its way to closing down, I reached back in for my rucksack and keys, hitting the fob as the door clunked shut — the yellow blink lighting up the brickwork next to the door. Strange I thought, normally at least the hallway light would be glowing back at me, or even the hustle of Anna inside as she made dinner. The whole place was black and cold, only the streetlight reaching out a dim faded beam towards the door.

Peering closer, a long vertical strip of shadow appears and disappears around the door, and as I walk down the steps, I can see its hinges gently swaying and knocking the frame, as the breeze from within the house edges it in and out. I push the door into the hallway.

'Anna?'

No reply.

'You there?'

Nothing still. The familiar hum of the heating and clatter from the kitchen is absent, only a small rustle of the blinds and a soft wind coming from downstairs. Behind me, a chirp appears as a cat edges into the hall and between my legs, looking up with wide eyes.

'What the hell's going on Hoops eh?'

I shut the door, resting it quietly in its frame behind me, moving inside to the top of the stairs. It's all quiet as I move down to the bottom of the house, and as I flick on the kitchen lights the first glimpse of the scene takes me back. Hooper wanders in ahead of me and begins to snake around the shattered plates and glassware over to his food dish, oblivious to the mess he's padded through.

At the back of the room I can see torn blinds sucking backwards through an open extension, and to my left the kitchen worktop tells a tale of chaos — broken oven dishes and scattered food have dropped to the floor from above, and a solitary knife stands vertical, its end piercing through the top layer of the laminate as it fell. A small, sweeping arc of blood trails away from the destruction and leads my eyes to the door beside the fridge, tilted open into the side of the house. Tank's bustling and snorting are absent from this picture.

'Anyone?'

I walk through, knowing already what I'm going to find. An empty room, more chaos, and what looks like an almighty fight between Tank and whoever has been through the house. Pictures are smashed on the floor and the back door is open, his bedding pulled through upturned water bowls.

The saving grace is the lack of more blood, with only heavy claw marks around the doorframe. Whatever has happened has happened with him in one piece, but this doesn't settle my heart rate anymore as I pull the blankets back through and lock up.

I turn to stare back down at the destruction, the stark realisation they've disappeared hitting hard.

Framed pictures are dashed on the floor, and our tranquil memories look back up at me through the fractured glass — I couldn't ask for a worse metaphor for my life right now.

Our happiness in pieces.

All gone through an open door.

Chapter Thirty-Nine

Skye signaled left, pulling the work van in towards the narrow opening of the building's courtyard. Her flat was on the second floor of three, and as she looked up before turning, she was glad to see the lights on in the living room. Hopefully that meant the timer had also turned the heating on. It had been a bitterly cold day out on the road in Northumberland.

Overall it had been a satisfying one, and she had promised herself a relaxing evening with the dog and a glass of wine or two. The court case against the breeder had finally been settled; a community sentence and a lifetime banning order on owning animals. Not the prison term she would have liked, but enough of a message to the community that they meant business when it counted. She had half thought about calling Mac before the drive home, to let him know how things had gone, but he was probably at home, relaxing and sitting down for a quiet and peaceful evening with Anna. It was best not to disturb him tonight.

As the van bumped the corner of the curb and tucked through the archway, the lights swung around the brickwork and opened into the small car park the building's occupants shared together: one reserved for each flat, no room for any extras. To her right, catching her eye, the disabled space normally reserved for the ground floor flat was occupied; a black transit sat facing outwards, its windscreen fogged and sagging heavily on the back wheels, edging right up to the wall as it obscured the blue sign behind it.

Shrugging it off, most likely workers finishing for the day, she flicked open the central console to grab her belongings: laptop, thermos and notepad, and tucking her phone into her jacket, she pulled the key from the engine and placed a hand on the door ready to get out. As the dashboard lights dimmed and shut off, the streetlight caught her eye in the mirror as it came through from the archway.

A shape moved across the shadows.

She froze.

All the panic of her attack flooded back to her, quickly joined by an adrenaline surge as the driver's door pulled open — a set of hands reaching into the van, grabbing and grappling at her jacket as they tore at her. As she spun and pulled away, the grip instead moved down to her legs, dragging them away from the footwell and out into the night. Seeing her only chance, she kicked heavily at the figure beneath her, sending it backwards into the car next to them, the thudding hit on the metalwork joined by a deep masculine growl as the body slumped down under the wheel arch.

It was fight or flight, and Skye wasn't taking any risks in the van by herself. She scrambled over the man — now pushing himself back up to his feet — and ran towards the building, hoping to God someone would have heard the commotion and called the Police.

As she sprinted towards the front door and lobby beyond, a second figure came from the passenger side, chasing close behind, quickly making up the distance between them as they crashed into the glass door and rattled it against the frame together. Long arms wrapped around her, and she twisted and turned against the grasp, pushing him back into the wall and freeing herself as her high-viz jacket tore off in his hands. She looked up: cold eyes stared back from a black balaclava, and he threw the yellow material back down on the ground behind them in frustration. Beyond, she could make out her first attacker, shakily getting up from the ground beside the van as he made his way over on groggy legs towards them, mumbling and swearing as he staggered the distance. The man in front of her looked too, and she saw her chance.

Still holding her keys, she wrapped them on the outside of her knuckles and punched straight into the centre of the masked face, cracking it towards the wall behind and causing a cry as the nose beneath split backwards with it, hands following upwards with the agony. She didn't need any more invitation to escape, and fumbled the keys into the door, shutting it just in time for the pair to slam against it, banging with closed fists as they realised they were locked out in the courtyard, facing her across the thick glass.

They didn't hang around.

Turning, they ran back to the black van and got in either side, the headlights glaring back through the porch door and lighting Skye up as she stood motionless in the foyer — breathing hard and fast, her mouth dry and her heart racing. As it swung and scraped the wall of the building's archway, scratching at the brickwork as it tore through, she could swear she heard the short burst of a scream and a dog's low bark go with it, the echo bouncing back to her through the opening as the engine strained and sped off.

Only when the courtyard fell back to darkness and the silence returned could she crumple downwards, head in her hands.

Eventually, as her nerves cooled, she looked out into the small shadowy courtyard: her torn jacket strewn outside, the work van beyond with its door open and hazard lights flashing, kicked on as she had struggled outwards, and what looked like the end of her thermos flask under the wheel of the car next to it.

She checked the pockets on her combats. Her phone and wallet were still there, and pulling them both out she soon found what she was looking for — the business card from the other day, from the female detective she had met at the council office. With a trembling hand she keyed in the number, and taking a deep breath, pressed to dial. The call connected after four rings.

'Hello, is that DI Rose?'

'Yes, speaking.'

'I'm sorry to bother you in the evening. It's Skye, I met you at the council offices, we talked about Steve. Do you remember?'

'Oh, that's right, Skye. How can I help, did you remember something useful? Are you okay, you sound a bit upset?'

'Not exactly DI Rose...' Skye went on to explain what had happened. She had stood up and was picking at the corner of a leaflet on the building's noticeboard. Something about a lost dog, it had been there for months. As she finished, Alice had already paused and composed herself. Either she was good at her job or none of this was coming as much of a surprise. Skye couldn't tell.

'Ok look, I can have a patrol car with you shortly, you get inside and we'll get those details checked if that's okay, you're not hurt, are you?'

'Actually, DI Rose, I was wondering if I could run something by you instead, something I've been suspecting recently. What I saw tonight made me think it wasn't a niggling doubt, and it's a reality, if that makes sense?'

'Ok, go on.'

Skye went ahead and explained her recent suspicions, and on the other end of the line, Alice took notes, mentally cross-referencing them back to her own.

After a minute or so she stopped her. She'd heard enough.

'Ok, here's what we're going to do. Give me a chance to call in a few favours, and if you're right, some back up. I'll be with you within the hour, okay?'

'Ok thank you. Thank you for listening.'

'Not a problem, but for God's sake Skye get inside your flat and lock the door properly. Only open it when you see me parked outside.'

Chapter Forty

I hunch over the work top, clawing at the wood.

I've searched the house. Under the bed, the wardrobes, I even lifted the hatch into the loft. All of them empty.

There's no trace of Anna anywhere. None of Tank either. Plucked from a perfect house and out into the darkness outside. God knows where, by God knows who.

All I'm left with is the chaos in the kitchen. The freezing wind from the open-door whips round with the rest of the despair. I can't believe it's come to this. The realisation of what I've done, what I've brought crashing down on our life starts to sink in. I've got no way of knowing what's happened. No way of finding out where she's been taken, no clues I can find in the debris around me.

I dig out my phone from my jacket pocket. My hand clammy on the case.

This was all on me now. I'd have to call the police. It was beyond sorting out; I sure as hell didn't have the resources to find out what had happened, never mind get her back safely.

Taking a drink of water, trying to get some moisture back into a dry mouth I sat down on one of the stools tucked under our worktop, opening the phone and hitting the call icon. What I wouldn't give to be sat here with Anna. Talking nonsense over dinner, laughing at the days we'd had. Not trembling, soaked with sweat.

No sooner had I opened the keypad to dial 999, it disappeared, replaced instead by an incoming call, number unknown.

'Hello…', my voice quiet and broken from the shock of the last few minutes.

'Good evening, Mac.' It was a local accent, deep and muffled, speaking firmly on the other end of the line.

'I can assume you're home now. Hope you don't mind us calling you on the personal phone. Figure I'd have more chance than on that burner you keep tucked away. We've had quite the party without you as you can tell, bitch of yours can struggle that's for sure. Must have your hands full with her pal. Anyway, she soon quietened down after some persuasion — sleeping like a baby now. You should see her, looks an absolute picture.'

I pushed out the stool and stood up, resting a hand down between the broken glass, the edges grinding into my palm.

'This has nothing to do with her you hear. You bring her back right now and we sort this out once and for all. Like real men.'

'Oh, you think I'm daft, do you? I've seen what you're capable of. No, we want you on our turf this time. And you're going to come alone. Don't you even think about calling the boys in blue either. We've got enough evidence on you from Davey to send you down for a long long time, trust me. No, if you ever want to see this one alive again you'll do exactly as we say. Same goes for this big beast you call a pet dog as well.'

I heard an iron bar hitting a cage over the phone line, the unmistakable snarl of Tank in the background.

'You know how difficult it's been not to just do this dumb dog right between the eyes? Figured we need him as insurance. In case it doesn't work out with pretty little Anna alone.'

The voice gave an address. I knew it well enough. The farm a few miles behind the house. The farm Tank always whimpered at as we walked by. No wonder he was terrified of the place. There all along, staring us right in the face.

'You come alone. You come now. Or the bitch and the dog get it.' The voice rang off before I could question the demand.

Fuck. Every inch of me wanted to phone the police. Hand myself in for what I've done — accept the punishment, save Anna and Tank. Lose them from my life while I rot away the rest of it in prison.

But what if it goes wrong? They see blue lights and that's it. They cut and run, leaving them both dead while they flee. Meanwhile I'm all alone and in a world of my own personal shit.

So maybe I do what they say and go alone, maybe there's a deal to be had. Only for the life of me I can't think what I could give them worth Anna and Tank. I've already crushed and torn down their new enterprise. I've already ripped out their beating heart. And now they want mine. It was terrifying.

A ginger head nudges my leg. Hooper, hungry as ever, looks up. I'd had him since getting back to the UK. My original G.

'What you reckon Hoops? Think dad can fix this one?'

The answer is another headbutt, and I brush the glass out of his way before he pads in it. Quint has joined us in the mess and sniffs around his brother, oblivious to the anxiety above knee level.

I feed them both. Who knows when I'll be back in the house at this rate, and I shut the lights off in the kitchen after I've swept up the shards of broken glass. Moving up the stairs I pad myself down and take out my belongings, dropping them in the key bowl beside the front door. Phone, wallet, anything that can identify me if I don't make it back, and I lock the house.

Hopefully I'll return. Hopefully with Anna and Tank.

***

Alice was only seconds off the phone from Andy Jordan when Skye had rang, having spent the previous twenty minutes on a conference call with DS Bell and Diane Petty. A trio of calls – each more rewarding than the next.

He had come up trumps with his morning's work. A trip to one of the region's most prestigious golf clubs had found him flashing a warrant card and taking the janitor to the men's locker room, all on the pretence of a reported burglary, but when left to it he had proceeded to identify and enter the personal lockers of Alice's two main suspects. No burner phones, but in the second locker the missing USB from the corner shop, marked with the owner's name. There was even paperwork dating back to Ronnie Macfarlane's original trial.

Jackpot thought Alice. Jackpot.

The icing on the bent copper cake however was the police uniform, hanging up, pristine and pressed. No doubt the same one used to dupe the shop owner for the CCTV.

As instructed, Andy had left it all in place — this was for direction only; she didn't want to scupper her official warrant when it came through or jeopardise any future trial — never mind have him busying about and getting busted by any of the golf club members whilst on site. As charming as he could be, he didn't have the tact to get out of that scenario. Not at least without some serious questions coming up anyway. No, the knowledge it was there, ready to officially uncover when the warrant came through was all she needed for now.

Samantha and Diane had been more rewarding in their official capacity however. The personal mobiles of her new suspects matched each other point for point on multiple GPS locations with the two burner phones in the group chat.

Gotcha.

She had closed the last call from Skye and held the phone in her hand, tapping it softly against her nose. Clearly she wasn't the straight forward girl she'd taken her for at their first encounter. Andy could learn a thing or two from her instincts.

She re-opened the phone and brought up the contacts list, scrolling down to a colleague in digital forensics. One who she knew was working late and owed her a favour or two.

After thirty seconds or so negotiation, and the promises of a few drinks next time the team was out, she had convinced him to open live GPS tracking on three mobiles: 'S', 'J' and her infiltrator, Phone X. Soon enough, as requested, the link was live on her tablet.

It was a stroke of luck. Simon Trench had clearly gone AWOL and walked away from the group, as two burners were live and moving in the same location, travelling westwards about ten miles north of where she was, oblivious to her tracking. Phone X was absent however, historical data showing nothing for two days. Not a good sign for its owner.

She collected her badge and keys, heading out onto the driveway, pausing to check the sat-nav for the drive north into Northumberland.

She put Skye's address in.

A buzz of excitement flooded through her. The case was well and truly alive now.

***

A flaking wooden sign hung underneath rotten wooden gallows, creaking ominously as it swung in the light breeze of the night. Stags Head Farm. Its track is dark and empty.

I had loaded up the car from the garage. The estate had creaked on its axle as I leant in and dropped the kit I needed. I had looked over and considered the Audi, it was bigger with more power, but something told me this was going to get messy. Messy enough to ruin the lease agreement. The petrol from the chainsaw was bound to stink it out as well — once this was done I didn't want that lecture from Anna about me ruining her nice car again. No, definitely a trip out for the vet mobile.

It bumped down the pot-holed road. Headlights off. Low revs.

Reaching the end, I turn off the ignition and roll to a stop alongside the large breeze block wall of the main shed. Looking out across the yard, small flickers of light span across the space from a wooden shed. This had to be it.

My heart quickened at the thought of Anna and Tank only yards away. My whole life trapped in there.

I shut the internal lights off and ease out of the driver's side door. No point in closing it, I rest it against the frame, zipping the keys into the dark jacket I'm wearing, padding myself down to make sure I'm not carrying anything loose or noisy.

Despite the cold my blood was electric, coursing through my veins, the static tingling at my fingertips. The fight or flight reflex battling deep down inside me to show its true nature. I took deep breaths. I had to get under control.

Doubling back in the opposite direction, around the shed and silage store, I still see no sign of life outside. No patrols, no movement, just deathly quiet, only the faint metal creak of an abandoned trailer to my right. The farmhouse is locked up tight, dark and deserted. It doesn't look like any other company is about to spring out in my direction.

I continue round over to the smaller shed, careful not to step into any of the shafts of light making their way out into the night. Shadows dance across the narrow gaps in the slats, and peering through a knothole at shoulder height, I can see what I need to inside. The interior isn't inviting by any stretch of the imagination.

***

It wasn't long, twenty minutes or so, and Alice was arriving at Skye's address, parking on the kerb outside and calling her to come down. She appeared, dressed in dark clothes as instructed, and was waved over to the idling car, its window down.

'You still okay?'

She got in the passenger side and sat down. As she clicked the belt into place she was handed a tablet, the screen showing a darkened map with two small beacons, flashing a dull pulse as they sat static on the grid. She soon recognised it as the Northumberland coastline; the roads she knew like the back of her hand traced out in a neon green web in front of her.

'Now this isn't strictly by the book you understand, not exactly a gold star in my ledger, but I could do with the corroboration. Especially if this is what we think it is.'

Alice looked ahead, thinking about waiting for tomorrow's warrant to be executed instead, the satisfaction of nailing them both in broad daylight with her team. But with both hands on the wheel she soon decided otherwise — both phones were in play, it was now or never. The endgame was in sight.

She turned to Skye.

'If you're right, and they're out for blood tonight, this will get dangerous. I've called ahead, should be backup in the area if we need it. Phoned in a few favours with the duty ARV in case. Never a daft idea to have those lads around trust me.'

Skye sat quietly in the passenger seat, the words streaming over her head like another language, watching as two blips on the map screen flashed in the same spot, not moving, hovering out in the countryside, out there in the middle of nowhere. As Alice reversed out and into the road however, setting off with a jolt, it didn't take her long to work out they were headed in their direction.

Back in the direction of her attackers.

***

I see two upright figures, facing away and heads down, both hunched together over what looks like a phone, the small aperture in the wood giving away only so much. What I can also see is Anna, duct tape around her mouth and wrists, lying in a ball on the floor to their right. Over by the far wall and tucked under a horizontal beam, Tank is in a thick metalled mesh cage, pacing back and forth in the tight space.

My gaze goes back to Anna: I watch her chest rise and fall, her eyes only loosely shut. This was no voluntary slumber. Bruises and cuts mark her gentle face. She looks in one piece though, and so does Tank. At least one thing this situation had going for me.

The bad news was both figures were blocking the main entrance; if I wanted in, I was going to have to go through them first.

My saving grace was I couldn't see anyone else. One against two was manageable, and if I could get Tank into this equation it would be game over for them. Looking at them now, huddled with the phone between them, it was clear they hadn't heard me pull up, or if they had, they were still playing it cool.

I gently back away from the shed, retracing my steps around the buildings before moving to the car and opening the boot.

The scene behind me wasn't great, but I had a plan, as well as the element of surprise at least. The old knock on the door and a polite hello wasn't exactly going to set the right tone for the safe release of my partner, or indeed the amicable return of my faithful hound, so it was time to get creative. Something they weren't expecting. Something they wouldn't think was possible.

I pick out the axe and chainsaw, gently shutting the boot.

The shed's main door handle sits at waist height, a thick loop of iron sitting either side. Turning the axe over in my hands, I clank it through — barring the door from opening within.

Understandably, the conversation inside stops.

Moving around the corner, aware of the shadows darting across the slats as they move towards the blocked door, I pick up the chainsaw, and flicking the safety off it kick starts into life with a few pulls on the starter; the sound of its shrill throaty revs soon tearing into the bitter freezing air surrounding the farmyard. I place it back down on the ground to idle. Raised voices shout from within as I walk back round to the front, picking up the petrol can I usually keep the saw's fuel in, giving the big double door a good soaking.

It continues to jolt from inside. The handle of the axe still taking the strain as it flexes with every shoulder barge, but as I throw a lit match and the flames take hold, the door stills and begins to crackle and spit its sparks back out into the yard at me.

This place was going up.

***

It wasn't long before Alice was turning the car off the main dual carriageway and down onto the unlit country road heading back east towards the coast. They had checked the GPS markers on the tablet — both were static but still active a few miles away, with satellite maps showing them on a farm. Alice had not yet mentioned the third GPS signal, her 'infiltrator', and she was hoping Skye wouldn't have noticed it flickering on and off the screen a few miles back before appearing at the farm. Someone else was in play here. This was it.

About two miles out they pulled over.

'Okay, here's how it's going to go down. I get out the car, you don't. I engage with them and call the shots; you stay put and observe only. Okay? If shit hits the fan, you call 999 and explain who you are and what we're doing. It's unofficial but still above board so you won't get into any bother.'

Alice popped the boot and pulled out a dark gym bag, unzipping it and taking out her police issue stab vest, pulling it on before getting back in the driver seat and closing the door.

'Right, now we see what's what.'

She engaged first gear and pulled up the shallow incline, towards the brow of a small hill with a rolling valley below, beyond which the farm buildings were situated on the map.

They were immediately met by the sight of a flickering yellow glow to the east, lighting up the sky between them and the coast, growing brighter and brighter as the distance narrowed.

'What the?' Skye muttered. 'Is that where we're supposed to be headed? Looks lit up like Christmas from here.'

'More than that Skye, I'd say it was on fire. Shit. This wasn't part of the plan.'

***

By this point I can assume the two are confused. I'm burning my own partner and pet alive along with them. Panic should have set in, thinking about how to save their own necks than deal with their ransom demands —

so I take the opportunity to move around to the rear, picking the chainsaw up again on my way past.

The slats are all but rotten in parts, so looking through to get my bearings, and to make sure I'm not going to chop a dog in half, I make short horizontal work of the rear wall and kick in the rest. I find myself staring at the back of the desperate kidnappers, fully focused on tackling the blaze in front of them.

My racing pulse has slowed to an ice-cold beat.

I'm in control again.

I grab Anna and pull her backwards, back in the direction of a wide-eyed Tank — he knows what's coming now. The new movement catches the figures' attention, and they both spin round to face me, stood over her, stirring from unconsciousness.

'Very good Mac. Very good.'

The smaller, wider of the figures shouted over the roar of the burning wood, the edges of the bark roughened by the smoke.

'Thought you were going to let us all burn there for a minute. Smart boy. Very smart.'

The figure stood in front of me — without his mask, without his group chat or his killer dogs — left me in no doubt this was 'S'. Suddenly it all made sense. The knowledge, the inside info, it all clicked into place in the seconds it took for him to open his mouth and speak. Weeks of wonder dissipated as he talked.

Steve the Dog Warden.

'Didn't see that coming did you mate.' He smiled, oblivious to the fire raging behind him as it engulfed the front wall and crept up to the beams above. The collapsing door framing his silhouette in bright yellow.

'I thought for a while you might have figured out who I was, but I can see by the dumb, shit-stained look on your face you didn't have a clue all along. What did I tell you Alex, arrogant bastards these vets.'

The other figure smiled through smoke-stained tears. Smiled with all the confidence of a man holding a pistol at his side, the butt of which he raised up and scratched the side of his head with.

'I tell you what Steve, I like this guy.' He pointed the muzzle at me. 'Even made us an escape route and saved us the bother of lighting his private funeral pyre, how thoughtful.'

Bollocks. I hadn't figured on a weapon. Chainsaw versus firearm was not a competition with long odds for sure. I stepped back but immediately clanked against the dog cage.

'I don't get it. Who's 'J' if you're Alex.'

Stalling for time was my only option if I was to get Anna and Tank free and out of the building.

'J stands for Jamieson. Alex Jamieson.' He was shouting now above the noise. 'Her majesty's constabulary Jamieson if it helps answers your questions. Been watching you for a few weeks you fucking idiot. Steve and I go way back — didn't take us long to realise what you were up to, especially after you walked through that shop's CCTV like the giant Scottish tit you are.'

The fire was raging, furious it couldn't go any faster, the flames clawing the inside of the roof as it tore through the eaves of the old wooden farm building. Clearly this wasn't a conversation that would last too long, and both Steve and Jamieson looked upwards and came to the same conclusion. Beneath my feet Anna was still stirring and looking up at me. Confusion turning to panic as she realised the roof above me was swimming yellow with a sea of flames.

'Well, we'd love to stay and chat, but I guess the pair of you are going to have to leave behind some evidence for me to find tomorrow. It'll be a pleasure covering this one up I can tell you.'

He raised the gun — deftly flicking the safety off — but Steve clearly had other plans, turning sharply to his friend.

'Easy Alex, we agreed he'd be mine; you get the bitch after if you want.'

Looking at me now, he motioned for the pistol from Jamieson.

'You see Mac I'd promised myself after Ronnie I'd put a bullet between the eyes of the fucker who did that, and I do so hate to break my word.'

Alex lowered the muzzle, shrugging to himself as he passed it into the left hand of Steve.

I allowed my hand to reach down, finding the catch on the cage.

Tank nudges a wet nose through the bars, scratching at the concrete, testing the metal.

I slid it through its housing, watching as a blur of dog surged past; enough to put me off balance as I dropped down to reach the idling chainsaw. Tank was accelerating now, at full pace as he covered the distance to Steve, who quickly stepped back as the gun found his right hand, around the same time as 60kg of mastiff arrived and leapt upwards to his neck.

A free left swung upwards in defence, only to find jaws clamping and piercing through the skin of his forearm as the two met. Alex turned in horror to his friend as the flesh began to tear away, and the whole grisly package, Tank and Steve, fell backwards onto the concrete floor behind them.

Anna was rousing below me, the urgency of the situation coming into view, and began dragging herself forward, inch by inch to the hole in the back wall. I lifted the chainsaw and moved towards Alex, wrestling with the collar around Tank's thick neck as he desperately tried to drag him away. Underneath, Steve was still taking the mauling remarkably well despite his shredded and limp forearm — tougher than I would have given him credit for — but panic set in as Tank finally crunched through the bones, exposing his unprotected neck.

As he gasped in agony for a final time he slapped his right arm down onto the concrete. I saw the aim.

The next few seconds played out in horrifying slow-motion and I was frozen to the spot, torn between helping Anna and running to Tank. The pistol was about 6 inches above his palm on the concrete, and with a third straining attempt he took hold of the butt at the same time as jaws took their final crushing bite. Before I could make up the distance to stop him, Steve pulled the pistol around in an arc and discharged it into Tank's side. One heavy shot into his abdomen. It happened so quickly.

Tank absorbed the blow and weakened, sinking down on his victim, eyes glazing over as guttural choking gave way to the gurgling flow of blood from his mouth, the gun falling from Steve's grip beside him. His big soft head fell to the side, his two big gentle eyes looking up at me as he tried to work out what was happening to him.

Jamieson saw it happen as well, and realising it was one versus one turned and faced me, the flames raging higher and higher behind him. I was his escape route. His way out of this inferno. The front of the wooden shed would soon collapse and fall, the smoke beginning to choke us both. It was a last chance.

He ran at me with both arms open. The sight of Tank lying lifeless beyond him fuelled a rage deeper down than any fire could ever reach, and I swung the chainsaw low at his legs, catching them both as I revved the motor on impact, the chain ripping the material and taking plenty of skin with it. He screamed and collapsed to his knees, flailing with his hands at new flesh wounds, smearing blood back over himself in a frantic panic. Only once the handle crushed through his temple, whipping him flat out on the concrete did he lie still. Out cold.

I dropped the saw and moved towards Tank. Eyes closed, head sunk to the side.

Behind me though Anna screamed as a burning timber beam fell and struck the floor beside her. The splinters shattered out over the concrete, stopping me in my tracks.

I realised we had no choice but to get out, so I ran to her, grabbing her by the shoulders and out through the hole in the back wall as the roof dropped around us. We fell about twenty feet from the building — the whole thing was ablaze and huge sections were collapsing inwards and falling from the sides, the fire accelerating by the minute.

'Anna, I've got to go back for Tank. I've got to. He's still in there.'

'Mac don't. You'll never get back out. Leave him, we can't help him. He's gone. Please.'

I rolled over onto my front, I knew she'd seen the gunshot as well as I had, but I was still bracing myself to run back in. I couldn't leave him. No way. Not Tank. The guy had saved my life twice, and now Anna's. Without him I'd have been dead and buried long ago. Even if he was gone, I couldn't leave him in there to get swept up with Steve and Alex's ashes tomorrow.

As I pulled up onto my feet however the front of the building crashed downwards with a screeching tear of wood. A giant plume of yellow embers threw itself back up into the darkness, lighting up the yard as they drifted around us. I realised it wouldn't be long before the rest of the building fell in as well.

I felt Anna tugging at my leg and looked down to see her pointing back towards the road. I knew again she was going to tell me to leave, to get in the car with her and get out of there, but instead she was pointing out beyond the farm.

'Look.'

A blue flashing light lit the trees of the road, and it moved towards the farm track entrance. A single vehicle: too small to be a fire engine or a police convoy. What the hell? I looked back down at Anna.

'Anna we can't be found here. I'll explain later. We just can't be here.'

'And Tank?'

He was microchipped to our address. More questions. Fuck. I looked at the wooden shed, or what was left of it anyway. It was entirely ablaze with pillars of flames erupting all over the roof.

'Shit.' I turned to Anna. She understood the pain without asking.

'Go get the car.'

She stumbled over, keys in her hand and got in. The blue light was getting nearer, nearly at the track entrance. I turned back to face the burning building for one final time.

***

The closer they got, the more obvious the flames were as they reached up into the sky. They danced and lit up the remainder of the yard: a larger shed, a few outhouses, and a farmhouse — all dark and no sign of life, black windows contrasting against the stormy sea of yellow cast around them.

'Shit, we need to stop and call this in. No way we're headed into this without back-up.' Alice pulled over and dialled a number on her phone, first to the switchboard for the fire service, then second her nearby ARV, calling in the favour for back up.

They started off towards the farm, this time with Alice's rarely used flashing blue light pulsing from its position on the dashboard. About a mile out they could see the building falling apart, one side crashing down in a heap with a burst of light and embers — bad news for anyone unlucky enough to be inside.

'Look!' Skye exclaimed. They both saw it. Two tiny figures, what could have only been twenty or thirty feet from the building, running out from the blaze.

'Is it them?'

'Possibly.' Alice squinted ahead, trying to focus her eyes. 'Whatever happens, you stay in the vehicle, okay? You hear me? You stay in this car Skye.'

They reached the main entrance to the farm about thirty seconds later and pulled in, the flaming building much clearer as it steered into view ahead of them at the other end of the track. The wooden structure was collapsing around itself, the fire roaring around the roof, chimneys of flames bursting through the gaps they created. There was no sign of the two figures they had seen, but they had been beyond and around the other side, hopefully having retreated further back.

Alice had slowed down on the uneven road — she couldn't risk sliding off into the hedgerow — and on the screen held up by Skye the GPS markers were still flashing, showing dead centre in the middle of the building ahead. Hopefully it was a time delay from the satellite, but something told her they were still inside, crisping as flames engulfed them.

They were only a hundred metres away when a set of headlights pulled out, full beams, dazzling them both as they flew towards them. Running into the ditch as she swerved they both ducked towards the centre console, Alice's hand barely on the steering wheel. Closing their eyes as the vehicle tore towards them, its engine strained and gravel flew as it bounced over the track.

Alice braced for a collision, while Skye turned her head away towards the back of the car, opening her eyes as it screamed past, stones rattling against the bodywork as it left them rocking alone on the track, teetering on the edge.

'Who the hell was that?' She cried as she sat upright. Looking at the screen two GPS markers were still dead ahead in the middle of the farmyard, and a third was moving in the opposite direction. 'You see who it was?'

Skye was still looking back down the track at the taillights as they sped away and disappeared.

She had watched throughout as it had all flown past, only partially catching sight of the car as it went — but some fleeting recognition resonated with her as it bounced and fishtailed down the potholed road, the full beams dancing against the hedgerows either side. Perhaps it was nothing, but the smoke of a memory was drifting in there now. A silhouette she couldn't place.

She turned back to Alice, back into the front seat. The feeling burned away as soon as it had come.

'No, no sorry, nothing. Nothing at all.' She looked ahead with Alice, still not sure who or what she had seen. She strained forward to look in the side mirror, but the car was long gone, way away on to the B-Road that led away east.

'Well, whoever it was wasn't hanging around. Let's get up there and wait for the back-up, see if anything else crawled out alive.'

They slowed as they approached the burning building, edging round the flaming mess with a wide berth. Alice's mobile rang and she answered, confirming ARV support was inbound and would be with them within minutes. The building was clearly done for, collapsing in on itself in front of them, but at least the fire service was following.

'Jesus!' Skye exclaimed from the passenger seat, pointing ahead to a slumped figure in the yard, chest heaving and both hands grasping at the dirt in front of it.

They both got out and ran over. The body fell over to one side, prostrate and looking skywards, gulping deep breaths of air as hands clawed at smoke filled eyes. Lower down they could see wounded legs, bleeding through ragged tears in the material. It was Alex.

Alice shouted down at her colleague.

'Bloody hell. Alex? Alex it's me, Alice. It's okay, you're safe. Skye grab me a blanket from the car, quickly.'

'Alice, what the hell are you doing here?' Alex was coming to his senses and pushing himself up from the dirt, rubbing his eyes as the pain of smoke kicked in again. The light from the flames lit up the bruises and blood on his face, his torn smouldering clothes hanging loosely around his shoulders.

'I'd ask you the same question Alex, but I reckon we both know the answer don't we.'

Alex looked back down at the ground, realising what she must have known. How she must have found herself here.

'I know it was you who took the CCTV from Markwell's murder. Shop owner as well as positive ID'd you to me. I also know you shut down the link to the dog fighting as quickly as it came up, and you've been trying to put requests in on the same mobile we've been tracking, the one that led us here, and to you. I daresay it's just driven off down the track with its owner. Who is it Alex? Who? Who is so important for you to find and throw your career away on?'

'You've got nothing Alice, circumstantial all of it.'

But Alex looked beaten. He knew she wasn't naïve. He fell back on the dirt, hands over his face.

'Who else are we going to find in there?' Alice continued. 'Your 'friend' from the golf club, Steve?'

They looked at the collapsing building, and then over at Alice's car, Skye's face looking out over the dashboard as she scrabbled around for a blanket.

'You think we wouldn't put that one together ourselves? The pair of you old buddies. Just happening to be investigating the same thing you were both trying to hide?'

Blue lights were racing down the track, Armed Response Vehicles, with the larger silhouette of a fire engine behind it. Skidding to a halt on the uneven dirt of the yard, the uniformed team got out and raced over to the pair on the ground.

'Ma'am? Everything all right?'

'Secure the perimeter, make sure no one else is on site. We've already had one car tear past us on the way in, I doubt we'll see it again. And tell the fire crew as well to expect a body in there. I'm willing to bet a certain Animal Welfare Officer is lying in there. This one was too chicken shit to help him out.'

'If you're referring to Steve he was long gone.' Alex muttered, groaning at the end of the sentence as he tried to move. He knew exactly what they would find.

'This wouldn't be the same Steve we had a tip off for?'

'Sergeant?'

'Called in about thirty minutes ago ma'am. Caller didn't leave their name; switchboard have the number though. Farm near here, securing the scene with local units when you called ma'am. Some kind of fighting pit in a shed, dried blood all over the shop and some half-arsed attempts to clear it up. No sign of any bodies, only a rotting dog in the middle of it all.'

The Sergeant lifted his hand and wiped a smoke drenched tear from his eyes as he spoke. It was choking everyone.

'Forensics are en route to tape everything up now. An almighty dust up it looked like to me, had one of the local boys looking over what might be a shallow grave on the perimeter as well. Nasty.'

'And the Steve part?'

'Yeah, tip off reckoned he was responsible for it all ma'am, used the name BloodSport or something like that, told us where to find the evidence and how many bodies there would be.'

Alice looked back at Alex.

'Well let's hope for your sake they don't find anything about you, or did you forget to clear that part up? You two planning on heading back there to finish later were we, after you had dealt with your problem here?'

'No comment Alice. No bloody comment.'

'Get him cuffed Sergeant. Get him out of my sight'

Skye had now appeared again at Alice's side, and they watched as the fire crew tackled what was left of the building. Alex watched too from the back of the ARV's 4x4, the dejection and defeat painted all over his face. They stood still as the flames subsided and died, and soon, from within the smouldering skeleton of the shed, a firefighter held up a fist, to signal a body. Minutes later, once it was safe, they entered the embers and retrieved a smoking corpse.

Sure enough, it was the barely recognisable form of Steve who was lifted out and brought into the yard. Alice moved over as Skye turned her head away, sickened at the sight of him.

With a gloved hand and holding her breath to avoid the stench of charred flesh, she went through the pockets of his crisped and blackened clothing, eventually finding what she was looking for, a black smartphone, melted and disfigured. She sighed, depositing it into an evidence bag held by the sergeant.

'Search Alex. If he doesn't have one of these on him he's ditched it somewhere nearby, okay?'

They dutifully carried out the search on Alex, but he was clean.

'Keep looking Sergeant, it's here somewhere. If it's not out here in the dirt, it's in there. I need that device.'

Alice turned to face Alex, who had been hauled out of the 4x4 ready to be put in a van. She could feel a speech coming on, but one look at him told her it would be a waste of breath. He was beaten, half choked to death on smoke and God knows what had happened to his legs. It would be a while before he said anything else useful.

'Okay get him out of here and back to the station to see a medic, and for god's sake cover up the body will you — before one of us is sick.'

Skye

Skye lay in bed. A week had gone by and she was still unable to get a good night's sleep; the morning's light had been pouring in for hours. She hadn't even bothered to shut the curtains the night before, crawling into bed after another long evening with a bottle of wine and a few vodkas.

Dark, blood-spattered images from the farm were still seared into her memory, projected onto the inside of her eyelids every time she tried to sleep. Steve's body charred and lifeless, a world away from the man she had worked with for years, haunted her wherever she went.

The police officer, Alex he had been called, stuck there too — his head hung low, the victory all but beaten out of him. She was in no doubt he was one of her attempted kidnappers a week ago, and the possibilities of what would have happened still ran riot in her imagination. She could have been in that fire, in one of those shallow graves, or worse, thrown to the dogs.

Ghostly, degraded thoughts followed her round her home like a black dog, treading after her own footsteps from room to room.

There was however a growing feeling of peace, that it was over, that it had reached its conclusion.

Last night she had had her first contact from Alice since the night of the fire. She had done enough a week ago to assure her she would be safe, but the phone call had begun to put her mind at rest, once and for all.

She had gone back to the station that night to find Alex, who it turned out was a long-term colleague of hers, and shortly after he was arrested and booked into the custody suite for the night. Only the medic had been allowed in to see him.

'I thought I would try give him at least some degree of professional courtesy, not that he deserved it, but by that point I was too tired to make a show of it. Booked him in and we left him for the night, went back in the morning for the first interview.'

'Did he explain himself?'.

'Not as such. He's playing the fool, which I know he's not, but he knows the system well enough to stay quiet until trial, he knows we can't pin anything extra on him for now.'

'Did he say anything about Steve at least?'

'Hasn't uttered a single thing about him. Not a peep. No comments every question we ask him. We've traced their friendship — goes all the way back about fifteen years — both local lads, it looks like they were on the same golf team for the club and went from there. Where the hell they got into this dog fighting business I don't know; luckily it looks like they were just getting started and nothing major yet, seems like our mystery man put a stop to it early.'

'Are you any further forward on who he was?'

'Can't say we are Skye.' Alice paused. 'There's no specific mention of a name in the group chat up until we picked up Ronnie Macfarlane's burner phone, and the two we picked up from Steve and Alex were corrupted by the fire, it's only partial SIM numbers and the GPS tracking confirms it was them: all recent data is gone along with the rest of it. Not even the wizards at the tech lab could extract anything. No, that information is well and truly lost.'

'And so what about the Phone X, from the mystery guy, he was the third marker I saw, wasn't he?'

Alice had paused again. Skye hadn't missed a beat that night.

'Long gone as well, I'm afraid. It briefly turned up at the farm, presumably after calling in the other location, then whizzed past us on the track and disappeared not long after. I would be betting short odds it's been well and truly destroyed.'

'So you've got no idea who it was?'

'At the moment no. Until Alex or Simon Trench start talking we're fresh out — if Simon even knows anything in the first place that is. I can't even guarantee it wasn't a setup from within the group itself, cleaning house and tidying up the loose ends. It's still an open narrative put it that way.'

'Jesus. Some shame.'

'You're not wrong.

'Surely there are other clues. Things left behind elsewhere? It couldn't have all been organised on those two phones, could it? No one's that careful.'

'Well funny you should mention it, it was the next bit to tell you. Two days after the arrest we executed warrants on Steve and Alex's homes: both as clean as a whistle. No personal phone devices, laptops, tablets, nothing. Not a trace.'

'Nothing?'

'Nothing. Even had the sense to clean out their golf club lockers too before we could get back to them.'

Alice had left out Andy Jordan's secret trip the day before.

'But how would they have known. They wouldn't have been expecting a police visit, would they? Whatever they were doing up at the farm wasn't supposed to attract the attention it did surely?'

'No, which is my sticking point. Once the red tape of the internal inquiry is out the way, I'm either looking for some secret stash they had — or worse — they've a guardian angel we don't know about, some bigger help pulling strings and clearing up for them.'

Alice had paused, her frustration showing through, the late nights grinding down her patience.

'I sincerely hope it's the former, the thought of more bent coppers interfering on my patch is one I can do without let me tell you. One was bad enough, never mind working out who another mystery suspect is. No, unless something shows up from the three bodies at the other farm we're not too far off where I started with this one. And I've a funny feeling they'll turn out clean as well once I've dug into them.'

Alice had finished off the conversation not long after. It had been late, and she had wanted to get out of the office. Long days preparing for the internal enquiry were taking their toll, and besides, there was only so much she could tell her. Something about some of her pauses however, as short as they were, made Skye think there was more to this than Alice had been letting on. The silent sounds of cogs whirring had left a trace of doubt in her mind, like there were other pieces to fall into place, things she could not talk about or explain.

Still, at least it was all out in the open. Her fear and anxiety over Davey Markwell had finally ended as well. It had been gruesome to hear how he had met his end, but a cruel and guilty satisfaction had filled her when Alice had explained everything on their drive home. His retribution, his torture at the hands their mystery suspect. Chillingly welcome.

They had signed off by agreeing an interview date for the inquiry — Skye would have a small degree of input it would seem after all — but for now she was free to have her paid time off. Something the council bosses had been more than keen to organise in the aftermath of Steve's awful crimes.

So, she lay in bed, hung-over, hazy, and in desperate need of a cup of tea, staring out of the window with the curtains wide open, playing out the scene in her head once more, thinking back to the blazing building and the car flying past them on the single-track road. The 'mystery man'.

Only the more she had thought about it, the more a feeling of déjà vu swarmed around in her. The car, the silhouette in the driver's seat. At first a blur but becoming clearer and clearer as she replayed it in her mind, staring at it from DI Rose's passenger seat as they both tilted over the side of the ditch, Alice panicking in the driver's seat, Skye staring straight at it.

No, as the week went on, it was more than a fading memory. It was coming to life. A familiar feeling surrounded her, making her feel safe inside.

She rolled over in bed and picked up her phone from the side table.

Plenty of notifications: two from her mum checking she was still okay, and multiple updates from the regional paper's online app.

Ignoring all these she opened the message screen, scrolling down to click on a previous thread to write out a new message. One she had been meaning to write for few days now. One she hoped would reach someone safe and sound.

Two words.

And of course, an 'x'.

Tank

A machine clicked and hissed behind me. Coffee.

Beside me, the garden and woods were framed by the window, frost dusting its sills and drawing the eye outside. It was only eight or so in the morning and the life out there was quiet: a few birds had already darted through gaps and landed on the lawn, and as the low sun slowly burned a path through the trees to lift the morning's dew, I daydreamed a different storyline to the one I was living. One where the birds were just birds, one where narratives weren't dark and terrifying.

I had been awake for hours. I had been all week. What I used to call sleep still escaped me. Peaceful days of stirring awake, sun filtering through the bedroom blinds whilst covers were pulled back over my head; far off memories for now. This thing hadn't left me yet. This grief.

I added milk to a mug, slowly watching as the coffee swirled upwards and turned to a familiar brown cloud. I thought about taking one up to Anna as she lay in bed, but I thought better of it. Better to let her rest.

I had slipped out in the darkness of the early morning, looking at her asleep as I pushed the covers over to keep her warm. She was so peaceful, eyelids flickering as if they might open, some gentle dream playing out behind them, and I thought of the terrors that had plagued my own shallow rest. It was better to be awake. I could control awake.

I threw a thick coat over my shoulders. Wandering out into the garden, and around to the side where I kept the compost, I stopped beside the recently overturned earth there. It was drying out and slowly blending in with the rest of the soil, losing its sharpness as autumn's long dead leaves blew over it.

It was only the wooden cross at the far end that still marked it out as a grave.

I sighed as Paulie came down from the fence and padded over to my feet, not ready to hunt yet. I reached down and tickled his ear.

'I hope it was worth it eh Paulie. What do you reckon?'

He didn't say much, only rubbed his little white whiskers against my leg and looked up. I took a long sip of coffee and breathed out into the cold crisp air, the fog of caffeine lifting in the breeze as it disappeared.

I dug around and pulled out my phone, checking it for the hundredth time that week. Local news was top of my searches, and it would stay that way for a long time to come. It was still the same feed, still the same storyline: local corrupt policeman and his accomplice defeated by hero Detective. I was still missing from the headlines. No mention of my motives or murders. No mention of the mess I had created. Paulie headbutted my leg again. Chirped his happy story into the garden.

I hoped it was worth it. I did. What had started as a small, beaten-up dog had quickly turned into a nightmare of my own doing. I didn't regret Davey, or Ronnie for that matter, or any of them come to think of it. But looking down at the little wooden cross, I couldn't help thinking about the real cost of it.

I turned to the back gate and its path beyond, thinking of all the walks I had enjoyed with Tank, his big, padding paws knocking the twigs and leaves out of my path as I followed on behind him, grateful now for his company over the last few weeks. The solitude and wordless friendship we had enjoyed, all the time exploring new and old places together.

I thought too of my gratitude to him, for finding me at the farm, for fighting my corner and saving my life on that wintry night when I was about to die alone. For saving Anna as well when I could not. For never having to ask him to be there, he just was.

I thought too of the possibility — some ethereal daydream as I stared at the fog slowly lifting from the dene — that all those animals, the broken and the dying that I had taken through their last moments; those warm furry souls who had lost their battles and come to me exhausted with life, that they had somehow come back to find me through Tank. A little spark of energy left behind in the ether when we said goodbye. I looked down at Paulie, his puffy ginger face staring back up from the leaves. This was getting a bit mushy for so early in the morning.

But as I stood in the garden, surrounded by the freezing morning air and fighting back a long overdue tear, I thought mostly about running back into the burning building for him when I should have been escaping.

Throwing his big lifeless weight over my shoulder, running out into the darkness with the flames behind us, the building crashing down as I ran with him to the car.

I thought about how frail he looked as Anna and I heaved him into the backseat, racing to the clinic as she held him still in her arms, those big soulful eyes so dull and helpless — flicking and focusing on the short space in front of him as his life fought deep inside to stay with us.

I thought about how I lifted his big bulk into the operating theatre, as Anna opened surgical packs and turned lights on.

I thought about the litres of fluid and blood transfusions, and surgery that felt like hours finding that bullet.

I also thought about lying with him in the house while he was sedated, painful, and struggling to heal for us. His bed not big enough for both of us.

Mostly I thought, looking at the back gate and path, about Tank, and how I wished I could have done better for him — to pay him back for all his trust in me as his big new friend.

I sighed, drinking what was now a cold coffee, wincing as the bitter taste went down and throwing out gritty dregs into the undergrowth. Quint the cat had appeared from the open side door and was in the undergrowth to my right, raking up the dirt and bark, readying to take aim with his morning's business.

'Do that here pal and you're dead meat…'

I hunched down and brushed away the fallen leaves from the grave in front of us. The lettering on the wooden cross was washing away, and as I cursed myself again for using the wrong paint, the sound of footsteps on the grass behind me got louder and louder. Looking up at the house the curtains were still drawn. It can only mean one thing.

'I see you finally worked out that cage big man. Thought I told you to rest those stitches and have a lie in?'

Tank has hobbled past, and much to Quint's dismay is peeing all over his pristine new toilet hole.

'I'm not sure he likes that. C'mere you.'

He falls in beside me, and we look down at the earth in front of the washed out cross.

The word 'Bella' is still there in the faded paint.

'I've got the feeling you two would have got on pal. She was all fight when it had counted, only right she came home with us eh.'

He seemed to grasp I was talking to him, panting and grinning beside me. His medical pet shirt tight, keeping him warm in the morning air.

'Come on then, let's go get your drugs sorted eh.'

We headed slowly inside, Tank groaning as he took the three small steps upwards, ready for another nap as well as his painkillers. As I quietly closed the door behind, a pocket vibrated as my phone came back to life in my overcoat. I took it out and looked down at the screen, it was glowing with a new message.

A familiar name. A feeling of déjà vu.

It was from Skye:

'Thank you x'

End

About the Author

Joseph Ward lives and works in Northumberland under another name. He is a real-life Veterinary Surgeon and lives a quiet, non-vigilante life with his family and pets, penning fiction in his spare time when he's not vetting. He doesn't really kill naughty clients, but they do sometimes get a stern look when they've been awfully silly and not listened to his wise words. He would like to remind all closet heroes that the Police are quite lovely and always worth speaking to in the event you come across organised crime when you're at work. Whatever you do, don't track them down one by one and do something you might regret. Honestly.

Printed in Great Britain
by Amazon